Bewitched by the Sea Monster

Stephanie E. Donohue

Published by Evermore, an imprint of Never and Ever Publishing https://neverandeverbooks.com/

Edited by Joyce at Rejoyce Literary https://www.rejoyceliteraryediting.com/home

Proofread by Line & Letter Editing https://lineandletterediting.com/

Cover art Vivian Valentin https://www.instagram.com/vivianvalentinart/

In *Bewitched by the Sea Monster,* the main character is at the tail end of an unhealthy/toxic relationship when she meets the Loch Ness Monster. Although she makes the decision to end the relationship before anything naughty business happens, this could still be brushing a a little bit into cheating territory.

Gifts & Games
Lodging W1 - W5°
Shops
Lobby & Brew & Bites
Health Clinic & Spa
Misty Mages & Boat Tours
Kelpie Pond
Alicorn Stables
Lodging E1 - E5°
Niverwick Isle

*To everyone peeking and wondering if there's gonna
be Nessie dick in this book...*

There is.
You're welcome.

CONTENTS

1

Words are hard.

They came easily to me. Once. A long time ago. Great waves of words, spoken too quickly for most to grasp.

Now they slip away. Most I've let slip. They are meaningless. Noise to break the silence.

But some I'm lost without.

Indigo. My love.

Alistair. My name.

Onyx. The one who stole my words.

These I repeat as I swim in the murky waters I now call home.

Indigo.

Alistair.

Onyx.

There is little life beneath these waters. Most creatures flee. *After* seeing me. I am too big. They feel…*fear*. Of me. I can't calm them, not when all I know are words, and they don't understand them.

And my words slip. More each day.

Indigo.

Alistair.

Onyx.

I fear the day I lose all my words. The day I stare into the waters with nothing in my head. When all I have is feeling. The ache in my belly that tells me to eat. The restlessness in my fins that pushes me to travel. The burn of my runes when I am being called to the surface.

I fear the day I lose my words.

But I also *long* for it.

When all the words are gone, I won't remember to miss them.

It will be easier. To spend the rest of my days wandering the waters as a mindless creature.

Cursed.

I am cursed.

Cursed to lose my life. My *words*.

Cursed to hold a broken heart that will never heal, even as my memories slip.

Cursed.

"Good afternoon, Mr. Hollingdale. This is Pippi calling from—yes, sir. Pippi. Like the movie. Yep. Oh yes, I've got the big red hair and everything…Don't often wear pigtails, but I guarantee they'd stick up just like Pippi Longstocking's." I leaned back in my office chair, fighting to grasp the phone in my sweat-slicked hand. My smile was so forced, so *phony*, it made my cheekbones hurt.

But the phony smile helped tilt my voice into a chipper pitch.

"Ahhh, I'll bet I just aged myself getting that reference though, huh?" Old, stuffy Mr. James Hollingdale wheezed into my ear. "Young-sounding thing like you probably don't get many men your age talking about such an old movie."

Young-sounding thing…Gosh.

My chipper must've been leaning closer to chipmunk if he thought my near-geriatric thirty-five-year-old self *young*.

I cleared my throat and swiveled a bit in my chair. "My mom *loved* Pippi Longstocking. The books, movies, the cartoons, everything. So it makes me happy when people get the reference."

A little white lie never hurt anyone.

My mom had, indeed, adored Pippi Longstocking. And I'd seen every single edition—had basically grown up with pigtail Pippi. But the references didn't bring me any joy. There were too many bad memories there.

But I wasn't about to unload my childhood traumas on Mr. Hollingdale. Because this stuffy old toadstool was the lead for one of my biggest clients—VitalTech Supplies—and I was about to tell him we'd screwed the whole dang pooch, and then left it out on a rainy day to rot.

"Pippi," he formed my name around a wheezing laugh. "I love it. I've seen your emails before, but I always thought there was a typo in your signature, so I've been calling you *Pippa* in my head."

DING!

My eyes dropped to my computer, focusing on the big block of text clunking up the message screen; the exchanges Andy— the actual project manager for the VitalTech account—and I had been swapping all day.

Andy: In short...we're fucked. Thoroughly. And James Hollingdale has been punching my goddamn number every fifteen minutes like clockwork. I don't even know how to explain this one. I sure as shit don't know how to keep him from blowing his top.

Me: You want me to try and soften the blow?

Andy: Would you? Please?

Me: I can try! Hollingdale's always been nice to me via email and seems the talkative type. Maybe if I chat him up first, it won't be as bad?

Andy: Yes. Please. See what you can do.

Beneath that old stuff, Andy had snuck a new update in.

Andy: ...Parts are backordered. Lead time up to sixteen weeks.

Oh. Fudge.

"It's lovely to speak with you, Pippi," Mr. Hollingdale half panted into my ear, "and *meet* you. Electronically, of course, but phone calls are always preferable to emailing."

Said every middle-aged white man ever.

My skin crawled, berating me for the rude thought. And my heart dropped to my toes with the next *DING* from the message app.

Andy: The order is confirmed to be unsalvageable. We need to wait for the back-ordered parts.

"So, I'm not going to complain about hearing your lovely voice, Pippi," Mr. Hollingdale continued, "but I was expecting *Andrew* to call. I've been trying to reach him *all day.*"

"Andy's...busy at the moment." I winced as a slew of angry and exhausted emojis exploded over my screen with Andy's next chat. "And, well, there's no easy way to serve this pill, Mr. Hollingdale. We've unfortunately run into some issues with your order."

Some issues.

Sure.

You see, here at Sunstone Industry, we made circuit boards. But not just *any* circuit boards; we used parts from Celesta and Elysium...and SorcerSoft, before they'd gone belly up. Companies run by Sorcerers that made parts slathered in runes and infused with *magic.*

We built that magic into the circuit boards, then shipped them to places like VitalTech, who used them to make diagnostic machines so advanced, they could do full body scans of a roomful of people and pinpoint who had cancer, who was diabetic, who had hypertension, whose heart was about to fail, and much more.

Magic.

Life-saving magic.

And Sunstone *boasted* about how we hired *professionals*— using esteemed techs who were well-versed in magic and technology—and placed quality at the echelon of our business.

But somehow, we built an entire gosh-darn order of boards *the wrong way.*

It wasn't caught until we did the final testing, and the boards fritzed.

And then, our *esteemed professionals* broke half the pieces trying to disconnect and reassemble the boards. So now we were up shit's creek and we *might've* had a paddle to get us out, like rushing new builds through the plant. *Might've.* If half the parts weren't on back order.

Couldn't build a board without parts.

"That doesn't sound good," Mr. Hollingdale sniffed in my ear. "What kind of issues are we talking about, Pippi?"

"Well, you see..." I drummed my fingers against the desk. Fiddled with the fat cat pen holder my fellow project coordinator, Kai, had gotten me for our white elephant gift exchange at Yuletide last year. Flipped through my notebook, my eyes catching on the scribblings I'd made in the corner yesterday morning. The start of a story. An angsty office romance I'd thought up while watching two of my married coworkers flirt in a meeting.

And they were *not* married to each other.

What happens if you meet the right person at the wrong time? What happens if the person who uplifts you, soothes your soul, and makes you whole wasn't the one you married?

Do you risk it all at the call of your soulmate? Or do you play it safe and stay with the life partner you chose—even if that partner is slowly suffocating the light out of you?

Stars, that was terrible.

"Yes, Pippi?" Mr. Hollingdale pressed.

"We...uhh...." My eyes kept roaming. Looking at my email. Scanning the heads of the people in the cubicles around me, I noticed Kai's spiky brown hair bobbing along to the music coming out of his earbuds and Jessa's slick, shimmering curtain of blond hair, which sparkled under the too-bright fluorescent lights.

I was looking for something—a miracle. A shining knight who'd swoop in and save me. A gentle way to deliver the bombshell. *Something.*

But there was nothing. No one.

My hands left sweat streaks on top of my bland, grey desk as I went back to drumming my fingers. "Mr. Hollingdale, I'm afraid we're not going to make your ship date."

"No?" A sniffy response. Not angry, not yet. Because he probably figured I'd come back with something like, "Yeah, we're gonna be about a week late."

The actual date would gast all his freaking flabbers.

"No." I watched the patterns my sweaty fingers left on the desk. "There was an issue in production. A...well...a *large* issue. But I want to make it clear that this was *our* mistake, and no extra costs will be incurred on your end."

A big wet sigh heaved into my ear. "What kind of delay are we talking here, Pippa?"

So much for all that talk about how he likes my name.

DING!

My heart jumped at Andy's newest message, hoping—*praying*—it'd be good news. But then my eyes absorbed the text, and my heart flattened itself beneath my feet and died.

Andy: Right now, the best ETA on shipping is August fourteenth.

I gulped.

August fourteenth was *four months* from now.

This order was supposed to ship this *Monday*.

"Pippa?" Mr. Hollingdale's voice thinned. Still not angry, but annoyed.

DING!

Jessa: If the news is that bad, have him call Andy for an update.

I jerked my head up and met Jessa's big, watery blue eyes over the edge of the cubicle. She emitted a wave of righteous rage as she tucked her chin down, banging out another message on her keyboard.

DING!

Jessa: This was ANDY'S lead, Pippi. Not yours. HE is the project manager. You're only his coordinator.

My hands shook as I pecked out a quick, *Ouch. Harsh.*

Jessa's lip quirked when she zipped another message to me.

Jessa: You know what I mean. HE was the one who okayed the date. HE was the one who tried to rush it through production. Our quality control department sucks, sure, but HE rushed.

DING!

Andy: Tell Mr. Hollingdale we will do everything we can to move that lead time in.

Jessa: If Andy wants to keep shoving these jobs through and making these promises, he needs to own it when things get fucked. Stop letting him push it off on you. You're gonna end up with an ulcer, Pips. You're as white as a sheet.

"Pippa? What is our lead-time?"

Oh shoot.

Mr. Hollingdale was mad now.

And my stomach did kind of hurt, as knotted as it was with nerves and guilt.

DING!

Jessa: Ulcers are a bitch, Pips.

I don't have an ulcer, I typed back. *And I told Andy I'd take care of this.*

Jessa: I'd tell Andy lots of things. None of them nice.

I sighed. Pinched the bridge of my nose. Winced when my sweaty hands smeared my foundation. And said, in the sweetest, calmest voice I could muster, "Boards were *damaged* during the production process. Unfortunately, they're irreparable, so we'll need to go back in with new builds. Again, you'll incur no additional costs for this. But…well…some of the parts are backordered with lead times of fourteen weeks. But, Mr. Hollingdale, we will—"

"WHAT?"

The yell rattled my ear, making me jump dang near out of my chair.

Kai and Jessa both looked up.

"FOURTEEN WEEKS?! This is unacceptable. *Utterly* unacceptable. No. Absolutely not. Those boards can't go out past the end of this *month*, Pippa. *Fourteen weeks?* Where is Andrew? Where is your manager? I won't accept this. Absolutely not."

I blew out a long breath. One that burned as it left my mouth because I'd held it in so long, it'd festered inside of me.

"Mr. Hollingdale," I tried, tentatively.

He ignored me and kept right on yelling for a full ten

minutes, until he got fed up with my attempts to placate him and snarled, "This is un-fucking-believable." Then he hung up, probably to go haunt Andy.

Sorry, Andy. I cringed as I set my cell on the desk. *I tried.*

"AND WHERE THE fuck was Andy, huh?" Jessa fumed an hour later as she shoved her laptop into her creamy leather bag. *"Nowhere."* She waved her arm at the glass wall on our right—the PM offices. The big, lofty square rooms concealed behind old, discolored and half bent venetian blinds, which all the PMs kept drawn—they didn't want us low lifes peeping at them.

Andy's door was open, though, and the room was dark. Had been all day.

"It was a stressful day for him too, Jessa," I pointed out.

And, stars, I'd never been so grateful to see that clock hit 5:00 p.m.

My hands were still shaking.

Big ole tacky patches of sweat still clung to my blouse, mainly around my armpits and the small of my back, where the stress pool usually rolled to. Thankfully the blouse was navy blue cotton with big billowy sleeves that hid the worst of the moisture.

No one liked being yelled at. *No one.* It was an awful feeling, getting all pretzeled with guilt, having to stammer agreements that you were a dunce, and muttering apologies for a screw up you didn't even commit.

"Stressful. *Sure.*" Jessa sniffed and peered over her cubicle at me, watching as my jittering hands wrestled to fit my laptop into the infuriatingly narrow slot in my messenger bag. "I betcha last week's paycheck Andy turned his phone off, took the boys out for a drink, and ain't feeling one iota of *stress* about what just happened. He ain't gonna take any flack for it, is he?"

"He's gotten an earful. I'm sure." The laptop made a satisfying swish when it slid into place. I flipped the top of the bag over, not bothering to buckle it. Wasn't worth the effort of steadying my hands.

"Oh, he got an earful alright." Kai poked his nose over, beaming at us. "Y'all didn't hear Frank this morning."

"You mean our esteemed leader who was"—Jessa threw some air quotes up—"'*on calls*' from 8:00 a.m. to when he ducked out after lunch?"

"Uh-huh. That's the one. See, this is what happens when you ladies are *late* on the daily."

"We start at 8:00 a.m. and we clock in at 8:00 a.m.," Jessa huffed, "that ain't *late*."

"Listen, I'd rather handle the worst of the early morning freak outs from the comfort of my bed," I said, "and then mosey in at my own speed."

"You should *not* be answering emails at the ass crack of dawn." Contempt rippled off Jessa as she rolled her eyes at me. Not contempt at *me*. But at my actions.

"It makes my day a whole heck of a lot easier." I swiped my still-sweaty hands on my jeans. *"Usually."*

"Eh-hem," Kai cleared his throat. *"As I was saying*, if you *had* been here at an appropriate time, you would've seen Frank explode. Happened at 7:45 a.m. When *you* were probably still sleeping." Kai pointed at Jessa. Then he laughed and ducked when Jessa winged a pen at his head. "He got right in Andy's face with it," Kai continued. "I thought Andy was gonna *piss* himself. That's why he hasn't been back to his desk all day."

"Hmmmm…nnno." Jessa dragged the *n* of the no between her teeth. "The dude gets yelled at a bit but dumps the rest of the blame off on Pips? Nope. He still got off too easy."

Kai rolled his shoulders. "Not saying he didn't. Just saying he got shit-sprayed too."

"You're being a little harsh, Jessa," I said gently. "He rushed the job, sure, but it's not like he shoved faulty work orders through. Everything on our end was right. A mistake happened on the floor, as it does on occasion. That's all."

"And honestly…" Kai drummed his fingers against the top of the cubicle wall, and a rush of warm, comforting feelings extruded from him as he flashed a sideways smile. "If SorcerSoft was still around, they could've bailed him out. I *never* had a fourteen week lead with them."

"Yeah, I was thinking that earlier. They were always *so good* in a pinch," I said. "And, stars, do I miss those days."

"No comment. I ain't been in this prison as long as you two." Jessa grinned playfully. "So I've never worked with them."

"A shame." Kai laughed. "They were the *best*."

"They really were. Quick to respond. Super friendly. Their stuff was always quality too." I pursed my lips. "They were *too* good. Probably why they went belly up."

"Probably. We can't let the good guys roll in this wild world of ours. Anyway"—Kai hefted his laptop bag onto his shoulder—"shall I walk you ladies to your cars?"

"But of course." Jessa fluttered her eyes and reached across the wall to brush his knuckles.

"Us ladies would never manage the five-minute walk without a big, strapping gentleman to protect us," I teased.

Kai grinned and stepped away from his desk, rounding the wall to hook his arm around Jessa, and then hauling her to my cubicle, so he could scoop his other arm around me. "My motivations are hardly *decent*," he said with a fake posh accent. "I simply want to look *distinguished* with two of the finest ladies in the office on my arm."

"I think you need to lay off the *Bridgerton* binges, Kai." I giggled, hoping he couldn't feel how clammy and damp my sweaty swamp arm was.

"Never!" Kai declared.

It was, truly, a five-minute walk: straight out the side door, down a set of chipped and stained concrete steps, and across the black asphalt parking lot to our cars.

"Oh look!" Jessa squealed once we'd stepped outside. "*Sunlight*. Halle-freaking-lujah."

She'd said this every day this week.

And every day Kai and I hummed in agreement.

There was something magical about those first few days of spring, when we left work and found the parking lot bathed in warm, late afternoon sun, instead of the harsh, artificial illumination from the light poles.

"Oh, suck it all, I remember now!" Kai started.

Jessa and I both looked at him in confusion.

"I wanted to tell you something earlier, Pips." He wriggled his arm free of mine, springing his keys from his jeans pocket. "Lemme get my car started first…to make sure the POS actually starts."

He punched his clicker.

At the end of the row, his silver SUV blared in annoyance and then the engine gave a creaky grumble as it turned over.

"Abracadabra!" He waved his arm in a showman's style. "It's *magic*."

"Oh, golly gee. You're a Sorcerer? And you never told me?" Jessa poked him playfully.

Kai wiggled his fingers. "Wait 'til you see the spells I can cast with a keyboard. But as I was saying, about that whole VitalTech fiasco…I don't know if this'll make you feel better or worse, Pips, but I don't think us messing this order up is gonna make one iota of difference to their bottom line. They were already in boiling water."

"VitalTech is?" I asked.

"Yepper. And I'm guessing by your blank faces," Kai added, "that neither of you read the news bulletins?"

"Why would we?" Jessa mumbled.

"Insider information." Kai said.

"I think you're the only one who cares about that, Kai." I squeezed his arm.

"Maybe you *should* care." Kai harrumphed. "See, we started talking about how SorcerSoft went belly up, and it made me think of the news bulletin from the other day. Magix is coming for places like VitalTech too."

"You're kidding."

"Nope." He popped the *p*. "They're claiming the technology is *insidious*. Causing more harm to people than good. Like, go-in-with-a-broken-arm,-get-an-X-ray-and-come-out-with-termi-nal-cancer kinda claims."

"That," Jessa and I said, almost in unison, "is *horseshit*."

"But that's what happens when the Standies take money outta the Sorcerers' pockets."

"So that's the claim they're making? That people should pay *three times as much* to hire a Sorcerer?" I asked.

"Yepper."

"Unbelievable."

"Looks like it's gonna go to court. There's a sparkling new lawsuit."

"Well heavens. No wonder Mr. Hollingdale went full Oscar the Grouch." I blew out a breath. "Poor man. He was getting hammered by bad news on all ends, wasn't he?"

Standies were people like me, Kai, Jessa, and Andy, and probably Mr. Hollingdale. Normal folk. Hapless, some would say. People without an ounce of magic in their veins.

Sorcerers were the magic folk—the extraordinary. People who never had a care in the world because nothing in the world was inaccessible to them. Humans who were above technology.

Technology, after all, was for the Standies—to give us a sprinkle of magic. A *taste* of what it could be like. And some Sorcerers didn't even like us having that. It made us too independent for their tastes.

"He still shouldn't have yelled at you"—Jessa broke away, skipping over to the door of her car—"and I would've told him as much. No matter what he's got going on, ain't no excuse to take it out on you."

"The poor man was probably wound so tight, a hairpin would've snapped him. And I dropped a bomb on his head."

Jessa waggled her key in my face. "You're too damn nice,

Pips. That's your problem. You can't keep making excuses when people hurt you. Sometimes people are just buckets of shit who need to be chucked in the sewer."

Chirp. Chirp. Chirp.

"Oh, shoot!" The chirping of my cell phone had me jumping.

"See? He's got you so worked up, you're spooked at your own phone!" Jessa cried.

"I think I accidentally flipped it off silent," I said. "When do you ever hear my phone ring?"

Jessa sighed, conceding.

I shuffled the last few feet to my car and wrestled my phone out of my bag's front pocket. Seeing that text splashed across the screen after the afternoon I'd had…well, it was a bit like getting a juicy, extra chocolate-y cake at the end of a subpar dinner.

I grinned.

Jackson (my longtime boyfriend): How was your day? Mine was C.R.A.Z.Y. But I can't wait 'til I get home. Or until you get home…I'll race ya! Because I've got a surprise for you, babe. A big 'un.

Pippi

"Oh, goodness babe…that *hair*…" Jackson's warm laugh greeted me as I shoved open the creaky old door to our rancher.

I winced and peered down the hall, where he waited for me in the kitchen, beaming as he held a delicate crystal wine glass—one of my better thrift store finds—in each hand. Looking like every woman's wet dream fantasy: tall and strapping, with soft dirty blond hair brushing the tops of his ears, and big sparkling cyan blue eyes.

"Is it that bad?" I asked, my skin prickling with unease as I imagined the worst. My red curls were boisterous on a *good* day, when they gave me a Julia Roberts in *Pretty Woman* kinda style. On average, they had Merida from *Brave* vibes. At worst… Medusa. Today, after running clammy hands over my curls one too many times and baking them with the heat radiating off my sweaty and stressed body, this was probably a Medusa day.

"Eh, it's poofing, that's for sure." A smile curved Jackson's lips. "Might be close to the shaggy mane you had when we first met, but I don't think it tops it."

I sighed a little, dreamily.

We'd met at a club three years ago. Jessa had dragged me there for a country line dancing night, and I'd seen him after I'd spent a solid hour sweating it up on the dance floor.

He'd looked so achingly lovely, sitting at the bar with his prim and fitted jeans and button-up shirt, both ruffled just enough to make him appear less cosmic, and more human. He'd been suckling a beer—one of the local IPAs—and staring around the bar with his lazy, half-lidded eyes.

I had never seen a man so breathtaking.

But it was his mournfulness that'd called to my heart, setting me across the room toward him. It radiated off him in big plumes—like an old heater coughing out ripples of warm air.

A striking, sorrowful angel. That thought had crossed my mind when I'd sidled up to the bar next to him, feeling grungy in my ruffled rainbow blouse and black jeans, knowing my curls were likely poofed into a bouncy frizz halo. He hadn't looked at me. Not until I'd leaned over, unstuck my tongue from where it'd glued itself to the roof of my mouth, and muttered, "You doing okay?"

His eyes had flown to mine.

"That's not a pickup line," I'd said hastily, burning with embarrassment. "I swear. It'd be a pretty dang boring one if it was, huh? But that wasn't my intent. Honest. It's just...you looked sad, is all. I thought maybe there was something I could do to cheer you up. But I'll leave if...y'know..."

He had smiled at me then.

And stars above, that smile had *done* things to me.

Glee and awe and disbelief had cow-kicked me, stealing my next words. Those feelings still gave my gut a daily walloping every time I looked at him. Like now, even though his radiant smile was fading a bit.

"Judging by the wild mane, I'm guessing it was a rough day?" he asked as I kicked my shoes off at the door, chucked my keys into the bowl on the side table we kept in the foyer (the "shit table," we lovingly called it, since we dumped our shit on it when we came in), and walked down the hall into the kitchen.

"You can say that again." I slung my purse onto the sleek granite top of our little kitchen island, and took the glass of wine he held toward me. It was a chilled white—not my favorite (I was an oaky, dry-bodied red kinda gal), but it was crisp and refreshing and offered enough kick to burn some of the stress away. I took two deep sips and then sighed again. "Thank you."

"But of course." He took a gulping swig of his wine, draining nearly half the glass in one go.

I cringed.

Jackson was a champion chugger. He gulped most things down. Water. Beer. Soda. Piping hot tea and coffee—I still didn't understand how he hadn't scalded his throat. The habit was left over from the time he'd been in the military, where he'd had to race the clock at mealtimes.

I always worried he'd choke himself or get indigestion. But he never did. He didn't even have a belly pouch—his stomach was flat. Flat, flat, *flat*. Deliciously so.

If I ate and drank the way he did, I'd look pregnant. Such was the unfairness of being a woman.

"So..." Jackson reached over and ruffled my hair, beaming when the frazzled strands fluffed up under his hand. "Your rough day?"

"It was a flipping *nightmare*."

"Ah, c'mon, babe, I'm sure it wasn't *that* bad."

"Production messed up a $500K order, and we've gotta eat the cost of it."

Jackson pulled an "ouch" face and sucked a whistly bit of air through his teeth.

"And I got to deliver the bad news to our client." I took a bigger sip of wine, craving the headiness of it. The way it seeped into my veins and pumped hazy and fuzzy feelings into my brain, hankering for the buzz more than the taste.

"Why did *you* do that?" Jackson chugged the last of his wine down and then reached across the island for the bottle, pouring himself another glass—and topping off mine. Bless him.

"Andy was"—I pressed the rim of the glass to my chin—"dealing with the fallout on the floor."

Jackson humphed. "Oh boy, I'll betcha that was a *mess*. You probably got off easy, babe. Anyway"—he drummed his palms against the island, twisting his mouth into a slight pout, even as he brimmed with excited energy—"I was kinda hoping you'd be in a *good* mood for this news. Not sure it'll hit the same when you're sour."

I frowned. I was a little frazzled, sure. But had I been grouchy?

Shoot. I had been, hadn't I?

Probably pulled a proper bitch face when I'd walked in, huffing heavier than the wolf in the *Three Little Pigs*.

"All I needed was this." I held up the glass in a mock toast. "And maybe a little of this." I pressed my other hand to his chest as I stood on my tip, tip, tippytoes (Jackson was nearly a foot taller than me) and touched my mouth to his warm, soft lips. "And everything's right in the world again."

He nuzzled his nose to mine, gave my bum a playful swat and then scooted back, hefting his right bum cheek onto the island in the half sitting, half leaning, all sexy pose he did so well. "We're going on vacation, babe!" he exclaimed, jiggling the full glass of wine in his hand, making a liquid whirlpool slosh almost up to the brim.

"Oh?"

"Don't jump for joy or anything."

"I'm…I'm getting there. This is…Wow." I pressed my hand to his knee, squeezing. "I'm a little shocked, I think. Because I figured vacations were off the table until…" I raised my wine glass, gesturing toward the spacious kitchen, with its big white cabinets, gleaming, grey marble countertops and sparkling appliances (gleaming and sparkling because I scrubbed them within an inch of their life every day). And then I threw my arm a little wider, motioning to the whole of our spacious, three-bedroom home. The 2,200 square feet of prime real estate we'd pinched and squeezed and barely extruded enough money to be able to afford.

Jackson waved his hand. "This trip's barely gonna take a sip out of our savings. All we have to pay for is the airfare."

"Airfare?" I squealed.

"Yup. But that's it. Everything else I got covered. Mostly." He tucked a hand into the pocket of his trousers. "There's still food and extras and all, so we'll say it's about 80 percent covered. Enough to make this doable for us."

A spark of excitement sizzled low in my belly as I leaned against the counter next to him.

Airfare.

I ran through all the places we'd talked about going to someday—that elusive *someday* we figured would never actually come, but that we still *hoped* for.

Paris—the city I wanted to visit more than *anything.*

London.

Tokyo.

Even states within our own country. California. Tennessee. Washington.

"Ahhhh"—Jackson pointed his wine glass at me—"there's my happy girl!" He pulled his hand out of his pocket and brushed his thumb against my lips. "I thought we weren't going to see her tonight."

"Are you going to tell me where we're going?" I tipped my tongue out, giving the pad of his thumb a lick. "Or are you gonna keep teasing me?"

"Niverwick Isle." He tapped my lips.

I blinked. "I'm...*Where?*"

"Oh c'mon, babe. It's the *hottest* vacation destination. *Every-one's* been talking about it for the last few years. You *had* to have heard of it." His smile drooped.

Niverwick Isle.

I *had* heard of it. Sure, I had. Like he said, everyone was yapping about it. It took my brain a while to register it because it was so far down on the list of places we'd talked about visiting that it wasn't even *on* the list.

Niverwick was an island—a *remote* island—so shrouded in magic, nothing worked there. No cars, TVs, cell phones...nada. Zilch. Anything made after the year 1900 or so would fail to operate.

That included boats. Visitors had to take a big ole fashioned sail ship to get to the island.

Here was where there was a tiny—*teeny*—smidgeon of a problem.

Ships sailed on the ocean. And this ship would drop people off at a slab of rock *surrounded* by ocean.

And y'know who was *terrified* of the ocean. Like, staring-at-waves-on-TV-too-long-caused-palpitations kind of terrified?

This girl.

And you know what made the ocean *even scarier*?

The star attraction of Niverwick Isle.

"Supposedly spring is the best time to go too," Jackson prattled on. "Nessie's supposed to be more active. A few of the guys at work reckon the beast gets horny come spring." He chuckled. "Suns out, dicks out. Y'know? Probably true, I guess. There is only one Loch Ness Monster, so my man probably does start hankering for some pussy after pounding off to his own hand—er—claw—er—*fin* all winter."

Nessie.

The Loch Ness Monster.

The big, phallic-shaped sea dino who'd once been lobbed off as a prank. A hoax, staged by a bunch of drunk Standie Scotsmen trying to splash themselves on the front page, or fabricated by a drunk sailor who'd peeped Free Willy's willy bobbing atop the sea and thought he'd discovered a new monster.

Either way, Nessie was always called the whiskey monster—that only *really* existed at the bottom of a bottle. Until it'd been found—for real—a few years ago, chilling by a small hunk of land in the North Sea—a place that emanated so much magic, it killed any scrap of technology that came near it. A jumble of rocks and trees now known as Niverwick Isle.

Nessie was the reason the isle became the talk of the town. The reason people siphoned more than $10K from their bank accounts for a week's stay.

Nearly every person in my life wanted to go to the isle, but not a single one could afford it. Jessa lamented at least once a month that the Niverwick experience would be forever out of her reach.

If the price was all-inclusive, maybe it wouldn't have been so terrible. But no. That $10K price tag got you a *room* for a week. If you wanted food or drinks, you could pick from one of the two overpriced restaurants on the isle. Activities and tours were extra. And there was zero option to stay for less than a week to cut down on costs because the ship only sailed on Sundays. So you had to book from Sunday to Sunday. No exceptions.

And if someone had a medical emergency while on the island? Lucky for them, there was a health clinic on site. Most insurances wouldn't cover the stay though, since it was run by Sorcerer Healers instead of Standie doctors.

This was an *exorbitantly* priced vacation destination. No bones about it. The kind only rich folk could enjoy.

And here was Jackson, telling me all we had to pay was the air fare. And a few *extras*.

"Babe?" Jackson huffed. "Did you space out on me?"

I blinked, realizing I'd been staring at our fridge, and tilted my chin back to him, plastering a smile on my face. "A little. I think I'm just..."

Confused.

Disappointed.

"Overwhelmed," I said.

Jackson beamed and drank the last of his wine. "Weren't expecting to come home to this, were ya?"

"No..." I dragged the *o* out slightly. *Nooooo.* "This is—"

"Huge. Right?" He jittered.

"Absolutely. But I guess I'm a little..."

His happy energy soured.

"It's not bad," I said quickly. "Promise. I'm...It's...Are you sure we can afford this, Jackson?"

Indignation fanned from him. "Did I not say—"

"I know. I guess I'm confused about the *how* of it. Like, Jessa's looked into going—"

"Jessa?" He puckered his lips. "Is that your shopaholic friend who hemorrhaged her life savings?"

"That's not fair," I said. "She put a lot of money into her mom's care, and you *know* that."

He raised his hand in a "point taken" gesture.

"But, anyway, Jessa has been *dying* to go to Niverwick. Every time some travel place offers a package deal, she snags a quote. And it's always *extravagant*."

"Sure it is." Jackson rolled his shoulder. "If they dropped the prices, the place would be more crowded than an amusement park. They gotta keep the riffraff out somehow."

Riffraff.

As in, people like us. Who didn't have ten or more thousand smackeroos to drop on a vacation. And I must've made a face at that because Jackson mumbled an irritated, "You know what I mean, babe."

I didn't. But I nodded. Because he was excited, and his joy was infectious, and I *wanted* to bask in it. But…

"How?" I softened the question with a nuzzling kiss to his chin.

"Zohar. You know, my manager." He blew out a gusty sigh.

Because I must've made a face at him. *Again.* "Right. Yes. Of course." I just didn't quite see what Jackson's supervisor had to do with this trip.

"He and his wife have gone every year since opening, and he'd pre-booked this year. But I guess his wife got a bug up her ass and decided she wanted to go to Berlin instead. Imagine that, babe—*Berlin,* over Niverwick Isle."

Oh, I could imagine it alright.

I, too, would rather take a one week furlough in Berlin.

"Anyway, he went to cancel the trip, but it was too close—"

"Too close?"

"—for him to get a refund, so he was out the money anyway. And since I'd closed on the Serphent account for the company, he *offered* the trip to me. *Me.*" He popped up from his half seated position on the island and tapped his heels against the floor.

And I *gaped*.

Jackson worked sales—for grocery chains, mostly—bidding brands to different retailers. Serphent, one of the biggest grocer chains that sold *exclusively* to Sorcerers, had been a *massive* win for Jackson six months ago. Especially since he'd been a *Standie* who'd closed the deal.

I'd been a little—okay, a lot—miffed that he'd never gotten a raise for that. Zohar had thrown Jackson a piddly little pizza party and called it a year.

As if reading my mind, Jackson wagged his finger at me. "You see, babe, I *told* you Zohar had something big for me coming down the pipeline, but you didn't believe me, did you?"

"I *did*—"

"And I haven't even gotten to the best part yet! The booking" —Jackson created a mini drumroll with his heels—"is May first."

"May? That's *two weeks* away!"

"Sure is!" Jackson exclaimed.

"I-I don't…I might not be able to get that time off."

"You've got PTO in the bank, right?"

"Of course, but—"

"They've gotta give it to you then, babe. Just put the request in tomorrow."

"And if it's not approved? I just told you we're dealing with a crisis."

Jackson waved his hand dismissively. "It will be. It's not like you're the PM on the account. They'll manage just fine without you. C'mon, babe! Don't worry about it. *'Don't worry, be happy,'*" he trilled in a Bob Marley impression.

I snorted.

He smirked, plonked his wine glass down on the island, and gave my butt a friendly pinch.

And my snort turned into a full-scale laugh. Because his giddiness had twined around my belly, twisting it into a spinning dance that left my whole body fluttering.

That was what it felt like, anyway.

But the apprehensive knot tying up my chest refused to loosen.

"I am still a little worried," I started.

"Ugh, *babe*." Jackson groaned.

"Just of…I mean…I have to get on a *ship*?"

Jackson sighed gustily as he dropped to one knee in front of me—a very showboat move—

and grabbed my free hand, pressing wet, open-mouthed kisses to it. "I know you had that incident when you were a kid—"

"I almost drowned."

"But the ocean is not some big bad out to get ya. Okay? And the ship has life preservers. You won't drown, I promise." He smooched the back of my knuckles, threw on his handsome boyish grin, and said, "Would you, Pippi Long—"

Oh yeah. Dear old mom went there with my name.

"—do me the *honor* of accompanying me on this grand excursion to Niverwick Isle?"

How could I tell this man no? When he was on his knees before me, looking so unbelievably, painfully, handsome?

When he was so excited?

I'd get over my fear of the ocean. I'd shove it aside, beat it with a stick, do whatever I had to do to get it out of my head, and make this vacation epic for him.

"Yes. Absolutely." I tucked my wine glass more firmly against my chest. "I do have one condition, though."

His blue eyes peered up at me inquisitively.

And stars above, if he wasn't an exquisite sight, with the tight, form-fitting sleeves of his button-down rolled to his elbows, letting the veins and muscled definition of his forearms pop.

My belly somersaulted again.

An impish grin tilted up Jackson's face. I wondered if he could *feel* my arousal—the way my heart had quickened and the heavy heat that'd settled low, *low* in my stomach.

Because the feverish desire pouring off him was *staggering*.

Lovely. *Hot.* Goodness, it was hot. It overwhelmed me, *consumed* me, fanning the aching heat in my belly until I squirmed.

"Yes?" His eyes dragged along my body, savoring me. "Your condition is?"

"Well, I've had a really long day. As you know."

"Hmmmm." He suckled at the back of my knuckles—a move that could've, and *should've,* looked obscene. But he made it seductive. Made me imagine that mouth suckling on other parts of my body—parts that were now *screaming* with want.

"I could use a massage"

"Oh, could you?" Jackson huffed playfully.

"Hmm-hmmm. And maybe a nice hot bath."

"Sounds *wonderful.*"

"And you know what'd *really* make my day better? If I could find a hunky guy who'd be willing to assist me with all that. Do you happen to know a guy who'd do that for me, Jackson?"

Jackson's hand slid up, up, *up.* His hot, soft fingers snuck under my blouse, tracing alluring patterns over my belly. Patterns that had my muscles bunching and left me panting. "I think I know of a guy. And lucky you"—his hand grazed the underside of my left breast—"he's available tonight. And the only payment he requires"—he pinched my nipple—"is a blow job."

4

Pippi

"Eeeeeeuuuuppppuucccccckkk..." I grasped on to the coarse wood railing with all the strength I could muster as my guts hurled themselves overboard.

"*Fuck*, babe." Jackson's hands tapped my back. "How much more do you have left?"

None.

The answer should've been *none*.

I'd been on this ship not even an *hour*. And I'd done *nothing* but puke.

Which was *horrific*. Because A: this rickety wooden vessel had the *sketchiest* bathrooms I'd ever seen. They were toilet seats strapped over a hole.

A hole that led directly to the sea.

I'd crouched by one of those toilets when my stomach first started roiling. But the violent *WORUSH* of the sea whisking beneath the black hole had sent me bolting back to the deck. Where I'd been since, hurling my guts up. I'd cleared a quiet place for Jackson and me to stand, though, since most people had migrated elsewhere once they heard me exorcising my demons, a.k.a, my stomach.

But that led me to the second reason this was so wretched. B: Jackson was at a complete loss.

Uncertainty poured off him as he touched my back—cautiously—standing a little distance away, lest I misaim and splatter some of my demons all over him. "I don't think we're even halfway there." His voice was tight. "Maybe you should've taken the meds earlier."

I'd taken the motion sickness preventative exactly one hour before we boarded the boat. *Exactly.* I'd timed it down to the minute.

It hadn't helped.

Because it wasn't the motion that had my stomach in an uproar. It was the *ocean.*

Seeing it. Hearing it. *Smelling it.*

Oceans stunk. That briny odor grated at my nostrils and made my eyes water.

And all of it together—the sights, sounds, and smells—had made me sticky. *Sweaty.* And set my stomach panickedly working on its evacuation plan.

I heaved again, straining against the railing, squeezing my eyes shut so I wouldn't have to see the frothing waters beneath us.

Someone walked by with a humph of disgust.

"Babe, you should really be doing this *in the bathroom.*" Jackson's fingers fluttered against my shoulder. "Or at least below deck. People are starting to get upset. I know there's a bar down there…"

My stomach surged.

"…so I'm assuming there are some places to sit. That'd be better, right?"

I pressed my knuckles to my mouth, swallowing the fresh flood of bile and making sure it *stayed down* before I croaked, "That'd be *worse.*"

Worse because of the smell. At least up here on the deck, in open air, the brine wasn't overpowering.

Down there, with years of water sediment built into the cracks and crevices, and the sewage-salt scent mixing with the aroma of booze, and the clouds of perfume and cologne from the people crowding the bar…Nope.

Nope. Nope. Nope.

I braced my hands against the railing, forcing myself to stare at it—this weather-worn scrap of wood, with all its cock-eyed grains and gouges and sunspots. Instead of the churning, white-capped grey waters below.

"Should I get someone?" Jackson asked.

Stay calm.

You're okay.

Stay calm.

I drew a long, shuddering breath, trying the four-seven-eight method Jessa always swore by. It never did diddly-squat for me, but y'know, stranger things have happened.

Like me being on a boat. A creaking wooden boat. A boat old enough to be my grandfather. Probably old enough to be my grandfather's grandfather.

A boat that'd once been a stunning vessel—if the grainy old photos we'd seen at the loading dock had been any indicator—with glistening, black-painted wood and crisp white sails. A proud sailing ship, once master of these waters, now geriatric and feeble, reduced to ferrying tourists.

Ferrying them over a *monster-infested ocean.*

My stomach rumbled. I leaned over the railing, bracing, but only a watery belch came up.

"False alarm." I turned to Jackson and tried to smile, but all I felt were tears. And I was afraid that if I did anything—even crinkling my face into a grin—I'd start crying. And he already looked so upset.

"I'm going to get someone." Jackson's arm fell away from my back. "I'm sure there's *something* they can give you. You can't keep going like this, babe. You'll make yourself sick and ruin the whole trip for yourself." His hands dropped to the front of my shoulders. "Can you come back a bit? There's a bench right over here."

He guided me, and I followed, my feet feeling heavy and clumsy as I moved. I didn't *sit* when Jackson tugged me onto a bench. I *fell.*

To my right side, someone sniffed haughtily. The kind of snuffle someone made around an "unbelievable."

"I'm sure she's not the only one onboard getting seasick,"

Jackson snapped as he twisted, extracting our chunky carry-on backpack from his shoulders. "You don't have to act like she's *diseased.*"

"Jackson." I laid my hand over his arm. And I dared a glance at the snobby sniffer, once Jackson had his warm palm against mine.

A middle-aged woman got up from where she'd been seated on the other end of the bench and walked away, pulling up the collar of her coat to protect her neck from the wind. The gale had already snatched her hair, leaving the artfully bleached strands tousled, and the cold had painted her cheeks a deep rosy rouge.

It *was* cold up here, wasn't it? With the sea breeze whipping by and frost still nipping at spring's heels. I hadn't noticed before. Puking was a good workout, y'know?

I felt it now though, the icy air slashing at my overheated, sweat-slicked cheeks. It was *delightful.*

Jackson nudged his arm out from under my hand and unzipped the backpack, frowning as he rooted through our clothes, my polka dot bathroom bag, his saddle brown one, and got to the spare makeup pouch I'd thrown our medications into. "Well, this isn't doing shit," he grumbled at the medicine pack. "'Motion Sickness Relief' my ass." He shoved everything back into the bag and zipped it up. "I'm going to go see if I can get you anything stronger. You gonna be okay here for a second by yourself?"

No.

"Yes," I said. "I'll be okay."

"Okay. Stay away from the railing, though. We don't want you flipping overboard. If you need to hurl again..." He sighed. "Are you *sure* you wouldn't be better off below deck?"

"Positive," I mumbled. "I'll be fine, Jackson. Honest."

I won't be fine. I'm scared. Please don't leave, Jackson.

Jackson stood, scooting the backpack under the bench. "I'll be right back." And off he went.

Leaving me alone. On a boat. Out in the middle of the North Sea.

Waves rumbled and smacked forcefully against the ship's hull. Battering it. *Weakening* it. How many lickings could a boat like this take before it stopped ticking? Before the wood folded beneath the sea's might?

Sweat trickled down my back.

What would happen if this ship sank? Were there lifeboats on board? How many? And would they stand a chance against the sea's behemoth white-capped mountains? Or the monster who dwelled in its depths?

My belly gave another bubbly grumble. I squeezed my eyes shut, fighting to breathe around the mounting nausea. The panic. But I *couldn't.*

I was a child again, battling the sea's malicious grip and watching the shore drift farther, and farther, and farther away. Knowing that no matter how hard I paddled, how viciously I fought, the ocean had me, and it didn't much like relinquishing its victims.

Terror clawed at my insides.

Breathe. You're okay.

My lungs sputtered.

That was a long time ago.

You're not a kid anymore.

Chirp. Chirp. Chirp.

The sound of my phone in my pocket sent me rocketing clear off the bench. I squawked when my bum thumped back down.

A couple walking by stopped and stared at me. They were my age, give or take. Maybe a few years older—already on the downhill slide to the big four-oh.

I smiled at them—*shakily.* The man returned it, tucking his chin into a slight nod, sympathy emanating from him. The woman looked down her nose at me like I was a pile of riffraff.

Which, to be fair, I *felt* like riffraff, wearing my comfy jeans, which were a little (lot) on the baggy side and a little (lot) threadbare around the cuffs and waist. My puffer jacket was the most *gorgeous* shade of shimmering lilac, but it was a full size too big for me. (The smaller sizes had all been *boring* colors).

Jackson called this my purple Michelin Man coat. He wasn't wrong. But I sure loved the color.

Combine my outfit with my red curls, windblown into a tizzy puff, along with the pallid and sickly complexion my skin was likely boasting, and…Yeah. I didn't blame the woman for looking at me like that.

Chirp. Chirp. Chirp.

"Shoot." I jumped again when my cell gave another angry rattle. "I thought you were supposed to stop working out here."

My phone had one bar. One measly bar, a little nick at the top corner. And it was determined to use that last breath of life to torment me.

Notifications flooded the screen, papering themselves over the background image of Jackson and me on the day we moved into our house. Emails. From work.

Andy asked if I could review work orders before I got to the island. Mr. Hollingdale at VitalTech copied and pasted the same message and punched the Send button every hour with the subject line: *Please advise status.*

Several notifications that parts had shipped—*not* for the VitalTech order. *Unfortunately.* But for another hot job we had meandering through the plant. I forwarded those to Jessa.

Company BS emails—y'know, the "happy birthdays" where people had to hit Reply All and clutter everyone's inbox.

More emails from Andy, and texts from him too.

Andy: Pippi…please…these orders have to go ASAP. Jessa doesn't know the account.

Andy: I need you to look at them. We can't afford another fuck up.

Andy: ????

Andy: You're not on the island yet. The ferry doesn't get there until 4:00 p.m. local time. Please review these work orders.

I sighed.

To say Andy had been upset when I'd submitted my PTO and gotten it approved was the understatement of the year—he'd almost cried. Which had dang near made *me* cry.

"I'm happy for you, Pip," he'd said. "Don't think I'm not. It's… *Phew.* Bad timing. I don't know that I could do this without you."

I imagined him sitting in his office, frazzled and working his dark hair into a messy tuft as he tried to figure out the work orders.

And then there were the texts from Jessa and Kai.

Kai: Don't look at those work orders, Pip. You're on vacation.

Jessa: Fuck the work orders. First of all, how dare he think I can't approve them. I see more work orders in an hour than he's looked at in the ten years he's been here. Second of all, it ain't your problem right now. Third of all, he's a big boy. He'll be fine. DO NOT WORRY ABOUT WORK ON YOUR VACATION.

Kai: You don't need to forward the shipping emails. I got them—remember, all your emails are coming to me. Enjoy your trip.

Oops. I should've read this before I shot the notifications to Jessa's email.

Jessa: You know I'm mega jealous, right? Have I told you that? ENJOY IT. Seriously. I know it's not your dream vacation, but girl! You're heading to the land of magic. To be PAMPERED. Have fun. And make sure you have a few drinks for me. XOXO.

I smiled, opened her text and started to type a response, but—

Around the ship, a chorus of "ughs" and "I needed one more minute" snaked into the air.

"That's it then," a man somewhere to my right declared. "We've crossed the reef. No more cell phones, boys."

My phone locked up, briefly flashed a NO SIGNAL at the top, then cut to a spinning wheel of death before it shut down.

Welp. There went that.

A thread of terror wriggled in my stomach. Around me, some people cheered. Others lamented the loss of their phones…their cameras, mainly.

"See that fog up there?" some man said. "Wouldn't have been able to get pictures through that anyway."

The wriggling terror worm did a funky little jig in my gut.

I tucked my phone back into my pocket and put my head down, resting it between my knees. Tried to focus on anything, *anything,* but where we were. On the ocean, now totally cut off from the outside world…

"Color…"

"Colorful things…from the ground…"

That voice. I popped my head back up, swiveling this way and that.

Fifty or so people spanned the length of the deck (there were one hundred or more on this ship, but with a chunk of them boozing it up below), and everyone was talking. Clamoring. But none were *that* voice.

That voice tugged at something inside of me—something deep. Like a memory I'd lost and completely forgotten about until something dredged it back up.

Déjà vu, some called that sensation. Others swore it was old magic trying to reawaken in a person—wishful thinking, mostly. Nearly everyone wanted to be a Sorcerer, but less than five percent of the population had magic.

"What's their word?"

The voice tickled my brain just as a scream shattered the misty air. Not a scared one —although it spooked the life out of me. That squeal was pure, unadulterated excitement.

"Oh, ooooh, OOOOOHH!" A woman bellowed. "I saw it! Lionel! I *saw it!* Come quick! It's the monster!"

5

Alistair

Something is missing.

A *word.*

I'm always missing words. But I can *see* this one. An image of colors—ones that don't exist in these waters. The closest I come to seeing them is on the surface. When the…

Orb…

Sun.

When the *sun* rises. And when it sets.

This image, which I can see, but can't find the word for, has color. Lots of color.

The colors come from…

The ground?

A feeling scratches my insides.

Restlessness?

Is that the feeling?

Or is that what the feeling causes?

It's deeper, though, this feeling. It grips me. *Burns* me. Makes me billow and snort, in ways that scare the remaining water creatures. They *hide* when they hear me approaching.

And that hurts me.

I hate that I'm losing my words.

Hate that I'm so…*restless* at losing my words.

The waters around me stir, as though also restless with this unnamed emotion.

And the…

Dark thing…

Shadow.

The shadow floats overhead, stealing the sun.

It carries sound with it—human sounds.

Speaking.

They've passed over me before. The shadow and the speaking. Normally, I don't notice them unless I am called to visit the humans. Then I have no choice but to leave the depths of my water and surface to…

Amuse?

I surface to *amuse* the humans.

But no such call tugs at me today. The rune above my eye, which burns and pulls when I must amuse the humans, is cool and still.

But my restlessness drives me to follow the shadow. The speaking.

Perhaps, as humans speak their words, I will find the one I am aching for.

The colorful thing. A soft, soft, colorful thing.

It grows from the ground. On the warm days. After the ice leaves.

It is plucked from that ground. So it can be shared.

And I share it with people. With *Indigo* most of all.

I share *many*—groups of those colorful things.

It brings me *joy* to share them. Because it brings others joy to receive them.

And that's the image I see—a cluster of the colorful things, wrapped in a long, pale hand that had once been mine.

What is the *word*? Why can't I remember it?

I swim, following the waters left restless in the shadow's wake. And hope.

Maybe these humans will give me a word back.

As people flocked to the rear of the ship, where the woman was still stammering that she'd *seen* the monster, my belly pulled. Not up, as it'd been doing this whole ride. *Down.* As though an anchor had wrapped around my gut and was trying to rip it straight through the hull of the boat.

"Where is it?"

"It was there! *Right there.*"

"Where?"

"I don't *see* it."

"There's no way she saw it. Not with these waves."

"Wait! He's here! See there…Look at that big-ass shadow!"

"That's the shadow from the ship, you dolt."

The mass of people clamoring at the railing, shoving at each other as they tried to get a clear look at the monster, smudged my vision. Their screeches and hollers made my ears ring. Sweat ran in long, meandering lines down my back, making my skin prickle. Itch.

There was too much. Too much noise and movement. Too much *emotion.*

It was suffocating me.

My hands jiggled—a nervous tic that drove most people *insane.*

"Babe, why d'ya have to shake your hands like that?" Jackson had bemoaned on more than one occasion. "You look like you're about to explode."

Because it feels *like I'm about to explode*, I'd always wanted to say. But I could never explain the why of it. How sometimes I felt *too much*. More than what my body could handle. And the hand-jiggling helped get rid of the excess.

It wouldn't make sense to anyone. Because it didn't make sense to me. So I clasped my hands together instead, twisting my fingers around each other until my knuckles popped.

"That's him! That's his tail!"

"Daddy! I wanna see the lock monster."

A small blur warbled in my right peripheral just as a wave of impatient desperation niggled at me to turn that way.

A little boy—he couldn't have been older than six or seven—was half swallowed in the wall of adults along the railing. He stood between his parents, a tall, heavily muscled man and a willowy woman, and he kept tugging at the man's sleeve, crying, "Daddy! I wanna see!"

"Why can't I remember it?"

I blanched when that odd voice coiled around my brain again. And my stomach abruptly took another nosedive, leaving me doubled over, wondering if I was going to faint or vomit or do a bit of both.

"Miss, are ye alright?"

I choked out a startled *"gah"* in response to the man who'd spoken into my left ear.

"Apologies." A warm hand flattened over my shoulder as a bulky body shifted around to my front. "I didn't mean ta startle ye." He dropped to a crouch, leveling me with a concerned stare.

This man had the harsh, weather-wrinkled face of someone who'd spent most of his days exposed to the cruelest of nature's elements, but his slanted smile was soft, and his grey eyes kind. Tranquil energy curled off him, calming the riot in my heart and stomach. And he spoke with a fascinating brogue—not Scottish, or Irish, but something that sounded like those two accents had had a love child with a Welshman. A billowing navy jacket draped over his shoulders, with a big gold pin on the lapel that had the word *Valiant* inscribed in a half circle. The name of our ship.

Our captain? *Maybe?*

I smiled up at him, as best as I could manage with as shaky as I still felt. "I'm easily startled. While on this ship, at least. Although, heh…That's not really true. I'm a bit of a chicken on a *good* day."

The man huffed, "Ach, means yer a sensitive soul, eh? Or so thuy say."

"That's me." I winced when a wave smacked against the side of the boat—a wall of water big enough to make the vessel shudder. My belly gave a viscid twist. "My stomach's definitely being *extra* sensitive today."

"I thought ye looked a littlah green around the gills." The man reached into his pocket. "First time on the sea?"

"Ummm. First time as an *adult.*"

"Oh, aye? Had ye trouble on the sea as a child?"

"Not on a boat. Just…" I blew out a breath, trying, but failing, to expel the memory.

The memory of being small—too small to have been allowed to swim in the ocean, but also too small to have a fear of the sea, or the common sense to avoid it.

My mom and dad had been arguing that day. That was all they did until they finally split when I was ten. Even on vacation they kept their teeth in each other's jugulars, constantly bickering and gnawing. But that day, Dad had been *extra* vicious, and he'd taken some big, painful bites out of Mom, before he'd stormed away.

To soothe the raw wounds he'd left, Mom had turned to alcohol. Bought two six-packs of beer from a peddler on the boardwalk and guzzled them like she'd found water in the middle of the desert.

By the time I went out into the ocean, Mom had been in booze lala land. She hadn't seen me venture into the waves without my swimmies. Hadn't seen me shrieking with delight when the water bounced me up and down. Hadn't seen me wailing in panic when the undertow hauled me out to the deep.

The ocean very nearly claimed me that day. *Would* have

claimed me, if the lifeguard on duty hadn't spotted me flailing and come to my rescue.

"Eh?" the man beside me prompted gently.

"Yeah. Ummmm…The ocean kinda terrifies me. Not kinda. It *does* terrify me. I'd honestly rather be *anywhere* but here right now. I almost drowned when I was a kid. And, y'know…" I exhaled. "Well, *hopefully* you know. And I'm not just babbling like an idiot."

"Aye." The man gave another warm huff. "I know. Ye didna need to trouble yerself, lassie. The sea is a might not to be trifled with. Any who spend time with her knuws that. Here." He'd found the thing he'd been rummaging for in his pocket and handed it to me.

I stared at the little, label-less tin in his hand. "Ermmm…"

"Peppermint," he said.

"Ah. No offense, but I don't think my stomach can handle any food right now. Even a mint."

"It's fer yer nose." He tapped the top of his lip with his other hand, just below his nostrils. "The scent. Calms the illness from the sea."

"Oh, yeah. I guess I can try that. Thanks!" When I took the tin and opened it, a rush of peppermint rose from the Vaseline-like goop and walloped my nostrils.

It was almost *painfully* strong. My eyes watered. But it certainly drowned out the brine of the sea. So I dipped my fingers in and smeared the goo along my upper lip.

"Better?" the man asked when I sniffed and closed the tin.

"Better. Yeah. A little. Thank you."

He nodded and popped the tin back into his pocket.

"That's an interesting accent you've got there." I inhaled, drawing as much of the minty aroma as I could into my lungs. "Where are you from?"

He rolled his shoulder. "All over, really. Me pa was army, ye ken, so they didna fuss much for keepin' families in one place."

"Ah. I totally get that. My boyfriend was in the military too. Air Force. Did the four years. Said it felt too wasteful because it was all Standies who were enlisted. But it was always Sorcerers running everything—they never got their hands dirty though. They sent the Standies to fight and die, and half the people didn't even know what they were fighting *for*. Which…Sorry. I'm babbling. I do that sometimes. Especially when I'm nervous. And I've been a nervous wreck since I got on this thing." I thumped my heels against the floor.

The man rolled his shoulders again. "I wouldna say yer babblin' any. And ye wouldna be the first to be afeared on the passage." He shoved his hands into his pockets, protecting them from the chill. "Which is why I worried when I found ye alone. Did yer boyfriend not make the trip?"

"Oh no, he's here. Somewhere. He actually went looking for you and your magic peppermint oil. Well…I mean…he didn't *know* you had the magic peppermint oil, but he was hoping a worker would have something that'd help. So when you head back to…wherever, and you see a tall, worried looking man with blond hair—that's Jackson."

The man nodded. "Understandable. If ye think ye'll be needin' more of the peppermint, I can leave it with ye."

"No." My nose twitched, the skin around my nostrils tingling from the goop. "I'm good now. As good as I can be, anyway. I'll be better once we get to the island. Goodness, it's cold though, isn't it?" A vicious gale snaked its way across the deck, biting the back of my neck. "And the website said to expect mild to hot climates on the isle. They must have a different definition of *mild* and *hot*."

"The isle'll be warm," the man said. "Once we make landfall, the cold'll dissipate."

"*Really?* Uh…how?"

"Runes. Magic." His shoulder popped up in another half shrug. "Don't rightly ken how it all works, mind, but they keep the temperature fair. Canna do much for the fog though."

"AHH!"

The explosion of excited screeches made me jump—*again*— and set the man standing out of the crouch he'd been in.

"THERE!" a woman hollered. "That's *definitely* him. See the shadow—the fins!? Where's my phone? Oh *fuck*. Dead? *Ugh*."

"Where?"

"I see him!"

"He's half under the ship!"

"He's *bigger* than the ship."

A nervous chill rattled my spine. "You don't think they really see it, do you?" I turned to the man. "The Loch Ness Monster?"

"They might. But I'd not trouble yerself, lassie. He'll not be emergin' from the sea, nor will he bother this ship."

"You're sure? I mean, I'm not doubting your expertise, but I'd imagine he's a fairly sizable creature."

"Oh, aye. Forty American feet, as I heard it."

Forty American feet. The label for our silly, outdated metric system got me to smile, even as the number made me shiver. "And you don't think a forty-foot monster would ever...I don't know, throw a tantrum and smash this ship?"

"He might, if he weren't controlled."

"Controlled?"

"Aye. Runes. Magic. He canna breach the surface until commanded, which is usually dun when he's called to eat—they dunna let him eat the creatures from the deep, ye see—or if they want him seen on a tour. He canna touch this ship either—'less he wants to feel a right nasty bout of pain."

"That sounds..."

Cruel, I wanted to say, but didn't.

The man seemed to hear the unspoken word, though. "May not be the finest way of keepin' him. But he's kept, and safe. And the people are safe." He inclined his head to the gawkers hanging over the railing. "I suppose that's all that matters."

"I guess."

Something jangled in my belly though. Not really sympathy. Or nerves. Definitely not more upchuck (thank the stars). But I frowned, trying to place the odd feeling. And *why* I was feeling it.

"Ah," the man beside me muttered, his voice so low it was

almost lost under the next storm of *ohs* and *ahs* from the group. "This'll be yer boyfriend, eh? Tall fellow with yellow hair, like ye said."

I turned and exhaled when I saw Jackson rushing toward us from the front of the ship.

"That's him," I said.

"Then I'll leave ye be now." The man swiped a hand over his chin. "Yer in good hands, eh?"

"Very. Thank you. So very much. And I'm sorry, I was super rude, I never even asked for your name."

He tipped his head with a slow, gentle smile. "Caleb," he said.

"Caleb." I rolled it over on my tongue. "*Thank you.* For the magic peppermint oil." I tapped my nose. "And the company."

"My pleasure, lassie." He turned and prowled along the deck, watching the gaggle of people hanging over the rail with a concentrated knit in his brow.

"Babe!" Jackson jogged the last few feet and plopped onto the bench beside me. "Looks like I wasted my time trying to find help, huh? Help found you, but..." He clapped a hand to my thigh—and his fingers were *frigid.* Goodness. The cold stabbed through my jeans.

I chaffed at his knuckles, warming them.

"I saw the Loch Ness Monster! Or its shadow, anyway. I was in the perfect spot and watched it pass right under the ship. It was *huge.* E-*nor*-mous." Jackson was almost breathless with excitement.

And I was breathless too. With *not* excitement. "How big?"

"Easily bigger than this ship."

I gulped.

"And some of the guys over there were talking, and—" Jackson stopped and scowled when the little boy, excreting clouds of disappointment over being unable to see over the railing and having his pleas to be picked up ignored by his parents, began howling. "What a fucking brat," Jackson grumbled.

"He wants to see the monster too," I said. "But his legs are too little, and his parents were shutting him out. It's sad."

"They're not ignoring him now though, huh?"

As the little boy bunched his hands into fists and worked his gaping mouth around the torrent of emotion spewing out of him, his parents had finally turned to him. But rather than offering to lift him up so he could see, they scolded him, which only made him cry harder.

My heart thrashed against my chest, begging me to go to the boy and lift him over the railing so he could see. To do *something* to assuage his distress. My hands fidgeted.

Jackson heaved a hearty breath and clasped his fingers over my knuckles, stilling them. "Should we move you somewhere quieter?"

"I'm fine, Jackson." I shifted, tucking my feet up onto the bench and prying my hands loose so I could curl against his side.

"Are you still not feeling better?" Jackson asked.

No.

The nausea had passed, as had some of the panic. But the boy's explosive unhappiness was fueling my own distress, and a strange, wriggling emotion had begun coiling in my gut. I was afraid to move, lest my uproarious stomach start heaving again.

So I pressed my face into Jackson's neck, where it was warm and safe, and closed my eyes, mumbling. "I am better. Honest, Jackson. I'm just tired."

He exhaled and leaned back, letting me snuggle into him.

But that odd feeling kept writhing and twisting around my heart in a wild, painful dance.

And I suddenly, *desperately*, wanted to go home.

"**W**elcome to Niverwick Isle! Where magic, monsters, and marvel await!"

That welcome spiel was spoken *by a cat.*

As I shuffled with the other tourists down a long, bedraggled dock, I *swore* the bouts of repeated vomiting had done me in. Rendered me so dehydrated, so woozy, that I'd seen the bell-shaped cat shadow at the end of the dock and had a random blip of a thought (*That is the cutest pudge cat I've ever seen. And it's waiting for us. Maybe that's the guest services attendant Caleb said would meet us.*) that my brain tried to turn into reality.

Cats didn't talk. Not even on magic islands. *Right?*

Fog curled lazily around us, forming a thick, smoggy veil that was almost impossible to see through. The people at the front of our group, a mere six or so feet away, had turned into hazy smudge blobs, and there seemed to be nothing beyond the eroded surface of the dock—nothing but a wall of white, broken only by the little bell-shaped shadow.

My fingers dug into Jackson's arm when the warped planks of wood grumbled beneath our feet.

"I trust you've had a pleasant trip?" The cat's shadow moved, its head following our trek across the dock.

"Babe." Jackson's breath danced over my ear. "Did that cat just talk?"

"Oh good," I whispered back. "You heard that too?"

"Uh-huh."

"Thank the stars. I thought I was losing it."

The novelty of the talking cat didn't sink in for most folks, though. Not right away, at least. Some were so deep in conversations, they likely hadn't heard the welcome statement. And others were probably expecting to find a person lurking behind the veil of smog. But then the first cluster of people reached the end of the dock, and their whispered titters wove their way back to us.

"Aw, it's a cat!"

"It's talking?"

"Well, he's a *magical* cat. Obviously."

Waves belted the bottom of the dock, making the wood rasp in protest. I shivered when icy water flecked under the hems of my jeans and bit back the urge to cry in relief when the swirling curtains of fog thinned, revealing the craggy surface of the island.

The cat blinked at Jackson and me as we stepped off the dock and joined the group of people queuing around a dinky, pockmarked sign that read, "Welcome to Niverwick Isle! Please wait for an attendant."

"Welcome," the cat drawled.

He was a long and lanky orange tabby. A real handsome feller too, sitting all proud and tall, with his little pouchy cat belly sploshed over his feet. His wide, bottle-green eyes were sweet and innocent looking, and almost too big for his face.

"Oh, my!" A woman behind me cooed, excitement boinging off her as she shuffled flush against my back, peering over my shoulder at the cat. "How *precious*. I can't! Oh my goodness, I *cannot*."

"Don't know that I'd call it *precious*, Melany. It's a little creepy," another woman muttered.

"Pft, don't be silly, love," Melany trilled. "He's a *treasure*."

I had to smile.

The woman behind me smelled crisp and fresh—like the perfume counter at a high-end department store. All those fragrances that were decadent and sharp and rich and very, very, *very* expensive. And Melany looked the expensive and sophisticated sort. She was older, in her late-sixties, maybe early-seventies. Although I would never presume that a sophisticated dame, such as herself, would fall on the older end of the scale. So, I'd guess her age was around sixty. She was dressed to the nines in a cleanly pressed long skirt, which fluttered down to her booted ankles, a form-fitted suit jacket, and an elegant black coat. A neat plait of silvery hair twined over her left shoulder.

And here she was, this elegant woman, all hunched up against my back, probably getting some good whiffs of my sweat-rank skin and vomit breath.

But she smiled at me when she noticed I'd turned to look at her. A big, white-toothed grin that wrinkled the skin around her mouth and temple—skin untouched by either the chemicals the Standies often turned to or the cosmetic magic the Sorcerers could wield. Her sophisticated beauty was *au naturel.*

"Don't you just wanna march over there and give the cat a good smooshing?" I said to Melany, being mindful to keep my foul breath aimed away from her face.

"Yes." She gave my shoulder a giddy swat.

And I immediately decided I liked her. A lot.

Some people just gave off good vibes. Happy vibes.

"You are *not* smooshing that cat," Jackson hissed in my ear.

I stood on my tiptoes and nuzzled his neck, peppering little kisses there.

"I wonder if it's actually the cat talking, or if a Sorcerer is throwing his voice," Melany pondered out loud to her partner. "Remember when we went to that safari thing? And that handsome Sorcerer boy was doing voices for all the creatures. You were ready to scoop up that little raccoon."

Her partner sniffed and ran her hand down the front of her slate grey trousers. She looked a few years younger than Melany and had a softer kind of suave to her. From the artfully untidy bob of chocolate-and-grey-specked hair that brushed her cheeks, to the crooked smile she threw at Melany, down to the simple, but well-fitted trousers and peacoat she wore. "The racoon was cute—"

"So is this cat."

"—ter. Cuter than the cat."

Melany gave an overdramatic gasp. "That's it, love. We need to divorce. To say a racoon is cuter than this precious angel," she tutted. Warmly. *Jokingly.*

The other woman gave a *harrumph* that might've sounded stiff and snotty, if it wasn't so basked in love and affection.

And I officially liked both of them.

"This your first time on the island?" I angled myself to face them.

"Babe." Jackson pinched my arm.

"*Yes.*" Melany beamed at me. "It's so exciting, isn't it?"

Not the word I'd use. But... "Sure is," I said. "It's our first time as well, and Jackson's been telling me there are some other creatures here. I thought it was just the Loch Ness Monster... but I sometimes live under a rock." Truthfully, I hadn't been interested enough to dig into everything the island offered. "Is there anything you're really eager to see?"

"Babe, c'mon." Jackson hefted our backpack a little more firmly onto his shoulders and twined an arm around my waist, pulling my back against his chest. "You don't have to chat with everyone in line."

"It's just a little casual conversation," I said.

At the same time, Melany responded, laughing, "At the moment, I'm obsessed with this cat. But if you ask me again in fifteen minutes, I'll give you a different answer."

"And you'll get a different answer fifteen minutes after that." Her partner chuckled.

"Right!" the cat chirped again, making several people squeal and giggle. "If I could have your attention for a moment—"

Melany bounced. "*Oooooh*, look at its little mouth moving!"

"—so I can make sure everyone hears me." The cat stood, dropped into a long, languid stretch, and meandered closer to us, his little paws padding silently over the rocky surface.

Jackson stiffened against me and hissed sharply through his teeth.

"Zohar didn't tell you about the cat?" I whispered.

Jackson sniffled. "No."

"Oh no. He *should've*, considering—"

"He doesn't know I'm allergic," Jackson cut me off.

"Oh."

"Yeah."

Jackson, you see, had some whopping allergies. Cats made him sneeze and break out in hives. So did dogs. Anything with dander, really. It was why we didn't have any pets.

I had a bunny when we started dating. Good ole Roger (like Roger Rabbit, get it?). He was such a friendly, happy little floof, and I'd given him free roam of my one-bedroom apartment, which meant Jackson hadn't been able to come over to my place. He'd start sneezing his head off as soon as he walked in the door.

Thankfully, Jessa had been able to take Roger when Jackson and I'd gotten the house together. If she hadn't…

I mean, I would've kept him. For sure. My heart wouldn't have handled surrendering him to a shelter. But poor Jackson would've suffered for it.

I twisted my head and gave Jackson a peck on the cheek, careful not to blast my foul breath over his face. "Your antihistamines are in the medicine pouch," I said. "I wasn't thinking we'd have a cat attendant, but y'know, I packed *everything*. Just in case."

"What would I do without you?" Jackson turned his lips to my forehead.

"Live in misery, I suppose."

"Quiet, please." The cat's tiger-striped tail flicked as he circled our group.

"Sorry," I mumbled during one of his rotations.

The cat stopped, fixed me with a look that almost screamed, "don't talk to me, peasant," and carried on with his announcements. "Your bags are already being transported to your rooms. I know you were told to leave them behind, and for many that is a cause for concern. Rest assured, your belongings are well cared for and are waiting for you."

"The cats dragged them in, eh?" a man at the front of the group boomed.

"Hoo-hoo, that's incentive not to be a dick to the staff, eh, Chapman?" someone else crowed. "You might find a hairball in your boxers."

"Ugh," a woman grunted. "I do *not* want a cat touching my stuff. Do I have to pay extra for a human?"

"That'll be another $2K," a man chortled. "For the privilege of having your belongings be hair free."

"I"—the tip of the cat's tail gave us a haughty wave—"am merely your *guide.* Rest assured, travelers, there is an abundance of human employees on this isle. It is not run by cats."

"How amazing would that be if it *was* run by cats, though?" I whispered to Jackson. "If our rooms were in these big cat trees, and we slept in these giant, poofy cat beds. The food might not be so great. All seafood all the time, probably. But they'd have things like cat yoga and laser tag and—"

"Babe, pump the brakes on that imagination train." Jackson shuddered. "That's a *nightmare.*"

I laughed and snuggled more firmly against him.

"When you arrive at the lobby, each of you will be handed a brochure with information about the island," the cat carried on, raising his voice above the whispers and giggles. "I'd advise that you take the time to look through it. You'll find a map of the isle, as well as a list of all activities and tours."

"He is so *stinking cute,*" Melany cooed.

The cat's tail twitched again as his eyes rolled over us. "It is always a delight to see the joy and wonder my greeting leaves upon travelers," he said, in a flat voice that sounded anything *but* delighted.

"Do you think he'll let me pet him?" Melany asked.

The cat's ears flattened, as though he'd heard her query. And he turned, fixing her with a severe stare that said, very clearly, "pet at your own risk."

"I think that's a *no*." Melany's partner chuckled. "You'll just have to wait 'til we get home and give our fluffballs extra pets."

"Now..." the cat spoke around a jaw-cracking yawn. "I'm certain you are all hungry and weary and longing for your rooms. But I would like to offer a word of caution before we proceed. Niverwick Isle is home to many beasts, and I will emphasize that word—*home*. This is their home. You are their guests, and we expect guests to behave accordingly. There will be *no touching* of any of Niverwick's beasts. There will be no disturbances to their lives, or disruptions of their feeding. You may *observe*, you may not *interfere*. Is this in any way unclear?"

Melany blew out a disappointed breath.

I turned and flashed her a sympathetic smile.

"I do wish to assure you," the cat continued, raising his voice over the babbling, "that none of these beasts will cause you harm. We all coexist peacefully with our guests."

As long as our guests coexist peacefully with us. He didn't say that last part, but it was so heavily implied in his haughty stare that I heard it clear as day in my head.

"The walk to the lobby is short enough and easy to traverse," the cat carried on. "The walk to your lodging may be close, or may be far, but transportation will be available to you should you wish it."

"Ooh, bicycles?" I whispered to Jackson. "Do you think?"

"I suppose," he sighed.

"I'll cart you around, don't worry!"

Jackson couldn't ride a bike. But I *loved* going for bike rides, especially in fair weather—although maybe not weather as *sticky* as what the island was becoming.

I hadn't noticed the heat, at first, coming off the ship where the air had been so cold. The warmth had snuck up on me, but my jacket was starting to feel like a sauna.

As I wriggled out of Jackson's arms, getting ready to shrug the jacket off, the cat pulled a coinkydink and mentioned the weather. "Due to the magic coursing through the Isle, the air is often quite humid," he droned. "Unfortunately, there will be no central cooling systems in any of the buildings—we do apologize for that inconvenience—but we've been assured by previous guests that the heat is not intolerable."

"Better the heat than the cold," Jackson said.

I slipped my jacket all the way off, spot checking my blouse for any wayward puke stains. Thankfully, the blue-and-white checker material was in the clear—thank *goodness.* I adored this blouse, with its billowy sleeves and poofy shoulder pads. Lots of people said shoulder pads looked dated or silly. I had to agree to disagree with them. Because I flipping *loved* what they did to my profile—making me look proud and tall. Taller than my five feet, three inch frame, at least.

"Lovely blouse," Melany said.

I beamed over my shoulder at her. "Thank you!" I knew there was a reason I'd liked her.

"Now then"—the cat meandered to the front of the group, holding his tiger-striped tail as high as it would go—"with those unpleasantries out of the way, allow me to extend the warmest of welcomes to Niverwick Isle. May your stay be *extraordinary.* Follow me! And stay close, please. The fog can be dense and disorienting when you're not acclimated to it. But if you do fear yourself lost, do not hesitate to call out. You'll find my hearing is quite sharp."

There was a lot of scuffling and chattering as the group followed him into the mist.

"We've got a bloody *cat* for a tour guide. What a world. *What. A. World.*"

"I'm never looking at a cat the same way again."

"*...will I ever remember?*"

I stopped dead in my tracks as *that* voice snaked through my ears again. The same one I'd heard on the ship.

"Babe?" Jackson tugged on my arm.

"*...more words. Lost. Always lost.*"

That voice had an...accent. A delightful one to boot. It sounded British—a high brow sort of British, though. The sort that belonged more on the royals than on the common folk.

But it was also...familiar. I'd never heard it before. Ever. But my heart bounced in my chest as though it was a dear and long-lost friend speaking to me.

I peered behind me, watching the shifting current of faces as people lurched by, hastening to stay with the rest of the group. I saw no one I recognized. *No one.* But that *voice.*

"Pippi!" Jackson gave my arm a sharper tug. "C'mon. What are you doing?"

"I..." I swiped my sweaty palm over my jacket, making sure the sleeves were secured in their knot around my waist. "Thought I saw someone I knew."

Jackson's brow rose. "I doubt that."

"Right. Yeah. Because we're the riffraff slumming it with the royals, right?"

I had *no* idea where that came from. The comment and the snark. Both had just *burst* out of me.

Jackson's head whipped as though I'd slapped him. "Babe..."

"I'm sorry," I muttered, leaning up to peck his cheek. "I'm just...a little cranky right now. And a lot woozy. I need a nap."

He nodded. "Me too." He stroked a hand along my back, giving my rump a playful squeeze, before he took my arm again. "Almost there."

"Lost..."

My heart clenched as the voice echoed in my ear again.

"All. Lost."

y gut squiggled with nerves. Leftover from the ship, I assumed. Because, well, *anxiety*. It did strange things to the body. Like making it hear voices, apparently.

Because that was the *only* explanation I had for that weirdness.

But even as we trekked inland, and the whooshing of the sea faded into the distance, my belly still tumbled around itself.

And then I figured it was the island throwing me off kilter. Because the fog was…interesting. To say the least. Very *gothic*, with the way it draped around the spiky boulders and gravelly soil that made for most of the landscape.

"Is it always this foggy?" a woman asked at one point.

"Oh yes," came the cat's drizzling response. "Always. The only place you have a chance of seeing the sun is in the mountains at the northernmost point of the isle. We do have hiking trails—for beginner and experienced hikers. The brochure will give you more information."

That was somewhat depressing to hear.

I liked a little fog now and again. Liked the surrealness of it. The way it made me feel as though I'd stepped out of my world and into an alternate dimension where Dracula waited just behind the swirling mist—a *nice* Dracula, though. One who was kind and thoughtful and maybe a bit sad, as he struggled with his curse.

I'd always had a thing for a sweet, brooding hero.

But the thought of being consumed in this sticky fog and not seeing the sun, or the moon, or the stars for the entire week's stay...that was a tough pill to swallow.

It wasn't the reason I felt off, though. *Something* else had my emotions in an uproar. I just didn't know *what.*

"This is the lobby and Information Center." The cat's voice meandered through the smog, reaching us before the blurred shadow of the building emerged. "As well as Brew & Bites—one of our premier restaurants. Breakfast runs from 6:00 a.m. to 11:00 a.m. each morning, and dinner begins at 3:00 p.m. As a reminder, a breakfast buffet is included with your stay. Dinner is not."

"Oh, wow," Jackson gruffed as the building came into focus. *"That's* ugly."

I pursed my lips, almost, but not quite, agreeing with his assessment. "I wouldn't say that. It's unique."

"Yeah. Unique and *fugly.*"

"I wonder if it's that color to help people see it through the fog?"

The building was a sprawling Georgian-style structure, all rigid with harsh lines. But instead of the traditional brick, this place was made of pumpkin orange stone and framed with pastel yellow window casings and doors.

That orange was *something.* Something I wasn't sure I liked, but I commended it. Bright colors were fun, and that orange was like a splash of sunlight against the slate grey island.

The *inside,* however, was a bit generic.

A sweeping set of French doors led us into the lobby. Three candle-lit chandeliers hung suspended from the ceiling, casting a warm glow over the shimmering black marble floor. Glittering clusters of mahogany furniture were placed strategically around the room, offering lots of plush chairs for people to rest in, and plenty of tables to hold their food, drinks, or other knickknacks. Each table had a tired-looking vase of flowers, and a few bland historical-type paintings hung from the walls.

The cat bounded on top of an expansive lobby desk and

turned his back to us. Like, "I'm done with you, stupid peasants. Bother someone else now."

A large chalkboard took up most of the wall behind the desk, and a piece of chalk was scribbling names in big uniform letters.

Jackson and I both spent several seconds ogling that piece of chalk. Because it moved *by itself.*

"Magic!" Jackson squeezed my shoulder excitedly.

"Welcome!" A tall woman, with sleepy green eyes, stood behind the desk, waving at us. "We understand many of you have traveled a long way to be here and want to get to your rooms and rest. We'll have you there as soon as we can. To expedite this process, please check your name as it appears on the board—if you have trouble seeing or reading the board, kindly let a staff member know. If all looks well with your party, you'll see a cabin number appear next to your name. We ask that you please line up according to your cabin number. Cabins W1-W50 on my left, and E1-E50 on my right."

"That's really freaking cool." A tall man with short-cropped brown hair clapped his hands, amazement pouring off him. "How does it know all our names, though?"

The woman dragged her drowsy eyes to him. "We know the names of everyone who sets foot on the isle, Mr. Blakehurst."

Mr. Blakehurst blinked at her and then burst out laughing. "So freaking cool."

"There's us, babe!" Jackson jabbed his finger to a line at the bottom of the board.

Pippi Long. Jackson Taylor. E20.

Slight scuffling ensued for several minutes as people shifted to the right and left of the desk and sorted themselves into numerical order. Lots of "what number are you?" questions fluttered around. Some people emoted tendrils of frustration—at being delegated near the back of the line or having to keep asking about cabin numbers—while most teemed with excitement and awe.

My stomach kept doing its odd wriggling, though. Even as

Jackson wrapped his arms around me and pressed buoyant kisses to my brows and cheeks.

Something was off. But *what?*

"Very good!" the woman called when the shuffling lines stilled. "We're going to bring you up in order and get you checked in. Once you receive your key, kindly proceed through this door." She turned and pointed to a four-panel door to the left of the desk. "There will be transportation outside. Your bags are already in your rooms."

I did my best to ignore the jiggling in my belly as we checked in and received a pair of old-fashioned brass keys, before we were ushered out the door to await our ride.

"Please stay behind the railing," a tall and slightly gangly female attendant droned to the clusters of people coming out the door and fanning out along a ramp.

Jackson and I shuffled into place behind a family of six—a haggard-looking man and woman in their mid-to-late forties, and their exuberant crew of four children, all under the age of ten.

"Mom! Mom!" the youngest boy called as he bounced up and down along the rail. "I see it!"

"You don't see nuthin'," his older sister snuffed.

"I do too!"

"Do *not!*"

"DO TOO!"

Jackson heaved a big sigh. I patted his arm and gave the children's mother an empathetic smile as she chided the youngest one for screaming.

"You've a beautiful family," I said.

She looked up, surprised, and gave me a big, proud grin.

"But I see it for real! Mom! Look!" The youngest boy thrust his arm between the pillars of the railing and pointed into the fog.

And there *was* something there.

A *big* something.

The heavy *kerthunk-kerthunk-kerthunk-kerthunk* of hooves

clattered against the rocky terrain as two enormous black horses punched through the mist and trotted to the end of the ramp, where they came to a synchronized halt.

"A horse-drawn carriage!" one of the kids squealed.

The two horses were strapped to a big wooden wagon—spacious enough to seat several dozen people, with room to spare.

But the thing was…

They *weren't* horses.

Horses didn't usually have *horns.*

"Are they unicorns?" I breathed, turning to Jackson.

"Alicorns," the attendant said in an uninterested voice—the tone of someone who'd delivered a spiel one too many times. "They're quite docile, I assure you, and would love a head scratch or two, if you are so inclined to do so. Although we warn all travelers to mind their horns."

"We try to mind our own horns." The bulking beast on the right snorted.

"But we lament at their placement," added the one to the left. "We have no sight directly in front of our eyes. If one were to wander too close, they may not be seen."

The words were spoken lightly. *Amicably.* But they almost *seemed* threatening, because the beasts looked so malicious.

A silken coat of black fur blanketed the alicorns' hefty bodies, but the long feathers fanning out over their fetlocks were a moss green. That same green dyed the ends of their flowing manes. And each had a twisted emerald-and-black horn—easily two feet long, if not more—protruding from between their eyes, where they apparently had a big blind spot.

"Elmas and Aeolus are two of the ten domesticated alicorns on the isle," the attendant added, no doubt noticing the nervous silence smothering our group.

"I am Elmas." The alicorn on the right bobbed his head in a curt introduction. "For those who wish to not traverse the island on foot, you need only to call me or my herd."

"Each cottage has a bell outside the door," Aeolus added. "If you wish for a ride, all you need to do is ring it."

"Fret not"—Elmas lowered his head, whuffling out his nostrils gently, as his mossy green eyes scanned the worried crowd—"We shall see you safely to your cottages."

The attendant walked around to the back of the wagon and slid a ramp down. "There are benches on either side, and the wagon is wheelchair accessible. But please let me know if you need help with boarding."

And so, we took an alicorn-drawn wagon across the island to our room.

Which might've felt old-fashioned—as though we'd walked right out of the twenty-first century and dropped into an era of horse-drawn carriages and fashionable top hats—if it wasn't for the alicorns. Those big, otherworldly, *majestic* animals looked ridiculously out of place harnessed to a rickety wooden wagon.

But they were amiable, as they trotted around the island, stopping at each cottage and waiting patiently while people gathered themselves and offloaded. When questions were asked, the alicorns answered in friendly, upbeat voices.

"I love the colors on all the buildings here," I said after we'd rolled past the first batch of cottages, all painted in eclectic shades of hot pink, lapis blue, sunflower yellow, and dusky lavender. "Is there a particular reason they've been painted like this?"

"It was thought, when the island first opened, that it was too grey," Elmas answered. "Most found it wore on their moods and diminished their enjoyment of the island. So colors were added to the buildings."

"It also helps keep one from becoming disoriented in the fog," Aeolus added.

"Ah...that's what I thought. Thank you for clarifying!"

"Of course," Elmas and Aeolus said in unison.

Twenty minutes later, the wagon rolled to a stop outside the magenta-and-white cottage that would be our home for the next week—cottage E20.

"These cottages are adorable," I said, after Jackson and I had stepped off the wagon—and I'd given both alicorns a pet, thanking them for the safe journey across the island. "Don't you think?" I turned to Jackson.

He grimaced as he drew the key out of his pocket and strolled up the white-railinged porch to the front door. "I don't know if I'd call it *adorable.* Pink's a little too much."

"I think it's cute." I shrugged.

And the inside was even cuter.

The door opened to a little entryway that branched off to the right into a kitchenette—complete with a fire burning stove, some cupboards for utensils and dishware, and a corner table that could seat up to six. The left side led into a living room with a cushy sofa and an old-fashioned wooden rocking chair. A big, ornate coffee table sat in front of the sofa, and a book-shelf stretched the full length of the wall that separated the living room from the bedrooms.

The door to the left of the bookshelf led to a square room with two sets of bunk beds, while the door to the right brought us into the primary bedroom, with its airy balcony doors and sprawling king-sized bed.

Our bags waited for us in the primary bedroom. As I moved toward the suitcases, hoping the familiar routine of unpacking would settle my nerves, Jackson threw open the doors to the balcony and stepped outside.

"Babe!" he called, suddenly thrumming with glee. "Holy shit! We've got a waterfront property!"

My stomach plummeted. "What?"

"You gotta come see this!" He clapped the railing.

"I'd…I think I'd rather not."

"Don't be like that," he pouted. "We're on land here. And this" —he thumped his heel against the balcony—"is as solid as solid gets. It's safe, babe. C'mon."

I did. Only because he was so excited. And I looked over the railing, allowing my eyes to scale down the side of the cliff that held our tiny cottage out of the sea's jaws.

Below us, the sea roared, frothing and angry, shooting white-capped waves through the roving tendrils of fog. They looked like monsters. Big, hulking, frothing monsters, curling out of the bowels of Hell to rampage upon the earth.

"What a view, huh?" Jackson hooted.

"Looks like something out of a horror movie," I said.

He tutted and gave his eyes an affectionate roll. "You're being dramatic, babe."

"Am not." And I told him exactly what I'd thought about the monstrous waves, which had him clutching on to the rail and laughing—in that big, booming, unadulterated way he did when something really tickled his funny bone.

"That"—he swiped at the tears leaking from his eyes—"is *definitely* dramatic. And a little overdone, yeah?" He laughed again, warmly, and pulled me in for a bone-smashing hug. "I promise I won't let the big bad wolf of an ocean blow our cottage down." His lips brushed the top of my head, tickling me, and then they shifted down, seeking my mouth.

I pulled away.

Jackson emitted a grumbly growl.

"Puke breath," I reminded him. "My toothbrush is in the backpack."

"Ah." He swatted my rump and shifted the backpack off his shoulders.

I took it from him. "You wanna give me...ten minutes? To freshen up?"

Jackson grumbled and turned his mouth to the side of my neck, suckling and biting until I squirmed. "Can you make it five?" He nipped at my ear. "That bed is *begging* to be broken in."

"It is. But I'd like to check for bed bugs first..."

"Ugh, *babe.*"

"You know I feel better when I check."

"That's just...It's weird."

"Ten minutes! I promise." I giggled when he pulled me flush against him, grinding his crotch into mine. "Okay, maybe five."

"Better." He gripped my backside with two hands, squeezing

possessively, before he gave me another playful swat and sent me on my way.

"Pippi!" Jackson hollered. "They're *swimming* out in the water."

I blinked at my groggy reflection in the bathroom mirror as I hooked a hoop earring into my left ear. Groggy because I'd power napped for four hours, after Jackson and I had broken in our bed, and was still a little sleep drunk. "What?"

I'd misheard him. *Surely.*

"There's a whole group of them down there," he called.

"Down where?"

"In the water!"

My stomach, still very unsettled and wiggly, flipped itself around a loop-de-loop. "Are they mad?" I fastened my other earring into place and hastily zipped myself into my blue polka dot dress. "With those waves they'll drown!"

"The waves are gone." Jackson bounded into the bathroom, grinning from ear to ear, and drummed his fingers against the doorframe. "And it's super shallow. One lady walked almost clear across without it surpassing her waist. So I checked the map"—he whisked the brochure we'd gotten from the check-in desk out of his pocket—"and we're overlooking the inlet. Because this has tide times marked for the inlet, and the tide is definitely out right now. We should go swimming." He waggled his eyebrows.

"Wha—*No.* I-I just got dressed for dinner." I turned in a little half twirl, letting the dress swish around my ankles, as I fought the panic swilling in my stomach again.

He chuffed. "Not right now, obviously. After dinner, for sure. Maybe a little moonlit swim."

"Uh…"

"Tide should be out 'til midnight." Jackson shook the brochure.

"That's not...I mean...I didn't pack a bathing suit."

Jackson tucked his chin down, flashing me an impish grin. "For what I have planned, a bathing suit wouldn't last long, anyway. *Especially* with you looking like that." He dragged his eyes over my backside as I returned to the mirror to check on my still-drying hair.

"You're not looking too shabby yourself." I eyed his loose-fitting grey-washed jeans and pastel blue polo shirt—a shirt which was *deliciously* tight on him—hugging his broad shoulders and bulging pecs, leaving very little to the imagination.

Jackson grinned and puffed his chest out, preening.

I gave my bum a little shake and got rewarded with one of his sexy rumble laughs, deep and masculine, which usually lit spindles of desire in my veins. *Usually.*

At the moment, not even a full fireball of desire could thaw the icy feelings gnawing at my insides.

"I'd pull your hair back though," Jackson said, watching me in the mirror as I scrunched my curls. "It'll just get all poofy."

"Yeah," I sighed, conceding defeat, and busted out my scrunchie. "Humidity is not a friend to the curly-haired folk. So, what are you feeling like for dinner tonight?" I asked.

His brow rose.

"Get your head out of the gutter." I smiled. "Food. Real food. The Pippi buffet isn't open 'til later."

"Shame." His eyes skimmed my body. "Where do you wanna go for dinner?"

I shrugged. "I was looking at the menus earlier, and we've got bar food and uh, *more* bar food."

"Bar food it is then."

He strode forward, swooped my hair over my shoulder, and dragged his teeth lightly over the curve of my neck. "It's gonna be an *amazing* week." He drew back, gave my ass a not-so-gentle swat, and turned away. "Let's go get this bar food over with. I'm already hankering for my dessert."

9
Alistair

I still dream.

My sleep isn't the same as it once was. It's not as… *complete*.

No. That is not the word.

Or perhaps it is?

But I think there's another I want, for the sleep I once had. When I'd lie down and become unaware of everything around me.

Now my rest is *incomplete*. I am always aware of the waters' movements. The way they cool and roughen as they prepare for a storm.

A storm *is* coming.

I don't know when, but the waters do. And I will see when it arrives, even if I remain in my sleep.

I am never fully asleep. And yet, I can still dream.

Those dreams take me to faraway places, filled with light and color.

I see things I once knew but have long forgotten, like the great orb in the sky—the feeling of its light warming my skin.

There are faces too—*familiar* faces. Seeing them makes me… *hurt*.

No…

This is not the word I want either.

There's a *feeling* in my chest, and although it *causes* hurt, it has a different *word*.

But it's one of the many that have slipped away.

And the hurt deepens when *her* face appears in the dream.

Indigo.

I see her smiling, full of light. Of *joy*. It soothes me, as much as it hurts me.

Until the dream changes. And it *always* changes.

Her smiling face crumples in pain.

Moisture fills her eyes.

She screams for me. Reaches for me. Pleads for me to help her.

And I can't.

I want, more than anything, to save her. To guard her from the force that will rip her apart.

But I can't.

Because this dream is a memory. And memories can't change.

I am forced to watch, again, as she screams. Forced to watch, again, as she…*dies*.

I hate that this is a word I still remember.

Dies. Death.

I wish I could forget the hurt that comes from having a love die. But for all the words that have slipped away, the one I want to slip remains with me.

I watch Indigo die. Always. Whenever I sleep.

And I awaken from these dreams, restless and hurting. Surrounded by the dark waters. Doomed to never again feel the warmth of the orb in the sky or see the colors of the land.

Doomed to never see her smile again.

But tonight is different.

Because when I open my eyes, a woman stares back at me.

10

Pippi

I blamed the wine.

Downing an entire bottle made people complacent for stupid stuff, y'know?

And, *yes,* I'd swigged the bottle. The *whole* thing. Every last crimson drop.

Why?

Well, it was cheaper to get a bottle instead of a glass. So we had. And then Jackson had opted to get the stout on tap instead, leaving me with all 750 milliliters of Merlot.

"You can take the leftovers back to our room," Jackson had said. "We'll do a midnight toast or something."

There were no leftovers. Not of the wine. Or the dinner. Or the appetizer.

The afternoon of puking and anxiety attacks had left my belly an insatiable black hole.

But that bottle of wine was gonna get me in trouble.

Sober me never, ever, *ever* would have strolled her bare-naked bottom into the water. Tipsy me? Had trekked willingly down the little path through the cliffs and allowed Jackson to strip off my clothes. And I'd laughed when I peeled his off. Because my head was buzzy and light, and the fog and shadows had twined in a delectable drape around the hard, muscular planes of his body, teasing me by keeping all the best parts shrouded.

Now I smiled, nervously, when he grasped on to my arm and walked backward, guiding us into the plopping water.

"Someone is *going* to—*hiiiiicccc*—oh my goodness." I waved my arm in front of my face. "Was that a hiccup or a burp?"

Jackson laughed. "A hiccup."

"Well, that's good. I don't want to blast ya with half regirtated…refrigerated…refurburated—" Stars above, it was hard to drag words out of my wine-sloshed brain. "—*regurgitated* fish and chips."

"We definitely don't want that." Jackson splashed water at me, flecking it across my belly, and making me shiver. "The fishy smell might sic the Loch Ness Monster on our asses. *Kidding,* babe." He shook my arm, maybe sensing the tight chord of fear that snapped along my spine. "It's too shallow. No sea beast will dare venture here. And if it does"—he planted a beer-scented kiss on my cheek— "I'll protect you."

"And you're sure the…" I freed a hand, swishing it in a wave motion when the word I wanted died a slow, suffocating death inside my sozzled head.

"Tide?" Jackson supplied.

"Yeah. That. You're sure it'll stay out?"

"'Til near midnight. Yeah."

Near midnight? Or *at* midnight? Or *after* midnight? Specification words were important.

Unless he'd slipped one in and my brain had blipped it out? Which…*possible.*

I didn't even know what time it was, to be honest. It'd been nine*ish* when we went to get dinner. And still daylight*ish*—which had been a little weird, for spring. And I never would've pegged it as being that late if I hadn't glanced at the mechanical clock hanging in the living room of our cottage. A clock that had to be wound every day, or so read the instruction pamphlet on the coffee table.

But without phones, without digital watches, without computers…time just kinda slipped away.

Frigid water smacked against my calves. "You're sure we're not gonna get kicked out for this?" I asked.

"Kicked out of *where?*"

"Y'know"—I waved an arm behind me—"here."

Jackson shook his head. "How are they gonna kick us off the island if the ship doesn't come back 'til next Sunday?"

"I dunno. Maybe they'll make us swim?" I shuddered.

"We're fine, babe." He shimmied out a little further, making a heavy *splosh* as his ankles cut through the next weedy wave.

I squealed when the water splashed against my calves. "*Ooooh.* It's cold!"

"It is a bit, yeah."

"Too cold for me." I tugged back against him.

"Uh-uh." He scooped an arm around my waist and blew a playful raspberry against my cheek. "The cold just means we gotta go *fast.*"

Something built in my throat—a protest, a scream, a squawk, I wasn't sure. But it didn't matter. By the time it wriggled out of my mouth, Jackson had already whipped me forward and plunged us both neck-high into the frigid water.

The cold took the air, the voice, the *words*, right out of me. I gasped. Tried to suck in a breath. Couldn't. And started to flail.

"Head under"—Jackson pressed his palm to the top of my head—"real quick. It won't seem so cold after." And then he shoved me straight down into the curve of an oncoming wave.

Saltwater rushed up my nose and flooded my mouth. My eyes burned. My lungs seared. But, as panic snaked around my heart, Jackson pulled me back up, holding me flush against his chest as I sputtered.

"See?" He swiped the water out of my eyes, peppering little kisses over my cheek. "It's not so bad when you go quick, huh?"

"It's f-f-f-freezing." The words came out broken. Because my teeth were chattering and chomping them up.

"It's not so bad, actually." Jackson squeezed me tighter, slapping our slick, bare bodies against each other.

"So says the man w-who just had the cold s-s-steal his erection," I grouched.

Jackson had been proud and erect before we'd gotten into the water.

Now?

Limp. He was *totally* limp.

"Ah"—he rolled his hips into mine—"it'll warm back up again. Don't worry."

His cock gave a feeble twitch.

I snorted. "Sure it will."

"We won't stay in long, babe." He turned his mouth to the side of my neck, nibbling lightly. "But it *is* romantic, isn't it?"

It might have been. If the cold water wasn't biting at my skin so viciously. Or if the sky that stretched over us actually looked like the night sky—with glimmering moonlight and twinkling stars—instead of a big ball of dingy-grey fog fluff. Or maybe if we'd gotten another bottle of wine to pump some fuzzy heat into our systems…it might've been very romantic.

But, at current, it was almost torture.

And that icy plunge had evaporated my soupy buzz. So all I had now was the cold, the aches from shivering, and the tingling of my skin as the water ravaged it.

A wave splashed water up to my cheek. I trembled. Jackson pulled me closer to him and gave my neck a lovingly lavished bite.

"The water's higher than it looked earlier," I mumbled.

"Hmmmm." Beneath the water, his warm palm cupped my left breast, fondling it.

Another wave doused my face, more roughly this time. The water shoving at us and gyrating our bodies against each other.

Jackson groaned against the side of my neck. And it almost felt good—those sparks of pleasure as the water rocked him between my legs. But it'd feel *better* if we were out of this cold water. And in our warm, dry bed.

"Jackson." I swallowed as he gave my breast a hard squeeze, just before the rollicking water mashed us against each other again. "I don't like this. I-it's getting rough and it's *cold*. I wanna get out."

He turned his needy mouth to my jaw, biting. Gently, but insistent. "Alright. It *is* getting rough."

Reluctantly, he pulled away from me and pivoted, heading back to the cliff path. I blew out a relieved exhale and clung to his hand when the water bore down on us, trying to pull us back out. "Jackson"—my fingers threaded through his when a sticky, frightened belch rolled out of my chest—"I—"

The riotous water *howled* as it engorged itself, puffing into a towering wall.

My heart stopped.

The rotating wall hissed and lunged for us, smacking us off our feet.

My head plunged straight into the frothy surf.

Jackson's hand was whisked away. I heard him yell, just before the water flooded my ears, and then he was gone.

I reached for him, but my hands came up empty.

No.

No, no, no, no...

I forced my eyes open, even as the salt scalded them. All I saw was rippling, consuming darkness.

Please, no.

My feet flailed, mashing against the rock bottom for one solid, glorious second—a second where I got my legs under me and pushed my head above the surface. A second where I saw the curdling haze of fog above, and felt the stone under my feet, and thought, really, *really* thought that I had a chance to walk back to the cliffs.

Until the next wave thrust me back under.

I fought its hold, clawing my way back up to the surface once, twice. Each time staying up only long enough to draw a solitary lungful of air before the tide claimed me again. Pain exploded over my hips, my back, my arms as my flailing body parts pummeled into solid stone.

"JACKSON!" On my third or fourth or fifth time cresting the surface, I stayed up long enough to catch two breaths, and I used the second to scream his name—*pleaded* he help me.

"Hang on, Pippi!" his answering call filled my ears just before

I was hauled back under. And his voice had sounded so frighteningly far away.

By the time I got enough air to call for him again, he'd stopped answering.

I could no longer feel the rocky bottom. No matter how far the waves shoved me under, my feet never connected with stone.

My arms and legs didn't smash into any more rocks.

And when I crested the surface again—for longer this time, enough to take *four* inhales—I found myself surrounded by nothing but fog and sea.

The cliffs were gone.

Because the tide had dragged me out.

Oh…please.

Not again.

Please.

Panic raked poisonous nails over my throat and chest, closing my airways. Making my insides feel as though they'd been shredded with a cheese grater. Tears splotched my vision.

I fought to coerce my ravaged lungs into taking all the air they could muster. And I just managed to scream, "HELP!" before the water dunked me under again.

I flipped. And careened. A free fall. Like those weird dreams of stepping off a sidewalk and plummeting down a thousand-foot drop into nothing.

And then…

Just when I was sure the spinning would mash my brains against my skull and have them leak out my eye sockets, it stopped. I opened my eyes again and wriggled my arms and legs, trying to figure out if they had the strength to take me to the surface.

But I didn't know where the surface was.

It was all black—so deep, so consuming—I couldn't even see the tips of my own fingers, even when I waved them in front of my face.

Did I have a face anymore? Did I have arms? Legs?

Under this sea, suspended and weightless, feeling nothing but the screaming ache in my lungs, I wondered if I was already dead.

Until I saw it.

The big, orange orb peering at me through the dark.

An eye.

An eye as big as my *torso.*

And it was *inches* away.

A silent scream burst out of my mouth, expelling a current of bubbles and wasting the precious little air I had in my lungs. I didn't care.

A startled, rasping sound jangled in my ears.

The eye closed.

And now I had no freaking idea where the monster was. I couldn't see the body attached to that eye.

But it was *here.* Somewhere.

Go! Go, go, go! I screamed at my legs. Willing them to kick through the water. To propel me up. Or what I *hoped* was up. There was resistance, so it *had* to be up. It had to be the way to the surface.

My lungs bellowed—the pain so intense, so shocking, checkerspots danced in front of my eyes.

Go. Go!

My legs were heavy as I battered them through the water.

My arms shook as I grappled and clawed and dragged.

But no matter how far I swam, the surface never came. The water rushed around me, squeezing my body, beating the last dregs of strength out of me.

I wasn't going to make it.

I was going to die. In the middle of the ocean, thousands of miles away from home.

They'd never find my body.

Jackson would never get closure.

I would just...*disappear.* Poof. There one second, gone the next.

I stretched, pushing my hands up until my shoulder strained, praying I'd feel the break in the water.

Thwack.

Pain jarred my fingers as they smacked against something solid. And rough.

Stone.

It *had* to be.

I forced my rubbery legs to give me three more powerful kicks. And they pushed me high enough to get my hands more fully onto the stone. To feel the jagged peaks cutting into my palms. I grasped on to it, hauling myself up.

The air burned my throat when I popped my head out of the water and took that first big, gulping breath. It was a wonderful kind of pain, though. A pain that meant life—*salvation.*

I cried, choking on my breaths and heaving sea water out of my lungs, as I crawled more fully onto the rock. And then I lay there for a heartbeat, two, *twelve,* savoring each fiery inhale and the stickiness of the air against my skin. Marveling at the fog and the dark hunk of rock I was clinging to.

Safe.

I was out of the water. I was *safe.*

But not for long. The next wave announced its rampage with a resonant growl.

I didn't want to look. But I did, and I sobbed when the mountain of water loomed so very, *very,* tall above me. I wouldn't survive that.

The fact settled deep into my bones. I was not going to survive.

Beneath me, the rock gave a shudder. And then—

A scream tore out of me when the solid slab of stone moved, lifting me up until I was *taller* than the wave.

When the fizzing water broke against the face of the rock, all it did was tickle my backside with a few foamy flecks.

Impossible.

The rock moved again.

I started to slide, and my numb fingers wrestled to keep hold of the jagged piece I'd been clinging to.

Except now, with the saltwater cleared from my eyes, I could see the jut of rock I had my hands wrapped around wasn't a rock at all.

It was a horn. A big, curved, pointed *horn*.

The surface beneath me? Was gritty but pliable. Warm. *Alive.* And it shuddered as a thick, accented voice boomed between my ears.

"What were you d-doing?"

11

No...no...no...no, no, no, no, no.

I pivoted, dragging my knees against the coarse surface as I drank in my surroundings.

Two long horns curved out from either side of me, their tips pointing toward the sky. Short, spiky scales cascaded down the length of the rock, tapering off between two slotted nostrils, which were currently blowing steam into the air.

No. It *couldn't* be.

A series of twitches and spasms rolled under my hands, as though the rock had been tickled by my frenzied crab-crawling.

I stilled, resting on my hands and knees, struggling to keep my breathing steady as realization thrashed my bones.

This isn't a rock! It's...

The Loch Ness Monster!

Had to be. Its head, at least.

The nostrils flared again, making a soft flutter as they shot another jet of steam.

Stars above. I was sitting on the Loch Ness Monster's *head.*

"GAHHHH!" I bellowed.

The monster flinched. "Must you be...*noisy?*"

And that *voice.*

The phantom brogue, the one that'd haunted me since the ship ride, had been coming from *him?*

"No...nope, nope, na-ah." I shimmied down the narrowed tip of his snout and nosedived—*literally*—back into the water.

Because in that moment—that wild, panicked moment—I decided the sea was less terrifying than the beast.

But what I didn't realize?

How far down the sea actually was.

I'd expected to plop right into it. Instead, I plummeted—ten feet, at least—screaming the whole way, until...

Swish.

Back under the water I went, choking when my last wail opened the floodgates and saturated my lungs.

It *hurt.* I sobbed, exhausted and frantic, but the ocean guzzled my tears.

Big, blotchy white spots blossomed in front of my eyes.

"That..." A voice thrummed between my ears. "Was...s-s-si... *silly.*"

Thwack.

Something big and solid bashed into my bottom and pushed me up, lifting me clean out of the water.

I was right back where I'd started, on the head of the beast.

I didn't know *why* I expected that to go any differently. The Loch Ness Monster was a whopping *"forty American feet."* Even if I were an Olympic-level freestyler, all bedazzled in my gold medals, I'd *never* outswim him.

"Why?" the voice demanded while I barfed up lungfuls of ocean—and half my dinner. Probably all the wine.

"Why *what?*" I gagged. "Why did I try to swim away? Why am I crying? Or p-puking? Because of *you.*"

Beneath me, the monster shuddered.

In anger? Or hunger?

I was probably like a decadent slice of cheese to him—a delicious morsel of taste and texture—just enough to satisfy a craving that'd been itching at him.

I pictured him gnawing me between his teeth, savoring the squirt of juices (my blood) over his tongue, closing his eyes in ecstasy at the satisfying crunch of my bones as he chomped them.

A great hiccupping sob surged out of me.

The monster made a low sound, like a growl, as his flesh rippled beneath me. And I figured this was it. This was the moment he flung me into the air and macerated me between his teeth. Like a dog catching a treat off the tip of its nose.

"Can you…h-hear me?" That thick, aristocratic voice inundated my brain again.

My sobs stuttered. "I…ummm…uh…Yes. And listen, I'm *really* sorry I snapped at you. Really. I'm not a snapping person. Usually. I'm just…" My lower lip quivered, mashing my words. "Please don't eat me. *Please*. I'm sorry I disturbed your slumber. I didn't mean to…We were…Jackson and I….It was shallow…and then the wave came and…" My breath hitched. "Please don't eat me. It was an accident."

"Why would I…eat?"

Those rumbling words might've sounded kind, if they hadn't been so resonant—the deep timbre of a creature fifteen times my size—and so strained.

"Because that's what monsters *do*, isn't it? Stars, and I had flipping fish and chips tonight. I should've had the burger. Listen, I know I might smell like your regular diet, but I promise I won't taste the same. I'll probably be tough too—I spend most of my time sitting at a desk. Or…Oh no. That'd make the meat more tender, wouldn't it? Forget I said that. I— AGGGGHH!"

The monster whipped his head to the side—not harshly enough to send me tumbling, but quickly enough to have my belly catapulting.

"*Noisy*," he grunted.

"Please, please, please—*Ooompfh!*"

His head paused and gave a sharp, downward slant, a very "get the frick off" motion that sent me skidding down the tip of his nose and plopping onto his back.

I stood, swayed, and yelled when my feet flailed, struggling to get traction on the slimy slope.

"Hold"—he blew out a long breath and bumped his muzzle against the spikes on his spine—"here."

I grasped on to one of those spikes just in the nick of time. A wave smacked into him, its foamy crest nearly swallowing the hump of his back. Icy water chomped at my toes and pulled, trying to rip me back into the sea. I clung to that spike for dear life and...*Ugh*. It was *squishy*. Not a spike at all, more like a pliable pillar, with translucent flesh webbed in between...

A dorsal. He had a webbed dorsal.

"Better?" Warm, briny breath fanned across my body as the Loch Ness Monster stared down his nose at me.

And *no*. This was not better.

Because he looked absolutely massive from this angle.

The slope of his back rivaled the size of a ship—and this was only the top of it. Several dozen feet of scaly flesh remained concealed beneath the churlish waves. The webbed dorsal dotting his spine stretched clean over my head. And his *neck*...

I didn't even want to take a *guess* at how long his neck was, and he currently had it all smooshed into a U-shape so he could keep his eyes fixed on me.

His cold, mean-looking orange eyes.

Mean-looking because the exaggerated downward curve of his brow hung a permanent scowl over his snout. And that snarling face, partially shrouded by the wispy fog, was framed by those two wickedly sharp horns, which curved from either side of his temple.

The Loch Ness Monster was a colossal titan. Master of these violent seas.

And I was this teeny, tiny, little spec on his back.

A morsel. A cookie crumb.

The shiver had started in my lower back and spindled up my spine, fanning out along my shoulders. When the icy water grabbed at my feet again, the shakes exploded across my whole body.

The monster made a low noise and puffed another breath at me. Which smelled *foul*—oh my goodness, that was an odor to rot my stomach—but was blessedly warm. And it seemed deliberate, as though he was *trying* to thaw my frozen limbs.

"I won't *eat* you," he said. His mouth didn't move, though. "What were you *doing*?" he asked. Still no mouth movement.

My skin prickled.

The Loch Ness Monster cocked his head slightly, his nostrils fanning.

The waves pummeled the side of his body in quick succession, each one getting a little bigger. A little angrier. He didn't flinch.

"What were you doing?" he asked again, softly.

I stared up into his big, orange eyes, trying to ignore how impossibly and pathetically small I felt.

And how very, very, very exposed I was.

I glanced down at myself. At the bruising already splashed over my ribs and breasts, the blood seeping from the jagged gash in my thigh, the tangled mass of hair knotted over my shoulder, and the slick length of my bare skin.

Another uncomfortable prickle danced over me. *Go skinny-dipping, they said. It'll be fun, they said. Stupid.*

And it was stupid to be so worried about this. Considering the situation I was in, my bare-naked bottom was the least of my problems. But it bothered me all the same. Being naked before an enormous sea monster made me feel *more* vulnerable. Like I was a doe-eyed maiden set upon a sacrificial altar for the beast to ravage.

I crossed my arms over my chest and hunched my back when a cooling breeze tickled places that should *never* be exposed to a chilly sea breeze. But then another wave splashed over the monster's back and tried to ensnare my feet, and I had to abandon modesty for security as I clung to his dorsal. The wave receded, but not before it barfed up a steaming vat of seaweed over my feet.

And gosh…I was going full stupid tonight.

Because I snatched the seaweed up and slathered it over my front, trying to use it to cover my breasts and crotch in a makeshift bikini.

Which…didn't work. At all.

"Did you just…attempt to…clothe yourself w-with…*weed*?" the monster asked.

"No." I sniffed as the seaweed oozed down my boobs. "Okay, yes. But in my defense, I'm trying to work with what I have. And I don't have much."

A vibrating laugh rolled through the monster's body.

I made a panic-snatch for his dorsal, and the seaweed bikini gave up the ghost and slid off my body completely, fleeing into the next wave. Probably scarred for life now that I'd debauched its innocence.

The monster chuffed.

"That bikini worked way better in my head." I watched the last treacle of seaweed sidle down my thigh. "But then again, most things work better in my head."

"Why clothes…Why don't you have clothes?" He cocked his head again. Which helped a little, to soften the harsh shape of his face.

"Uh…" I blew out a breath. "It's really dumb, but I was skinny-dipping…"

"Skinny…dipping."

"Yeah. Y'know. Dipping into the water in your skinnies." I waved an arm down my naked front, wincing when the movement jiggled my breasts.

The monster saw it too. His eyes might've been bigger than my torso, but it was easy to tell when they hyper focused on something. They went still, and the black slits narrowed. *Lovely.*

Maybe *getting eaten* was off the table, but *getting ravaged* was still a card in play.

The monster's eyes shifted up, focusing on my face. "Why would you…?" He let the question hang.

"Because my boyfriend thought it would be fun…"

"B-boyfriend?"

"…and romantic. Like in the movies, y'know?"

"Movies?" He dragged this word out, "*Mooooovies?*"

"But it was *awful,*" I hucked. "So cold, and the water was too rough. But I *tried,* y'know? Because he was enjoying it, and I wanted to enjoy it too. But I didn't. And then…and…My side hurts…" It did. All of a sudden. In mid-sentence, the bruise on my side gave a deep, bone-aching throb. "I didn't even wanna be here. I wanna go home."

"Huh-h-home?"

It might've been annoying, having someone parrot my words. But when the monster did it...my heart gave a little tug.

He sounded the words out the way a toddler would. Like he'd heard them before, but had never attempted to say them, and maybe didn't fully understand their meaning, so he let them soak on his tongue for a bit before he attempted to string the syllables together.

"I'm sorry." I mopped at my face, before the salt water from the sea and my tears could dry into crusties on my cheeks. "I talk a lot and fast when I'm nervous."

The monster's nostrils flared as he blew another heat puff over me, chasing the cold from my skin. "Where were you... skinny-dipping?" he asked.

"Ummm. I'm not 100 percent sure. Jackson said it was an inlet? The tide was out when we went in, so it was shallow."

"Ah."

"You know where that is, then?"

"Yes. I can't go there."

"Oh, I wasn't—"

"The storm will make it d-d-dangerous. For you. The waters will be r-rough. And you would need to climb..."

"Storm?" I angled my head back, peering up through the fog. It was impossible to tell what the sky looked like, with all the misty film covering it, but there wasn't any rain. No rolling thunder or flashes of lightning.

The monster tilted his head, gesturing toward the frothing waters. "The waters feel it."

This time, it was my turn to go, "Ah."

The storm was coming, and the ocean was throwing a rabble-rouser party in anticipation.

"I can take you near...the..." Tension rippled down his back. "I don't know its word. "You walked it. When you left the..." He trailed off with a sigh. "You walked it. To arrive on land."

"The...Are you talking about the dock?"

"*Yes.*" There was joy in that word, as though I'd given him the answer to a puzzle he'd been laboring over. "Yes. The *dock.* I can take you near it. But I can't go close to it. Even under...I can't get close. You'll have to swim."

"You're...you're *helping me?*" I asked, shocked.

He tucked his chin in a nod.

"I...*Thank you,* really. I-I thought Jackson was going to be taking me home in a body bag—"

"Body...bag?"

"It's a saying. Body bags are what they wrap dead people in. Although to put me in one, they would've had to find me, and the sea might not've left any of me behind. So, thank you."

The monster whuffled. "We should go now. Would you feel..." He paused again. "S-s-safe...*er.* Saf*er,* on my head?"

I stared up at his devilish face.

No. The answer should have been no. I shouldn't have felt safe anywhere near him.

But he asked the question so gently, as though he was genuinely trying to figure out how to best calm my nerves.

It soothed me and had a broken, "Yes," tumbling from my lips.

He whuffled and gingerly lowered his head until the tip of his nose brushed my hip. "Climb," he said.

But I didn't. Not immediately. Because when I reached out, touching my fingers to the tip of his nose, something curdled my insides.

Sadness. The kind that destroyed—swept over you like a black plague—ravaging your body and leeching the life from your bones.

I ripped my hand back. The sorrow faded.

"What's w-wrong?" His nostrils fanned.

You're in pain, aren't you? I'm so sorry. Who do you grieve for? Is there anything I can do to help? If he'd been human, I might've asked those questions. But they seemed far too intimate to hurl at a sea beast. So I swallowed them down and said, "Nothing. It's just…D-do you have a name?" A slightly less prodding question to start with. "If you're gonna be wearing me on your head like a naked human hat…I mean, in my book, that's pretty personal, no? I like to know what to call people—or, well, you're not *people*, but you get the idea—when things get personal. And I've just been calling you 'monster' in my head. But it doesn't seem right to keep calling you that. So I figured I'd ask…Do you have a name?"

The monster made a low rattle, a noise that visibly traveled along the length of his throat, making his scales vibrate.

"Or, if that's too personal, I—"

"Alistair," he said.

"Alistair." Golly, no wonder he had such a posh-sounding accent. The voice had to live up to the posh-er name. "It's beautiful."

"And you"—Alistair nudged his nose against my hip—"have a name?"

"Pippi."

"Pippiiii," he dragged my name out. "Pippi." A laugh burbled in his throat. "Yours is b-b-beautiful too."

12

Pippi

"Pippi." My name rumbled through Alistair as he cut through the angering sea, holding his head just high enough to keep me out of the water's reach.

"Pippiiii." He kept chewing on it, trying to get a feel for all its textures and tastes, maybe hoping the repetition would make it stick better to his brain.

"Pip-ee." Okay. This was actually adorable. It shouldn't have been, but delight warmed my insides all the same.

Which, I mean, at least I was warm *somewhere*. Because a chilling current now snaked through the air, and icy water still clung to my body, leeching the feeling out of my extremities.

And the thought of having to slide off Alistair's head and get back into those frigid, rabid waves…

"Pippi," Alistair said, "you're…s-shivering?"

And that catch around *shivering*, the uncertainty when he finally got it out, as though he wasn't sure it was the right word…Stars. Why, *why* did I find him so endearing?

"Can you feel that?" I muttered.

I *was* shivering. Big body-quaking shivers—a fruitless attempt to thaw my frozen limbs.

"Yes," Alistair said. "Are you c-cold?"

"Freezing."

"Free-zing." He gnawed on the word, and then gruffed a sincere, "I'm sorry."

"There's no need for you to be sorry," I said. "It wasn't your fault I went for a swim in my birthday suit. Although"—I tightened my arm around his horn for balance when he bobbed up and down with a choppy set of waves—"I didn't think it'd be *this* cold."

"The warmer months haven't arrived," Alistair said. "They haven't...released the cold from the waters."

"I know. I was freezing the whole ship ride to the island. But the island itself is so warm you kinda forget it's still only May."

"May..."

"Yeah. The month. Or...You probably don't know the months, do you?"

"I do, some," he said. "September. November. D-D-December. Ember. Juember. Ju-uly."

A chortle wriggled out of me. Not because listening to him struggle was funny, but because of how July had clunked up the roll he'd been on with the 'ember months.

One of those things was not like the other. Although "Juember" had a nice ring to it.

"May," Alistair concluded, either not noticing my laugh, or choosing not to comment on it. "What are the words for the others?"

I rattled them off.

He slowly repeated each one. And once I'd gone through the whole list, he recited all twelve months on his own, brimming with pride when he made it all the way back to December.

"That was—" I started to congratulate him but ended up biting the words off with a squawk when a big clap of thunder exploded overhead.

"You're s-safe." Alistair's voice twined around me, easing my galloping heart. "We're nearly there."

Nearly there. He'd been swimming for several minutes, and he wasn't a slowpoke, but we were only *"nearly there."*

I swallowed. Or tried to. But my mouth had gone so dry, the lump in my throat had gotten so big, it was hard to swallow. "The ocean took me out far, didn't it?"

A hum vibrated through Alistair. "The waters are s-strong... *est*. Strong*est* before a storm. But I wouldn't test their strength. Even when there's no storm."

"Well, no worries there. It's like the saying: fuck me once, shame on you. Fuck me twice, shame on me. Or, well, that's the Jackson version of that saying, at least. He didn't think 'fool me' packed the same punch, so he added some flavor. Y'know?"

"I'm not sure..."

"Means if something bites me once, I don't generally give it a chance to bite again."

He said nothing to that, just romped up and down, bobbing through the cantankerous waters.

I wondered if it was hard for him to swim with his head held up. It had to be the equivalent of a person walking with their chin pointing at the sky. And I knew from experience—usually from my trips to cities with stunning architecture to gawp at— that my upper back would scream if I had to carry that posture for any length of time. I couldn't imagine walking like that while trying to balance something on my forehead. Something that moved. And talked incessantly. And shivered so hard, its teeth made *click-click-click* sounds.

Bless him. Truly. I started to say that—another babbling thank you—but he belatedly responded to my last statement.

"Fuck," he drizzled the word out, "doesn't mean bite."

I choked.

"It means s-s-s..." He sighed.

Oh no. I knew exactly what he was trying to sound out. "Sex?"

"Yes. *Sex.* It means sex. Unless I have the word wrong. I sometimes confuse them..."

"Oh, no, we're on the same word page here." My choke turned into a giggle. And then a full-fledged laugh. The kind that tickled your insides, left your belly muscles aching, and had the world looking a little brighter than it had a few seconds before. "Like...Yes, generally, fuck means sex. Not always *good* sex though, sometimes it's the bad sort, the kind that's forced on you when you don't want it. That's why it's used in the saying. I just said 'bite' because...well, most bites are also unwanted.

Except the ones that are. So there's good fucking and bad, and good biting and bad, y'know?"

Stars help me…I was talking sex with the *flipping Loch Ness Monster*. What a vacation this was. One for the freaking books.

"Ah," Alistair said.

A zap of frustration hit me then—*his* frustration.

The kind of exasperation I usually got first thing in the morning when I was trying to make sense of a complicated email before the coffee kick-started my brain.

He knew the words. But was aggravated that they kept muddling on him.

"Where did you learn to speak?" I asked. "Your English is great, by the way. *Impeccable*. I'm just a little curious where, or how, or *why* you've learned to speak it."

"I don't speak," Alistair said. "Not anymore."

Which was not the answer I was expecting. "Oh, but you do. You are. To me."

"This isn't speaking," he said. "I've no *voice*. Not for a long time."

"But I can *hear* you."

"Yes."

"But you're not actually talking?"

"No."

Which would explain why his mouth didn't move. "Then how—"

Alistair came to an abrupt stop, his body arching back with a pained hiss and wagging his head from side to side, as though something had walloped him across the face.

My feet slipped and skittered, fighting for balance. The coarse scrape of his scales and nubbly ends of his spikes slashed at my heels, making my eyes water. The death grip I had on his horn was the only thing that kept me from plummeting off him.

"I'm sorry," he grunted breathlessly as he stilled, giving me a chance to right myself. "But I can go no further. Your dock is there."

I squinted. But through the curdling fog and revolving hills of water, I couldn't see anything. We might've been feet away from the dock. Or miles away from it.

And the way he'd stopped—so suddenly, and with that hiss of pain...It was like he'd smacked into a wall. Or maybe not even something as solid as a wall, more like those electric fences that zapped the bejesus out of dogs when they got too close.

I ran my hand over Alistair's horn. "Are you okay?"

Alistair made a noncommittal warble. "I can go no further," he repeated.

Acidic ice plopped into my belly. This was what Caleb had meant. When he said the Loch Ness Monster was *controlled* with runes and magic. I thought it'd sounded cruel then. But now that I'd seen his pain...

"You should go." Alistair lowered his head, dunking his nose into the surf, bringing me closer to the water.

I recoiled.

"The water will only get more angry." He prodded gently. "Right now, it's still f-forgiving. It will carry you most of the way."

Icy water slashed at my back as the sea swelled, preparing to spit a series of massive waves at the isle. And I meant *massive*—those waves rose to staggering heights.

BANG!

Thunder bellowed overhead.

Zzzzaaappp.

For one second, one mercifully brief, terrifying second, lightning speared through the fog, casting a wide ray of illumination over the sea.

It looked *evil.*

Brutish black waters leapt for the heavens, hissing when the skies spat them back down to earth. Jilted and wrathful, they turned their rage toward land.

The dock, only a few feet away, was barely, *barely,* high enough to avoid the waves' snapping teeth.

I shrank back, clinging to Alistair's horn.

"Pippi…" A wave swallowed Alistair's face, making him sputter. He exhaled, blowing a fountain of water out of his nostrils, and murmured, "Go."

"Are you going to be alright? With the storm?"

Why on earth had I asked that question? He *lived* in the sea!

Alistair blew out again, sending a jet of misty water into the air. "I've lived through many storms, Pippi," he said.

"Right. Yeah. Just…I'm not normally near an ocean during a storm—or at all, really—I kinda hate it. It's just too big and unpredictable and…"

I'm scared. Of being on an island in the storm. Of the ocean.

I'm worried for you. Because the sea is far bigger than even your forty American feet.

You're kind. It'd break my heart to see you hurt.

I'm scared.

But I didn't say any of that. "Sorry. I'm being stupid. And I'm sure you want me off your head—"

"You're not s-stupid," Alistair said, "to fear the waters. Never stupid. But you're safe." He paused, extruded another jet of water, and added, "I'll stay here until you're on land."

And that was surprisingly comforting, to know he wasn't going to dump and ditch me. "Making sure the lady gets home safely. You're a proper gentleman, Alistair."

"*Gentleman…*" He savored the word. "I try to be."

"You are." I ran my hand over his horn—wondering if he could feel my touch, and if he knew it was meant to be a comfort—and shimmied down, getting ready to slide off his head. But as my toes twinkled the top of the water, I froze again. Another question rolled over my tongue—a question that seemed asinine, but one that refused to be swallowed back down. "Can I see you again?"

A twitch rolled over Alistair's hide.

"I mean," I amended, "I'm guessing I'll *see you*—that's the point of being on this island, isn't it? But is there a way to just have it be the two of us? Like this? Except without me having to nearly drown—I'd rather *not* be in the water. Maybe over by the inlet? If the tide's in and it's not stormy, can you go there?"

Alistair said nothing for a long moment.

I chewed at my lip, wondering what had gotten into my head and hashed my brain into this pulp of stupidity.

And then...

"I can swim there. In the inlet. When the water is calm. And when it's filled," he said.

Anticipation tingled in my veins. "Would you want to meet me there? Maybe tomorrow night?"

"I can."

"Okay, it's a date. Well not a *date.* But..."

Gosh, Pippi, stop digging the stupid hole and get your soggy behind into the water!

My belly swam with nerves—as unsettled and rollicky as the waves—as I scooched myself down the side of Alistair's head and into the water, still clutching on to him.

His orange eye followed me, watching my every move.

"Tomorrow?" I verified.

"Tomorrow," he agreed.

"And you'll..." I grappled for him when a wave ballooned beneath me, shooting my body up, up, up, and then sending it crashing back down. "You'll wait? I'll call back once I'm on the dock. But while I'm in the water..."

"I'll be here," he confirmed.

"Okay. Thank you. Again." And there was nothing else for it.

I let go. And swam like a fish wriggling out of a shark's mouth.

Or, well, I *tried* to have that kind of pep in my kick, but the glacial waters bore down on my lungs, making it feel like I was drowning, even with my head above the surface. My frozen limbs pawed sluggishly, too heavy for a proper doggy paddle.

Alistair nudged me with the tip of his nose, giving me a boost. "Let the waters take you," he said.

And boy, did the waters take me. Up at first, until vertigo danced around my head, and then shooting me forward.

I would've screamed, if I wasn't fighting so hard to breathe against the cold.

A hulk of wood whizzed out of the soupy air.

The dock.

It was almost within arm's reach.

All I had to do was swim, swim, *swim*...I paddled and kicked, dragging my numb body through the water.

So close...so close...I stretched a hand out.

The wave I rode began to crest, the top turning over into itself, creating a vicious, frothy vat.

But I was *there*. My hand brushed against a solid pillar, and I clung to it with all my might, wrapping my arms and legs around it.

The wave grouched and tried to slurp me under the dock. I cried out.

"You're alright," Alistair called. "Hold on. Let it pass."

With a growl, the water released my legs and barreled forward.

"Climb, Pippi," Alistair said.

And I did, battering my numb fingers until they bent, twining them around the handholds on the side of the pillars. Forcing my feet to push, push, *push*.

I gasped when I hauled myself up onto the solid surface of the dock. But I didn't give my wobbly legs a break. *Not yet,* I pleaded with them. Not yet.

The warped and weathered wood sliced at the undersides of my feet as I made a mad dash for land. Water plumed into the air when the wave crashed into the side of the island, soaking the dock, and sending bitter pellets to slice at my legs, my sides, my back. But I didn't care.

As soon as I got myself far enough on to land to feel safe from the ocean's grasp, I sank bonelessly down, curling myself into a fetal position.

My heart thundered. Every beat struck painfully against my chest and made a heavy hammering sound between my ears.

Tremors danced along my body. And my voice, when I tried to call back to Alistair, came out in a croak, "I-I'm...I'm here."

"I know." That wonderfully accented voice caressed my frenzied mind. "And I'm glad. You're safe, Pippi."

13

*P*ippi.

A new name. And new words to come with the name.

Pippi.

It is hard. To let her go. But I *have* to. She belongs on land. And even I can't keep her safe from the waters in a storm.

"I-I'm...I'm here," she calls.

"I know. And I'm glad. You're safe, Pippi."

I *am* glad. But I'm also *not* glad. I want to call her back. While she is with me, I feel...

Different.

But...*not* different.

My mind is clearer. I fight less to find words. And she fills my head with new words and old ones. Words that had slipped but have now returned.

I feel more...like *myself.*

I've forgotten what it is to speak to another—to have my questions answered. To be asked questions in turn. To hear someone laugh over words I've spoken.

I hear humans laugh nearly every day. I see their smiles and joy when I am called to the surface to amuse them. Once, those sounds and faces would make *me* feel joy. I *like* to make humans smile and laugh.

But that joy slipped. Vanished, with many of my words. I can't say *why.*

Maybe I've grown tired. Maybe I ache too much to speak

with the humans, not just amuse them. Maybe I let too much of myself slip.

But I haven't felt joy...

Until Pippi *laughs*. And it's...the *sound* of her voice, the *knowing* that she's scared, and lost, but trusts me enough to *laugh*.

My heart stirs. How long has it been? Since I felt this...the *stirring?* The *ache* of seeing someone so...so...

There is a word, to capture the feeling...

Enthrilling?

No.

Enthralling.

Yes.

The tilt of her head when she smiles—a full, genuine smile. It is off, her smile.

No...

"Off" isn't the word.

Or perhaps it is?

She smiles more on one side...

Crooked.

Her smile is *crooked*. And the shape of it enthralls me.

But her eyes enthrall me most of all. Their softness. Warmth. *Kindness.*

I wish I had more words for the way I feel.

"Tomorrow," we promise.

We'll meet again...*tomorrow.*

It's been a long time since I've felt the drag of a day, the waiting for a *tomorrow.*

In truth, I allow those words to slip.

Today.

Tomorrow.

Yes-yes-yeserday...yesterday.

They are meaningless to me. Or they *were*. But now I have a tomorrow to yearn for.

Tomorrow.

Tomorrow I will hear her voice again.

Tomorrow I will converse.

Tomorrow I will remember what it is to feel myself.

Something inside of me tightens—a feeling I would not have had a word for before. But now the word comes easily.

Impatience.

I remember now.

Impatience.

And I remember how very long it is, to wait for a tomorrow.

14

Pippi

How I managed to get back to our cottage without getting lost, and without people getting an eyeful of my full moon and its orbs (my bare bottom and other assets), I had no clue.

But I did.

I cut my feet to ribbons—the gravelly island soil was *not* conducive to barefooted moonlit strolls. I also got startled half to death each time the thunder teed off, and my side ached something fierce by the time I arrived at our magenta cottage. But I made it.

A light flashed in my face as soon as I opened the door.

"PIPPI!" Jackson plonked his candelabra on to the entryway table and yanked me into the foyer. "I was *just* going to see where I could scrounge up some fucking help. I've been scoping the shoreline for an *hour*. And I couldn't call anyone. And *fuck…*" He shoved the door shut and stroked my arm.

I threw myself at him, wrapping him into a rough hug. My side screamed in protest. The pain nearly knocked the wind out of me, but I gulped down my cry, shoved the discomfort down, and held on to him.

"I thought you were *dead*," he hissed.

Guilt mangled my stomach. And I, all at once, felt like scum. Worse. Like the used gum that mucked up the bottom of some-one's shoe.

Because he'd been so worried about me.

But I hadn't really thought of him.

Well, I *had.* But not to the same extent. I hadn't wrung myself wretched wondering if he was dead. Something inside my gut, my heart, had assumed he was okay, even though I'd had nothing to support that. Jackson had been ravaged by the same wave, he'd merely been closer to the rock face.

"Where did the tide take you?" Jackson pressed. "Why didn't you *answer* me when I was calling for you? How did you—you're *bleeding*. Fuck. I'm going to see if I can find the medical clinic."

"Don't!" I grabbed for his arm when he made to move past me. *"Please."*

"Babe, you've got blood running down your leg," Jackson pointed out.

And I did, from the big, loose-lipped gash that ringed my thigh. It throbbed—a heavy, thudding pulse that jack-rabbited along my leg.

"I'll be okay. Honest," I insisted at Jackson's dubious face. "But I…"

I don't want to advertise that we were skinny-dipping. It's embarrassing. If no one knows, I'd rather keep it that way.

I don't want to be asked to give a play-by-play of what happened when the ocean took me.

I met the Loch Ness Monster tonight, and he was so kind. But I'm worried he'll get in trouble if I tell people he helped me. I don't think he's supposed to interact with us like that.

"I'm tired, Jackson." I buried my face into his chest, letting my tears dribble onto his shirt.

He'd slithered back into the clothes he'd worn to dinner, but his shirt was inside out. It smelled briny, and musky, as though the rocks and sea salt air had rubbed off his cologne.

"I want a hot shower and clean clothes," I mumbled. "And I want you to take me to bed. I don't wanna stumble around in the dark trying to find the medical clinic. It's going to storm…"

On cue, a pop of thunder rattled the walls of our cottage.

"Oh yeah. That's gonna be a big 'un." Jackson tapped my back when I flinched at the noise. "We'll see how you are tomorrow and go from there. I know gnarly vacation infections are a great watercooler topic, but I think we'd rather save that for another time, yeah?"

"Yeah. Preferably never." I exhaled, slowly, trying to release the tension in my gut. But between my nerves and Jackson's stress, no breathing technique stood a chance at unraveling that anxious knot.

I shivered. And shivering made my bones feel as though they'd been chiseled with a nail file. So I nuzzled into Jackson, trying to drink up his body heat. "Jackson, you won't believe—" I started, searching for the words to describe Alistair.

But at the same time, Jackson said, "I hate to be the bearer of bad reminders, but there's no hot water in these showers."

My nerve-knotted stomach plummeted. "Oh no."

We had plumbing in this cottage, sure. Flushing toilets, showers, sinks, the works. But it was all old fashioned and there was no electricity, so the water got lukewarm at best.

And I really, really, *really* wanted a scalding hot shower. I wanted it so bad, it hurt. Wanted it so bad, I cried.

"Hey now"—Jackson prodded my back—"none of that. It's toasty in here, and we do have a kettle, remember? And tea bags."

I blew out a shaky, and very moist, breath. "I forgot all about the kettle. Could you throw it on while I shower? And give me the biggest cup they have."

"I'll make *two* cups."

"Thank you. I love you." I pressed a sloppy kiss to his neck.

He rested his chin atop my head. "I know."

"OW!"

I yelped, clapping a hand to my side when the crazy lady shoved her palm against my ribs and made my bones crunch.

"Broken ribs too. Tsk-tsk." The sallow-faced Healer (named

Alana, also known as *crazy lady)* walked to the black and white counter tucked into the corner of the healing room. "Fortunately, nothing is displaced, and the wounds are shallow, so this tonic'll have you right as rain in a few hours." She flung her latex gloves off and began pulling vials and powders out of the cabinets.

"Thank fuck." Jackson clenched my hand. He'd been beside himself that morning when I'd woken up too stiff to bend, my feet burning too much to walk, and the gash in my thigh still oozing blood—even after I'd cleaned and bandaged it. So off to the health clinic we'd gone. Where the solitary Healer—a Sorceress with a penchant for tonic mixing—scowled and scuffed her way through the patient list, of which there'd been three: a round-faced boy, no older than six or seven, who'd developed a fever overnight; a middle-aged woman who said she had a stomach flu (judging by the tequila scent wafting off her, I'd guess that flu bug came from the bottom of a bottle); and me.

It stunk here, in this small, white-walled room. Mainly with an overpowering herbal aroma, but there was a faint sour milk scent too, likely emanating from one of the vials Alana lined up on the counter.

"How is it you came to find yourself with these injuries?" Alana asked as she dropped a pinch of neon green liquid into a glass beaker.

Jackson and I looked at each other.

"You might as well come out with it." She swished the liquid around. "If there's a risk of tetanus from those cuts, it's better to let me know now than wait 'til you're home and have to deal with *Standie* doctors."

Such disdain in her voice. *Standie doctors.*

Sure, they weren't as quick to heal or as efficient at diagnosing as the Sorcerers. But they did the best they could and offered salvation and relief to the millions of Standies who couldn't afford the exorbitant fees to be treated by a Sorcerer.

At our silence, Alana paused and turned, staring down her

nose at where I sat on the exam table, my bare and mangled feet hanging over the edge. Jackson stood with his hip propped against the table beside me, looking utterly nonchalant, but his agitation pricked and prodded at me.

"Doing something you weren't supposed to, huh?" Alana tutted and turned away with a low, *"American* Standies..."

"I didn't know we weren't supposed to swim in the inlet," I muttered. There. The truth. But not entirely. Swimming. Not skinny-dipping.

Alana sighed and opened the cabinet above her head, grabbing another vial. "You're not. It's in the brochure you're given when you check in, but you Standies never bother to read the fine print, do you? That's what gets you into trouble. Us Sorcerers are taught to mind those warnings when we're young. Don't read the fine print on an enchantment and you'll flip your bones outside your skin. It's happened," she added after a glance at my horrified face. "Especially with cosmetic enchantments. And it's a right nightmare to reverse. So we make sure to read fine print, whereas Standies flippantly ignore such warnings. Must be nice."

"T-there were other people in the water, though." I looked at Jackson, silently pleading for his help.

"And if other people decide to jump into the mouth of the sea beast, are you going to follow them? Thinking it's safe?" Alana scoffed.

Yes. The word rose in my head.

Yes. Because it would *be safe. With Alistair.*

But I chewed that sentence up and swallowed it.

Jackson said nothing.

"Hmmm. Well, here." Alana thrust the beaker of bubbling, bright green liquid under my nose. "Drink that—*all of it,*" she added when I sniffed and recoiled.

It wasn't the *worst* thing I'd ever smelled, but it was a bit like rancid seaweed that'd washed ashore and festered in the sand and sun for days.

The taste was worse. Because the liquid was bubbly, so it

couldn't be tossed down like a shot, and it was so salty, and bitter, and...*Yuck.*

I took a sip. Squeezed my lips shut when the bubbles fizzed against the roof of my mouth, and swallowed the biggest mouthful I could manage.

"Good." Alana turned away, placing her vials back into the cabinets.

I took another gulp. And then another. The drink did *not* get better with repeated exposure.

"You'll want to take it easy for today," Alana added.

"We were just going to see the alicorn stables," Jackson said.

I glanced up at him after I downed my next sip. "We were?"

"Yeah, remember we were talking about it at dinner. I booked us for a tour."

Had he told me that? Cold sweat prickled my temple—either a reaction of the fizzing drink making my insides feel poppy, or the realization that I had some blind patches in my memory from last night. Like, I *remembered* the night. All the events of it. But little details—like what we'd talked about at dinner—were fuzzy.

"I wouldn't push it, even for a tour. Not with the state your feet are in," Alana said. "It'll hurt when they start healing. My advice would be to take the day to sit at the bar and *read your welcome brochure.* But you do whatever you feel is best. I'll just warn you that it'll be painful, the healing. And that's all I can do. But *certainly*"—she paused, and pivoted, giving us another haughty down-the-nose stare—"do *not* make any further attempts to swim in the inlet. I know the waters are shallow there, and it's tempting. I know we have a tidal chart. But if you had read the fine print, you'd know that the tide is not always accurate on the isle. There's too much magic"—she twirled her finger above her head, indicating the air around us—"it messes with the force of nature. *Drink up.*" She turned that twirling finger to me.

Because I had stopped drinking the tonic. It'd made my stomach feel funny and I'd hoped a little break would settle it.

It didn't. So I downed the rest as fast as I could and handed the beaker back to Alana, who whisked it out of my hand and stuck it into a bin for cleaning. "There now, you'll be all healed up in a few hours. The front desk takes cash or check payments —no credit cards on the isle. I *hope* you're aware of that, but we get a good number of people who aren't."

"I brought a checkbook." Jackson patted his pants pocket.

We'd both put money into our shared checking account for this trip. Enough, we figured, to cover everything we wanted to do, twice over.

But the number we got hit with as we checked out of the clinic...Well, I wasn't sure if it was the tonic that made my belly feel as though it'd sprouted jumping beans, or the realization that our little skinny-dipping venture had eaten a quarter of our vacation fund.

15

Pippi

lana had not been lying when she'd said the healing would hurt. Boy, did it.

It had started at the breakfast buffet, when the potion fizzing in my stomach had left me so bloated and gassy, I'd almost retched trying to force down a piece of toast. We'd hung out at Brew & Bites for at least an hour afterward, waiting for our tour, which had a 10:00 a.m. start. By the time we left, the burbling in my belly had eased.

Nothing had healed, though. The wound on my thigh hadn't even started to scab. I had to rewrap it in the bathroom when blood seeped through the bandages and made small ink blot patterns on my frilly skirt. Teal paired well with most colors. Crimson was not one of them.

Thankfully, I was able to flag down a staff member who got me a tin of dust—*magical* dust. I sprinkled it over my skirt, waited exactly sixty seconds, as directed, rinsed it off and… *Voila.* No more bloodstains.

"Ye can keep that," the robust female staff member told me when I stuttered my thank yous and tried to give the tin back. "We get shipments of 'em near weekly, so ye'll not be putting us out none."

I smiled, patted her arm in thanks, and tucked the tin into my pocket, mentally calculating how much use I'd be able to get out of the dust. Magical stain removers would come in *very* handy.

With my dress saved, and the bloat deflating, I felt better when we headed for the tour.

But a scorching ache crept into my bones—the sort of deep, gnawing pain you'd get with a fever—as we lined up outside the alicorn stables. And it sharpened, until it felt like I had glass shards burrowing into my feet, razor blades peeling the flesh off my thigh, and a chain saw grinding my ribs.

I'd smiled, though, at the gathering crowd, and had managed to dig up some laughter when our enigmatic tour guide chucked some cheesy jokes at us.

"Can anyone tell me why Mayo would be the best name for any horse, alicorn, and all equines?" The broad-chested guide swiveled his hazel eyes around the group. "Anyone? Because when they talk, you can declare, 'Mayo neighs!'"

The cluster of kids in our group giggled. The adults mainly rolled their eyes, but we all gave him a good-natured chuckle. And then we were off, on an hour walking tour that I remembered *none* of.

I was so focused on ignoring the pain, on smiling and trying to look like a happy-go-lucky tourist, that there wasn't any room left in my brain to absorb information.

Some parts stuck, sure. Like how very big the black furred alicorns looked while they rested in their airy box stalls, and how gentle they were when they were asked to step out into the aisle. Children ran around them, shrieking in delight, while everyone else poked and prodded and asked questions. The alicorns stood still, allowing the touches, and cordially answered each query.

The stables themselves were pristine, with spotless cobblestone floors and glistening black doors on the box stalls. Five gold chandeliers dangled overhead, suspended from the arched mahogany rafters. Above that, the ceiling opened to an expansive skylight, which coaxed as much illumination as it could from the fog-swaddled sky.

Afterward, as we took the wagon back to our cottage, Jackson buzzed with excitement. "I did *not* know all that. About how these creatures...*are*. Were. Did you?"

I clung to his exuberance nearly as tightly as I clung to his hand, trying to distract myself from the proverbial knives flaying ribbons of skin off my thigh. "Ummmm...which thing was that again?"

"Where they came from."

"Ah." Had that been a tour topic?

Jackson chuckled and tapped his thumb against my knuckles. "Did we lose you for a bit at that part? Or...wait, that might've been when you were off petting that alicorn with the blue mane."

I vaguely remembered that. I had gravitated to one of the alicorns who'd had doleful eyes and seemed a little forlorn, and I'd given him neck scritches, hoping to cheer him up. But I couldn't recall if he'd had blue in his mane.

"They were saying it's some kinda old magic," Jackson said. "When magic was a lot more common and not regulated. That five hundred or whatever years ago, the people on this island, back when it was part of Scotland, got cursed. "

"But that's *illegal*. To curse people." Sorcerers had been executed for doing so. It was rare, when one tried to circumvent the law and drop a curse on someone, but it got splashed all across every news channel, magazine, blogging site, and social media feed when it happened.

"Yeah, now it is, but it wasn't then. Because the town here got cursed. Everyone who died there couldn't just *die,* they had to come back as something else. So thousands of people kicked the bucket and resprouted as alicorns and banshees, and basically the full mythical creature alphabet. And then they all... disappeared."

"Disappeared?"

"Yeah. I guess everyone figured they'd died-died. And that was that." He tapped my thigh. "This is our stop!"

My brain sputtered as I clambered off the wagon beside him. "I...Wait, are these...The alicorns and all...they're not those people from five hundred years ago? Are they?"

The two alicorns pulling the wagon whuffled, as though they'd heard me.

"Stars, that was rude. Sor—" I pivoted to face them, but they'd already turned away, pulling the wagon of chattering tourists to the next stop. "—ry. Sorry."

"They might be five-hundred-year-old farts." Jackson shrugged. "Or might be those people banged out a bunch of kids, and these are their offspring. No one knows. Not even the creatures."

"How can they not know?"

"The spell that held them here. Up until it was lifted six years ago, it was fucking with their memories."

My stomach tilted—either from the sorrow that slammed me at the thought of that alicorn with the doleful eyes, of *Alistair* being trapped here for five hundred years, or from the vicious bite of pain that savaged my bones.

I swayed.

"Whoa, babe." Jackson grabbed my arm. "You doing okay?"

No. My bones are being crushed into dust and my skin is on fire.

"I'm achy," I said.

"I guess that's a sign the healing stuff's working, though, right? It's about fucking time, too. Do we have any Tylenol you can take?" He led me to the door of our cottage.

"Yeah." I had already popped some. It'd done nothing.

"Well—" Jackson started but cut off when a voice to our right trilled, "Yooo-hooo!"

I turned. Melany and her partner were at the door to their cottage, a mere two lots down from ours. Close enough to make out their shapes in the fog, although I had to squint to make sure it was them. And then I smiled, even as my bones gave an exhausted grind.

Because I liked them. Genuinely. Melany with her vibrant joy, and her partner with her gentle snark. They were good people. Granted I didn't really *know* them, but sometimes you didn't need to memorize a person's life history to know you'd found a friend.

"Good afternoon!" I waved at them. "Having a good trip so far?"

"Lovely." Melany gave a contented sigh. "We just returned from the fields. Sarah was drawing the will-o'-the-wisps!" Melany motioned enthusiastically to her partner, who smiled and held up a worn leather sketchbook.

"I don't know that this does them justice though." Sarah tapped her sketchbook against her thigh.

"They were so *gorgeous*. Especially in the fog like that." Melany heaved a dreamy sigh. "And so is your drawing, love. I can't wait to see it painted. I hope you'll not sell this one."

"This one is all for you." Sarah's mouth quirked into a warm smile when Melany made a happy sound. "Anyway, just because I'm a curious nosey body, I have to know, where have you two come from?" she asked Jackson and me.

"The alicorn stables," we answered in unison.

"Ohhhh, the tour?" Melany trilled. "How was it?"

"The stables are gorgeous," I said.

"We'll have to do that." Melany turned to Sarah, who shrugged, smiled, and said, "Sure thing."

"And maybe we should find the will-o'-the-wisps tomorrow?" I looked at Jackson, who rolled his shoulder.

"I know it's a bit warm and muggy and all, and not really *hot tea* weather, but would you two like to join us for a cup?" Melany asked. "Or a *cuppa*, as the Brits call it. I love how that rolls off the tongue."

The pain gnawing at my bones gave a particularly vicious munch, preemptively scolding me for the words it knew I would say. "A cup of tea sounds *fabulous* right now."

Melany grinned.

Jackson's brow pinched.

I took pity on him. "I'm sure you'd rather not chitchat with us gals, huh? That's fine, you don't have to. Maybe you can figure out which bar fare we're gonna have for lunch?"

"You sure you're up for a tea visit?"

No. I want to sprawl out on the bed and zonk out until at least *tomorrow.*

"I won't be long. Fifteen, twenty minutes tops." I stood on my toes, dropping a nuzzling kiss to his lips.

"Do you want greasy or *extra* greasy for lunch?" he asked.

My stomach balked. "Hmmm, tough choice. But I'll have to go with plain greasy." I flashed what I hoped was a smile and not a grimace, as I strolled across the gap of stony terrain that separated our cottage from Melany and Sarah's.

"I'm so tickled we caught you today." Euphoria warbled off Melany in big, galumphing waves as I approached. "I was telling Sarah this morning that you were such a dear and we needed to kidnap you from the hubby at some point."

"We wouldn't have actually kidnapped you." Sarah gave my shoulder a friendly pat as she ushered me into their cottage. "But we *might've* held you under ransom."

This time, my smile felt a little looser because their happiness was infectious.

"Apologies for the disarray," Melany added once we shuffled through the door.

Their cottage was a different color—canary yellow and sky blue—but the interior layout was exactly the same as ours. It had a more *lived-in* feel though, with clutter on the kitchen counter, clothes strung over the back of the couch, and food scattered over the coffee table. It was inviting. Made it feel more like a home, rather than a generic isle cottage.

"We've never been much for housekeeping." Sarah dumped her sketchbook onto the sofa.

"I like it," I said. "My mom had a saying that a house wasn't a home until it'd been broken in with some clutter."

"Oh, well we have more than 'some clutter' here." Sarah laughed. "I like everything out in the open, so I don't forget it."

"And if I put something away, I'll forget where *away* is half the time," Melany added.

"I feel that." I laughed. "Especially when you're not at home and don't know all the drawers and closets."

"Exactly!" Melany plucked the iron teakettle off the wood-burning stove and carried it over to the sink. She swooshed it around once she'd filled it—a weird quirk I also had; like, I *knew* the kettle was full because I'd just watched the faucet fill it, but I still sloshed the water around to double-check.

I smiled. I *knew* I had good reasons for liking these two.

"If you don't mind me asking…Pippi, your name's Pippi, right?"

"Sure is."

"Thought that was what I heard. You had Sarah singing the Pippi Longstocking theme song last night."

"I loved that show when I was a kid." Sarah chuckled.

"But I wanted to make sure it was Pipp*i* and not Pipp*a*," Melany finished.

"Nope, it's Pippi. And my mom was a big fan of the show too," I said to Sarah. "I could sing the theme song with you." Truthfully, I'd rather never hear that tune again. But I did have every word memorized.

"Don't tempt her." Melany opened the wood-burning stove, making sure the big ball of orange flame that blazed without heating the rest of the room (magic) was still going strong before she placed the tea kettle on top. "She's a horrid singer. You are, love, no offense meant. But thankfully you didn't need to serenade me to win my heart. As I was saying, you look a bit under the weather, Pippi. Now it's no judgement, we've all been there, but if you're fighting your way through a hangover, we do have some stuff that'll help."

Oh, shoot. Apparently, I hadn't been doing as good a job at hiding my winces and twitches as I'd hoped. "I'm okay," I said, even as the healing soles of my feet sent a particularly nasty zap of pain through my entire skeletal structure. "Or I *will* be okay. We had a bit of an *oops* last night and I banged up my ribs and got a few nicks and scrapes."

"Oh dear," Melany said.

"Did you go to the clinic?" Sarah lowered herself onto the couch and motioned for me to sit.

I sat, grateful to be off my poor, throbbing feet. "Yes, and that's probably why I look"—I waved my hand in front of my face—"however I look."

"Pallid," Sarah said.

"Pinched," Melany supplied.

"Goodness. That bad, huh? And here I was trying to go for pretty and placid. But anyway, the clinic made the pain worse."

"Ah, they gave you a tonic." Sarah nodded. "Wretched, that is. I was fortunate, or *unfortunate*, enough to have one six years ago…or was it seven?" She looked to Melany.

"I believe it was ten, love." Melany crossed the room and plopped into the rocking chair.

"It's not been *that* long," Sarah huffed.

"You were still in your forties."

"Was I? Ah, but it doesn't matter much though. We were in Seattle and this Sorcerer teleported right on top of me—knocked me into oncoming traffic."

"Oh no!" I whispered.

"It was *horrific*." Melany shuddered.

"Broke my leg in three places," Sarah continued.

"And your collarbone," Melany said.

"*And* my collarbone. I had a wicked concussion too. Would've taken me months to get back on my feet after that. But because there were witnesses to the Sorcerer having caused the accident, he had to cover my care. So I got to see a Sorcerer healer. Was back on my feet within a day, but I remember the pain of the tonic." She pursed her lips. "It's *awful*. Worth it, sure. Saves ya a lot of hassle and headache as opposed to doing it the Standie way. But I'm surprised you're up and about if you were given a tonic this morning."

I shrugged. "If I stayed in bed, I'd just be thinking about how miserable I feel. Y'know?" How bold of me to ask that last question when *I* didn't even know.

But Sarah and Melany both hummed at my statement, as though agreeing.

"If you don't mind me asking"—Melany elegantly crossed

her legs—"how did you get yourself banged up enough to need a tonic?"

Embarrassment prickled my cheeks. And I thanked the stars and all the cosmic entities of the universe that my mom had given me her reddish complexion because I never looked pink-cheeked with embarrassment if my cheeks were always pink. "We tried to go swimming," I said. "In the inlet outside. And the tide came in earlier than expected so I played pinball with the rocks."

"Oh my," Melany said.

Sarah laughed. "Damn. That had to be terrifying."

My stomach swam as the memory rushed back—of being stuck beneath the surface, drowning, while the current smashed my body up. But the swimming turned to a gentle flutter as my brain reminded me where the misadventure had taken me: to Alistair.

"I'm surprised you didn't hear screaming last night." I swallowed the fizzy feelings down. "From me or Jackson. He got belted around too. Not as bad, though."

"Honestly, hon, you could've thrown a rave outside our bedroom, and I wouldn't have heard a thing. I was exhau—Oh, dang it!" Melany leapt to her feet when the tea kettle let out a wailing cry. "That scared the life half out of me."

"You need help?" Sarah asked.

"No, dear. You sit and enjoy our guest. I'll be just a moment."

"I did actually hear something last night, now that you mention it," Sarah said to me. "Not much of something. And I'd just been reading about the banshees on the isle, so I figured it was my head playing tricks on me."

"There are banshees on the isle?" I blanched. I really, *really* should've researched this place more.

"Yep, two of them! There's a full history on them in here." Sarah plucked the glossy brochure off the coffee table and handed it to me. "They do nighttime haunt tours to see them—ear protection included, of course."

"Huh." I stared down at the shining leaflet. "Welcome to

Niverwick Isle" stretched across the front in big, loopy letters, "where magic, myths, and monsters await."

And...*Stars.* I hadn't even noticed this yesterday.

But beneath the slogan, and the few scripts of testimonials (*"Best. Vacation. Ever."*) was a picture of Alistair. A painting, one that made him look fierce: a dark green serpent, slithering through the seas, his orange eyes searching for their next kill.

A chill rattled my spine.

"It's horrid looking, isn't it?" Melany swooped back over with three mugs of tea balanced precariously between her hands. "I know Nessie's the centerpiece, but I'm not sure that I want to see him if he looks like *that.*"

He doesn't. Well...okay. He does a little bit. But his eyes aren't that mean.

"They should've put Marvin as their centerpiece." Melany placed my cup in front of me.

I blinked and tore my eyes away from Alistair's painting. "Marvin?"

"The cat," Sarah said. "Melany stalked him last night."

"I did *not.* I just saw him walking in front of us and asked his name. And it's adorable. Such a proper name for a proper fellow. We should find a way to abscond him, Sarah."

"Marvin stays on the island," Sarah said dryly. "And we *certainly* don't need another cat. The ones we have are enough pains in the ass."

"Oh, shush." Melany clicked her tongue. "You *adore* our munchkins, and you know it."

"I will admit to no such thing." The wave of affection and love that cascaded off Sarah as she said those words had my own chest pinging with happiness.

But then I glanced back at Alistair's painting and a barb of sorrow shot into my heart. I traced the tip of his snout, where his lips were curled over his teeth. And I wondered how long he'd been stuck here, alone, with no one to talk to. No friends, family, lovers. Only the sea...and now the gaping tourists.

I circled my thumb over his eye. *No wonder you felt so sad.*

16

"Oh…Sh—" I squealed when a rock careened out from under my foot, sending me thumping onto my keister and sliding a good foot or two down the meandering cliff path.

"—*oot*," I finished when I came to a stop, precariously close to the edge. "Shoot. Ouch." Blood glittered on my hands from the scrape the rocks had left on my palms. "I take that back. *Shit* is the word I need."

My bruises and nicks from last night's misadventure had *just* healed. And here I was, sitting at a bend in the cliff path at half past the witching hour (the old superstition us Standies had about 3:00 a.m.) and banging myself up, *again*.

"*How did you get these cuts on your hands, babe?*" I muttered in the best Jackson impression I could muster while my voice was shaking. "Well, you know, Jackson…I was climbing around the cliffs in the dead of night to go meet the Loch Ness Monster in secret, instead of staying in bed with you where I belong. Why? Because I'm an *idiot*, apparently."

My stomach churned as I plucked little pebbles off my palm and did my best to wipe off the worst of the blood—thank all the stars I'd had the foresight to wear my lone pair of black jeans.

And it was my nerves, for sure, that had me so frazzled and miserable. Because only a few spindly layers of craggy stone separated me from the whooshing ocean below. And any time I was this close to the sea, getting suffocated by the brine, I wasn't a happy camper.

But guilt also chewed at me because I hadn't told Jackson

about Alistair, and I didn't know *why*. I'd started to. Several times, during lunch, while we'd perused the little gift mart, when we'd wandered by to stare longingly at the exorbitantly expensive spa, and when we'd settled in for dinner. But I'd never actually gotten the words out. And I should have.

It was wrong. To be here, while Jackson slept unaware.

It was wrong to *be here* in general. Especially when the fine print in the brochure stated:

"Many of our cottages border the inlet, and although it may be tempting to dip your toes into the water while the tide is out, we heavily caution against doing so. Tides around the isle can be unpredictable—the sea does not have a mind to be gentle to our esteemed guests, no matter how much we wish it so. There are paths winding down the cliff face, should you like to brave a closer look at the waters, but be wary—these paths are not so easily trodden, and Niverwick Isle is not liable for any damages to person or property from any of our island attractions or on our grounds."

Which, the short explanation meant: *It's dangerous. If you don't want to take our word for it, that's cool. But just know you can't sue us if you die.*

Sweat creepy-crawled down my chest and congregated in a big, sticky vat beneath my breasts. It made me itch, especially when the fine, silken material of my red and gold blouse plastered itself to my wet skin. I fanned my non-bleeding hand in front of my face, getting at least *some* air moving. But gosh, it was humid tonight.

Or maybe my anxiety was radiating me from the inside out.

Or maybe it was a bit of both.

ROAR!

SMACK!

HISS!

Mist splattered over me as a wave pummeled the cliffs with enough force to rattle the ground beneath my butt.

I jolted and, for a terrifying moment, the world teetered sideways on me.

My bleeding hand pulsed with pain when I braced it on the ground, trying to keep my upper body from wilting beneath the vertigo.

It won't come up this high. You're fine. Even if it does, you can climb higher.

You already made it down, you can make it back up.

Pain lanced my chest. *Breathe!*

A sluggish breeze tickled my cheeks but offered no relief from the moist heat. I *swore* it'd not been this hot before. Muggy, sure. But not unbearably so. Not until now.

Maybe I took a nosedive off the cliffs, and I'm already dead. And got chucked into Hell for arranging a secret rendezvous behind my boyfriend's back.

Gosh, wouldn't that be a nightmare? An eternity spent in the fog, dangling just above the jaws of the sea.

My swallow felt more like an involuntary spasm.

"Pippi?"

I screamed when that accented voice blanketed itself over my brain.

"I'm sorry!" Alistair said. "I'm sorry. I didn't mean to s-scare you."

"It's…You didn't. I'm just…" I peered into the dark, barely making out the undulating outline of the water below. "You're down there, right? Or, I guess you wouldn't have to be that close, for your…would we call it telepathy? The way you speak to me? Oh, I guess it doesn't matter. You probably can't even hear me."

"I can. Hear you."

I squinted again, and the shape of the curdling sea was a little clearer, with my eyes adjusting to the gloom, but Alistair's behemoth outline was nowhere to be seen.

"I'm beneath the water." Alistair's voice caressed my brain, answering my unasked question. "I can't surface here."

"Is it the magic again? Preventing you?"

"Yes."

I gnawed on the inside of my cheek. "It's not hurting you

now, though. Right? Or is the inlet completely off limits like the dock was?"

"I can be here. Under the waters. It will only hurt if I surface."

"Good. That's…I wonder why, though. They could probably make a killing and charge double the price for inlet-facing cottages if they came with the chance to get Nessie all to one's self. Or, well…I guess that would be a massive liability though, huh?"

"Lia…lie-a-billl-a-tee." He stewed over each syllable. "I *know* this word. *Liability*. I *know* it. But not its meaning."

Something jangled inside of my chest. Sympathy, sure. Because I felt his frustration, and I knew how maddening it was to have something on the fringes of your mind that you just couldn't quite grasp. But there was also this sense of…wrongness? Deja vu?

"It's legal jargon," I said. "Basically means you're responsible for something or someone. The isle is responsible for us—the tourists. So, if something happens—like if one of us goes for a naked joy ride on their star attraction and gets hurt—they don't wanna get sued. So they write some half-baked warning in their brochure, and make sure you can't pop up to tempt people, and…Yeah. It's a protection against stupid people doing stupid things."

"Ah. I see." Although his tone suggested that he was still puzzling some of the details out. But then he chuckled and parroted one of my other statements. "'N-naked joy ride.' Is that what you'd call our meeting?"

"I mean, if the shoe fits."

"Does it?"

"Doesn't it?'

"I don't know. What's a 'joy ride?'"

"Literally just going for a ride to find joy," I said. "There's no place you have to be, no destination in mind. You're just cruising along the freeway to have a good time."

"And you were having a g-good time?" I could hear the

sarcasm in his voice, and my brain was flooded with an image of a posh, dark-haired man raising a skeptical eyebrow.

"I mean, *no*," I admitted. "It was an experience, sure. But I could've done without the broken ribs and sliced up feet."

Silence stretched between us, fractured only by the rushing of the sea.

Worry curdled the air. Not mine. *His.*

"You were hurt badly?" he prodded.

"Yeah. Not from anything you did, though," I said. "Honest. You prevented me from getting banged up worse. The ocean knocked me around pretty good before I got to you."

"Ahhh…" He dragged the sound out.

"And you were hurt too," I added. "Trying to bring me to the dock. That magic…it doesn't hurt for long, does it?"

"No. The pain is q-q-*quick*. Quick. It doesn't last."

"Well, thank the stars for that." I sighed and wiped at the treacly stream of blood still oozing from my palm. "But even quick pain is no fun. And it doesn't seem right, this isle, and the magic they zap you with." I blew out a breath big enough to ruffle the curls that swirled over my forehead. "I've only been here a *day*, and I can't wait to go home. I didn't even want to *come*, if I'm being honest. But Jackson was so excited, and I wanted to be too, but—"

"J-Jackson?"

"My boyfriend. Umm, like a significant other. A mate?"

Alistair gave me another drawling "*ahhh*." "Didn't you speak him…*tell* him? That you're not…not…*un*. Happy. That you're *un*happy."

Unease crawled up my throat. "I didn't say I was unhappy."

"You didn't have to."

"Oh no. Do I sound miserable? Or look it?" I combed my hands through my hair and winced when I remembered one palm was covered in blood, and sighed. "I'm not. Miserable. Honest. It's just been a weird couple of days. And the isle is weird. And I am *terrified* of the ocean. I was getting heart palpations just sitting here. And I came into this trip stressed—we had this crisis at work right before I left. So I'm just off-kilter, I think. And everyone gets the urge to run back home when they're off-kilter. Y'know?"

To this, Alistair said nothing.

But I'd said that all very fast, and he needed time to mull words over.

"Sorry," I said after a long beat of silence. "That was a lot. I know. I babble sometimes. It's a problem."

"It's not a problem," Alistair finally said. "You don't need to be sorry. *I'm* sorry."

Which was not what I was expecting. "What are *you* sorry for?"

"That you're u-unhappy. That you're scared of the water," Alistair said. "And that I want to k-keep you near the water. I like speaking—talking—I like *talking* to you. But I don't want you to be scared."

And there went that pesky jiggling in my chest again, the same as I'd felt when I'd first arrived on the isle. But it sharpened into a wriggling worm wrapped in barbed armor.

It *hurt* this time.

I jittered my hand, trying to shake off the excess feeling. And then I hissed a "sorry," when I caught myself doing it, and turned to popping my knuckles instead. But then I smeared blood everywhere, groaned, and parked my hands under my bottom.

The wriggling in my chest continued. From Alistair's emotions: sorrow and fear and hope and desperation. But from my emotions too. The shame of what I'd been putting poor Jackson through the last couple of days. Fear—always fear—when I could hear the rumble of waves and smell the stench burbling from the sea. Curiosity, of this tentative new friendship, and desire, to see where it might lead.

"Pippi?" Alistair pressed gently.

And maybe it was his kindness that had my mouth spouting this absolutely foolish question. "Can you surface anywhere near the rocks?"

"I can," he said. "On the other side."

Likely, the part that faced the open sea, where there weren't any tourist cottages.

"Could you take me there? If I..." Stars, this was *absurd*. "If I climbed down to you, could you take me to a spot where you could surface? It feels wrong talking to you like this. Like I'm taking advantage of the fact that I can't see you, so I'm just prattling on. And I think I *like* talking to you too. But I want to converse properly. Y'know?"

An incoming wave chuffed and huffed, chortling at my brazenness.

Alistair said nothing.

Doubt and disgust wound thorny vines around my belly. What was I thinking?

I opened my mouth, getting ready to blurt a *never mind*. But the words shriveled when Alistair finally spoke, "I would like that very much."

17

Alistair

"Could you take me there?" A simple question.

"I would like that very much." A simple answer.

But the words feel…

Heavy?

I'm certain that's not the word I want.

"I'm terrified of the ocean…"

"Could you take me there?"

It all feels…

Big. Her question. That she fears the waters but trusts me to keep her safe. It all feels big and heavy and…

Once, in another life, another *world*, I'm told I am…

What's the word?

Emotional.

I can't recall *who* said this. I see a stern face forming the words. It's someone I know, but their name has slipped.

"You're too emotional, Alistair."

"You trust too easily."

"You give your heart too quickly. It's going to get you in trouble someday."

I've forgotten how *deeply* I can feel.

But as I stare through the waters at Pippi, watching her… fur…?

No. It's not fur that falls over her shoulder. It has a different word.

Hair?

Yes.

Watching her *hair* move when the air hits it.

It's colorful, her hair, and it enthralls me. How bright it looks against the dark rocks, the way it moves in the air, like a dance.

Those emotions I've once been told would cause trouble, the emotions I've forgotten how to feel, fill me again. I'm alive, in a way I haven't been for so long.

Pippi pauses, her eyes darkening as she stares at the water.

Fear.

You don't have to.

I want to tell her.

You belong to the land. And the land is where you should stay.

I don't want you to be scared.

I'm selfish. For bringing you into the water when you fear it.

But I don't say those things.

"You're so selfish, Alistair!"

Indigo's face comes to me. Her eyes are watery as she yells those words.

"You're selfish!"

And I am. I never mean to be. But I am.

That selfishness hurt others. Hurt those I cared for the most.

Pippi moves again, her flippers—feet—her *feet* moving slowly against the stone. Her eyes roam now. Looking for me?

I blow out. The shooting water draws her gaze. Her mouth moves into a crooked smile, and her *eyes...*

The trust in them feels heavy too.

I am selfish. But I am determined to never let that selfishness hurt Pippi.

I just want one night.

"You won't let me drown, right?" she asks.

"Never."

18

Pippi

"You won't let me drown, right?" Those words gurgled out of my throat as water danced over my toes. I'd climbed down the cliff, shed my shoes, rolled my jeans up to my knees, and had been prepared to step into the water, but now I had a major case of cold feet—*literally*.

Because the waves seethed and snarled at the intrusion to their space. The air thickened and the salt from the sea clogged my nose, making it hard to breathe. Even when a treacly breeze wandered through, my blouse and jeans were plastered to my skin, like slimy armor, guarding me from the cool air.

Why, why, *why* was I doing this?

"*Never,*" Alistair said.

"Never what?"

"I'll never let you drown. I'm right here. You're safe."

This said as another wave munched up the rock face, shooting a fizzing slosh of water over my feet and horking up a bit of sea gunk for good measure.

I made a noise halfway between a cry and a gag.

"Are you alright?" Alistair asked.

No.

I wasn't sure if the sludgy stuff hugging my toes was seaweed, the guts of a dead fish, or something else entirely. And I didn't *want* to know.

So I verified, "You're still here, right?"

"Yes. Beneath you," Alistair responded. "You'll step off the rock and onto my head." When I didn't move, he added, "I like wearing you as a hat, it's…fesh…fash…*fashionable.*"

A surprised laugh bubbled out of my stomach, expelling some of the fear and doubt with it. "Well"—I licked my lips as the next wave receded—"this hat is decorated quite nicely for you tonight."

"Oh yes?"

"Yup." My foot plinked into the water, sinking down, down, almost to my knee before it connected with something coarse, and warm. His head. "I've got my Levi's on—and a vintage blouse." My second foot went in, scraping down next to the first. "I found it in a thrift store. It's the real deal—still had tags on it and everything. A Ralph Lauren, circa the early '90s. So, yeah. I'm always proud when I find stuff like this. I'm a bit of a thrifter nerd."

"It looks…*lovely*. It's almost the same as your hair. The color. R-r-run…" A soft jet of water plumed when he sighed.

"Red?" I supplied.

"Yes! Red. Like your hair. Both are lovely."

The way he complimented me was quite lovely. Goodness. With that accent, and the way the words rolled off his tongue… er…well, *would've* rolled off, if he was speaking.

Lovely.

That was a dangerous sort of voice. With its deep timbre dropping almost to a purr, and the words spoken with such reverence—like I was truly the loveliest thing he'd seen in his life.

That was a voice that got girls in trouble.

"You're a bit of a flirt, huh?" I asked.

"Flirt. Flirt? Flirt," he chanted the word. "I've been called that before."

"I'm sure you have."

"Is it a good thing? Or bad?"

"I guess we're both gonna find out." That sounded *way more* coy than I'd intended.

I was almost thankful when a wave blasted my knees, reminding me that I was standing in the ocean, on a sea beast's head, and should not have been flirting.

"You're safe, Pippi," Alistair soothed.

I exhaled, trying to convince my brain of that, even as my heart leapt into my throat when the next wave leered at me. It was bigger than the others, and it looked mean, with the way it panted and steamrolled. Like the big bad wolf, storming over to huff and puff and blow the pig's houses down.

"Can you take hold of my horn?" Alistair asked.

"Your—" My tongue stuck to the roof of my mouth when the wave rampaged closer.

"My horn," Alistair repeated. "It should be beside you."

My eyes fell to the right, where the tip of his horn curved out of the water, rising almost to my hip. I scooted over and grasped it for dear life, even as it made the scrape on my hand burn.

The wave, thankfully, huffed and puffed too much and winded itself by the time it hit the rocks. It made a great hiss as it splashed ice water up to my waist, but it was too weak to make a proper grab at my legs.

"Goodness, that's *cold*." My back tightened around a shiver. I swore the water temperature had dropped at least ten degrees since last night.

Or maybe my fevered skin just made it *seem* colder.

"I'm sorry," Alistair said. And a punch of *something* went through my gut. A strange, flavored emotion that was a bit like sadness, joy, regret, disgust, and hope being sautéed in a big skillet.

I almost bent down to stroke the top of his head, to offer what little comfort I could. But I looked back at the cliffs first, to make sure my shoes had stayed out of the wave's teeth, and I blanched.

Because the cliffs were several feet away.

Alistair had started swimming. So smoothly, I didn't even feel the movement. But he was quick. Within seconds, the dark fog swallowed the cliffs.

I dug my fingers into the hard, almost fingernail-like texture of Alistair's horn. "It's easier for you to swim underwater." It wasn't a question, just me thinking out loud.

But he humored me with an answer. "It's quicker. Although I don't find it d-difficult to swim above the surface. It's different."

"I guess it would be. Yeah. Like someone doing freestyle versus a backstroke."

He hummed, as if agreeing.

Wet, salty air walloped my cheeks as he glided through the inlet.

Stars above, this had to be a sight. With me zipping over the choppy current like Aladdin flying out of the Cave of Wonders on his magic carpet.

A deep and nervous, but highly amused, bray exploded out of me.

Alistair blanched. And then erupted in a trumpeting chuckle that shook his entire body, made the waves jiggle, and probably had the cliffs shuddering.

I clung to his horn but somehow, miraculously, didn't feel frightened of the gyrating ocean. I was too busy fighting off my random giggle attack.

"Was that"—Alistair's body vibrated again—"a *laugh?*"

"No." But another great, hiccupping guffaw rolled up my throat. "Okay, *yes.* But I could ask you the same question, Mr. Sonic Boom. How many fish did you send into hiding with that sound bomb?"

"A few."

"I'll bet."

"How many humans do you f-frighten with that laugh?" he asked.

"None."

"D-doubtful."

I choked on the next chortle. "Excuse me?"

"I've heard a sound like that before," he said. "When a w-w-*whale* was dying."

And, well, since he liked my braying guffaw so much, I decided to give him an encore.

And he answered with another of his sonic booms.

"I'm sorry," he added as I leaned against his horn, clutching at my aching stomach. "That was r-rude of me to speak of your laugh that way."

"Are you kidding?" I wheezed. "That was...I haven't laughed like that in"—I exhaled and gave my screaming stomach muscles a rub—"years. Probably. So thank you for that."

"I wasn't the reason you started laughing."

"You sort of were. Because I was thinking about how ridiculous I'd look right now if someone managed to peep me through their window. If they could see me through the fog, that is."

Alistair paused. Then laughed again, softly this time. "It would be a s-sight, wouldn't it?"

"Oh, yes. I'd probably be the talk of everyone's vacation. But then you'd be in trouble because you'd have the whole isle lining up for a ride."

Alistair made a gushing sound, as though he'd chuckled around a mouthful of water. "So I should make sure to r-return you before daylight?"

"Yes. I guess so. When the clock runs out, the magic runs out, just like a proper fairy tale. Well, I mean...the magic isn't going to run out. And this isn't a fairy tale. But you get what I mean. I hope? Or...I'm probably talking gibberish."

"Fairrrrryyyy tale. Fairy tale." He harrumphed, then asked, "Like Cinderella?"

And I dang near slipped off his head when the shock shook me. "Yes! Like Cinderella. Exactly. Which...Goodness. I'm a little bamboozled that you know what Cinderella is."

"I know most of it," Alistair said. "It's a l-l-love story. She has to return by...it wasn't daylight...*midnight*. She has to return by midnight. And she loses a shhh-suh-shoe."

"Yup, that covers all the bases. But...*Oh!*" I squealed when Alistair's head lifted out of the water. It was a gentle movement, done in a way that wouldn't jostle me, but the surprise of suddenly being several feet above the sea twisted my insides. "I guess we've arrived?"

He made an affirmative chuff and lowered his head, touching the edge of his snoot against a big flat ledge that wrapped around the grey-stoned cliffs like a balcony.

"Thank you. For the ride," I said as I gingerly strolled down the length of his nose—trying to be mindful of where I placed my feet. Both so I didn't impale my soles on the spikes framing his face, and so I didn't accidentally smoosh a sensitive part of his nasal bone that would set him sneezing.

After hearing his laugh, I didn't think the sea or the residents on the isle would survive an Alistair sneezing fit.

"It was my pleasure," Alistair said. He drew away once I was securely on the ledge. And turning around to face him—seeing the way he *towered,* with his neck scaling halfway up the cliff walls, even when a big chunk of his body remained submerged beneath the water...

My heart faltered. He was certainly a formidable sight. And I saw more of him now, from this angle, than I had last night.

A thick blanket of dark green scales swaddled the top portions of his body, while lighter ones peppered the underside of his neck. The translucent webbed dorsal curving along his back likely acted as a sail, lending him speed. And his head, despite being twice the size of my entire body, was delicate looking, with its long, narrow-snooted shape. Snakelike. A head capable of whipping quickly through the water to snatch its prey.

My mouth went bone dry. "I somehow forgot how big you are."

He blinked.

"Don't get me wrong, though"—I waved my arm, hoping I hadn't just stuck a barb in his feelings—"you're gorgeous. Really. It's just..." I clutched a hand to my chest when my heart gave a nervous flutter. "I think it's that survival instinct humans have, you know? Our senses know we can't fight a monster, so our brain starts pushing us to run. Not that you're a monster, though. Well, you *are,* but not a bad monster. And I *know* that. But my nerves are taking a while to get the memo."

Alistair blew out a chuckling breath that fluttered his nostrils and sent a warm waft of air over my wet, and very cold, feet. There were gills, on either side of his neck, just underneath his cheeks. I hadn't noticed them before—and likely wouldn't have noticed them now, if his breathy laugh hadn't set them fluttering like streamers tied to a fan.

"I'm sorry"—I threw him a wry grin—"I'm still a little frazzled. And very tired. And I sometimes lose my filter."

"You always say sorry for talking." Alistair tucked his head slightly to the side—almost like a dog, tilting and craning and trying to figure out when it would get that tantalizing piece of cheese. "Why?"

"Because I do it too much when I'm nervous or excited or whatever. Jackson calls me 'motor mouth' sometimes."

"Your b-boyfriend?"

"Yes."

"Does he not like your talking?"

"Oh no, he does. He gets a kick out of it, mostly. But sometimes I think he wishes he could get some words in."

Another warm breath fanned over my toes. "I don't mind you talking," Alistair said. "I remember…words when you speak. Words that have slipped. Some that slipped so long ago, I don't remember forgetting them."

Pain kicked my gut. *Emotional* pain. The sort of distress someone got when they found an old photo album and started flipping through the pages, seeing the faces of all the loved ones they'd lost.

You poor thing.

I stepped forward. He watched me, his eyes going a bit crossed as they tried to follow my movement.

"May I?" I stretched my arm forward, fingers curling toward the tip of his snout.

His nostrils fluttered as he nudged his head forward, gently meeting my hand.

"You're sad, aren't you?" I rubbed at the hard, spiked scales atop his snoot.

He blinked again.

"I hear it sometimes, with the way you say certain things. You sound sad."

I feel your sadness too, but I usually don't tell people that. They think it's weird.

"Do I?" He billowed, dancing thin tendrils of his hot breath over the sleeves of my blouse.

"Not always. Or even most of the time. But sometimes, yeah, you do." I ran my hand up and down the gap between his nostrils, marveling at his face's textures, which were hard like granite in some areas, where the scales jutted into spikes, but squishy and pliable in others.

Alistair whuffled.

The knot of distress he left in my gut loosened.

"I don't mean to pry," I said. "Believe me. I know if I've got something gnawing at me, I don't always like strangers poking around. But sometimes it helps to talk about it, even if it hurts at first. So if you ever want to slough off some of your pain onto someone else, I'll listen."

The gills along his neck ruffled as he bobbed ever so slightly up and down in time with the sea, but his eyes remained stationary, fixed on me.

"I think…" he started and then paused for a long beat.

I said nothing, intent on giving him time. But when I stopped stroking his nose, he pushed his snout forward, seeking the contact. So I kept going, running my hand up and down along the ridges of his face.

"I think," he started again, and paused, but only for a moment this time. "I think I'd like to wait until I…can find the words. Too many have slipped."

"Of course." I rubbed his muzzle. "We can keep it light

tonight. Maybe you can tell me how you heard about Cinderella. And then *I* can tell you about the retelling I wrote when I was in high school."

"R-r-retelling?"

"Yeah. Like, I took the story of Cinderella but put my own spin on it. And it was *terrible.*"

"You wrote it?"

"Uh-huh. I wanted to be a writer when I was a kid. Still do, if I'm being honest. I've always had a big imagination—which isn't always great when you start imagining bad things." *Like you whipping that snakelike head around and ripping me off these rocks, dragging me to your underwater realm, and keeping me as your sex slave.*

I shook that nasty thought off and said, "But I haven't actually written anything since college. I just haven't had the time."

Alistair must have noticed my shudder, because another one of his hot breaths fanned over me. This one was unfortunate, though, because it hit me in unison with a breeze, which lifted the hem of my blouse, and sent Alistair's hot air dancing across my belly.

And it *tickled.* I squirmed and bit back a laugh.

The black slits of Alistair's eyes narrowed. He cocked his head, aiming his next breezy breath into my neck, where it grabbed a big tuft of my hair, making it stand up on end.

I squealed.

One of those deep, sonic boom chuckles reverberated out of him, rattling the stone beneath my feet.

"I'd like to hear your story," he said, bumping his nose apologetically against my hip when our laughter cooled.

"Uh-uh, no sir. You're going first." I cautiously lowered myself down, letting my feet dangle over the edge.

Alistair ruffled and rested his chin against the ledge beside me, his orange eyes fixed on my face.

When I touched him, stroking between the spikes on his cheek, he sighed, lavishing the contact.

You poor, poor thing.

I kept petting his face, giving him the touches and affection he was so obviously craving. "So, Cinderella, I have a ton of questions, but there's one I'm gonna need you to be honest about, Alistair. You don't turn into a pumpkin when the clock strikes midnight, right?"

19

Pippi

Regret tasted like rancid eggs, especially when it flavored my tongue first thing in the morning.

It wasn't visiting Alistair that I regretted. It'd been, to use his phrase, *lovely*, to talk with him, even if I did sacrifice a night of sleep for it. He was sweet, and he'd been so happy to have the company, which had made *me* happy. Because I hated to see such a kind creature so sad.

The regret was for the secrecy. The fact that I hadn't yet told Jackson about Alistair. That I chickened out every time I searched for the words. It was *awful*, what I was doing to him.

"Babe. Hey."

I blinked when Jackson waved his hand in front of my face.

I'd been blankly staring, watching people shuffle to and from the breakfast buffet without absorbing any of it.

"Earth to Pippi. You with me?" he asked.

I dropped my hand from where it'd been (barely) holding my lead-weighted head upright on the table and beamed at him. "Of course."

He raised an eyebrow as he speared his fork into his fried eggs. "Didn't seem like you were."

"Well, I might've gotten a little distracted with people watching," I said. "And ogling up the premium buffet."

Jackson twisted, shooting his eyes over to the row of black-clothed tables on the other side of the room. "Yeah. Their stuff does look good, doesn't it?" He turned back to his slightly rubbery fried egg with a sigh.

Brew & Bites had two breakfast buffets. The premium one

was at the far end of the cavernous, high-raftered room, wrapped around the big arched windows that overlooked the foggy path to the docks. That buffet looked and smelled delectable. Cooks worked behind the black-clothed tables to prepare waffles, meats, eggs, and fish, while baristas hustled to keep up with the orders for cappuccinos, lattes, and other specialty coffees. People had to wait in lines for their meals, sure, since all the cooking was done over old coal burners, but everything they received was fresh and piping hot. And once they'd finished with their five-star breakfast, they could mosey back up to peruse the dessert table, where fruits and breakfast pastries were scattered in a colorful array.

I would've gotten quite pleasantly plump this week, if we'd had access to that buffet. Sadly (or maybe fortunately), we didn't. It was for premium guests—the spattering of people who were willing to pay extra to get the good food. The rest of us riffraff got the regular buffet at the opposite end of the room, nestled against the wall between the bathrooms and the staff lounge. And we had some scrumptious fare to choose from too, like muffins, bread, cereal, and a hot bar that had rubbery eggs and sausage. And our coffee was super-duper fancy: tepid brown water that trickled from old carafes.

All that said, it wasn't a *bad* breakfast. A regular old continental fare. But it sure felt like slop when that other glorious buffet was in eyesight, which was by design—to tease people with the better food until they forked over the money.

It was an excellent marketing ploy.

"Babe!" Jackson snapped his fingers. "I lost you again."

"Sorry." I leaned back in my chair, trying to straighten myself up, but I cracked my shoulders against the unyielding wood and winced, sending my fork sliding out of my slackened fingers. It made an awful clatter when it pinged off the end of my plate.

Jackson frowned. "What's going on with you?"

"Nothing."

He pursed his lips.

"Really," I insisted. "I feel fine. Just a little groggy this morning."

Jackson cut another small sliver off his egg. "You're sure that's all it is?"

"Positive." I plucked my muffin off the plate and tore myself a piece, eating it to prove my point.

"Shit, babe!" Jackson abruptly dropped his fork and lurched across the table, snatching my right wrist and shaking the muffin out of my grasp. "When did you do this?" He turned my hand over, exposing the scrape the rock had gouged into my palm last night.

I wriggled my arm, silently asking him to release me.

He tightened his hold.

"I slipped in the shower." The brambly lie scraped the top layer off my tongue as it rolled out of my mouth.

"You fell?"

"No. Nothing like that. I just…y'know…" I raised my other hand, miming me bracing myself against the wall. "The tile there's kinda coarse, so it scraped my hand up."

His fingers dug into my wrist. "You're lucky it wasn't a full fall. Did you get dizzy or something? The shower's not that slippery, with the mat in there."

"I'm fine, Jackson. I just slipped."

Guilt caged my heart between its spindly teeth and bit until the organ gushed blood.

I couldn't even feel Jackson's emotions when he released my arm and finished his egg. I was too busy drowning in my own bloody shame.

"You're *sure*? Because I don't know if we can swing another trip to the clinic."

"We don't have to." I forced another bite of muffin down and reached across the table, brushing Jackson's knuckles. "Honest. I'm okay. I just need some extra coffee, some sugar"—I held up the muffin in a *cheers* gesture—"and maybe some fun, and I'll be right as rain. So, what's on the agenda today?"

"Well, I'd wanted to take the boat tour, but that's already

gone. They only run onc a day, and only open bookings the day of, so those spots go quick. There're some other tours, but..." Jackson tapped his fork against his plate. "We're gonna have to be a bit picky about what we do. That clinic ate such a big chunk of our funds."

"I'm sorry."

"It's not your fault they charge an arm and leg." Jackson gusted a heavy breath.

But it feels *like my fault.*

If I'd been a better swimmer, or if I'd just put my foot down and said no when the skinny-dipping didn't feel right, we wouldn't be having this conversation.

I hated this. How strained we felt, with money bearing down on our shoulders, and guilt and disappointment creating a toxic plume over our heads. Around us, the room was filled with the sound of laughter, as happy tourists stuffed their faces and fervently discussed their plans for the day. But there was no laughter at our table. And seeing dismay creasing Jackson's brow and forming spindly lines around his mouth hurt my heart.

"Well, how about we just walk around the island today? Do some exploring on our own? It could be fun," I added when he frowned. "Melany and Sarah did that yesterday, and they saw all sorts of things."

"Who?" Jackson asked.

"Melany and Sarah. Our neighbors. The ones I had tea with yesterday."

"Ah. Yeah. The odd couple." Jackson chuckled

"I wouldn't call them that," I said. "They're sweet."

"You think *everyone* is sweet. And, don't get me wrong, I love that about you, and they probably are very nice. I'll give you that. But they are a bit odd, yeah?"

It was my turn to frown. "What makes them odd, exactly?"

"Well"—Jackson leaned back in his chair—"you know..." He waved his hand.

And the only thing I *knew* at that moment was that he didn't have an explanation.

But before he could scrounge for an answer, a shrill *DING-DING-DING* filled the room. The sound of an old dinner bell, the sort that came from a metal triangle.

An immaculately dressed woman who worked the front desk of the lobby during the day strode around the room, banging the metal stick against the dinner bell. She was a tiny wisp of a thing, but she had a personality that made her seem like a giant—a no-nonsense, straight-backed, I-may-be-small-but-I-can-still-kick-your-butt vibe. And she was throwing that off in waves as she shushed anyone who still whispered or giggled.

"I apologize," she said, "for disturbing your meal. I promise I'll only take a moment of your time." The dinner bell made a soft, echoing ding as she tucked it under her arm. "Unfortunately, all tours scheduled for this afternoon have been canceled. You will be refunded"—her voice rose above the unhappy gurgling—"and the tours will be rescheduled. Please understand, this is an extraordinary event—we have *never* canceled tours before on the isle, and you can rest assured knowing this will not happen again during your stay. We have some special guests arriving this afternoon, which necessitated the cancellation of the day's itineraries."

More murmurings filled the restaurant, but there was an air of intrigue now.

Jackson shifted in his seat, his eagerness reached across the table to lug me in the gut.

"Mr. Rune Bloodworth will be arriving at noon," the woman concluded.

That name meant nothing to me. But evidently it should have, because the chittering in the room increased. And Jackson sat so straight in his chair, he looked like he'd grown to a man twice his height.

"He is bringing several delegates," the woman prattled on, "to celebrate the five-year anniversary of the isle's opening. We do apologize for not making you aware of these events sooner, but there is good news...*Quiet* please." She waggled the dinner bell when the overlapping voices threatened to drown her out. "Please, a moment more of your time is all I ask. Since you are our esteemed guests, and your visit overlaps with the isle's anniversary, Mr. Bloodworth has ordered a feast for this evening. Every guest is invited to attend—free of charge."

"Thankfully she added that last bit in, huh?" I turned to Jackson with a soft laugh. "It wouldn't have been very good news if we'd had to pay a thousand bucks a head to go to this dinner."

Jackson wasn't even looking at me, he was *intently* watching the woman. His palpable excitement rocketed broiling, feverish waves into me.

Then she waved her arm, sending the dinner bell chiming pleasantly and said, "That's all. Enjoy your meals." And he deflated, as though he hadn't taken a breath during her announcement.

A wave of zeal rammed into me then, from Jackson and just about everyone in the room. Slamming into me with enough force to steal my breath for a heartbeat. Two. Three.

Panic curdled under the happy current.

My panic.

Happiness was a wondrous emotion, but it could be woven into a heavy blanket when there was too much of it. And that blanket was stifling me.

Sweat dribbled down my back and formed sticky puddles under my thighs. Beneath the white-washed jeans I wore, my skin prickled. My hand moved, joggling, trying to bounce off some of the excess emotion so I could *breathe.*

"Babe, you look like you're trying to fly." Jackson's chuckling voice sounded like it was miles away.

I tucked my hands between my legs and braced, focusing on taking shallow, steady breaths, until the feelings ebbed. "This Rune Bloodworth, is he a celebrity?" I managed to ask.

Jackson laughed and shook his head. "Pippi, I love you, but

sometimes I *swear* you live under a rock. How do you not know who he is?"

I shrugged.

"He's the owner of Magix."

"Oh." That name rang a bell. Magix, after all, was the corporation that *shredded* any business, Sorcerer-run or otherwise, that offered services for Standies. Like my client at work, VitalTech.

"Are they having a company retreat?" I swiveled my gaze around the undulating masses of people in the restaurant. "Seems an odd place for them to pick. I never hear of any Sorcerers vacationing here. Have you?"

Jackson rolled his eyes. "Magix *owns* Niverwick Isle."

"They do?"

"Yes!"

"But I thought they were all in on that 'Sorcerer for hire' stuff. That's what's putting one of my clients at risk."

"They *are*," Jackson said. "But they also have subsidiaries and conglomerates. And one of them is Niverwick. So, yeah, he might not directly work in the tourism sector, but Rune Bloodworth owns this island."

"Ooookay."

"And it's *huge* that he's coming here." Jackson jiggled his knee under the table, too giddy to be still. "I'd heard some rumors, gossip stuff, mostly, and I'd *hoped* they were true, but he's never been to the island before. And we're going to have dinner with him." He thumped his palms against the table. "This could be an *opportunity*. Rune Bloodworth is a genius. They say two minutes with him—just two minutes—and you can get doors opened for you that might've stayed closed your entire life."

"Well, sure, he's a Sorcerer, right? They can do whatever they want."

"He's not the richest CEO in the world just because he's a Sorcerer. He knows how to create opportunity, and he can do it for other people. The stories I've heard… And for him to come here…" His eyes glimmered as he clapped his hand against his thigh.

Disquiet crawled inside my chest. I didn't like this, and I couldn't pinpoint *why*. Something just didn't feel right.

But I swallowed the doubt down and forced a smile on my face. "I guess you're thinking of approaching him?"

"Um, *yes!*" Jackson said. "This could be…*Well,* if I get those two minutes, everything could change for us. *Everything.*"

20

Pippa

"*B*ehind the line!"

Marvin the cat had a set of pipes on him. His slinky, orange-coated body was totally buried behind the wall of people in front of me, but his command rang loud and clear over the throng.

The crowd shifted back, people hissing and cursing as toes got trod on and ankles got dinged. Jackson grasped my arm, tucking me against his side to keep me safe from the shuffling feet.

"I didn't think it'd be this crowded," I muttered.

Jackson scoffed in disbelief. "It's *Rune Bloodworth*. And they canceled all the tours, so everyone had an open schedule. That's why I wanted to get here earlier."

We'd made only a quick pit stop to our cottage after breakfast so I could change out of my jeans and slip into a graffiti summer dress. The mugginess had been dialed up to ten, and I'd started to feel itchy in my jeans.

Although, to be fair, Jackson said the humidity was still tolerable, and no one else was complaining. So most, if not all, of my sticky feelings were self-induced. Emotions jacked up my internal body temperature, making me less tolerable to the outside heat.

Regardless, I'd needed only a minute to change. We'd descended upon the dock at 11:30 a.m. to find the area jam-packed. And nobody was allowed *on* the dock—the closest we could get was about a dozen feet away. Too far to see the ocean through the foggy veneer.

Marvin had been waiting for us all to arrive too. He'd politely asked that we stay a distance from the sea. When people got brazen and started shoving closer, he'd hissed at us to step back. When people refused to heed that warning, he'd summoned a piece of chalk (likely the same magic chalk that wrote on the lobby board) to create a long line over the rocks.

"Nobody," he'd said, "is to wander past this point."

Someone had, of course, tested his boundary. The man who'd skipped over the line had received a slanted scratch on his ankle.

"Stupid, bloody gremlin!" the man had yelped. "How *dare—*"

"The safety of our guests is our utmost priority," Marvin had droned. "And I am permitted to use whatever means necessary to ensure that safety. Loitering on the dock during the disembarkation could pose a hazard to yourself and those arriving on the isle. I apologize for the scratch." This said in a tone that suggested he was not one bit sorry. "You will be compensated with a free tonic from the health clinic."

"Does that include a rabies shot?" Someone guffawed.

"Not. Funny." The man gnashed his teeth around the words.

But people now tried to stay behind the line. If they squiggled themselves too close to it, one shout from Marvin sent them all fluttering back.

Jackson tucked his arm around my waist, keeping me flush against his side, in case he needed to rescue me from more stomping feet. It was a sweet gesture. And normally, a squeezy, protective Jackson would've left butterflies fluttering in my belly.

But today? The heat of his palm seared through my dress and blistered my skin. Sweat moistened the areas of my back that were stuck to his scorching chest. The press of the crowd dragged at my nerves and left my emotions in a big thorny tumbleweed.

"I wonder if they'll be on the *Valiant*." Jackson bounced lightly. "Obviously they won't ever be on the ship *with* us, but we could still *technically* say we sailed on the same ship. Pretty cool, huh?"

"Very cool." I fanned lightly at my face. "But I'm a little surprised they need a ship. They couldn't teleport here?"

I felt his shrug. "Maybe they can't? The magic on the isle could be blocking their internal GPS, or whatever they use."

"Oh! I think I see it!" a woman in front of us trilled.

"That's a wisp of fog, hun," came her husband's response.

"Oh."

"It is beholden to me," drawled Marvin, "to remind you, yet again, that you are not to approach Mr. Bloodworth or any of his delegates when they disembark from the ship. You were given time to acclimate upon your arrival. We ask that you allow the same for them."

"I definitely see something," the woman crowed again. "There, to the left a little…"

People slogged into each other, straining to see, and a narrow gap opened in front of me. There, smudged against the foggy horizon, was a ship-shaped shadow.

Jackson squeezed my hip. But, at the same time, a jaw of fear clamped around my heart.

I jolted.

"You…" Thin tendrils of Alistair's voice brushed against my mind, so laden with shock—with *panic*—they zapped me with the same voltage as a cattle prod.

Jackson pulled me in for a bone-crushing hug, maybe mistaking my spasm for anticipation. And I welcomed that hug, and the security it provided, when sorrow flooded my chest. A great, yawning sorrow, the kind that ran so deep it couldn't be soothed by tears.

"Why are you here?" I closed my eyes, bracing against the onslaught of pain that accompanied Alistair's voice.

Something was wrong.

I could hear it…*feel* it.

"That is definitely them!" Jackson whooped.

I opened my eyes. And jumped when I realized Marvin had

meandered through the legs of the tittering onlookers and was sitting near my feet, staring up at me.

He blinked. In that slow, sluggish way cats did. Like they found your presence to be insufferable.

But I *swore* he knew what I was feeling. That green gaze was just a little too shrewd.

"I...I...You..."

Marvin's tail twitched in time with each of my stutters.

"Babe, wha—Oh, *shit!*" Jackson snatched at my hip, hauling me away from Marvin. "The fuck, man?" he grumbled. "We're not even near your stupid line."

Marvin turned, stuck his tiger-striped tail into the air, and wove back through the crowd.

"I don't think he came over to scold you, Jackson." I fought to keep my words steady. "He's probably patrolling."

"I know. But I'd be spending half the day sneezing if it'd rubbed against my leg or swatted, or did whatever it is that cats do."

Marvin turned when he reached the front of the group and found a gap to peer at us through.

"Do you think it can hear me?" Jackson hissed.

Marvin gave a slow, purposeful blink.

"Unfortunately, yes," I said. "But I'm sure he won't hold your allergies against you."

Marvin looked, very much, like he would hold them against Jackson.

With a grunt, the smudged shape of the ship ground to a stop at the end of the dock.

Anticipation made the air soupy, so thick and chunky, every breath was a battle to get down. And in between my slurping inhales, I felt Alistair, the pinpricks of his panic puncturing holes into my gut.

I squirmed, battling with the urge to do...*something.*

If only I could communicate with him the telepathic way he communicated with me.

Ssssssssnnnaaappp.

A hissing snap and a bright flash of light made half the people in the crowd flinch.

"Sorry!" a man on my left side grumbled as he fiddled with the camera in his hand. "Stupid thing's got a mind of its own."

The camera he had was the only sort that worked on the isle: a vintage, all-manual type that'd gone out of style one hundred or so years ago. Anything digital, or even anything using a battery, went kaput as soon as it landed on the isle. So not many people had cameras.

And those who did, didn't rightly know how to work them. As evidenced by the man's cursing as he fiddled with the knobs and buttons, trying to figure out how to snap a picture.

And he certainly had no chance of sorting his camera in time to catch the big entourage's arrival.

Ssswwwwisshhh.

A man teleported in front of our group, flashing us a thousand-watt smile as he shook some invisible ruffles out of his Hawaiian shirt. "Well, *this* is unexpected!"

"It's Rune!" Jackson breathed in my ear.

There weren't many people who could wear a red, green, and yellow Hawaiian shirt, paired with khaki shorts, and still look suave. But Rune Bloodworth was one of those people.

He was a bull of a man in his late forties, and his age showed in the grey hair dusting the light brown strands at his temple and the deep laugh lines around his eyes and mouth. Things that were enough to peg him as an adult in the middle of his life, not enough to actually age him or drag down his devilishly good looks. And he wielded that devilish charm well, as he preened and strutted closer to our group, throwing a dashing smile at everyone who hooted and uttered cries of "welcome."

And I had, indeed, seen him before. His squared and masculine face had been plastered across many supermarket tabloids. Those bright amber eyes of his had judged me whenever I'd grabbed a piece of chocolate from the register racks. But I'd never realized who he was. Until now.

"This is a welcome group, yes?" Rune clapped his hands and

chuckled. *"Excellent.* I love it. Although I'm sure you all have other things you want to do. I would loathe to keep any of you from your vacation. But I do appreciate the welcome."

A gaggle of other men and women teleported around him as he spoke, all dressed in their Sunday best: suits and ties for the men, and snappy business skirts and dresses for the women.

Apparently, the big head honcho was the only one who got to have a dress down day on the company retreat. Although he *had* been nice enough to let the men wear colorful ties.

"We should get drinks. Marvin. Marvin! Where's that blasted —Oh, hahaha," Rune boomed.

Through the twisting mass of limbs and torsos in front of me, I watched as Marvin sauntered up and sat at Rune's feet.

"That's right!" Rune said. "I keep forgetting you're *small.*"

Marvin's tail twitched.

"These fine folks deserve a drink for standing out here in this smog to make us feel welcome. Don't you agree, Marv?"

"I suppose," Marvin drawled.

"Open a tab in my name. And take these folks to the…er… Brew & Bites. Is that it?'

"Yes."

"Take them there and get them a round of drinks." Rune clapped his hands. "We really do appreciate you being here, ladies and gents, and all others. As I'm sure you can imagine, we are *ecstatic* to visit the isle with you."

I swore my eyebrows were going to fly off my face with the way they shot up at that statement. Not a single person in that group of Sorcerers, outside of Rune, looked *excited* to be here.

"And it's incredible to see that excitement reflected back to us. To be shown such love." Rune patted a hand over his heart. "Amazing. Absolutely amazing. Oh, come now, Onyx, it *is* uplifting, isn't it?"

A woman had finished her long stroll down the dock and came to a harrumphing stop behind the cluster of Sorcerers. She'd been the only one to walk the dock, instead of teleporting from the ship. And the only one to look at the swarm of onlookers with open disdain on her face.

"She's excited too. I promise." Rune laughed. "She just likes to keep people guessing."

If looks could kill, Onyx's would've melted the skin right off his face.

But in all fairness, she was the sort of woman who made the resting bitch face look breathtaking. She was tall and willowy with rich black hair (fitting, for her name) and big green eyes. Everything about her was delicate, from the angular curve of her jawbone, to her spindly wrists, to her lean and shapely legs. She was like a model, and she dressed the part, donned in a silken green wrap dress, paired with a glittering diamond choke necklace, and big hoop earrings. Silver rings glittered from six of her fingers as well.

She turned her eyes over our group—the Standie tourists of the isle—scoffed, and walked away, heading for the lobby.

People murmured as she passed.

"Do you know who that is?" Jackson asked.

"Onyx?" I repeated her name.

"Onyx Thornheart. Yeah. He *made* her. She was a nobody—born without magic to a Sorcerer family, working the nine-to-five grind with the rest of us. Then she got in with Rune and now she's up there with the richest women in the world. I'm telling you, babe, this is why everyone's out here today. Rune Bloodworth changes lives."

"Onyx." The mournfulness in Alistair's voice and the needles of despair he fired into my heart had me digging my teeth into my lips to keep from crying out.

Onyx stopped dead in her tracks and turned, raising her eyes toward the ocean.

Had she heard him too?

Rune called to her, jokingly telling the group that, "Onyx here has been dying for a drink since we left the states. Haven't you, Onyx?"

"Onyx." It took every ounce of willpower I possessed to keep my feet rooted when my body itched so fiercely to move. To run to the sea and offer whatever comfort I could give to Alistair. To make a dash for Onyx to ask if she really *could* hear him and then demand to know why he was so upset over her being here.

But I did nothing. Except to lean back into Jackson's arms and suckle what comfort I could get from his embrace.

After a heartbeat, two, three, Onyx smirked and turned away from the sea.

21

Alistair

Once I belonged to the land. I belonged to the *humans.*

That life feels distant. The colors and sounds of it. The noise. The feeling of *belonging.* Of having companionship. The sensation of having strong legs. Of walking.

I miss walking.

It feels…*felt*…purpose…ful. *Purposeful.*

To place my feet against the ground and *walk* somewhere.

So much of my life now is…*un*purposeful.

I move, because the waters and my body don't allow stillness. But I am never *going* anywhere. I can't.

I miss walking. And I've forgotten how much I've missed it. But the image haunts me today: the place I lived on the land. A place far from the waters. Where the orb in the sky…

Sun.

That's its word.

The *sun.*

Where the sun is seen—it *shines.* And I feel its light warming my back.

That sun does not shine here. Not over these waters or the land.

I miss that too. The sun.

There are the tastes on land…food. So much food. I see some of it still, in the hands of the humans I am called to amuse. Burgers. Sand…werches-witches-*sandwiches.*

Chips.

They are my favorite.

Chips.

In my old life, I ate them until my belly hurt.

Now, food is given to me at the start of the daylight hours and the end. I am given creatures of the water, the food this body needs. But it's not the food I want.

Nothing here is what I want.

I want my legs, the sun, the food…*everything.*

But instead, I swim. Forcefully twisting my body through the waters until I hurt. I hope the hurt will hide the want, but it doesn't.

The other creatures flee, frightened by my strange movements.

I want to call to them. *I won't hurt you. I'm sorry.*

"What are you sorry for?"

Pippi's voice.

I miss her.

I *shouldn't.* She belongs to a land far from here, a place where she has *friends* and *work* and *wineries* and *a house*—all the things she speaks of to me. Things that sound…

Lovely.

Like her, the way she looks in her red shirt, with her red hair. *Lovely.*

Those lovely things are hurting me now.

I still, allowing the waters to strike and pull at my body as I look to the surface, wanting to be there. To feel land beneath my feet, the sun on my skin. To open my mouth and *speak.* To find words easily. To walk with Pippi across the land, where she is unafraid, and see the lovely things she speaks of. To find my own lovely things: friends and homes and love.

I want to *live.* Instead of exist.

A shadow covers the surface, turning the waters against me.

The rune above my eye is cool. I am not being called to amuse the humans. And this is not the day humans arrive on the land—I know this because of Pippi. Because I know how many tomorrows I have until the shadow carries her away and brings others in her place.

This shadow should not be here today.

It's wrong.

I swim, following the shadow.

I see the humans staring at me, and my heart turns colder.

I *know* them—

The mark on my face burns. A deep, deep, deep hurt that consumes me. Blackens my sight. I cry and pull back. *Too close.* I am too close to the shadow.

Fleeing to deeper waters takes the hurt away.

But then I see *her*.

She stares down at me, her eyes hurting me nearly as deeply as the rune.

I know her face.

It haunts me when I dream.

The last face I saw before I became what I am.

The face that *screams* at me, telling me I'll never walk the land again.

Onyx.

"Alistair! Can you….no, you probably can't, huh? *Ugggggh,* what am I *doing?*"

Being crazy.

That was what I was doing.

I'd snuck out of the cottage while Jackson showered and got himself ready for dinner.

Well, I hadn't *fully* snuck. I'd told him I was going for a walk. (*"Really, babe? Now? Well, whatever. Be careful."* That had been his exact response). I just hadn't disclosed *where* I was walking to: the dock. I'd gone clean across it, even as the sloshing water underneath made my stomach flop and grumble. And I now stood alone in the middle of a fog so gelatinous, it seemed to have swallowed up the rest of the world.

The head of a wave struck the edge of the dock, spitting a wad of foam and muck onto the edge of my skirt.

I squeaked and glared at the fizzing glob oozing over the graffiti print. "Ugh, *great.* Guess it's a good thing I didn't change yet."

"Pippi?"

My heart leapt into my throat when Alistair's voice filtered between my ears.

"Alistair?" I called again. "Can you hear me?"

"I can."

Something was wrong.

His words were thicker. Slurred, almost. Not in the way people got when they'd had one drink too many. This resembled a watery lisp that stained a voice after a prolonged bout of crying. And his emotions were muted, as though the tears had drained him dry.

Oh, Alistair.

As a smaller wave swilled at the posts of the dock, munching on the wood with all the power of a chihuahua chomping on a tree trunk, a heavy *plop* sounded to my right.

I turned my head that way.

Alistair's orange eye cut right through the fog. So vibrant, it could've been a beam of light shining from a boat or a lighthouse.

The sight of that large luminous eye would've been petrifying—a scene straight from a horror movie—if I hadn't known that harsh stare belonged to the kindest of creatures.

"Are you alright, Pippi?" he asked.

"That's actually the question I was going to ask you," I said.

"You s-screamed," Alistair continued.

"I...Oh. Yeah. No. That wasn't a scream. Well, it *was*. But just because my skirt got wet. Nothing else."

"You l-look..." he stuttered. Sighed. "There is a word for this...your... *color* is not the same."

"My color?"

"Your face."

Which didn't help, until he added the next bit.

"It doesn't *have* color."

"Oh. Pale? Is that the word you were looking for?"

"Yes!" He exhaled. "*Pale.* You look pale. And is that not...for humans...it means they're not well?"

"I mean, *yes*"—I tapped my fingers against my cheeks—"but in my case, it's just from fatigue. But thank you for pointing out that I should put some makeup on tonight so I don't look like a corpse at dinner."

"That was *not*...I..." Alistair waffled. "Corpses are...*dead*."

"They sure are."

"You don't look dead."

"Like the walking dead, maybe."

"And m-make...up...makeup...Is that paint?"

"Also yes. You see my plan now, huh? I'm going to paint some color on my face so I don't look like a zombie. Kidding," I added, softening my voice when Alistair's eye rolled, looking pained. "I'm kidding, Alistair. It's a joke. I'm—" I bolted backward when another wave belched sizzling water over the top of the dock. "I *am* fine. Completely. Just a little tired. And a lot worried about you. Are you okay, Alistair?"

He blinked. "Yes."

"You didn't sound okay earlier. When Rune Bloodworth and his posse came to town."

"Ah." Alistair's voice shriveled a bit.

"You seemed upset."

"I was."

"Are you still?"

He paused for a moment, considering. "Yes."

I inched forward, hating that he was so far away and that his eye was the only part of him I could see. Hating that there was pain in his voice and I didn't know what to do or say to make it better. "I'm sorry, Alistair. Is there anything I can do? I'm a good listener, if you want to vent."

A swelling wave rose in front of Alistair's eye, temporarily dousing its light. "How do you always seem to know when I'm s-sad?"

"I just do. I've always been able to tell with people. Which, I mean, you're not *people*. But you get my point...I hope."

He said nothing. Just stared at me. *Through* me.

Heat danced over my skin.

Alistair's eye rolled slowly, drinking me in. But he wasn't only savoring the dips and curves of my body. He was searching deeper. Into my heart. My mind. My *soul*. Trying to read me, understand me, know me.

He was stripping me down.

Or, at least, that was what it *felt* like, with his eye peeling through my layers, leaving me bare, more naked than even I'd been on the night we met.

It was kind of thrilling.

And…arousing?

Heat spiked low in my belly—a heat that *reveled* in being pinned down and exposed.

I swallowed.

What on earth?

Alistair's slitted pupils narrowed.

And I swore he knew my thoughts had fallen into a gutter. But he blinked again and said in the sweetest, tenderest voice, "May I tell you something?"

I swallowed again, willing my body to calm down. "Sure."

"Do you…Can…" he blustered. Took a moment to collect himself and said, "There is a word for you…for what you *feel*. What you are. But it has slipped."

"There've been a lot of words used for me. Depends on who you ask. My dad probably had about the best of the bunch, though. *That*," I added when the slit in Alistair's eye narrowed, "is a story for another time."

Never.

It's a story for never.

"It's not c-c-c…" A gusty sigh quivered the water around him. "*Normal.* It's not normal. To feel what you feel."

"No. It's not. Which is why I generally don't advertise it." I crossed my arms over my chest as a cold wash of reality trickled over my head.

It suddenly wasn't arousing to have his gaze expose me, *study me*, like this.

It was humiliating.

"I'm sorry," Alistair's whisper caressed my brain, soothing the nerves his stare had flayed raw. "I didn't mean to u-u-upset you."

"You didn't. I'm tired. And cranky, I think. And…"

"Unhappy?"

"Worried," I said. "About *you*. I felt you earlier, Alistair, when the Brady Bunch—"

"B-Brady. Bunch."

"—arrived."

"Brady Bunch. I know this." His eye bobbed behind another wave.

"It's a show." I shrugged. "Another of Mom's favorites. About a dysfunctional family. So I'm being ironic when I call the motley crew of snobby Sorcerers the Brady Bunch. I'm really talking about Rune Bloodworth and all his henchmen and henchwomen. Like Onyx."

Pain squiggled in my chest.

Alistair's pain.

He seemed to realize the agony worm had escaped, though, because he immediately clamped down on it, drawing it away from me.

"You know her?" I asked.

His eye closed, and the world got a little bleaker, scarier without its light. "I do."

"Did she—"

"I w-wish…want…don't…don't want to speak of Onyx." Alistair's eye opened a small, weary crack. "Not now. I'm sorry, Pippi."

"Don't be sorry. I get it. Believe me. So I guess we're both leaving stories for another time, huh?"

He hummed in agreement.

"We'll have to meet again then, right?"

He said nothing.

"Tomorrow night?"

Good grief, Pippi, get the hint and leave the poor guy alone!

But before my brain could shoot those needly barbs of doubt into my bloodstream, Alistair said, "I'd like that." In a voice filled with hope—the sort you held your breath for, because you were afraid that any slight movement, even an exhale, would pulverize the thing you'd been clinging to.

My heart gave a heavy, hollow thump. "Tomorrow night, then. But if you want to talk sooner…well, I'll be here all week. And you can probably just…*talk*. I don't know what sort of range you have, but I've heard you from different parts of the isle, so we can test that range, if you'd like?"

Silence.

"Well," I cleared my throat. "I'll see you tomorrow."

As I moved to leave, he called to me.

"Pippi!"

I turned, scuffling my feet around to avoid getting pissed and spat on by the waves.

"You're...what you are...what you *feel*...it...give me a m-m-moment. Please..."

His frustration wrapped a boiling band around my body. Aggravation at knowing what he *wanted* to say but having to hunt for the words as they swam away.

"Take your time," I said. "It's okay. Just take a breath and give yourself a moment to think it through. I'll wait."

"Be c-c-careful," he finally stammered. "With your h-h-h-h-heart. *Heart.* Don't let anyone d-d-d-destroy it."

Oh, Alistair. You're thirty-five years too late for that sage advice.

But I smiled. "I could say the same about *your* heart, Alistair. I hate to think of you in pain. So, I'll tell you what. For the next week, we'll look out for each other, yeah? I'll guard your heart, and you can guard mine. And we'll...I guess we'll see where we are by the time I go home. Sound like a plan?"

He said nothing, but he didn't need to. He let me feel his answer.

And it left me almost giddy.

"Ooooh! Mushroom ravioli?" At first, I thought my gritty and sleep-heavy eyes were deceiving me. I blinked once. Twice. But the chafing dish was still filled with creamy mushroom sauce and the freshest raviolis I'd ever seen.

It was *real* food, not deep-fried, grease-saturated bar fare. And it was my *favorite* dish. Mushrooms were an obsession, and my mom had transplanted the *pasta-equals-comfort-food* belief into me. So, mushrooms and pasta, after the last couple of days I'd had, were like gifts sent from the stars.

"They're really good. I'm actually here for seconds." The woman behind me shouted in my ear as I ladled the steaming raviolis onto my plate.

Shouted, only because the jarring noise inside the Brew & Bites didn't allow for civil volumes. You either screamed above it, or you drowned in it.

It was the noise from the people—all one hundred or so folks currently on the island were stuffed into the restaurant, so dozens of lines of conversation overlapped each other, creating a big, puffy talk wave. And even that had to fight to rise above the tide of bagpipe music.

The woman next to me, burly and middle-aged, with a handsome face and sweet green eyes, was thoroughly jangled by all the commotion, and trying her best to hide it.

"The bagpipes are a little much, aren't they?" I asked her in the lowest conspiratorial whisper I could manage, with those jaunty strings of music billowing in the air.

She offered me a relieved smile—grateful that she had

someone to commiserate with. "They're *a lot* much. And not very good."

I tucked my chin toward the windows on the far side of the room, where the bagpipes hovered in the air, blowing themselves hoarse.

Who needed musicians when you had magic, right?

Except humans might've read the room a little better and chosen not to blast a bold Scottish war soundtrack over people stuffing their faces. It wasn't terrible music, but the heavy, dramatic notes gave the impression that we were about to be attacked.

I understood the woman's discomfort.

Some of it was my discomfort as well. The pinpricks of an overexertion headache had poked into the back of my head when Jackson and I first arrived ten minutes ago, and I knew I'd have a full-blown wallop of a headache by the end of the night.

So my plan? Stuff myself with as much mushroom ravioli and wine as I could, before the headache turned my stomach against me.

"I wonder if they think war music is good for digestion?" I yelled to the woman over the last wailing chord of the song. "Maybe they'll switch to some zen tunes for dessert."

Her shoulders scrunched with tension. "I hope so."

I gave her arm a light nudge, a silent beckon for her to hang in there, and to seek solitude if she couldn't hang any longer. And she seemed a little calmer when I turned away from the buffet and headed back to my table, so I hoped some of my messaging had gotten through.

Jackson and I had picked a table in the center of the room, thankfully some distance from the bouncing bagpipes (although the space did nothing to dampen the noise), and Jackson had manned the fort (and guarded my glass of wine) while I'd perused the buffet.

"Ugh," Jackson groaned lightly when I slid into my chair with my packed plate. "There's a fungus among us." He flashed me one of his handsome, boyish grins as he took a pull from his beer.

And then...

I squinted, sure the hazy fatigue over my eyes was playing tricks on me. "Jackson...are you *smoking*?"

He winked as he raised the chunky cigar to his lips again and inhaled. "Kian was handing these out."

"Kian?"

"Yeah. Kian Reed." At my blank face, Jackson waved the cigar. "He works logistics at Magix."

"Ah." I tucked my napkin into my lap, fighting the squirm of irritation in my chest.

I didn't particularly care if he smoked, especially since it was just a cigar—not much harm was going to come from it. But there was a dark thought burrowing into my brain, one that said he looked ridiculous, puffing on the end of that cigar, with his chin popped up in the air.

It turned my insides sour with shame to have my brain wander that way, but I couldn't *not* think it now.

My eyes burned as I turned the long edge of my fork into the ravioli, cutting a bite-sized sliver. And I hoped, as Jackson swiveled his head around to give me a loose, loving smile, that he couldn't see those thoughts on my face, or feel them assaulting his own emotions.

"There's prime rib up there," I said, my voice turning to my customer service chipmunk style. Thankfully, the headbanging battle anthem circulating around the room softened the chirp.

"Is there?" Jackson's eyes brightened. "And someone was walking around with lobster."

"Oh, yeah. I saw that up there too and thought about grabbing some, but the mushrooms won."

Jackson pulled an *ick* face. He hated mushrooms with the same fervor I loved them with.

"Everything looked delicious, though," I added. "*Everything.* You might need to roll me out of here at the end of the night."

"We'll probably be rolling each other." Jackson went a little cross-eyed as a woman sauntered by the table clutching two plates, one stacked high with oysters, the other weighed down by the biggest, juiciest steak I'd ever seen. "Oh shit, that does look good! Here, hold this!"

"Jackson, wha—" I grunted when he plonked the cigar out of his mouth and shoved it into my left hand. It was gross—all slimy and hot where he'd had his mouth around it—and lazy tendrils of smoke tickled my nostrils. "What am I supposed to do with this?"

"Just hold it. So I can go get food."

A few fat ash flakes tumbled off the end of the cigar and fluttered over my plate. "Don't they have places you can put these? Ashtrays or something?"

Jackson gulped the last half of his beer and motioned to our black-clothed table. "Do you see an ashtray here?"

"They probably have some at the bar."

"Yeah, and it'll take me as long to get an ashtray as it will to get my food. Just hold it for a few minutes. Please."

"Maybe you should've waited until *after* dinner to light this."

The bitterness in my voice shook me to my very core.

That was *mean*. The snappish way I'd hissed that. *Mean.*

It was the way my mom used to throw words at my dad when she was mad and hankering for a fight.

Jackson, thankfully, had already started walking toward the buffet line. If he heard me over the rallying music, it would've only been snippets.

But *I'd* heard the words. And had felt the heat behind them.

My lip quivered as I dropped my fork and used my free hand to pluck up my wine glass. And I pulled a Jackson, downing the whole glass in three gulping swallows. It didn't help the headache situation, but it soothed my blistered emotions. So much so, that I grinned from ear to ear when Jackson came back to the table, and then I gave him a big, noisy kiss on the cheek when he reached over to take his cigar back.

His eyes brightened, and an impish grin cocked up one side

of his mouth as he bent and kissed me. Deeply. *Obscenely.* Suckling and nibbling until I strained against him, seeking more.

"You seem to be in a better mood, huh?" He drew away, caressing my bottom lip with his thumb. "Were those magical 'shrooms?"

"Might've been."

More like magical wine, chugged on a mostly empty stomach.

I nibbled on his thumb, sighing when he laughed and popped another warm kiss to my temple.

This is what it *should've* been, with us on vacation: happy and playful and mischievous and enjoying each other's company.

So why didn't I *feel* any of that?

Why didn't he?

Because when I reached for him, trying to find a ribbon of his warmth or affection to cling to, there was nothing. Excitement, sure. For the food and the party and the presence of the Sorcerers who were seated at the round pub tables by the windows—all of whom he knew by name and happily rattled those names off to me as he scooched his chair into the table and dug into his steak. But it was all superficial stuff. I couldn't find anything deeper.

Maybe this island was breaking him as much as it was breaking me, and we were both doing our best to hold ourselves together.

Vacation of a lifetime, I thought bitterly.

The music screeched to a halt—as though offended by my despondence.

As silence swaddled the room—with people sputtering out in mid-conversation and peering around, trying to figure out why the music had stopped—Rune Bloodworth sauntered past the buffet bar and clapped his hands.

"I know, I know." He rocked on the balls of his feet. "That was incredibly rude of me to kill that lovely music. It's only temporary, I promise. I just wanted to take a moment of your time to thank you, sincerely, for being here. When Onyx—I'm sure you all know my business partner, Onyx." He swept his hand out, gesturing to the windows behind me.

I twisted in my seat.

Onyx sat by herself on a stool at a round pub table at the end of the row. And while the other Sorcerers were sitting a little sloppy, with most shifted sideways or swinging their legs or leaning, Onyx was as straight as an arrow. No slouch curved her back, and she had her legs elegantly crossed at the ankle, with her feet resting on the lower rung of the stool. She wore a deep ocean-blue gown that sparkled beneath the candlelight and spilled to the floor like a glistering waterfall.

She stared out the window, a glass of red wine sitting untouched in front of her. When Rune called her name, she didn't look at him. Didn't react when all heads in the restaurant turned toward her.

"When Onyx came to me with an idea to open a resort on a remote island…Well, anyone who knows me knows I love to take risks." Rune's smile shone brighter than all the candles in the room. And it was infectious. I smiled back at him when he panned that grin over me. Everyone did. How could we not? "Without risk, there is no reward. I firmly believe that. But this was by far the biggest and most ambitious leap I'd ever taken. You all should have seen this island six years ago. It was *savage*. Cold and rainy 350 days of the year, and muggy the other fifteen. The ocean was beating the rocks down to dust, and the creatures…Well, let's just say they weren't *glammed up* and ready to take center stage."

A laughter trickled around the room.

"Just being here for a day would send anyone spiraling into a depression," Rune continued. "But Onyx had a vision. And she believed in it, and I believed in her, and now here we are"—he raised his whiskey glass—"feasting with one hundred and twenty-seven of the finest people in the world. Celebrating the five-year anniversary of Niverwick Isle's opening. So I am proposing a toast, one of many I'll propose tonight, I'm sure. I *am* fond of my toasts." He laughed. "To Onyx and her vision."

"Hear, hear!" someone said. A few other people clapped. And, one by one, glasses were thrust into the air.

Onyx still hadn't moved. Still hadn't touched her wine or acknowledged the toast.

"Oh, shit." Jackson laughed as he raised his empty beer glass. "We should've gotten a second round, huh?"

I peeled my gaze away from Onyx and lifted my also-empty wine glass. "Guess so. We were both lushes tonight."

"And to all of you," Rune concluded in his resonant voice, "for joining us." He turned, clinked his glass with a tall, balding man at a nearby table, and then declared, "Drink up!"

The gentle tinkling of glasses knocking against each other filled the room.

Jackson and I looked at each other, tapped our glasses together, and mimed drinking them down. And I laughed after, caught up in the playfulness, but Jackson had already slid his eyes back to Rune.

"Now then, Onyx..." Rune downed the rest of his whiskey and motioned for a waiter to come fill his glass. "Why don't you tell us how you discovered this place? It's quite a story." He gave the small, blonde waitress a gentle pat on the arm when she reached his side and refilled his glass. "And I certainly don't want to steal your thunder."

Onyx moved then, fixing Rune with a look that said, quite plainly, if he even attempted to steal anything from her, she would hit him with the force of a thousand lightning bolts.

Rune just waggled his eyebrows. "She is a bit shy, folks. Always putting in the work but never looking to take the credit. How about we give her a little applause? See if that encourages her?"

Clapping ricocheted around the cavernous room—the pitch so shrill, it drove an ice pick in between my ears.

I cringed.

Onyx rolled her eyes.

Rune placed his whiskey on a table and tapped his hands

against his thighs in a mock drumroll. "C'mon, Onyx. *You can do it!*"

Onyx blew out a frustrated breath, took a long pull from her wine glass, and said, "Me mam told me legends of this isle…"

Her voice was heavily, *heavily* accented with a brogue somewhere in the Scottish family. English that almost didn't sound English. If I didn't *really* focus on the words, and the shape of her mouth as she formed them, it was all incoherent jibber.

"Ye all know them now, eh? Legends of the curse that trapped humans in this town and turned them to beasts after they died," she continued. "Me mam thought we had ancestors in the town. Although if our ancestors all turned to beasts, I didna know how she figures we were born human."

Only a speckle of laughter followed that. Likely because most people were staring at Onyx with concentration, trying to make sense of her words.

"Ach, but I liked the stories well enuf. So I bartered for a trip here when I was in me twenties. Found the isle as Rune said." She flashed her cold eyes to him. "Savage. And I says to Rune—"

"That the legends can be real and accessible for everyone," Rune finished. "And I gotta say, folks, I had my doubts. Until…" He gestured back at Onyx, returning the proverbial mic he'd snagged from her.

"Until he saw the Loch Ness Monster." Onyx scowled through her finishing lines. "And I says to him that the reef will keep it to the isle, and runes will make the isle safe for people to visit."

"I love that brand of magic. *Runes.*" Rune thumped his chest. "There's a soft spot in my heart for them."

Several people laughed.

Onyx just rolled her eyes and pivoted back to the window.

What an odd exchange that had been. Which was fitting, I supposed, for this odd island.

"Anyway"—Rune waved his hand over to the bagpipes, sending them quivering on a long, mournful note—"I'll save the rest of my toasts for after dinner. Or…Wait! I have to do this first, folks, sorry." He made a cutthroat gesture with his hand and the bagpipes deflated with a whiny *eeeeeeee.* "Because speaking of dinner, everything you're eating tonight has been prepared by our very own Aranis Brightspark. Stand, please, Aranis. Take a bow."

A sprightly Sorcerer stood from a center pub table and waved self-consciously.

"Aranis is launching MagicBite next month," Rune said. "Aiming to make mealtimes magical, even for Standies. So if you're enjoying the food, make sure to watch for the launch. He's on most Standie social media platforms as well, if you'd like to give him a follow when you get home. Now, no more interruptions until everyone has a full belly." Up went his hand again, sending the bagpipes wailing with another battle song.

"I wonder if—" I turned to Jackson, starting to ask if he thought Rune took song requests.

But Jackson was gone.

He must've jumped up as soon as the music started and was now standing in a line at the bar, both our empty glasses in hand.

I sighed and popped a half-cooled bite of mushroom ravioli into my mouth.

24

"Pippi. Pippi, I…" Alistair's voice tickled my brain on the lonely wagon ride I'd taken back to my cottage. Lonely, only because the families with kids had left Brew & Bites earlier and most everyone else, including Jackson, were enjoying the after party, so I had the wagon all to myself.

I'd stayed as long as my pounding head would tolerate. And I'd tried not to be upset when Jackson had kissed my temple and told me to go on ahead without him after I'd mentioned going back to the cottage.

But I was a little upset. More than I had any right to be.

The two alicorns who pulled the wagon, a male and female pair named Blythe and Orielle, were friendly, maintaining soft, idle conversation as they carried me to my lodgings through the fog. On any other night, I would have engaged in small talk with them. But tonight, I was too tired, too raw, too…*off kilter*.

My emotions were jumbled into a brambly hairball. I couldn't tell which ones were mine, and which ones belonged to others. Like Alistair.

"Pippi…I'm sorry. I shouldn't keep calling you." My heart wept at the lonesome tenor of his voice. And I almost went to him—almost bypassed my cottage and wandered down the cliff path. But as I stood at the door, deliberating, my skull gave an awful, grinding thump, reminding me that I was overdue for a snooze session. And that was sometimes the best cure for every-thing that ailed the soul—a good, hard, uninterrupted night of sleep. Something I hadn't had since coming to the isle.

"I'm sorry, Alistair," I whispered as I went inside, changed into my pajamas (a.k.a., an old pair of Jackson's boxers and a holey T-shirt), kicked the blankets to the bottom of the bed, and stretched out over the pillows.

Alistair's voice continued to tease my brain—lightly, at first. Soft, whispered words, most of which started to sound like murmured gibberish. But then he grew more insistent. Demanding, almost.

"Pippi. You look lovely."

His voice dropped to a raspy whisper, one that had goose bumps exploding over my skin.

Stars, that accent of his, and the way it caressed each word…

It was *sinful.*

I rolled over, curling myself into a ball, and tried to ignore the spindles of arousal sparking in my belly as I drifted off.

Behind me, the bed dipped.

Jackson.

I sighed and scooted back, seeking him, the warm weight of his arms. The heat of his body. The comfort and affection and security, and…

My eyes burned when the bed gave a little shudder, and the weight disappeared.

Jackson never touched me.

I called for him, brokenly, hating the way my tears scraped my voice raw. But when I managed to lift my leaden head from the pillow and peer at the doorway of our bedroom, my heart slammed against my chest.

It was gone.

The door.

The whole *bedroom.*

There was nothing there. No walls, no bureaus, no windows. The suitcases we'd left piled in the corner had vanished. There was *nothing.* The edge of my mattress dipped off into an endless pool of inky black.

"Jackson?" I bolted upright.

Or, well, I *tried.* But something heavy and iron-solid pinned my body to the bed.

"Jackson!"

I swiveled my eyes around, but the black plagued my vision. I couldn't even make out the shape of whatever was holding me down.

"Jackson! Help!"

My heart turned into a heavy thrumming motor between my ears.

The thing pressed more fully against me, crushing me.

Every inhale became a struggle. My lungs were too smooshed to work properly. And I couldn't *move*. My wild attempts at flailing, at freeing myself, only locked me down tighter.

The black swelled around the fringes of my vision, an obsidian ocean puffing itself into a massive tsunami.

My cry came out in a warbling gag.

"Pippi?"

It wasn't Jackson who called to me.

"Alistair!" I bellowed. "Alistair! HELP!"

With a sticky roar, the black waves at the edges of my vision gyrated, contorting themselves as though in pain, and retreated.

The weight shoving into my chest vanished.

I was alone again, lying on my side, panting and sweating as I tracked the trickles of color returning to the walls around me.

The mattress dipped again.

I stiffened. But a warm hand pressed against the small of my back, kneading gently.

"Jackson." I shuddered and arched into him.

"You're safe, Pippi."

Oh no.

My blood turned to ice—big, clunky cubes that clinked and clanked their way through my body, smashing bruises and welts into my insides.

That wasn't Jackson's voice.

It was Alistair's.

His hand slipped under the covers and up my shirt, splaying his warm palm against the skin of my back. He chuffed when I shivered and scooted closer, pressing more of his hot body against my suddenly frigid one.

"How are you—" I started to move, to turn, and found that I no longer had control over my body. When I asked my limbs to move, they didn't.

"You're safe, Pippi." Alistair rubbed my back. "You're safe."

I stiffened anyway, straining to lift my arms, my legs, my head off the bed.

Alistair crooned to me, muttering velvety gibberish until I stilled.

"Your voice should be illegal," I snapped at him.

He laughed—a deep, rich, and unadulterated chuckle.

And an image plastered itself across my eyes, only for a second—barely long enough for me to drink in the details. Of a man. A tall, handsome man. Naked, his muscles taut and rippling around his booming laughter.

And he was laughing because I'd shoved him onto a bed.

My bed.

The man's face was blurred. No matter how I scraped and dug at the image, I couldn't get his facial features to focus. But the rest of his long-limbed body was in *sharp* detail. Every cord of muscle bunching and coiling as he shimmied himself back on the mattress. His belly fluttered when he propped himself onto his elbows and reached for me, beckoning me to join him.

I stretched my fingers toward him, giggling when he latched his around them and pulled, gently, flipping me onto my back.

Stars. Above.

Literally.

He'd flipped me right out of my bedroom.

I lay on my back, staring up at an indigo sky encrusted with twinkling stars and illuminated by the ivory moon.

But I still couldn't move.

I couldn't lift my head.

Couldn't look at anything except those stars.

And someone was touching me, stroking the insides of my thighs—

Thighs that were *bare*.

"You're safe." Alistair dragged that sinful voice over my brain when I started to squirm. "Pippi. You're safe."

"What's...How...Wait!" I cried.

Because he'd pulled away.

"*Wait!* Don't leave!" My hands scrabbled.

His fingers found mine and he held on, tightly, with the same force I was gripping him with.

But he still slipped away.

I dragged my nails into his knuckles, sobbing when I couldn't *feel* them.

I might as well have been holding a wisp of smoke.

"Pippi..."

His voice filled me. But it was different this time. Strained. The exquisite groan of a man who'd been pleasured and teased to the very edge of release.

What on earth...?

And I saw him. Clear as day.

That long-limbed man lying beneath me, panting and groaning, his body slick with sweat, his muscles coiling, as I—

No.

Goodness.

No.

This is wrong.

This is...

"Oh!"

The twisted, tortured sound clawed out of my throat as molten pleasure pooled between my thighs. A fire stoked by the soft scrape of a man's tongue.

I arched, hissing.

Laughter rumbled from between my legs, sending pulsating vibrations through my core—an area that was now *screaming* with the need to release.

I had never been this aroused.

Never.

Never had the suckle of a man's mouth brought me so, so, so

very close to orgasm. Not like that, anyway. That *suddenly*—the fierceness of it stole my breath and made my vision blur.

The mouth moved away, and the sudden coolness between my legs had me twisting and sobbing. Until those warm lips touched my brow. My cheeks. The tip of my nose. My lips. Soft, nuzzling kisses. Playful, in the way they tickled and shaped themselves into a smile whenever I giggled. Comforting, in the way they murmured words against my skin. Words spoken in Alistair's voice that didn't make any logical sense—random phrases slapped haphazardly into sentences—but that were spoken with such reverence, they left me dizzy.

They were words meant to be *felt*. Not heard.

Expressions of loss and hope. Declarations of love. A plea for connection, and whispers of relief when affection was given freely.

It was thrilling. Heartwarming. Arousing.

My goodness, was it arousing.

When those lips returned to the pulsating area between my legs, I cried.

I was going to come.

Hard.

I was going to come *hard*.

I whimpered. Bucked my hips. Grunted. Did everything I could to just keep him moving…a little…just a little…

"Oh!"

My eyes flew open.

"Oh. Shit."

The curse tumbled out of me as I stared at the dark interior of our cottage, panting—heaving, more like it—as my hips rocked against…

My own hand.

The realization—that I'd been dreaming and masturbating in my sleep—hit just as the orgasm rolled over me. And it was intense—the kind of orgasm that had your toes curling and sent you to the stratosphere. But there was no joy in it.

Only sorrow.

Because that hadn't just been a hot and wild wet dream. It'd been a soft and beautiful love story, one I wanted to stay in forever.

I sat up, shuddering from the shock waves of pleasure, and patted my hand along the bed. Empty. Cold.

Jackson wasn't here.

The cottage was still and quiet.

I drew my knees up to my chin, hugging my legs as my body thrummed with aftershocks and my heart sobbed, wishing everything in that dream—the sense of connection I'd felt, the love, the companionship, *everything*—had been real.

I DECIDED THE NEXT MORNING, as I got ready to go to the kelpie show Jackson had booked, that the dream hadn't happened.

I'd never think of it, speak of it, or acknowledge it. With one exception: I'd confront Alistair tonight. Only because I *had* heard him before I fell asleep, and I wanted to make sure he wasn't planting pornos into my head. My gut was telling me he didn't, though. That all the R-rated imagery had been my own imagination. Which was maybe proof that I needed my head examined.

Regardless, I screwed a smile onto my face, banished the bad thoughts from my brain, and went to the show *determined* to be a happy-go-lucky tourist. Even if I was *pretending* happiness, maybe that was the gateway to *feeling* happiness.

"Oooh my gosh!" I shrieked with laughter and clung to Jackson's arm as the kelpie rose out of its pond. "It's terrifying!"

"It's awesome." Jackson chuckled.

The tall, sickly-looking horse slunk its way out of the pond, swiveling its pale yellow eyes over the rows of bleachers ringing around its waters in a half-moon shape. Its spindly teeth gnashed. Moisture oozed off the stringy moss dangling from its pale green fur.

There wasn't any fog coverage inside this dome at the base of the mountains, and I actually *missed* those misting clouds. They would've, at least, softened the monstrous, unnatural appearance of the kelpie.

Around us, children squealed. Adults gasped.

I leaned more fully into Jackson, my skin prickling when the kelpie's eyes landed on me. It stared for a heartbeat. Two. Then slithered away, zeroing its gaze on a little girl, who screamed and buried her face into her mother's shoulder.

The kelpie flicked its seaweed tail and bellowed—a trumpeting whinny that had half the people in the stands, including me, clapping hands over our ears. Then it slapped its forehooves into the water, creating a big, splashing wave, and it…

Transformed.

The strings of moss twined around its shifting body and twisting limbs. The splashes of water glittered over its paling flesh. And when it straightened up out of the water, shaking droplets out of its hair, it was no longer a horse, but a lovely, long-legged woman.

"Oh wow." Jackson laughed.

The woman chuckled and blew a kiss at the audience, wagging her finger at the men who whooped a little too loud.

"I wonder if that hurts her?" I asked. "Changing forms like that?"

"I'm sure it doesn't." Jackson drummed his feet against the bottom of the bleachers.

The woman bowed and waved her arms, summoning four more kelpies from the pond. They flanked her, two on either side, as she stretched her hand over the water, bidding it to move and shape itself into a long bullwhip.

For several moments she played the part of horse trainer, putting the four kelpies through piaffes and prances, and wielding her magic over the water to make aquatic jumps for them to bound over. She'd feign surprise whenever one of the kelpies *accidentally* crashed into a jump and transformed into a woman behind its splashing wreckage. And then she contorted herself back into her horse form and leapt over watery fences that had to be as tall as Jackson.

At the end, all five kelpies turned to their horse forms and summoned a towering wall of water in the middle of the pond.

They sailed over it in unison.

People roared.

The kelpies sank into the pond upon landing, disappearing beneath its surface in one big plop.

As the riotous cheers ricocheted through the dome, another kelpie rose from the water—a taller, ganglier horse with rippling blue flesh and ribbons of seaweed plastered to her forehead. As the crowd cheered, the kelpie whinnied and pranced up to the left-side section of the bleachers, where she stuck her head over the divider, and blew bubbles out of her nose, inciting a bunch of excited squawks from the kids sitting nearby. Then she returned to the pond, where she pranced in place for a moment before she snapped into a squared halt. A shudder ripped through her.

The ribbons of moss and seaweed dribbled down her body. Her skin melted, trickling down her bones as they cracked and crunched and reforged themselves.

I cringed. "Goodness, that looks awful."

The kelpie laughed as she shook the last of her horse limbs away and straightened into a tall, silvery-haired woman. She spun herself into a delicate dance, skimming the edges of her mossy skirt through the water to create cascading fountains around her.

It was entrancing. Hypnotizing.

There was freedom in her dance, in the way she poured herself into each fluid movement. But there was pain in it too—the agony as she tried to convey a message, knowing most of the meaning would be lost in translation.

Tears welled in my eyes.

"It makes you feel like you're in a tragic fairy tale. Doesn't it?" I whispered to Jackson.

Whispered, because the audience had gone silent, watching the kelpie's pirouetting dance.

"I guess." Jackson shrugged. "She definitely knows how to work a crowd."

The kelpie, basking in the audience's rapture, leapt and pivoted through the twinkling fountains of water that had formed around her. Then she stopped. *Abruptly.* As though someone had fitted a hook to her midsection and hauled back, bringing her dance to a clumsy, sudden end.

I frowned.

People hooted with enough force to shake the ground beneath us.

Jackson sprang to his feet, mashing his hands together and whistling.

The kelpie stared at us, her chest heaving.

"Why'd she stop like that?" I asked Jackson as I got to my feet.

"Because the dance ended," Jackson said.

"It didn't look like it ended, though. It was like…" When Alistair had gotten too close to the dock and the magic had burned him.

Why burn *her*, though? Had she gone on too long with her dance? Were these creatures so rigidly controlled, they got punished for toeing a time schedule?

"Encore!" people shouted.

The kelpie shook her head, dropped into another curtsey, and dove into the depths of the pond.

"Well!" The man who ran the kelpie exhibit stepped out from where he'd been resting against the bleachers, and beamed at the crowd, waiting until the resonant applause quieted before he continued, "What a performance, huh? I'll tell you, I've been here five years, and these lovely ladies *still* take my breath away. Now, if you enjoyed today's performance and you're a big kelpie fan, don't forget to check out the gift shop. The funds go not only to making the environment better for our lovely ladies"—he swept his arm over the pond—"but can also help us expand this experience in the future."

And there it was again: that sour emotion, wriggling around inside my chest.

"Ooh, babe." Jackson jerked my arm when the commencement speech ended and people began to move. "I didn't realize Kian was going to be here!"

"Who?"

"Kian Reed," Jackson said. "We met him last night, rem—Oh, well, wait." He squinted. "You were at the buffet when he gave me the cigar, and the smoke ring contest might've been after you left—"

"Smoke ring contest?"

"But he's a cool dude. You'd like him."

I turned, shifting through the crowd to see who he was pointing at. My eyes instead snagged on the familiar forms of Melany and Sarah as they stood from the bleachers directly opposite us.

Melany saw me too, and she gave a great beaming smile as she waved.

"Melany and Sarah are here too," I said. "This was a popular show today."

This time it was Jackson's turn to go "Whooo?" Like an owl. "Oh. *Them*," he chuffed after he followed my gaze.

"Don't be rude," I chided. "They're sweet people. I like them."

"Of course you do."

I whipped my head around, stunned by the harsh way he'd responded. "I'm sorry?"

Jackson shifted and stared ruefully down at his feet. "You like everyone, Pippi. But yeah. Whatever. We can go say hi to them too. But Kian's right this way, so why don't we hit him up first? I really think you'll like him. We'll be just five minutes. Then I'm all ears for girl talk."

My smile was so forced it hurt. "Yeah. Okay. Sure. Where is he?"

"Right over here. C'mon."

As we descended the steps, I caught Melany's eye again. She cocked her head toward Sarah, motioning for me to join them.

I pointed at Jackson and shrugged.

And she laughed, waving her arm like she understood completely, before she pointed at the pond and gave me two big thumbs up. Behind her, Sarah huffed and tried to pull the "Oh-em-gee, I can't believe I made this loony tune my life partner" sort of face, but she was smiling too. And when she slung her arm around Melany's shoulders, pulling her in for a kiss…

My heart *hurt.* Suddenly, and viciously, as though someone had fired a bullet clean through it.

Jackson and I didn't have that.

That warmth, and affection, and *love* that poured off Melany and Sarah, the way they looked at each other, full of adoration and awe.

Had Jackson *ever* looked at me like that?

Had I ever looked at *him* that way?

My gut squirmed.

Oh no.

I turned to Jackson, searching for his eyes, his emotions, anything I could grasp on to. Anything that would tell me I was wrong.

But he had his gaze fixed on Kian. And even when I clawed at his hand, silently begging him to *look at me,* he offered me only a brief, lukewarm glance.

25

"*How do you always seem to know when I'm s-sad?*"
   "*I just do. I've always been able to tell with people.*"

It's…

What's the word?

Restless?

No. It's not strong enough.

Maddening?

Yes.

Maddening. It's *maddening* to have a word within my reach—a word I can *see* but can't grasp. The more I try, the more it slips.

There is a word. For what Pippi feels. What she *is*. I know it. *Knew* it…once. But now it keeps slipping.

And she *doesn't* seem to know.

Which makes the maddening *worse*. Because I can't speak… *tell* her that she isn't alone in those feelings. I can't…wane-warn—I can't *warn* her of how easily she can be hurt.

Perhaps she already has been hurt.

I snarl into the waters, wishing they were hard. A solid object to strike my head against. Maybe that will stop the words from slipping. Or force all of them to slip, so I stop fighting for the ones I half remember.

I *know* what she is.

I want to *tell* her.

But I *can't*.

And it's *maddening*.

Maybe that's why the dream comes to me, after my restless body stills into a restless sleep. Because I can't stop thinking of her. Can't stop worrying. Can't stop seeing her hurt, with me in the waters, unable to help her. Unable, even, to give a proper warning.

Useless.

In the dream, I am not useless.

I am human again. I walk the land beside her. I speak easily.

And she is lovely. Smiling at me, her face lit by...

The sun?

No.

The light is too soft to be from the sun.

It's the other orb. The one that sits in the sky in the dark hours.

Moon.

Moonlight.

Her face is lit by *moonlight*.

She laughs—at something I've said, although the words coming out of my mouth are meaningless. But I laugh too. And I reach for her—slowly. Hoping. Unsure. Wanting to feel her, but not sure if she wants the same.

When she reaches back for me, I am...

Relieved.

That she allows my touches. And that she returns them.

And I don't stop touching her.

Her hair, first. The lovely red hair, which has me enthralled.

My human...

Fins?

Fingers.

My human *fingers* touch her hair, while my mouth...

I know this word...

Kisses.

My mouth *kisses* the top of her head. Her nose. Her cheeks. Before settling on her mouth. All the while, my hands continue touching. *Feeling* her, in a way I'll never be able to do while in this body. But in the dream, I can.

And she can touch me. *Feel me.* Which she does, in ways that make me...

Restless.

No.

Desperate.

Once, I knew these feelings well. The desperation. The joy. The…

The…

Pleasure.

Of being with someone. Of exploring each other. *Learning.* Teasing. Laughing.

Once, I had felt all of this.

But it has been so long. I've forgotten how to feel this way.

Pippi has reminded me.

And the dream reminds me that the things I feel can never be mine. Not truly.

26

The worst part of an oncoming storm was the inevitability. Knowing that what was about to hit would be catastrophic but not being able to do a gosh darn thing to stop it.

There'd been a tension storm grouching over me and Jackson for days. Weeks. Years, maybe. That storm was making landfall, whether I was ready or not.

But, as with most hurricanes, it started with stillness. The peaceful calm before, when the sun still shone and you hoped the winds would move the storm in the other direction.

I spent most of the wagon ride back to our cottage curled against Jackson, my head resting on his shoulder, my knees tucked up. Holding on, as I listened to him talk without really absorbing anything.

Around us were a half dozen or so other tourists. A family of four sat near the front of the wagon. The youngest girl played with her new kelpie stuffie while her older sister whined that she hadn't been allowed to get anything from the shop.

"You picked the water bottle," her mom admonished. "And we agreed you would each get only one souvenir."

"But the stuffies are *cuter*."

"Well, hon, next time you'll consider waiting, instead of buying the first thing you like."

An older couple sat near them, smiling fondly at the two little girls, even as they were gripped by some fierce nostalgic blues. Reminiscing, maybe, about when their kids had been that young.

Another young couple sat diagonally from us, wrapped around each other, the way I was coiled around Jackson. But they couldn't have been more different from us. Because I felt the adoration pouring off them. The contentment. And joy. They were young, and on the vacation of a lifetime, and so in love, they were nearly delirious with it.

And then there was me and Jackson; with him distracted, talking about Kian and Magix, and me holding so tightly to him —clinging on to what we had, as hollow as it was, and wondering if I was strong enough to hold on. To hold us together.

"I was surprised at you, though," Jackson said to me at one point, giving my back a light, reprimanding tap. "You barely said a word to him. Normally I can't get you to stop talking to people. I get he's not your usual charity case type."

"Charity case type?"

"But I figured you'd like him."

"I didn't say I didn't like him."

Truthfully, all I remembered of Kian Reed was his dimpled smile and high-energy personality. Whatever we'd talked about, whatever I'd said or didn't say, was all mashed up in my head.

"You sure didn't seem like you *did* like him." Jackson expelled exasperation in big, radioactive waves.

Exasperation at *me.*

Because I hadn't behaved the way he'd expected me to in front of his new friend.

I bristled, but tried—really, *really* tried—to keep the hurt out of my voice when I said, "Even if I didn't like him, at least I was polite, and went over with you to say hello. Which is more than I can say for you."

Jackson stiffened. "The fuck is that supposed to mean?"

The fact you call the people I want to talk to "charity cases." And treat them like they're lesser riffraff. I gnawed at my lip, keeping the words contained. Those kinds of words would start a fight.

And I wasn't sure I had the strength for a fight.

"Nothing," I said instead. "I just wish I'd had time to introduce you to Melany and Sarah. They would've loved you." And I pressed my face into the side of his neck, seeking solace, comfort, hoping he would let it go.

But he was tense and turbulent, and the longer I stayed silent, the rumblier his emotions got.

So I turned away from him, staring at the landscape—what little I could see of it through the fog. I was fed up with this stupid fog. It was oppressive—a dark curtain of depression, snuffing the light out of me.

I wanted to see the sun. The stars. The sky.

I wanted to be away from this island.

I wanted to be home. Safe from this storm teeing up to destroy me.

"Anyway"—Jackson poked my knee, drawing my attention back to him—"I was thinking…you have that black dress with you, right?"

I frowned. "I have a black one with white polka dots."

"Damn, that's the only one you brought? I was hoping you had the nicer one with you. The one you wore to the New Year's party."

I tried to swallow the irritation clawing up my throat. *Tried.* "The cocktail dress?"

"Yeah. You look hot in that one."

"That's more of a black-tie dress."

"So?"

"Did you bring a tux with you?"

"No."

"So why would I have brought a cocktail dress?"

Jackson sniffed. "I thought you'd want to dress up for dinner."

"I *do* like dressing up for dinner. That's why I brought a whole stack of outfits," I said. "They're just not black-tie, dry-clean only dresses."

Jackson gusted heavily.

As the wagon slowed, the family at the front, maybe catching some fizzling shocks from our brewing storm, preemptively moved to offload before we'd fully stopped. The mom flashed Jackson and me a strange look as she herded her daughters past.

I dropped my voice to a whisper when the family disembarked and the wagon lurched forward. "Are the clothes I brought that dreadful?"

"You *know* it's not that," Jackson huffed. "I like showing you off. And that black dress…*Mmm*…all the men would've been jealous. That I get to have you, when they don't."

I like showing you off.

Like I was one of the beasts on the island, all diapered up for an audience to *ooh* and *ahh* over.

I wondered if the creatures of Niverwick felt this kind of lousy every time they were paraded in front of spectators.

And if they did…which, if I was being honest, I was certain they did…

How horrific did that make us? Me. Jackson. Everyone on this island. People who looked at living, breathing creatures like they were inanimate displays. Art pieces slapped onto a wall to give us a few seconds of entertainment.

In his defense, this was nothing new for Jackson. Scheduling a dinner. Asking me to wear a certain outfit. Strolling to the event with me on his arm and proudly declaring to everyone that I was his. He'd done it all before back home.

It used to fill me with pride. I'd clutch his arm and smile until my cheeks hurt.

It'd gotten old though. Most things did.

The staleness turned to indifference.

And now the indifference was souring into resentment.

"Could we have dinner with Melany and Sarah tomorrow?" I asked him.

Jackson rolled his shoulder in a half shrug. But didn't answer.

I scoffed. The wagon grinding to a stop by our cottage covered the noise, but Jackson must have seen the irritation on my face, because his puckered into a scowl.

I stood before he could say anything, suddenly very mindful

of everyone around us, watching warily, not wanting to be caught in the whirlwind.

It was amazing, the way we all had an innate sense when something bad was about to go down.

"Babe!" Jackson's voice was a husky growl.

I stepped off the wagon and walked around to the two alicorns—Eos and Valeria, they'd said during their introductions. "Thank you," I whispered to them.

Eos, the taller and more finely built of the two, turned her head toward me, billowing worriedly. "Are you alright, miss?"

"Fine. I'm…" I touched a hand to Eos' shoulder in what was meant to be a thank you pat, but the despair that flooded my heart at the contact had me ripping my hand away with a grunt.

"You don't look well." Valeria swished her tail and turned her nose to me. "We can take you to the health clinic if—"

"She's fine." Jackson's hand clenched my shoulder—hard—before he smiled at Eos and Valeria. "I'll take care of her from here. Thank you, ladies." He stepped to my side so he could give the alicorns a bow.

They whuffled, charmed, as most were, by Jackson's smile.

"Just remember, we're a call away," Valeria added. "If you need us."

"Thank you." I nodded at them.

"Okay, Pippi, what on earth is going on with you?' Jackson asked after the wagon rolled away.

I walked to our cottage, wrapping my arms around my midsection to hold my slithering stomach in place. "Nothing. I just find it interesting that we always go to dinner or events with the people *you* want to go with. But when *I* want to have dinner with someone, you just…brush it off."

This time, it was Jackson's turn to scoff. And the wagon was gone, so he didn't have any creaking wheels to hide the sound.

I inserted the key, stepped inside the cottage and turned, biting on my lower lip to keep it still, so the stare I fixed him with was more stern than sobby.

"Babe." Jackson shut the door behind him. "*What* is the big deal? You've known those two ladies for what, a day?"

"About as long as you've known Kian," I said.

"Yeah, but he's…well…"

"He's what? Male? Old? Richer? A Sorcerer? What makes him better than Melany or Sarah?"

"He's…Well, he's opportunity."

"So people are only worth your time if you can climb up on their shoulders and better your lot in life? Is that what you're saying?"

"No. What the fuck, Pippi? Is that really what you think of me? That I'm a leech looking for someone to bleed dry?"

No.

Say no.

I'm sorry.

This is stupid.

I'm being stupid.

Say no, Pippi.

But my mouth betrayed me. "I don't know."

Jackson's eyes blew wide.

Anger exploded in my chest—*his* anger. A white-hot rage that escalated so quickly it left me disoriented. I stumbled back, leaning against the wall for support.

"Well," he said, his voice low. Dangerously low. "Thanks. You really know how to stroke a guy's ego, huh?"

"I'm sorry," I whispered. "That was so very mean."

"No shit." He bent, ripped his shoes off, chucked the left one at the wall, and propped his hands on his hips, his chest heaving. "Seriously, Pippi, what the fuck? Are you this mad because I wouldn't talk to those two stupid chicks?"

"Don't call them stupid."

"I'm sorry. Would you prefer if I called them eccentric old bats?"

An icy thorn twined around my stomach, making my gut ache. For a heartbeat, two, three, I stared at him. This beautiful, god-like man, with his handsome, masculine squared jaw.

Sometimes I'd lay awake at night, caressing that jaw while he slept. Marveling, usually, that such an ethereal creature would deign to share a bed with a mere mortal like me.

His big cyan eyes—how many times had I gotten lost in those blue depths?

The lush, bowed curve of his lips. How many times had I suckled on them, dragging their velvety softness between my teeth? How many times had I lavished their petal-soft caresses on my skin?

I'd loved this man. Loved him with everything I had. My heart, my soul, my mind, *everything*. I had been so full of Jackson, I'd almost forgotten Pippi existed.

But now, as I stared at him in the small, cozy foyer of our vacation cottage, I didn't know if I truly loved him anymore. I didn't know if I was so desperate to hold on to what we had because I still cared, or if I'd simply spent so many years building a life around this man that I didn't know who I was without him.

When those realizations hit, they hurt. A deep, gnawing sort of ache that drilled into every bone in my body, and left me shaking, bleeding, *broken*.

The tears snuck up on me, oozing out before I could stop them.

"You're crying? Unbelievable." Jackson pinched the bridge of his nose. "You started this, Pippi!"

"I know, I—"

"You're the one who threw the fucking insults *at me*."

"I *know*, Jackson. I'm—"

"You know what, no. We're *not* doing this now." He bull-dozed past me, shoving his shoulder into mine. Hard. Almost enough to hurt.

"Jackson—" I reached for him.

He shrugged me away.

"Jackson, please. Let's take a second here. To cool off. A-and" —a hiccup rattled my chest—"I think we should talk."

"Why?" he snarled at me. "So you can tell me what a big, stupid leech I am?"

"I didn't mean it that way."

"Could've fooled me."

"Jackson, please—" I bit off, flinching, when he stormed back toward me.

And in that half a second, as he crossed the room, his face contorted into an ugly snarl, and his rage struck my heart in big, sizzling zaps of lightning, I almost wondered if he'd hit me.

He didn't.

But he put his face right into mine, letting me see what my words had done to him, as he hissed, "We're *not* doing this. Not here. Not now. If you don't want to go to dinner, *fine*. Whatever. I'll tell them you're sick or tired or too embarrassed to be seen with your leech of a boyfriend."

"I'll go to dinner, Jackson, I never said I wouldn't."

"Well, maybe you shouldn't. Because if you go, you'll complain about something and make me feel like the bad guy. So I'll go. *Alone.* You can get room service. Or hook up with the two kooky dingbats you love so much. I don't fucking care." With a disgruntled sigh, he stomped into the bedroom.

The bathroom door slammed. Hard. With a resounding SMACK that shuddered every wall in the cottage.

I flinched, wrapped my arms more securely around myself, and waited until I heard the trickle of the shower running before I sank to the floor.

27

Pippi

We'll be okay.

People fight all the time. Bigger fights than we had. Meaner. And they cool off and make up.

We'll be okay.

But my parents fought too, hadn't they? And they were never okay.

We're different.

I can patch things up in the morning. But should I?

These thoughts had bounced around in my head all night. They'd first invaded when Jackson, dressed in black jeans and a mint green polo shirt, left for dinner, muttering that I should *"not bother waiting up."* They'd staged an assault as I sat on our bed, crying until my eyes hurt, and they'd chased me into my sleep and haunted my dreams. And they continued to drill into my brain when I woke up and blearily looked at the clock on the wall.

The midnight hour had come and gone.

And Jackson was nowhere.

His side of the bed was undisturbed, and his clothes were strewn where he'd left them. In the bathroom his cologne, shaving cream, toothbrush, lint roller, and comb remained scattered over the sink. He never tidied after himself. Didn't need to, really. I usually hit the bathroom after him and put everything away.

I hadn't done that tonight, though.

And he hadn't come back to set anything straight.

Anything. His stuff. Or our fight.

Near seven hours now, since he'd gone.

Did he even want to set things straight?

Did I?

We'll be okay.

It was around that time, sniffling in our empty cottage, that I got myself together, shimmied into a red swirl blouse and jean capris, and left. To go meet Alistair.

And when Jackson came back tonight—*if* he came back…

Let him worry.

It was a nice night. Warm, with a breeze that was still a little too sticky, and a lot too salty, for my taste. But it felt less like the sweltering sauna that it had been the last few days. Or maybe my internal body temperature had cooled. The epic crying session had wiped out the negative emotions I'd been frothing over.

Either way, it was almost pleasant, climbing down the cliff path, and sitting, once I'd gone as low as I dared, to wait for Alistair.

It would've been *more* pleasant if those barbarous thoughts had stopped ravaging my brain.

What have I done?

Why did I do it?

I've been saying how much I want to go home. If I keep this up, I might not have *a home by the time we leave here.*

And that brought on the waterworks again.

I felt him several seconds before he called my name. His hope was soft and delicate as it reached for me, like a ribbon of fine silk.

"Pippi?" Alistair murmured.

"I'm"—a watery hitch fractured my words—"here."

A pause. Then, "You're c-c-crying?" he said in the tenderest voice.

"Y-y-yes." And I cried harder.

Because the sound of my tears had left him in turmoil.

And his turmoil fanned mine.

It was a vicious cycle.

"What's wrong?" Alistair's voice soothed.

"*Everything*," I said.

"I'm sorry."

And those weren't flat words spat out to be polite. Alistair was truly, deeply sorry, even if he didn't know what he was sorry for.

"Me too." No matter how many tears I mopped up, more kept coming. "I made such a mess. And I don't know *why*...I mean, I do. But I should've done it differently. Or just kept my mouth shut and...Stars. I used to think that about my mom. That she should've kept her mouth shut. And now I-I've thrown it all away. It feels like. And..." Salt blossomed over my tongue when I slurped a mouthful of tears. "My head hurts." It did. The raw, skull-flaying ache that crying left behind.

"I'm sorry." Alistair himself sounded close to tears. "What can I do? Pippi? To...help?"

"Can we go somewhere?" I asked. "I don't wanna be here right now. So can we go somewhere? *Anywhere.* Your favorite place, as long as it's not underwater. Although, honestly, drowning would probably solve all my problems—"

"Do *not*"—Alistair's voice rose to a frantic bellow—"say that, Pippi. Ever. Please."

Horror, heartache, and fear flooded my chest. The agony had me sucking in a great galumphing breath. And then I panicked when the air got stuck in the base of my throat. Because my lungs were drowning in the swamp of caustic emotion.

Tacky sweat dribbled down my back. I straightened. Grappled at the rocks. Started to see checker spots.

But then the sensation vanished. My lungs worked freely. My head cleared.

Because Alistair had pulled his torment away from me.

"I'm sorry." His voice tentatively stroked my brain. "I'm sorry. That was ru-rude. To yell. I didn't mean to scare you."

"You didn't," I said. "Honest. You didn't scare me."

"Good. I—"

"You've lost someone." It wasn't a question. People only

experienced that sort of misery when someone they loved had been ripped out of their life.

"I have. But I shouldn't…You…I—"

A hot pool of his frustration swamped my chest.

"Take your time," I reminded him. "I know I talk fast, Alistair. But you don't have to keep pace with me. Take your time with the words. I'll wait."

The pool cooled and dwindled away.

"I spoke…talked fast too." Alistair sighed. "Once."

"Was that back when you were honing your flirting skills?"

He laughed. "Yes."

"A speedy smooth talker. With a hot British accent. You must've had all the ladies lined up. Probably the gents, too."

He paused, nibbling on the words, trying to figure out their textures and flavors. And then, in a voice deliberately dropped a few octaves he asked, "You think my…ack-ak-acc-sent. Accent. Is *hot?*"

And I laughed. A very messy and wet laugh that left my throat a little raw and sent some flaming ice picks into my brain. But it dried the tears, better than my sleeves or hands could've done. "Yes. Your accent is hot. More than that, it's decadent."

There's a reason I had a wet dream of you whispering sweet nothings to me.

I wasn't quite rebounded enough to tackle that conversation, though. Not yet.

"I like your ack-accent too." He kept his voice low and husky.

"Now you're milking it."

He dropped to a purry growl. "You say my name n-n-nice. *Alistairrrrrr.*"

A shriek of laughter rocketed out of me.

"Oh dear. There must be another whale d-dying nearby," Alistair rumbled.

And I was *gone.* Laughing until I wheezed. Until my stomach ached and I started crying again. Good tears this time, though.

Healing tears. The sort that nourished the soul, rather than drained it.

Alistair murmured to me as I fought off the giggle attack. Nothing to set me off again. Just support, to help me down from my high, and keep me from crashing back into despair.

"You do have a lovely laugh, Pippi."

Ahhh, there was that word.

Lovely. I'd never hear it the same way again.

I swiped at my sticky eyes. "Thank you. Not for the compliment. Well…I mean…thanks for that too. But double thank you for the goofing. I *really* needed that."

A pulse of joy thrummed through me.

"I'm sorry, I…What you felt. Earlier. I should have…Cun-con-controlled it." Alistair stumbled over the words. "And not yelled. I'm sorry."

"Honestly, Alistair, I'm glad you let me feel that. We've all got nerves that flare when someone trounces on them. I didn't know you had a nerve there. I'm sorry."

"You *couldn't* know. When I haven't told you."

"I know. And I'd like to fix that. The things we don't know about each other. I'm not on this island long, so we're having to speed run this friendship. But I like you, Alistair. And I'd *like* to know you. As much as I can."

His hope was back, twining its silken chords around my heart. "I'd like that too. And Pippi, I had to th-think. But you wanted to go. Leave. To a f-favorite place. Do you still?"

"Absolutely."

"I know where to take you."

28

We didn't talk much as Alistair cut through the sea. Carrying me on his head, even though I had offered to boot myself to his back.

He'd scoffed a gentle, "You're my favorite hat, Pippi."

So I'd taken my customary place atop his brow, holding on to his horn—or *trying* to, anyway. I shook so hard, my hands kept jittering off it.

Jackson's probably back now, right? Isn't last call usually at 2:00 a.m.? Or is that not a thing here?

He'll worry himself sick when he comes back and finds the cottage empty.

I shouldn't be doing this.

A soft rumble echoed through Alistair—almost like a purr. Not necessarily one of contentment. More an offer of comfort—a reminder that he was there.

I dug my nails into the coarse texture of his horn.

I'm a terrible person.

Once we left the inlet, and the magic forcing Alistair beneath the surface lifted, he raised his head above the water. But we still didn't talk.

The rabid waves hissed and snarled, trying to stop our progression, and Alistair plowed right through them, while the fog bore down, thickening to a gummy mist.

Eventually, the waves conceded defeat and flattened themselves into sporadic lumps, but the fog refused to relinquish its hold. It snuffed out my sight and oozed into my lungs like molasses—I couldn't see anything beyond the dark, scaly slope of Alistair's head.

There was only sound out here, like the *whoosh-sploshing* of the water against Alistair's bulk. His breathing, rhythmic and steady, mixed with my labored wheezing.

His movements slowed and another of those comforting purrs pulsated through him as he said, "Look up, Pippi. Can you see?"

I angled my chin back, expecting to find more warbling curtains of fog.

Instead…

"*Oh!*" The ragged gasp ripped from my lungs. Because stars glittered overhead.

Dull stars, of course. Ribbons of smog wove between the twinkling lights and snaked around the waning moon, diminishing most of their brilliance. But, in that moment, after *days* of not being able to see the sky, the sight of those distant, twinkling lights had a big, slithering ball of emotion clogging the back of my throat.

I had *never* seen a starry sky that looked as gorgeous and as awe-inspiring as this one.

"This is the only place to see the lights," Alistair said. "Sometimes even here they're hidden. But this is a good night. And the orb…the moon is out."

"It's gorgeous, Alistair!"

"It is," he murmured. "*Lovely.*"

Oh goodness.

He had to use *that* word, huh?

Heat scorched my cheeks.

And, well, I'd been fixing to ask this.

"Can you…" My tongue stuck to the roof of my mouth, and I had to work to pry it free. "Can you… peep people's dreams? Or…" Gosh, this wasn't coming out right. "*Give* them dreams?"

"No?" Confusion wrinkled Alistair's voice.

"It's just…I had a dream last night…about the stars…and *you—*"

"And me?"

"—and then tonight you surprise me with this. Which, it's a great surprise. I love it. Truly. I've been *really* missing the sky. And I've always enjoyed sitting under the stars on a nice night. Jackson usually doesn't, but...that's not the point. I'm so very grateful you've brought me here. But it made me wonder about the dream. Y'know?"

If the poor guy wasn't confused before, he certainly was now.

"I think so," Alistair said slowly.

"I'm sorry. Babbling." I ran a hand through my hair, wincing when my sweaty palm stuck to the curls. "It's what I'm good at."

He quieted for a heartbeat. Two.

Some very loud heartbeats. My organ had a motor on it that would put a monster truck to shame.

"I...You dreamed of *me*?"

He said this kindly, but with a flirtatious lilt.

"Yes." I had to smile. "I dreamed of *you*."

He made an interested whuffle. "I hope I wasn't being...na... n-n-n-n-*naughty*."

How did his brain go right to that?

How?

Was I that obvious?

"No comment," I muttered.

He laughed. "Oh dear, I *was* n-naughty!"

"I didn't say that!"

"But you didn't *not* speak it."

"I...We...you know...Do you? Did you...*make* me dream that?" An uncomfortable, viscid heat seeped under my armpits. *Please no.* This would be...the *invasion* of privacy...

A soft, pacifying emotion fluttered in my chest.

"No, Pippi." Alistair's voice lost all its playful sparkle. It was earnest now. "I don't...I *can't*...make you s-see dreams. Even if I can...*could*, I wouldn't. Your dreams are safe."

I exhaled, blowing some of the tension out. "Okay. Good. I didn't think you did. But...thank you."

He hummed, and said, in a voice nearly as hesitant as mine had been, "I also dreamed, though."

"You did?"

"Yes."

"Of me?"

"Yes."

"Goodness. And you're sure you didn't—"

"No. I p-p-promise, Pippi. I wouldn't."

"Okay. I believe you. But…huh. Interesting. Maybe there was something in the air last night? With all the magic in this place…I dunno. Can magic scramble dreams like that?"

"Perhaps," Alistair said, in a tone that suggested he had no flipping clue but was trying to reassure me all the same.

"Hmmm, okay. Now *I* have to ask, were you naughty in your dream?"

"No." A shudder ripped through him. "But *you* were."

And those three little words? Spoken in that husky accent? And the shudder he'd spoken them around?

Stars. Above.

Small, but persistent, tendrils of arousal tugged at my belly, nearly making me squirm.

A terrible human being.

That was what I was.

Jackson, my *boyfriend*, would worry his brains out when he found me missing, and I was getting all hot and bothered imagining what naughty things I did in Alistair's dream.

Guilt took a big, bloody chaw out of my heart. As I hemorrhaged, lightheadedness rushed over me. My knees buckled.

"Pippi?" Alistair called when I plopped on my bum.

"I'm okay," I said.

But I wasn't.

Not really.

I tucked my knees up to my chest, trying to physically hold myself together.

"Would you like to speak…*talk*?" Alistair asked.

"In a minute." Right now, I had to fight to keep my guts in place.

"Okay."

I pressed my forehead to my knees.

Alistair made low, thrumming noises. Reminding me, again, that he was there. But he otherwise let silence fall over us.

And the motions of his body, as he bobbed his head in time with the waves, combined with his gentle noises were comforting. Like being rocked to sleep, smooshed safely in the arms of someone you loved, while they murmured reassurances in your ear.

Which was a thought that set me crying. *Again.*

Because it made me realize I'd never had that kind of loving security with Jackson. Or anyone, really. I'd had to go halfway across the world and perch on the head of a sea beast to find those kinds of feelings.

How pathetic.

"Pippi?" Alistair whispered.

"I'm sorry." I wiped a hand over my face. "I'm lousy company tonight, aren't I?"

"You could never be lou-lousy," Alistair said. "I only wish I could help."

"This helps, actually. Being here. With you. It's helped. Even though it doesn't look it." I scrubbed more tears away and laughed. Bitterly. "My mom used to say tears were how our souls shed their scars. I guess I've got a lot of scars. And they're not even…I mean…" I sighed. Chewed on my lip, rolling it between my teeth until the pinprick of pain plugged the worst of the flood. "I said I wanted to make tonight about knowing each other. But I'm not always good at…" I waved my arm over myself, remembered he couldn't see me since I was above his eyes, and amended, "I'm not good at talking about me. So, this is gonna be different. I guess. A story. Maybe if I make it all a little less personal, it won't be so weird. Y'know?"

"I think I do," Alistair said.

I sighed. Got my nerves in a big ole snarl, trying to figure out where to start. But then I felt Alistair. His calm. And I grasped on to it, suckling at his emotions, leeching off them, until my own stilled.

And then I knew where I had to begin.

"There was this girl once," I said. "She had young parents. Her mom'd only been seventeen and her dad two months past his eighteenth birthday when she was born. They'd loved each other then, when they were young and idealistic. But as the years passed, they drifted apart. And they fought. *Constantly.* Stewing in their own bitterness. And they pulled the girl into the pot to stew along with them. Because she could feel their emotions, and to be constantly boiling in anger and hate and disappointment—it wore on her. She did anything she could think of to turn the burner off. Singing, dancing, making her parents cards and drawings, acting out scenes from her mom's favorite shows—even though the girl *hated* those shows— because her mom used to put them on to drown out the sounds of fighting. The girl tried *everything*. And she had some success, at first. When her parents focused on her, they calmed. But eventually it stopped working, and nothing the girl did helped anymore."

It was easier talking like this. Pretending I was talking about a fictional girl in a fictional drama.

It was easier to pretend this wasn't my life.

"The girl's parents finally went their separate ways. But they'd inflicted wounds upon each other that would never heal. Her once fanciful mom turned bitter and sad. Her father decided he'd rather pretend he'd never had a daughter. But the girl kept trying to please them both. Because that was all she knew how to do.

"She went through high school and worked her tush off to get straight A's, and started looking at colleges, even though she didn't want to. She had other dreams. To explore the world. Write a book. Live a life for herself for the first time. But her mother, who'd been so bitter for so long, was proud and boastful of her daughter going to college. And the girl liked when the people around her were happy. So she forsook her dreams and went to school."

The next words thickened, turning to syrup in my throat. I had to *really* fight to choke them out. "Then the girl's mom got sick. And there was nothing the doctors could do, nothing the girl could do. So she kept going to school, kept showing her mom the near perfect grades. And her mom was content when she died. *Proud.* The girl told herself she was at peace too, even though she wished she had spent those last months living a life with her mom, instead of grinding away at a college degree."

The sob hurt as it punched through my chest. And I mean *punched*. It came out with enough force to rattle my bones. Even Alistair flinched, caught off guard by my keen. He chuffed, billowing out a gentle fountain of steam from his nostrils, comforting me, but he said nothing as I collected myself and finished the story.

"After college it was off to corporate America, where the girl kept busting her bum, bending over backward to make her bosses happy, to keep her clients content, and to make sure her friends and coworkers never wanted for help or companionship. And when..."—a foul, lemony taste swished over my tongue—"when she met the man who flipped her world upside down, she bent over backward for him too. Making sure she was cheery when he had a bad day, watching the movies and shows he wanted to watch, going where he wanted to go, acting the way he wanted her to act, dressing the way he wanted her to dress..." I pressed a hand to my mouth to still the trembling. "Because she loved him. With her w-whole heart. But that love was draining her, and she didn't even realize it. Until..."

My heart was about ready to break out of my chest. I laid my hand over it, trying to cajole it into slowing. "The girl was taken to a faraway land. A *magic* land. And it was like she woke up. For the first time, she looked at her life and realized she hadn't been living. She'd been sinking into a quagmire, struggling with the weight of keeping everyone happy. And that quagmire is going to consume her sooner, rather than later. But it's home. Everything she has, everything she loves, or thought she loved, is in there. And if she starts f-fighting to be free of it, she'll lose everything. And that *terrifies* her. But she knows if she stays, the swamp is going to consume her, and that scares her too. But at least she'd be home, you know? She'd be home…and there's comfort in being at home, even if it's suffocating her. And… Gosh, saying all this…Phew! What a sad little story my life makes, huh? The girl who lived for others but forgot to live for herself. *Pathetic.*"

I sniffled. Had a hiccupping sensation that I thought was bringing more tears. But surprised myself when I belched a laugh. A bitter, humorless, lifeless chuckle. The kind people forced out in awkward situations when they didn't know what else to do or say.

"I'm sorry, Pippi," Alistair said, in that gruff, sincere way of his. Like he was pouring his whole heart into the apology.

"It's not even worth being sorry over. It's just sad. A pitiful story with a pitiful ending." I absently reached down, rubbing my hand over the spiky scales on his head.

He gurgled contentedly. "Your story hasn't ended."

"No. It hasn't. There's still another chapter to cover the tense and awkward trip back home, which the irate boyfriend is probably gonna boot her out of—"

"That won't be the end," Alistair said. "Only a-a p-p-plot twist. The girl *thinks* her story ends sad. But she hurts. For a little. And then finds her joy."

I traced my fingers over the point in one of the scales, suddenly so flooded with affection, I felt buoyant—ready to slide off his head and float above the water.

It was his affection for me.

But also my fondness for him. This lovely, sad, sweet creature.

What a pair we made.

Two lost and lonely souls.

Except my lost and lonely feelings were all self-inflicted. I'd chosen the path that led me into my quagmire, and the only binds holding me there were the ones I created.

Alistair was imprisoned by outside forces. And it was heart-breaking.

He had so much heart and personality. He deserved so much better than to be isolated to this dinky little island full of vapid tourists. People who only ever saw him as a thing. Not the wonderful, charismatic being he was.

And I suddenly hated that I was sitting on his head. Able to feel him, but not able to *see* him. Not able to make eye contact.

When I talked to people, I made eye contact.

Alistair should be treated the same way.

I rose to my feet.

"Pippi?" Alistair prodded.

"How cold is the water?"

A questioning ripple squiggled through him.

"I don't like that I'm always talking over you." I wiped at my nose. "I want to talk *to* you. On level...well, I can't say *level ground.* But y'know what I mean...do you?"

"I...think." Alistair's dry tone implied he didn't understand one bit but was trying to humor me. "Are you sure you wish to be in the water?"

"It seems c-calm," this lie said, as I watched three janky waves break themselves over Alistair's hide.

"It is. Calm," Alistair said.

"Good. Yeah, I want to be in the water then. With you. Unless..." I peered over at the small, white-capped mounds of waves. "There's nothing down there, right?"

"I've heard there's a sea beast."

His drizzling sarcasm teased a laugh out of me. "You don't say?"

"He's fuh-frrr-friendly."

"Well, I hope so."

"But he likes women. With red hair."

"Oh, gee. Guess I'm toast, huh?"

We both burst out laughing.

"I should've clarified," I said. "There's nothing *else* down there, right? Besides your snarky tush? Niverwick isn't, I dunno, hiding its next star attraction under the sea. Right?"

"I'm alone. You're safe, Pippi, in these waters with me. Always."

And I felt that safety in the very core of my being.

For the first time in my life, I stared down at the ocean without getting sticky with fear and dread.

"You're safe," Alistair reminded me as he lowered his head, shortening the drop.

"I know." I pinched my nose shut between my forefinger and thumb and plunged into the sea.

29

Alistair

Trust is beautiful. And cruel.

To have Pippi stare at me with trust when near the waters.

She fears the waters. And I hate the way fear looks. The way it darkens her gaze and swallows the green in her eyes.

The green that is *more* than green, because it has other colors in it. But I don't know the words for them. I'm lucky I remember green.

I don't understand why some…complex words come back, or stay, when easy ones slip.

The word *juxtaposition* comes back to me. I'm dozing, and my mind is calm, and the word is there, as though it had never slipped. But I still don't know the words for all the colors. Or the colorful things that grow in the ground. Or the words to tell Pippi what she is.

But I know *juxtaposition*. A word I don't *need*.

It's maddening.

I've gotten…d-distracted.

Again.

Which is maybe a sign I'm becoming more like *me*.

"Alistair, your brain is like a six-lane road with no traffic control. Pure. Chaos."

Indigo's voice. Laughing. And scolding, because something had slipped from me, although I don't remember what.

"I couldn't be inside your head, love. I'd get dizzy."

"That's why I have you. To keep me grounded." My old voice. Speaking with warmth. *Love.*

It makes my chest hurt. The remembering.

But looking at Pippi makes my chest hurt too.

Because she is asking to join me in the water. And she is not...*un*afraid. She's unafraid.

Because she *trusts* me.

And her trust brings me joy, even as it causes hurt.

Because there is love there too.

Falling in love.

How...a-a-accurate.

It does feel that way: like falling. The same feeling I get when I dive deep in the waters. Usually when I am fed by the one—a human male, who finds amusement in watching me hunt for my food. He sends it to the bottom of the waters. And tells me he will take it away if I don't find it in time. So I dive. I don't want the food, but I hurt without it.

As I dive, my stomach feels strange, as though it doesn't move with my body.

And I feel that way whenever Pippi looks at me. Whenever I look at her.

The feeling of diving, farther and farther into the waters. But leaving my stomach behind.

Diving in love.

And when she tells me of her life. Trusting me with the things that make her hurt. When she comes to me sad. And lets me make her happy. When she smiles and laughs, and when the joy makes her eyes...*bright*. When she touches me. Offering comfort. C-c-c-companion...ship. *Companionship*.

I dive. Deeper and deeper. Until there are no waters left. I'm no longer *diving* in love. I am *in* love.

And I suddenly hurt...*ache*...*desire* to tell her everything.

The love I'd had before and destroyed. The trust I'd nurtured and shattered.

I want to tell her about these wounds in my heart that will never fully heal.

There is so much I want to say.

So much I can't.

Because I don't have the words.

And because the mark above my eye aches, reminding me there are things I am for-for-*forbidden* from remembering.

30

Pippi

*I*ce turned its nails into my skin and scraped, peeling off several layers.

At least, that was how it felt when I plunged into the sea.

I sputtered. And choked. And made some very attractive *heeeeeeeeeeee* sounds.

Warm air danced over my head as Alistair billowed worriedly.

"This…" I gasped, fighting to get enough air to talk. "This really clears your sinuses, huh?" I paddled through the water, gurgling when a wave whacked my face, and ended up swimming smack into Alistair's side. "Ooops." I flattened my palms against the craggy surface of his scaly hide and pushed myself back, angling my head up…and up…and *up* to look at him.

Stars, he was huge.

Even when his neck arched down and the tip of his snout was just above my brow, I had to crane myself way back to look him in the eye.

"How's the weather up there?" I asked. "Any warmer than it is down here?"

He made a low, grumbly snort and dropped his head down, dipping his nose below the surface.

"Guess—*Eeeeekk*!" Screeching laughter exploded out of me.

Because Alistair had blown a jet of warm water at me. And it *tickled* as it cycloned around my legs and torpedoed up the hem of my shirt, making the top poof out of the water like a pudgy balloon.

Then it was Alistair's turn to laugh when the shirt slapped lightly against my cheeks.

"Better?" he asked, chortling.

"Oh, yes. *Loads.*" I smooshed the top of my engorged shirt down until it sagged back against my skin. "Why get a life jacket when I've got a sea dino to inflate my blouse?"

Alistair's eyes blinked differently when they were half submerged in water. Rather than the eyelids closing from top and bottom, clear membranes swiped across the eyes from the side.

Which was…freaky.

"Sea…dino?" Alistair blinked again.

"Yeah. Well. I mean, you kinda look like Littlefoot from *The Land Before Time*, you know? Just less *cutesy.*"

"I think I'm cute."

"Hmmm…" I ran my hand over his shoulder. "Not as cute as Littlefoot. And he's, you know, *little.*"

Alistair scooted his head a little closer to me. "But can he do this?" He blew out, sending a geyser of water straight into the air.

I squealed as that mist tumbled down, pelleting me lightly over the head. "Goofball."

He responded with a sonic boom laugh—and the ocean took offense to having an Alistair detonate in its waters. It retaliated by shooting a barrage of tall, choppy waves at us.

I scrabbled when the waves sloshed over me and raked my nails into Alistair's shoulder, fighting the slimy pull of the water.

"You're safe, Pippi." Alistair touched his snout to my side, holding me steady.

"I know," I said. "But could you maybe wait until I'm *not* in the water to launch a tsunami?"

"Sssssssooooooo-nam-eeee," he gargled the word. "Those are… *large* waves."

"Sure are."

"Much larger than the ones that just passed."

"Hmmm, those got pretty close to tsunami level."

"Hmmm," he lightly mimicked me. "I think not."

I splashed him, grinning when he chuckled.

"You, sir," I added, "might be big enough to dismiss monstrous waves, but did you ever see what happens to people when they get flattened by a tsunami?"

"It's bad, I'm sure," Alistair drawled.

"They're *pulverized*. Every bone broken. Skin flayed to ribbons."

"Oh dear."

And that got me.

The slightly high pitched *"Oh dear,"* like he was Winnie the Pooh, hemming and hawing over the empty honey jar.

I cackled, and then ended up swallowing a big, salty mouthful of seawater, which turned my giggle into more of a barking gag.

Alistair snuffled gently. "Careful, Pippi. The b-b-b-banshees make that sound. When they m-mate."

I choked again.

"One of them might answer your m-mating cry."

I laughed.

And *laughed.*

Until my stomach hurt and I had to hold onto Alistair for dear life because the giddiness turned my muscles to goop. Until I had tears streaming down my face and I was gagging—both on the air, and on the sea.

"This is *your* fault." I sneezed when a vat of water flumed up my nose.

"I'm very sorry." Alistair vibrated with a low, non-tsunami inducing chuckle and sent another warm puff of air over my head.

It took several minutes for the giggles to subside.

And several more for me to catch my breath.

"You've color in your cheeks again," Alistair told me.

"Did I not before?" I pressed a hand onto his side for support when the next wave swelled.

"No. Except where you'd scratched...*rubbed* your eyes. You were pa-pale. But you have more color now."

"Laughing will do that to ya." I stroked my hands over his shoulder, letting my fingers bump and bounce over his scales. Smiling when his contentment poured into my heart, shielding me from the bitterness of the sea.

My fingers caught on a jagged pucker of skin, near the base of his throat, and the heat radiating from it nearly scorched my fingertips.

I frowned, pulling my hand away.

"It's a rune," Alistair said.

"Magic?" I tapped my fingers against the crinkled line, hissing when it sizzled my skin.

"Yes. That one stops me from eating."

"It stops you from *eating*?"

"I can only eat when I'm fed. If I eat from the waters, outside of my feedings, I won't be able to swallow. I-I'll..." He sighed. "There's a missing word...when something you eat doesn't *stay...*"

"Regurgitate? Vomit? Puke?" I supplied.

"Yes."

My hand was numb as it slid away from his neck. "That's *barbaric!*"

"They do not want me to eat from the waters. The creatures...if I eat all of them, others won't...they won't live here. The waters need the creatures."

If that was supposed to reassure me, it didn't.

I squinted at him, my eyes tracing the shape of the rune. It blended well. The jagged line flowed with the curve of his scales and the slope of his neck. If I hadn't felt it, I never would've known it was there.

I flattened my hand against it, gritting my teeth through the stinging pain.

This was cruel.

Malicious.

Demeaning.

To not even let him feed himself.

To make him barf if he dared to go against his schedule.

A bitter, lemony taste flooded my mouth. *Hate.*

I actually, legitimately, hated the people who ran this stupid island.

"Pippi?" Alistair ruffled my hair with another soft breath.

"It's not right." I pulled my hand away when the searing pain escalated to unbearable levels. And scowled when I flipped my palm over and found not a single burn or blotch of red.

"It is what it is." A nonchalant statement, betrayed by the deep, bone-aching sorrow radiating off him.

"And you've other runes? They keep you from surfacing?"

"Yes. From surfacing. From getting too close to ships. Or the dock. Or other areas." He turned, pointing the tip of his nose at something I couldn't see through the fog. "From crossing the r-r-r-reef."

So that was why the stars shone here.

He'd taken me to the reef, to the very edge of Niverwick's magical border.

To the very edge of his cage.

That lemony taste turned acidic. "And those runes…are they also on your neck?"

"No. They are above my eyes." He cocked his chin slightly sideways, as though showing me, but there was no way I'd be able to see them. Not in the dark, and not when the runes camouflaged themselves so well.

"Alistair, I'm so sorry," I whispered.

A distressed sound escaped him. "Don't be. Pippi. Please. This isn't your…g-g-guilt. It's not yours to feel."

"I feel it anyway." I touched a hand to the burning rune again, forcing myself to savor the pain. "Does it hurt?"

"No," he murmured. "It only hurts when it's…ack-act-activated."

"What about other things? When they force you to stay under the surface? Even if you're doing what you're told and don't activate the rune, does it hurt you? Like, so, okay…I watched one of those nature documentaries a while back about whales. And I didn't realize they were *air breathing.* I'd always assumed sea things breathed water. But whales suffocate if they can't surface."

"I am not a whale, Pippi." Alistair chuckled.

"Well, I *know* that."

"I'm way…there's a word. C-coo-*cooler.*"

And he stressed that word too, in a '90s surfer boy style. "*Cooooollllllerrrr.*"

"Oh jeeze, you're really hamming it up tonight, aren't you?" I asked.

He blew out a big breath, sending the gills on the side of his neck fluttering like sparkly green streamers.

"Yes." I laughed. "You're right. You're way cooler than a whale. And *prettier.*"

Alistair tucked his chin up and puffed his chest out.

"Did that stroke your ego enough?"

"A bit more won't hurt." He laughed when I gave his shoulder a tap. "But, no, Pippi. Being under the surface, staying there, it does not hurt me. I can b-breathe air. Or water. Both are e-e-easy."

"Well, thank the stars for that, at least." I kneaded my hands into the areas around the rune, wishing the magic was a big muscle knot that I could work out with a deep tissue massage. Or a line of ink that I could scrub away. But it was more of a brand—burnt *deeply* into his flesh. A blistering wound that would never heal.

But I tried to make it feel better.

Alistair nuzzled the tip of his nose to my head, and a warm river of tranquility trickled through my chest.

He *loved* this.

Being touched. Shown affection.

He was basking in it.

So I kept going. Grinding my knuckles into the tall, slippery slopes of his shoulder. Applying as much pressure as I had the strength for, although I knew my massages wouldn't penetrate his thick hide. At best, the digging touches probably felt like a light brush to him.

His shoulder, when I worked my hands lower, slipping them beneath the water, never stopped moving. Hard bands of muscle coiled and rolled beneath my palms. And the sloped plane of it seemed endless. Even when I'd dropped my hands past my waist, they were still squarely on his shoulder. I nudged my paddling legs closer, brushing my bare feet against him and stretching my toes to see if they could feel the end of his shoulder.

They couldn't.

"Do you have flappers?" I blurted, suddenly itching with curiosity. "Like in all the Loch Ness Monster paintings? Or are you more like a big sea serpent? Slithering around without legs?"

Alistair chuffed. "I have flappers."

I dragged my toes along his side, reaching as far down as I dared.

"They're beneath your fins—*feet*. They're beneath your feet."

I stopped paddling, letting myself sink down to my chin.

My toes still traced the rolling shape of Alistair's shoulder.

"Would you like to see them?" Alistair asked.

"I wouldn't be able to. If they're that far down, I'd have to dive. And I am *not* diving that far. Nope. Even if I did, the water's too...*Eeeek!*" I bit off, gasping, when Alistair abruptly plunged headfirst into the water.

His body slithered in an *impossibly* long arch, following his head down, down, *down*...

It seemed never ending.

Forty American feet never looked so long.

His butt rose into the air as his front sank down. And he had a *tail,* a thin, whippy tail that he flicked in a little wave before his bum finally disappeared beneath the surface.

And then I was alone, doggy paddling against the waves, surrounded by the dark, knobby expanse of the sea.

Little sparkles of fear singed my belly and stunned my

muscles, locking them. Only for a heartbeat, but long enough to give the waves a chance to stuff me under the surface.

I kicked, thrusting my head as high as it would go above water.

Overhead, the stars twinkled through the curdling fog soup. Teasing me with how far away they were. Making me feel the insurmountable distance between me and them.

The surface seemed just as insurmountable when you were trapped beneath the sea, as I'd been the other night.

"Pippi." Alistair threw me a solid rope of calm.

I clung to it.

"You're safe," he said.

And then—

A *sploosh* to my right had me scrabbling, twining my head that way.

A long, curved flapper poked out of the water, wiggling at me.

"They're not my most a-a-a-*attractive* part," Alistair said. "But since you want to see..."

A second flapper popped up beside the first.

And, with a heavy *sploosh,* two stouter flappers emerged and began waggling to my left side.

And I almost laugh-cried in relief.

Because those flappers were caging me. Protecting me.

Alistair had gone under the water, but he hadn't gone far, staying directly beneath me.

The first flapper twisted into a seductive wave. And now that I'd calmed, and didn't have checkerspots bouncing over my eyes, I could get a proper look at those appendages.

"Oh, Alistair." I laughed. "You might win the ugliest feet award."

Alistair's flapper paused and straightened in mock shock. "You don't find them attractive?"

Not even a little.

They were, in a word, *horrid*—wrinkled green-scaled limbs wrapped in a thick layer of crusty barnacles.

"I mean, they're not a deal-breaker. As long as you keep your socks on." I grinned.

"Ah."

With a sticky *schlup,* all four flappers disappeared, only to reemerge several seconds later with tangles of hissing seaweed twined around them. "Better?"

Stars above.

He really was a goofball, wasn't he?

A certified class clown.

It made me giddy.

"Perfect," I said. "The socks do the trick."

"Good." Alistair gave all four flappers a vigorous shake. Blobs of seaweed pelted my head.

"Alistair!" I shrieked with laughter.

He chuckled and whisked his flappers back under the water.

"Ugh." I raised one hand to my head, grimacing at the hot goo of the seaweed. "My poor hair…Oh gosh, you're back."

Alistair's two curved horns pinged above the surface. But the rest of his head rose slowly, following the bloom of the next wave. The water split itself over his forehead, trickling down on either side of his face, creating a rain shower over his eyes. But he didn't seem to notice. He slowly, *slowly,* allowed the rest of his head to rise, turning those orange eyes to me.

And his face.

Goodness…

He drew his lips back, putting his razor-sharp fangs on full display. It might've looked menacing, if he wasn't overexaggerating an overbite, and deliberately making himself cross-eyed.

That was a doofus face.

And he amped the doofus up several more notches with his chirpy *"Boo!"*

"You"—I wheezed and flailed in between bouts of giggling—"are a derp." I spat out a mouthful of water. "Has anyone told you that?"

"Deeeeeeerrrrrppppp."

"Oh my goodness."

"I used to hear…not that word, but others. I think they're the same." Alistair dipped his chin back into the water and sidled forward, scooping his nose under me. "You're cold," he added as he raised the rest of his head out of the water—gently, so I didn't flop and pinwheel myself back into the ocean.

I scooted back to my usual place between his horns.

Alistair gave a long, contented hum.

"Do people not ever see your derpy side?" I asked.

"Pardon?"

"You said you *used* to hear you were a derp. Do you not anymore?"

His purrs rattled to a stop. "No. Not for a long time."

And there was his sorrow again, cutting through my bones, making me *ache.* For things like home. Or my friends. For the comfort of a simpler life.

I lowered myself into a sitting position and reached down, rubbing my hands over the top of his head. "I'm sorry…"

"Don't—" he began.

"I'm sorry that I can *feel* your pain," I continued, "but I don't know how to ease it. And you eased mine. I wish I could do the same for you. But I'm not sure how. So I'm sorry."

Silence stretched between us for several long heartbeats.

"Pippi, I-I…"

Alistair started. And stuttered to a stop.

"How…"

Again, he chewed on a word and then spat it back out.

"I wish…"

I kept stroking the top of his head, giving him the time, the space, to sort his thoughts.

"I think…" His words were syrupy as he started speaking for the fourth time. "I'd like to tell you my story now."

31

"*O*nce, I *dreamed*," Alistair started slowly. Hesitantly. As though forcibly having to drag each word from the bowels of his brain. "Too much. I got l-lost in the dreams sometimes. Especially when they were big. And I had a *big* dream. I saw a...split...a divide in the world. And I wanted to...connect...*bridge* the divide. Everyone thought I'd fail. That the dream was too much. I tried anyway. And I made it real. But it took from me. *Stole.* My t-t-time. Days. Life. *Indigo.*"

Sadness knifed into my belly as that soft—so, so, so softly—spoken name tumbled through my ears.

Indigo.

"I met her before the dream con-consumed me. She wa-was...." he stuttered. Sighed, billowing the air through his nostrils in a rushing roar. "*Everything.* I loved her. And I should've..." He shuddered around a zap of despair. "I should have ended the dream. But I got lost in it. In the dream. The work. The *vision.* Lost. My head i-ignoring my heart. I was s-s-s-selfish. Stupid. My love started to slip, and I was too lost to see it."

"Oh, Alistair." I stroked his head, offering what comfort I could.

"This dream...it...worked. In ways I didn't...But it—" Alistair choked, trying to chew too many words at once and getting them all stuck in his throat.

"Take a breath," I said. "Give yourself a few seconds."

His entire body shook around his inhale. And quivered on his exhale.

"I miss...speaking...talking...quickly," he huffed.

"I would too."

"I h-h-hate that I can't—" he bit off, making a sound like he was hocking the stuck words from his throat.

Molten trickles of frustration seeped into my chest.

I flattened my palm against the top of his head, wishing I could pour peace into him, the way he always fed calmness into me. I wanted to *hold* him. Wrap him in a big, squishy hug. Press myself flush against him until he felt the pace of my breathing and could coerce his lungs to follow the same rhythm.

But I couldn't do *anything*, except perch on top of his head and hope he got some comfort from my presence. And maybe he did. Because after several long heartbeats, Alistair soothed himself enough to speak again.

"The dream worked. But the more it worked, the more it d-d-demanded. I kept giving. The dream kept wanting. And Indigo..." A ruffly sigh escaped him. "She kept f-f-forgiving. When she shouldn't have. She stayed. When she shouldn't have. She deserved more. Someone who wasn't always lost. She died. The dream...what I had *made* with this dream...it...it took her. And I wasn't there. I couldn't stop it. She died. Alone."

My blood turned to ice. "Oh, Alistair, I'm—"

"Please don't be sorry," he said with uncharacteristic brusqueness. "Not for me. Be sorry for Indigo. For the *innocents*. I deserve my hurt."

"No, you don't—"

"Indigo was innocent. And I should have..." His flesh undulated around a flinch. "May I offer advice, Pippi? For you?"

I blinked. "Uh, sure."

"You spoke of being trapped. In that qua-quag-*quagmire. I* was a quagmire. Once. I trapped Indigo. And was the b-burden that made her sink faster. I didn't mean to be, but every day I wish...that I'd let her go. Or she'd b-broken away from me. Every day. I loved her. Letting her go would've hurt me. But I'd be h-h-happy for the hurt now. If it made her happy. But I..." His voice broke. "I can't help Indigo. Not anymore. I *can* help you. And I wish this for you, Pippi. Break free of your quagmire. Maybe you won't lose...your...b-boyfriend. Maybe he's lost like I was. And doesn't know he has you trapped. But if you do lose...it won't be forever. You'll be free. And will be happy again. But to *never* be free...I don't want that for you."

And yup, the waterworks had started again.

Alistair stiffened. "You're crying. I didn't mean—"

"It's okay, Alistair. It's okay. You didn't make me cry. *I* made me cry. With everything that's...well, with everything that happened with Jackson. The timing of this is so terrible. With us being here."

"If you wait for a good time, you'll *always* wait," Alistair said.

"Look at you coming in with the sage advice."

"Well, I am the wise-est...*wisest* sea beast. And the *coolest* and *cutest*."

"And the most egotistical. Can't forget that."

"I like a different word. C-c-confident."

"Overly confident, maybe." I rubbed at the tears tickling my cheeks and curled my knees into my chest, both to warm my body—although the sticky, humid air had already thawed me out—and because I suddenly felt off-kilter. Placed back under a spotlight, when I wasn't prepared to be there. "How did we end up circling back to my trauma?" I asked. "This was supposed to be *your* turn to offload some pain."

"My hurts are old," Alistair said. "Yours are fresh. And I'd like to help. If I can."

I rested my chin against my knees. "You have. Everything about this night—you have helped, Alistair. I've never *laughed* like I have tonight. Never felt so..."

Content.

Safe.

Silly.

Happy.

"...free."

Alistair warbled. "Good."

I leaned back, watching as a pudgy puff of fog trickled off the nearly full moon. "Would you tell me about Indigo?"

Confusion surged through him.

"She was important to you. And anyone who's important to you is important to me. I'd like to hear about her. Whatever you feel comfortable sharing."

He quieted for a moment. Not in a tense way that suggested I'd trounced too far over the line. This was a reflective silence as he organized what he wanted to say.

"She grew...*things*," he began. "This word is missing. Colorful things. They grow in the ground."

"Uh..."

"They smell nice."

"Flowers?"

"Yes! *Flowers.* Flowers. What an *easy* word. And it kept slipping." He harrumphed.

"Sometimes I lose track of stupid-simple words too," I said. "I think they're the *easiest* ones to lose. Big, complicated words tend to stick in your brain, but the simple ones blend too much and get lost in the crowd. So...flowers? She grew flowers?"

"Yes. Flowers. Indigo loved them. Loved making them grow. I used to pick them for her. From different places. Different flowers...ones that didn't grow where we...our home. I'd pick them. And she'd care for them. And they'd grow." A soft laugh burbled through him. "I used to...j-j-joke that she got as lost in her flowers as I did in my dream. And she said the difference was...she was a woman. Women got themselves less...*unlost* better than men."

"Oh, yeah, she's not wrong. Women generally multitask better."

"Multi. Task. Yes." Alistair laughed. "I don't do it well. Indigo did." He stopped for a moment. And then in a sad, broken voice said, "I miss her."

"I'm sure you do. She sounds wonderful."

"She was."

He didn't say anything else.

Maybe rooting through the crevices of his brain, hunting for words, had left him weary. Or maybe he wanted to keep these scars to himself. We all had wounds other people would never truly understand, and trying to explain ripped those cuts back open. Left them bleeding. Raw.

So for several moments we silently watched the stars. Listened to the ocean grumble and splash. Absorbed each other's company and comfort.

"I'd love to see a shooting star," I said after a long stretch. "I've never seen one, except in movies. But people swear they've as much magic as the Sorcerers. That even a Standie can ask something of a shooting star and have it come true."

"They are," Alistair said, "*magical.* But they don't come here." His head shifted slightly as he tilted his chin up, eyes drawn to the sky. "I've never seen one. And I come here often. I *like* looking at the stars. It's...p-pe—"

"Peaceful?" I finished.

"Yes."

"I think so too." I lay down between his horns, pillowing my hands under my head, so I could keep staring at the sky without getting a neck crick. "Sometimes life gets turbulent. But even when everything's flinging around and flipping upside down, the stars are always there. Always steady and quiet. Always *shining.* Clouds and fog might cover their light, but nothing snuffs them out. They're eternal. And steadfast. And assured. Everything we're not."

Alistair made another one of his purring sounds.

"I used to sneak out on the roof when I was a kid. When my parents argued into the dead of night. And I'd watch the stars until I fell asleep. I even made up a story. When I was in, I dunno, middle school? Maybe a little older. It was before my parents split—can't remember if it was before we moved—their last-ditch effort to save their marriage. Anyway, I wrote this terrible story. A romance. About a human boy who was lonely and sad. He saw a shooting star one night and wished it would bring him a friend. And the star sympathized with him, so she came to him herself. Offered him companionship and love and lost her heart to him in the process. But in answering the boy's wish, she trapped herself on Earth. And she thought she'd be happy there, with this boy she loved. But he didn't love her back. He used her, taking more and more of her stardust until she had none left to give him. And—"

Oh goodness.

Now I remembered why I'd blotted out this story from my memory.

The *ending*.

"What happened?" Alistair prodded.

"She…well, she lived a while on Earth, despairing more each year," I said. "Eventually she took her own life, thinking death would bring her back home. But it didn't. She just became dust."

Alistair gasped and grouched, "That is awful."

"Yeah, kid me was a little emo." I smiled. "I was super unhappy at that point in my life, though. Which was why I started writing. To escape my own life. Occasionally I got vindictive and made my characters suffer. It's therapeutic to do that. I should probably do it again."

"You don't write anymore?"

"No. Haven't for a long time. I always *want* to, but there's never really a good time to sit and work a story out."

"If you always wait for a good time…" Alistair started.

"I'll always be waiting. Yeah. You hit me with that sage advice already tonight. It's goo-goo-goo—" A jaw-cracking yawn split the word. *"Good."*

"You're tired."

"Yeah." I dragged a hand over my raw, heavy-lidded eyes. "Lying down was probably a bad idea." But I didn't have the strength to get back up. Not when my muscles had turned into a big, goopy puddle.

"You can sleep," Alistair said.

"I probably won't." I blinked blearily at the stars. "They are pretty. The stars. And you look pretty too, when the moon hits you." My tongue struggled to carry those leaden words. "I should start writing again."

"You should."

"No more sad endings, though."

"No. Ha-happy endings only."

"I can manage that." I closed my eyes, because it was too much effort to keep them open. "Hey, Alistair?"

He hummed softly.

"I really like you."

"I like you as well."

"I wish you were human, though…"

Sleep wrenched me beneath the surface. And I didn't have the strength to swim, so I sank.

Alistair's mournful response followed me down. Words I was convinced my snoozing brain had muddled and reshaped.

"I am human."

32

Pippi

"*I am human.*"

In the dream, it was a man saying those words. The tall, long-limbed man sat with me beneath the stars, his body glowing beneath the moonlight as we listened to the waves tumble beneath the inlet cliffs. I turned to him as he spoke, wanting to *see* him. But no matter how I squinted and strained, the details of his face kept slipping out of my brain. Like creamy yolk sludging off a half-cooked egg.

"You're not human, though," I said to him.

The man huffed and pulled me to him, nestling my rump between his thighs and twining his arms around my torso. Wrapping every part of his body around me.

"I am." His chin rested atop my head. "Pippi!"

His voice sounded different when he said my name. Distant. As though he'd slipped away from me.

I nestled back, burrowing myself into him. But his warmth vanished.

"Pippi. Wake up."

I jolted, my eyes springing open, and I grimaced when my cheek scraped against the scraggy scales on Alistair's head. "Was I asleep?" I croaked, dumbfounded. My voice definitely *sounded* sleep squeaky. I had grit in my eyes—my very swollen and puffy eyes—and wet drool painted my cheek.

"You were," Alistair said. "And you s-s-s-snore. Did you know that?"

Err…yeah. Jackson might've mentioned that at one point.

"It's…*cute.*"

I wiped the drool from my chin on the sleeve of my crusty shirt—crusty, because it'd dried with the salt from the sea clinging onto the fabric, making it gritty and stiff.

Gross.

I sneezed when a bit of the salt flaked off and floated up my nose. And then I sneezed again, because the first one didn't clear the gunk out. And then three more times, because my nose was generally a jerk when I first woke up and threw a hissy fit over every particle of dirt and dust it had to inhale.

"Oh dear." Alistair laughed once the fit had subsided. "Waking hurts?"

"It does today." Because I'd been *sound* asleep. A slumber so deep, it was almost a coma.

I yawned—wide enough to make my jaw pop—and stretched my hands over my head as I sat up. Surprisingly, my back wasn't sore. My hips didn't creak. All the aches and pains I usually had first thing in the morning weren't there.

Apparently, Alistair made for a comfy mattress.

My hair though...*Yikes.*

The dried salt had my curls sticking up in a porcupine style.

"Ugh." I finger-combed the strands, wincing when they crunched. "Jeeze, I'm sorry, Alistair. I spent half the night crying, and then I passed out on you. I wasn't very good company, huh?"

"You were lovely," he said.

"H-h-how long was I o-o-o-out?" This yawn started as a quiver in my belly and it rolled upward, gathering momentum, until it wrenched my mouth open and escaped.

"A while. And I didn't want to wake you. But it's nearing orb...sun-sunrise."

Wakefulness crashed over me like an icy wave. "It *is*!? Oh no. I...Gosh, Alistair, I'm so sorry. I really didn't mean to stay out this late! I *have* to get back."

"You're nearly back, Pippi," Alistair soothed. "But I can't stay above the surface. And I didn't want to go under while you slept..."

"Oh." It took a few seconds before realization actually hit me. "*Oh.* Yeah. Well, thank you for the heads up." I clambered to my feet, clutching onto his horn for support. "No one likes to wake up with a soggy bottom, eh?"

He purred an affirmative as his head sank beneath the surface.

I tried not to squeal when the frigid water slashed into my bare feet.

Tried.

"Sorry," he murmured.

"No worries." I shook my left foot, trying to get the blood flowing back to my toes. "I can't believe I passed out like that."

"You needed it. The sleep."

"Yeah, I guess." I chewed on my lip as Alistair passed the jagged cliffs bordering the inlet.

Those craggy rocks had been in my dream too, and they'd looked just as malicious beneath a sparkling blanket of moonlight as they did swaddled in curtains of fog. The dream man had been beautiful, though, with his skin glowing under the ethereal light. And he'd felt as solid, warm, and real as the rocks around us.

But he wasn't.

"I am human."

The man was a wish. My heart's mournful, desperate desire for Alistair—this charming creature I'd grown so attached to—to be a human. Someone I could take with me, *away* from this island. Someone I could share a life with.

In just a scant handful of days, I'd somehow forged a connection with Alistair that ran deeper than any other. But I couldn't keep him.

We were two lonely souls that lifted each other up. We belonged together.

But we *couldn't* be together.

So I dreamed of him as a human man. And grieved when that dream ended.

"We're here. Pippi," Alistair said.

I blinked. Realized I'd been blankly staring at my hand, where it was curled around his horn, and looked up.

My eyes immediately found the cliff path that would lead to my cottage. My tennis shoes were still scattered there, one teetering close to the edge while the other was thrown back against the rocks. Because I'd ripped them off with shaky hands and had been too blinded by tears to notice where I'd chucked them.

My mouth suddenly went dry. Painfully so. The sort of dry that hurt to swallow.

I didn't want to leave Alistair—leave this magical, emotional, exhausting, *wonderful* night we'd shared.

I didn't want to go back to Jackson and confront…*everything*. The argument. Our relationship. All the wounds and blisters that would hurt when we dug into them, but that all needed to be lanced to heal.

"It will be alright, Pippi," Alistair said when I hesitated.

I nodded and clambered up onto the cliffs. "Yeah. We'll… we'll work it out, I'm sure. But he's gotta be furious that I didn't come home last night. And made him worry."

"He won't be m-mad," Alistair assured me. "Once he sees you're okay."

I nodded, even as doubt curdled in my belly.

My fingers were stiff as I grabbed my shoes and slipped them back over my feet, wincing at the slimy feeling of shoving wet toes into damp pleather. And the shaking got worse as I set to my hair, trying, and failing, to look a little less like Medusa's rabid pet porcupine.

"Guess we're going with a braid." But my hands *struggled* with that simple plait. The stiff strands of hair kept springing out of the twines. My fingers kept getting the chunks tangled. I imagined in the end, it looked less like a braid and more like a half-melted cotton candy spiral. But it would have to do.

"How do I look?" I asked Alistair as I straightened my shirt and flexed my legs to get the stiffness out of my jeans. "From what you can see, anyway? Am I presentable? Or am I—Oh shoot. I didn't have makeup on, did I?" I wiped my hand over my cheeks. "Phew. Okay. I took it off earlier. Forgot about that. Drunk raccoon face averted."

"You look lovely, Pippi." Alistair's sadness nestled into my chest, cuddling against my own sorrow. "Always."

JACKSON WASN'T in the cottage when I got there.

And guilt gnawed at me.

I'd been so selfish last night.

I changed quickly, squirming out of my sea salt stiff clothes and shimmying into the skirt and blouse I'd worn yesterday, chewing at my lip the whole time, and telling myself that I needed to take these few minutes to put myself together. So when I found him, I wouldn't stink of the sea and have him half out of his mind worrying if I'd tried to drown myself.

And I took thirty seconds to reassess myself in the mirror. My hair wasn't so bad—the sloppy braid almost looked stylish—but my face.

Stars.

Puffy red eyes peered back at me from the mirror. Red stained my cheeks as well—either from the scrub of saltwater against my skin, the tears, or both.

This was going to be a heavy makeup day, for sure. Cold compresses for the eyes. Lots of concealer. And then no one would know I'd spent the night bawling and swapping sob stories with the Loch Ness Monster.

But, for now, I wiped the cakey flakes of dried salt off my cheeks and headed out the door.

I didn't have to go far to find Jackson.

He meandered through the fog, his hands grappling to free the key from his pocket. Wrath engulfed his beautiful eyes when he glanced up and saw me standing in the open door.

"Jackson!" I called, waving my arm. "I'm—"

"Decided to come back, have you?" He scowled as he slammed the key back into his pocket.

"I—"

"I figured you were bunking with your gal pals. So I went to breakfast without you. Sorry."

Breakfast?

I glanced up at the fog over our heads. "It's barely dawn."

"Kian and some of the others went for a pre-dawn hike up in the mountains. We got to Brew & Bites just as they started serving breakfast. I would've invited you, but you bailed on me. We saw the banshees and the will-o'-the-wisps, by the way. So, I hope your little tantrum was worth missing out on an awesome experience."

"Tantrum?"

"But at least you're here, and I won't have to go drag you out of the chicks' house. Did you cool your heels any? I hope so." He knocked his shoulder into mine as he bulldozed into the cottage.

Rage peeled off him in big, hot, lashing waves. They struck me harder than his body had—hard enough to have me flopping back into the doorway.

Jackson never turned his eyes to me. He strode toward our bedroom, peeling his shirt over his head.

I followed him. Numbly.

"You can shower after me," he snapped. "And you need to be ready to leave by 10:00 a.m."

"I..." The words choked me. There were too many spiraling up my throat too fast for my brain to process. "W-w-w-we..."

Goodness, is this how Alistair feels when trying to speak?

Poor thing.

I cleared my throat, knocking the words loose, and swallowing the ones I didn't need. "Jackson," I whispered, "can we talk?"

"The boat tour takes off at 11:00 a.m. Unless you'd rather sit that out as well?" Jackson shrugged out of his pants and stomped into the bathroom. Over the hiss and rattle of the shower starting, he added, "But I paid for two tickets. And they were pricey. And you've already cost me a *fortune* on this trip, so it would be nice if you could stop PMS-ing for the day and go on the boat tour with me."

My gabbers were flasted. Thoroughly.

I couldn't even *think* straight.

It took me several seconds to realize I'd left the front door wide open.

Several more to have the sense to close it.

He'd gone *hiking*?

Ate breakfast.

Booked a boat tour.

There'd been no concern from him when he'd seen me standing at the door. No remorse or worry. Just anger and annoyance.

He hadn't cared where I was. Hadn't paused to wonder why I was upset. He'd just carried on with his trip and expected me to "*cool my heels*" and go along with it.

He didn't care. Maybe he never had.

And I'd felt *guilty* for going out with Alistair.

Now I hated that I'd felt guilty.

Hated myself for hating that I'd felt guilty.

What I'd done was wrong.

But Jackson…

Heat exploded over my skin, making me itch. And fume.

I stormed into the bathroom.

His towering shadow wriggled behind the thin shower curtain as he scrubbed at his hair.

I ripped the curtain aside.

"If you're thinking of using *sex* as an apology"—Jackson flicked shampoo out of his eyes—"you better get to your knees. I'm not interested in *anything* else."

"We need to talk," I snapped.

His eyes scorched into mine. "About *what*?"

"How about…"

The fact that you're a selfish prick.

And I was too stupid to see it.

"...L-last night," I said, after only a brief stutter. "And this trip. And *us.*"

Jackson stuck his head under the trickling water and angrily scrubbed the shampoo off. "I can't believe this. You're still sour. *Still?* For fuck's sake. What is the matter, Pippi?"

"I'm trying to tell you—"

"You haven't been right since we came here."

"Because I didn't *want* to come here."

He closed his eyes. "I swear to fucking...I surprise my girl-friend with a dream vacation—"

"This wasn't *my* dream vacation."

"—I bring her to a magical island—"

"—knowing she's terrified of the ocean. You forgot that part."

"And she decides to be an ungrateful bitch." He flicked water at me.

"Ungrateful?"

"I don't know what the fuck got into your head—" Jackson broke off, sudsing up a rag and scrubbing his body down. An action that, a week or so ago, might've left me salivating. And he was so deliberate about *how* he did it. Fondling his chest. His biceps. His cock.

But I'd never been so cold.

Sexually cold, at least.

The anger was broiling.

"—but I *miss* my happy girl," he finished.

"I don't think your happy girl has been *happy.* Not for a while."

He heaved a big sigh.

"We really need to talk about this, Jackson. I can give you some time so we can both cool off."

"We don't have time. We have to be at the dock in a few hours."

I bristled. "Why on *earth* would you buy—"

"Because everyone is going to be on this tour, Pippi!" Jackson threw his rag at me. "*Everyone.* And maybe you don't give a shit about the people *I* like, but can you at least appreciate that I enjoy their company?"

"Sure I can. When you start appreciating the same thing about my friends."

He rinsed himself, glaring at me the whole time, and then flicked the shower off. "Can you stop being selfish—"

"How *dare*—"

"—and be in a civil mood. Then maybe, *maybe,* I'll be civil for whatever pointless talk you wanna have." He snatched a towel off the hook.

And, before I could muster up an insult, Jackson walked out of the bathroom and slammed the door in my face.

33

Alistair

$\mathcal{I}$ am called to feed after Pippi leaves. So I go. But I don't eat. Much, at least. And after, I wait.

Wait to be called to amuse the humans.

Wait for the night to bring Pippi back to me.

But *she* comes to me first, climbing a rock path most humans are for…bidden. Forbidden from.

A part of me hopes she'll fall into the waters.

The rest of me regrets the cruel thought.

If she does fall, I will save her.

Because I do not hate Onyx. Even now.

Once, she had been a friend. I cared for her. And I don't forget that affection, even if she has.

Onyx sits on the rocks. "Well, I confess I'm disappointed, Alistair. I leave ye for five years and expect to return findin' ye a mindless beast. Instead, I come to this shite island and find yer a lovesick pup."

I struggle to understand her. Even words I know sound strange when she speaks with her ack-accent.

"There's no use hidin', Alistair. Ye know I can hear ye."

"I'm not…h-hiding." I rise to the surface.

She smiles. Not in a soft way. Like Pippi smiles. Or in a way that shows joy. Hers is…*cruel.*

Smiling because my curse makes her…

Not happy.

That's not the right word.

Satisfied.

"Now then…" she speaks more. Too many words, and too

quickly. They're meaningless to me. "Oh feck. Ye've gone pretty far, eh?" Another cruel smile. "Canna say as I'm unhappy about that, but I didna have the patience to talk stupid to ye. C'mere, ye oaf."

I move closer.

She pulls something from her shirt and blows it into my eye.

A powder. Herbs. Filled with magic.

The dust burns. The way the runes above my eyes do, blackening my vision, and making me pull away with a hiss.

But then…

I shake the hurt out of my eyes.

And find the world has cleared, for the first time in years.

Years.

My head is my own again: busy and chaotic, with too many trains of thought running on crisscrossing tracks.

I am thinking how desolate the sea is, with its muted color palette, as though the magic leeches the light and vibrancy out of this part of the world to fuel Niverwick Isle.

There's an empty feeling in my stomach, because I hadn't eaten my fish (breakfast of champions) and I *crave* food. Real food. Or, well, real *junk* food—chocolate, gummy bears, *pizza*, with every single topping they can cram on it (even anchovies), popcorn (American style, drowning in butter), sweet coffee, chips…a *carton* of chips. Enough to make even the beastly belly I have now ache.

As I tease myself with thoughts of food, I'm staring at Onyx and noticing how thin she's gotten, and how her eyes look hollow and sad.

But I'm thinking of Pippi too, and my heart is doing flips inside my chest. Because I'll be able to talk to her. Fully. She won't have to, in Onyx's words, *"speak stupid"* for me to understand. And I'm running through the conversations we've already had, lavishing over the words I hadn't known then, but do now.

What will she wear tonight, I'm wondering.

She has the most colorful clothes, and I've loved each outfit I've seen. The bright style gives this monotonous place some flavor, and each one highlights different parts of her hazel gaze. The red and gold blouse she wore when she met me at the inlet made her eyes dark—seductive, even if she wasn't trying to seduce me. The dress she wore on the dock had enhanced the green in her stare—and I wish I'd been able to see her closer, to drink in the way the colors brightened her eyes.

Of course, the clothes she *hadn't* worn on our first meeting had been equally entrancing—but thinking those thoughts will take away my right to call myself a gentleman.

A *"lovesick puppy,"* Onyx had called me.

She's right.

"It's good to know ye haven't changed, Alistair." Onyx pulls at my scattered mind until it focuses on her. "Thinking lots of thoughts?"

"Too many," I say. "As usual."

"Must have been nice for ye, eh? To be the sea beast and lose those human thoughts."

"No. I've *hated* it."

She laughs. Bitterly. "Mayhap if ye'd stop fightin' the spell and let it work, ye wouldna hate it, eh?"

I scoff.

"Well, I wouldna get too used to havin' yer thoughts again, Alistair. That was a potent potion. I mighta used all the isle's sage, and it was a sodden nightmare gettin' the mix together and findin' someone to cast over it. But I reckon it'll only last ye an hour—two, if yer lucky. It'll definitely wear itself off before yer new friend comes to meet ye."

I try not to acknowledge the disappointment, the *despair*, but the emotions dig at me before I can wrangle them, and I know Onyx has felt them.

Because Onyx and Pippi share something: that ability to *feel*.

They're Sensitives.

That's the word I tried so hard to remember the other night.

A *Sensitive*.

They're rare creatures, Sorcerers born without the ability to wield magic, but capable of feeling it.

Once, when magic was new, and humanity used it to hurt each other, Sensitives were valuable. Armies sent them into the thick of danger, to have them sense what spells and enchantments hovered in the air. They were, in a sense, human bloodhounds.

Nowadays, it's a curse to be born a Sensitive. Society has no use for them anymore, and their openness, their ability to feel so keenly, forces them to bear an insidious burden: the weight of human emotion.

Onyx, sensing where my thoughts have wandered, says, "Does she know what she is? Yer friend?"

"No," I say. "She knows what she can do but doesn't seem to understand *why*."

Onyx drums her fingers against the stone. "Maybe that's for the best, eh? I wondered how she got to be an adult while stayin' so...*nice*. *Ugh*. I've been watchin' her, Alistair. That woman yer lovesick for. She's always smilin', even when she's miserable. Always tryin' to make people happy. It makes me sick."

Anger burbles inside of me. "Kindness is not a crime, Onyx."

"No. But it's feckin' disgustin'."

"She's instinctively using her abilities, without understanding what they are, to help people. It's..." One of the things I adore about her, even if it worries me. "Admirable."

"Ye would say that," Onyx scoffs. "Because ye were born with wieldin' magic. It's not '*admirable*' what she's doin'. Puttin' herself through that for feckin' arseholes who dunna deserve it. She'd be better findin' just one or two to pour herself in and soddin' the rest. Of course"—Onyx's face twists into a feral scowl—"when someone destroys the thing she's poured herself into, it'll destroy her. Better to turn bitter than to drain yerself dry, eh?"

This...

This is why she's here.

Not to taunt me for the attachment I've formed with Pippi, but to see if there is still a knife in my heart. There is. There always will be. And she wants to twist it.

"I lost everything too, Onyx. When Indigo died," I remind her.

"No ye didn'."

"I *loved* her."

"Enough to let her rot at the bottom of the sea."

"I did *not* destroy that ship."

"Liar."

"Onyx, I swear to you—"

"Ye haven't changed one bit, have ye? Still insistin'—it was *yer* bloody feckin' ship, Alistair. Yer shiny new toy. Ye spent enough time tinkerin' with it. But the one time ye weren't on it and me sister was, it explodes. Coincidence, eh?"

I don't know how to answer that.

So I say nothing.

Saturn had been a ship born out of collaboration: an idea to combine the technology of Standies with the magic of Sorcerers. It was a luxury liner unlike any other, swift enough to sail the world in two weeks, but smooth enough that its passengers would not be rollicked by the speed in which they were traveling. While aboard *Saturn*, guests were treated to both magical marvels, while never having to give up the convenience of their modern lives, as they do at Niverwick Isle.

It wasn't *my* ship, per se. I hadn't drafted the concept, but I'd invested in the team who had. I'd helped launch it, and had spent several weeks sailing on it, answering media questions, entertaining guests, diagnosing and fixing its kinks. It was something I had taken great pride in.

Indigo had always been curious about these ventures I often found myself swept up in. Before *Saturn*, it had been an operating system. Before the operating system, it had been medical diagnostic equipment. Before that...

I don't remember.

But there was something.

There was always something. A project. An *obsession*. Something I'd pour over and work at until it was perfected.

The dreams, as I told Pippi, that I lost myself in.

But I've learned that you can only pour from one cup.

And while these projects consumed my brain, I neglected my heart.

"Alistair, it's just one night."

"Can you be here by 3:00 p.m.?"

"Do you have to work so late? Only...the fundraiser's tonight. I'd love for you to be there."

Indigo's voice fills me. Haunts me.

"We have a reservation tonight. Please don't forget."

"Will you come home? Please? I'm in a crummy mood and need one of your comfort burritos."

Comfort burritos.

I've *forgotten*.

It's what I called being wrapped in a blanket with another person, cozying up together until you roast...

A burrito.

"A burrito a day keeps the doctor away..."

Indigo and I had burritoed frequently. Until my mind, my ambition, my *selfishness* started to wreck our relationship.

Onyx laughs and says, "Ah, ye've got some memory comin' back, eh? Enjoyin' yer brain now, Alistair?"

No.

I know she knows that, so I don't say it.

"I always wondered what she saw in ye." Onyx sniffs.

"Likely the same thing you saw in me once," I say. "You hate me now, Onyx. But you didn't always."

Onyx purses her lips. "No. Yer right. I didna always. Ye were a bit of a buffoon. Likeable enough. Harmless, I thought. I didna figure ye for a selfish sort until it was too late. She already loved ye. Committed to spendin' her life with ye." She's crying now.

I look away.

Because seeing people cry makes *me* cry, but I can't shed tears while trapped in this monstrous body. Instead, they burn inside me, begging for a release they'll never find.

And this hurt goes deeper. Because when I see Onyx cry, my

mind thinks it's Indigo weeping. And I am pulled to comfort her. Ease her pain.

They are sisters—*twins.* Onyx's hair is longer, and she has a dimple in her chin, but she is otherwise identical to Indigo.

Or *was* identical.

Onyx is thirty-five now, whereas Indigo will forever be twenty-nine.

I close my eyes.

I've grieved her, my beautiful Indigo, with her keen humor and steadfast spirit. The calm to my chaos. The steady beating heart of our relationship. I've spent nights in a rage, hating myself for the part I played in her death. Other nights, I've mourned, wishing I'd been the one to die instead. If any magic existed that could trade one life for another, I would have *gladly* cast that spell. But it doesn't. And I can't. No matter how I wish for it, I can't trade fates with her.

I've pleaded for death to come for me anyway, to take me away from my broken heart.

I've hurt. And I've despaired. And I've healed. Accepted.

The final stage of grief, as they say.

I've accepted that I will never see her lazy smile, hear the syrupy drawl of her voice, or the pleasant way she hummed along to the Beatles. Indigo never did anything fast. She lived her life like the flowers she adored—slow, and steady, and savoring every moment. Her magic was that way too. Sluggish. Onyx used to joke that it was stolen magic, that Indigo had pilfered it from her in the womb. But it was just...Indigo.

I've accepted that she is gone.

I've healed as much as I could.

But I'll never stop missing her.

I'll never regret that I said yes when she suggested going with me on *Saturn's* next voyage. Her way of trying to reach me, to talk to me, while I'd been in the bowels of my obsession.

I'd told her to get on that ship.

And then I'd been *late.*

I can't even remember what I'd gotten held up with. A meeting, or something equally as stupid.

"The ship leaves in five minutes, Alistair. What do you mean you're still at the office?"

"There's been a crisis. I'm sorry, sweet, I have to get this sorted first. Can you see if they'll wait?"

"They said they won't."

"Drat it all to hell. It's okay. Listen, I can meet you after it sails."

"Meet me?"

"Yes."

"On the ocean?"

"Absolutely. All you'll need to do is get the coordinates from the captain and I can teleport there."

"Oh, Alistair. This is silly."

"You say silly, I say a fun challenge. I've always wanted to test my range."

"And if you don't have the range?"

"Then I guess I take a dunking in the sea, and you get to laugh at me. I think I've got this though. You go ahead, sweet. Enjoy the start of the cruise. Make sure you hunt down Rueben—he's the best bartender. And you can tell him I said that. Before you finish your first drink, I'll be there, yapping your ear off."

"I'm going to hold you to that. You know I love your yapping."

"I'll never understand why, but I love that you love it. And I love you. And I'll be there soon. I promise."

Twenty minutes.

I'd been twenty minutes late.

The call had come just as I'd left the office and prepared to teleport aboard the fast-moving ship.

Saturn was gone.

Destroyed.

Ripped to pieces that the ocean all too gratefully devoured.

There was nothing left.

No bodies to find. Only fragments of bone.

No pieces of the ship to excavate. Only scraps of metal.

"She should never have gotten on that ship," Onyx says.

"No," I agree. "She shouldn't have. *None* of them should have. She wasn't the only one who died, Onyx. But the others keep slipping…"

I know them now. Ruben, the broad-chested bartender with his easy smile and big laugh. The ship's crew—some of them were so young, like Silvia, fresh out of college and weighing whether she wanted to become a nurse or carry on her schooling to become a doctor. The passengers—a mere spattering of fifteen, including Indigo. Friends and family of the crew, since *Saturn* hadn't officially opened to the general public.

Sixty people had been on that ship.

Sixty people had lost their lives.

And then there were the others that were impacted. The families of the dead. My employees, innocent, but all punished alongside me.

On most days, the only one I remember is Indigo.

I hate it.

Hate that I've forgotten so many others.

But Onyx doesn't care about them. She never had.

"Indigo is the one I dream about," I tell Onyx. "Every night, I watch her board *Saturn*. And I *scream* at her to stay on the land. I'm running for her, trying to stop *Saturn* from sailing. But I can't. I watch it explode. And I see her caught in the explosion. She's scared and crying and begging for help. And I try to help her, but no matter how hard I run, or fast I swim, the sea takes her from me."

Tears rake across my brain.

Onyx's eyes are cold, like steel, when I bring my gaze back to her.

"I have these dreams every night," I say. "Even on the nights when I don't remember what a ship is, or why she was on one."

"Good," is all Onyx says.

"I don't know why *Saturn* exploded, Onyx. I tried, for weeks, to figure it out. I ran through the blueprints and talked to the staff from its previous voyage, asked them if they'd noticed anything. A flaw either in the magic or the technology, *something* that would've explained what happened. They hadn't. They said the ship had run like a dream. I wanted to know *why* it happened just as much as you did. But I never will, and it will *haunt* me. For however long I live. There were sixty people on that ship, Onyx. Their blood is on *my* hands. And I'll never forgive myself. That day destroyed me."

"Ach, it didna destroy much. Absolved of all blame—"

"In the eyes of the law, only."

"'Twas an accident, they said. Bollocks. It was *yer* ship, Alistair. Yer invention. It killed my sister. And ye walked a free man."

"The only thing that verdict did was keep me out of a physical jail. It didn't absolve me of anything."

"But it did. Everyone forgave ye, eh? Even the families of the other sods ye sent to die. They *pitied* ye. I seemed to be the only one to care yer were guilty."

"So because I couldn't rot in a steel jail cell, you trapped me in an aquatic one."

"Exactly."

"And what about the others? What unforgivable crimes did they commit to earn a place in jail beside me?"

She raises her chin. "They worked for ye, didn't they? Helped ye with that ship."

"Guilty by association, huh? *That's* cruel, Onyx."

She turns away from me.

"Have you found peace?" I press. "Now that we're off the streets, locked away, where we can't hurt anyone else?"

Her lip quivers. "Yes."

It's a lie.

I don't need her ability to sense her pain.

"I hope you do manage to find that peace, Onyx. Life is too short and too precious to live it in turmoil. But you should let the others go. Keep me here, if you must, but free them. They're innocent."

There is remorse in her eyes. "I can't."

And I know why.

She isn't the one who placed this curse.

She drafted it, I have no doubt. Onyx has a deep love and appreciation for magical history, and this curse is modeled closely after the one that struck the Scottish island all those centuries ago. The one that created the legends.

But Onyx is unable to wield the magic to enact such a curse. Someone else did. A Sorcerer, one powerful enough to weave an intricate spell, and reckless enough to break about a hundred laws and regulations.

A Sorcerer who will not willingly throw away the *assets* they risk so much for.

"Be careful, Onyx," I say, "with whoever you've chosen to work with. I don't want to see you get hurt."

And I mean that.

I am angry. But I have no hate in my heart, even for the one who damned me.

She stands then, agitated and restless. "Does your new love ken? What ye've done?"

"I've told her what I am able to," I say. "The parts and words I can remember."

"Ach, well, could be she thinks yer a bleedin' heart that needs her mendin', eh? A pity project for her to nurse while she rebounds from that sodden headed oaf she's—"

"That's enough." I am gentle, but firm in saying this. "Pippi has nothing to do with our fight."

"But ye'll put her in the middle of it anyway, eh?"

"She is leaving at the end of the week. And I'll be alone again. If you find yourself getting irritated with her, focus on how devastated I'll be when she's gone. That should cheer you up again."

Onyx places her hands upon her hips and stares down at me, contemplating.

The magic she's used to clear my head is fading. Slowly. Words haven't begun to slip, but my brain grows sluggish. Soon, I'll have only the fog again. And the feelings. And the few words I manage to cling to.

I try not to despair at that. But I do.

"You know," Onyx says, "I dunna think it matters."

"What doesn't?"

"What happened to that ship. You coulda handed me sharp proof that it was not yer doin'. That 'twas a beast from the sea that killed me sister, not yer negligence. And it wouldna mattered. Because she'd still be dead, and ye livin'. And I'd still hate ye for it. Now I've a ship to catch." She turns, preparing to climb back up the cliff. "Be careful with that sweet little Sensitive of yers, Alistair."

34

Pippi

*J*ackson *despised* my outfit.

When I'd emerged from the bathroom, wrapped in a billowy rainbow blouse, tucked into a hot pink skirt, he'd *scowled*. And I'd glared back, daring him to say something.

He hadn't.

But, goodness, I'd gotten some seething looks.

Even as we waited in the queue to board the ship, Jackson's eyes burned into me. And quivers of rage zapped my belly—*his* rage. The sort of anger that made you itch to grab someone and shake them until they yelled in pain.

It was violent. And so *extreme.*

I gnawed on the inside of my cheek and forced myself to look anywhere but at him.

The problem?

In avoiding Jackson, I kept seeing Alistair.

The boat tour was the premier activity on Niverwick Isle, since it got you up close and personal with the doofus dino (a.k.a.: their Loch Ness Monster; a.k.a.: Alistair). And they showcased him *everywhere.*

The odd, squiggly-shaped building called Misty Mages, which hosted both the tour departures *and* a dive bar, was painted a deep cerulean. Moss dangled from the gabled roof, and craggy, coral-colored stones bracketed the doors and windows. It was very obviously meant to look like the sea— especially with the way the one-story building curved in a loose wave around the docks—although it was far prettier than the actual ocean around Niverwick.

Inside the building, peppering the glossy lapis walls, were dozens of small, cartoon-y pictures of Alistair. All of them depicted him as a wild-eyed monster who savagely hunted the other beasts of the sea. They were all PG images, no blood or gore. Cartoon Alistair was just snarling viciously at whales and sharks and monster squids. But a grim black-and-white portrait of him cleaving a ship in half hung above the black marble table, where we all penciled our signatures on a waiver, agreeing to not sue Niverwick Isle, should the dreaded sea beast wreck our ship.

A little girl had bawled upon seeing that portrait.

I understood her fear.

Oh, stars, did I understand.

And I'd ached to comfort the girl, to tell her that Alistair was just a big, gentle derp. But her mom had quickly scooped her up and pulled her aside, murmuring assurances and singing until the girl calmed.

Outside, the Alistair assault continued. A towering mural of him scaled the full length of the cerulean wall on the backside of Misty Mages. His big, green-scaled body turpentined around the wiggly building, while his scathing orange eyes leered at the queue.

A few slots in front of us, a family waited with their two kids, and both boys *oohed* and *aahed* over the big mural. It got some huffs of appreciation from all the adults too.

I frowned at it.

This island needed to fire their stupid, violent artist.

Jackson had said nothing, not a *single word* since we'd left the cottage. But as we shuffled off the land and prepared to step onto the dock, he laughed darkly and flicked one of the A-frame signs that flashed a few final warnings at us.

This one had "Arms are a yummy snack" in bold orange letters that wove around a crude sketch of a Loch Ness Monster biting the arms off the stick figure tourist who'd waved them over the side of the boat. And under, in smaller writing, "For your safety, keep all arms and legs behind the rail. Absolutely no diving."

I wondered grimly, *sadly*, if Jackson had tapped that sign to indicate that he *hoped* I'd become sea monster food on this tour. But then he went right back to giving me the silent treatment, even as we strolled across the rickety dock to the smiling young attendant handing out goggles at the ship ramp. "Sorcerer's vision," he crowed as he handed two sets to Jackson.

Jackson smiled, thanked him, and chucked my goggles at my head once we boarded the ship.

They bonked off my cheek, hard, and I had to scramble to catch them.

Jackson kept walking. And I followed…until the ship rocked under my feet and my brain bulldozed past the anger and hurt to remind me where I was.

This ship was *substantially* smaller than the one we'd sailed to the isle on, built to hold only fifty adults, or so the max capacity sign at the entrance had said. And this old-fashioned vessel, boasting weather-worn wood from the 1800s, creaked its geriatric bones in the swaying dance of the sea.

My stomach slithered.

Alistair's down there, I reminded myself as I fought the swelling panic. *You're safe, Pippi, like he always says.*

Jackson cocked his head over his shoulder, saw me getting a little green around the gills, and walked back.

I reached for him.

"I hope you took your meds," he snapped as he snatched my hand.

"Yes." My teeth ground the word out.

He harrumphed and twisted his arm through mine, leading me across the ship deck.

I smiled, as best I could, with my stomach doing loop-de-loops and my lips quivering, and leaned into him, hating the pressure broiling between us.

I didn't want to fight. Or spend the rest of the trip scowling and throwing jabs at each other.

"Jackson"—I slung the goggles up on my shoulder and used my other hand to rub his arm—"can we—"

"Hey! Jackson!" a deep male voice called.

Jackson raised his goggles in a cheery wave. "Kian! Hello!"

Rune Bloodworth and the rest of the Sorcerers had an area roped off near the front of the ship—although the ropes weren't attached to anything. They floated in mid-air, joggling threateningly at any plebeians who dared to wander too close. And people were milling around it, ogling longingly at the minibar and snack tables lining the ship bow.

From the throng of Sorcerers, the dimpled Kian beckoned for us to join them.

The ropes exuded a droning fizz and slithered to the side when we approached, giving Jackson and I entry into the Sorcerer Club.

Jackson yanked me into his side, bending his head like he was going to smooch my cheek. Instead, he hissed in my ear, "Please do not puke in front of these guys. Use the bathrooms below deck. *Please.*"

Anger gashed my skin, no doubt leaving red patches over my cheeks and chest. And it possessed me to say something utterly wretched, "Maybe I'll puke on Rune Bloodworth's shoes."

Jackson said nothing. But the utter *contempt* that spilled into my stomach left me shaken.

"Jackson!" Kian seemed to not notice the tension sparking off us as he stepped forward and reached out his hand.

A boyish grin slipped over Jackson's face as he pivoted.

"Kian." He beamed, shaking his hand. "Thank you *so* much for snagging us spots today."

"Of course, of course." Kian turned his twinkling eyes to me. "And I'm glad the lovely Pippa was able to join us."

"Pip—" I started to say in an amiable correction.

But Jackson spoke over me. "She's finally feeling better."

"Oh, awesome. I'm very happy to hear that." When Kian let

go of Jackson's hand and reached for mine, I took it. Numbly. Not even feeling the handshake—not really. Not with the buzzing of my brain drowning out other sensations.

He'd called me *Pippa*.

An honest mistake; people did it all the time. But Jackson hadn't corrected him, nor had he let me correct him.

Almost as though he didn't *want* them to know my real name.

I turned to Jackson, when Kian left us for the mini bar, and reached for him. Physically, and emotionally as well. Trying to find something, *anything*, that would settle my souring stomach.

But when I touched his hand, a wave of animosity slammed into me.

I almost cried.

Jackson wouldn't look at me.

"Here we are!" Kian returned a few seconds later, handing a tall pint of beer to Jackson. "And for you, Pippa." He bowed slightly as he handed me a glass with clear, bubbly liquid. "A hard seltzer. My wife *loves* this flavor. It's peach something— what is this one again, hun?" He turned to where a group of women sprawled on stools by the minibar.

"Mango. Peach Mango!" quipped a tall and elegant-looking blonde woman.

"That's it." Kian pressed the glass into my hand. "But go easy on these, eh? Lest your man kick my ass for getting his girl sick again."

I screwed the happiest smile I could manage onto my face. "He's very protective."

"As he should be."

With an almighty *urrrrrrrggggg*, the ship teetered beneath my feet.

I clutched on to Jackson, and he held me steady. But the antipathy he kept expelling turned my stomach into an acidic wasteland.

A cacophony of whoops and hollers rose from the people

onboard the ship. Kian tucked his glass under his arm and whacked his hands together in thunderous applause.

"We're off!" Rune announced, as he thrust his own glass into the air. "A toast! To a successful voyage…*hopefully*," he added, with a booming laugh that sounded like Count von Count.

Muh-a-a-a-a.

"Cigar, Jackson?" Kian asked.

"Of course!" Jackson said.

"Excellent. Oh, and Pippa," Kian added, "feel free to hang out with these lovely ladies. Hun!" He drew his wife's attention again. "You've got room for one more, right?"

She beamed and nodded. "Always. Pippa, is it?"

"Pippi," I muttered automatically.

"Oh, *shit*. It's Pipp*i*? I'm sorry, I was calling you Pippa, wasn't I?" Kian turned toward me with a genuine look of remorse.

"It's no big deal. Honestly," I said. "It's—"

"She gets called Pippa all the time." Jackson drew me in for a flat hug. "I don't even notice when people get it wrong anymore. I always joke that she should change her name."

Do you? Always joke?

I've never once heard you say that.

"But then I remind him that we'd lose this fun conversation starter." I daubed a grin on my face, ignoring the throbbing pain it left in my cheeks, and angled my head up to stare at Jackson.

He smiled, but his eyes were hard. Cold.

A wrathful god wearing a mask of happiness.

"It's a conversation starter *for sure*," Kian said. "Pippi. Like the cartoon, right? The girl with the pigtails?"

"That's the one."

"My mom used to love that show," he said.

"Mine too." I pointed to my chest. "Obviously."

Kian chuckled. "That's awesome! We'll have to wrangle up the crew and do a coolness check, to see who gets the reference and who doesn't." He gave my hair a friendly ruffle.

And I…actually liked him. He had an easy-going temperament. A little boastful, maybe, but harmless. And he softened whenever he glanced at his wife.

I almost hated to admit that Jackson had been right about me taking to him. Then again, he'd accused me (rightfully) of liking *everyone*. But I wanted to extend this olive branch to him, a balm for the raw sores I'd inflicted on him this week.

I do like Kian, Jackson.

You were right. I'm sorry I acted like an ass when you mentioned this earlier.

Please forgive me.

I touched his arm, stood on my tiptoes, and started to whisper all of that into his ear.

Jackson shrugged me off and walked away.

35

Kian's wife was a doll of a woman named Elisabeth.

"Oh, gosh, what *lovely* hair," Elisabeth trilled as I wobbled over to where her group milled around a set of bar tables and stools—shining black furniture that *shouldn't* have been so stationary atop a bobbing ship. But I supposed they were bolted down by magic.

"Those *curls*. Hmm." Elisabeth sprang from her stool and fluffed her own silkily straight gold locks. "I'm *jealous*."

"I was actually thinking how much I'd love gorgeous hair like yours." The breeze had fluffed my curls into a tizzy. "I guess you always want what you don't have, right? But this humidity isn't kind to curly hair."

"That it is not." Elisabeth tutted and strode the short distance to the black-steeled minibar. "It's all the *salt* from the sea. It's rough on the skin too."

"Sea salt is only good for chocolate and French fries," I said.

"A-fucking-men, sister." A tall woman with strawberry blond waves raised her glass in a salute.

"I'm going to make that my life motto," Elisabeth said before she tapped her glass against the bar top. "*Mango seltzer*, please."

There was a *tink* as ice dropped into her glass, and a light *gloog-glug* as it filled itself to the brim with fizzy water.

I gaped.

Elisabeth laughed. "It takes some getting used to. Magic. And it *always* overfills the glasses." She raised her cup, slurping until the bubbly liquid was below the rim. "There. Now I can walk with it. The enchantment's on the minibar," she added. "So all you have to do is tell it what drink you want. Now"—she strode back to the stool she'd vacated and gave it a hearty thump—"come here, love. I'll do something with your hair to protect it from the dreadful sea spit."

"*Sea spit!*" the strawberry blonde woman trilled.

"Oh, you don't have to—" I ground my teeth when the sea gave a particularly hard buck, and the rocking of the ship sent my stomach crab-crawling up my throat. Only for a few seconds. Once the floor settled, the nausea did too, *thankfully.*

"Nonsense." Elisabeth insisted. "Sit. Please. I *love* doing hair."

"Too much," one of the women in the group chittered good-naturedly.

And, well, when Elisabeth's zeal tugged so hard at my heart, beckoning me to come closer, how could I not?

"I used to be a hairstylist, before I met Kian, of course. But *no one*"—Elisabeth *oohed* when I staggered onto her stool and she got her fingers in my curls—"had hair *this* gorgeous. And it's so thick!"

She spent at least an hour fiddling with my hair. Trying one updo, deciding she'd done a "*rubbish*" job. Taking it down. Crafting a second that she *liked* but didn't *love*. Then she got an idea for something she thought would look better, so the second updo got taken down so she could twine my strands into their final form.

All the while, she and the other women gossiped. It was all mindless prattle. Nothing mean-spirited, just "Did you see so-and-so is dating who's-em-what's it?" kinda things.

I joined in a little. Whenever my stomach felt steady enough to risk a bit of conversation. But mostly, I listened and slow-sipped the seltzer, wishing it *wasn't* spiked, because the fruity bubbles helped slow my reeling belly.

"Onyx, dear," Elisabeth called suddenly. "Would you like to join us?"

I turned.

This ship had warped wooden benches scattered about the

deck. Three dotted the arch of the bow, and Onyx rose from one of them, tossing her book down as she cradled her empty cup and made for the minibar. She didn't acknowledge Elisabeth's invitation as she banged her glass on the bar, curtly asked for a beer, and bolted back to her bench.

"Fussy bitch, that one." One of the women harrumphed.

Onyx lounged on the bench and buried her nose back in her book.

Stars bless her steady stomach. I'd *never* be able to read on a ship.

"I heard she's *livid* about this island," Elisabeth whispered. "Didn't even want to come."

"Wasn't it…I mean…I thought Rune Bloodworth said it was *her* idea?" I asked.

"It was." A handsome, almond-colored-skinned woman said. "But she had a very different pitch."

"She wanted it to be less a tourist thing, right?" Elisabeth asked.

"Yup. A retreat or something." The almond-colored-skinned woman shrugged. "Rune saw more money in tourism."

"So he overruled her?" I asked.

"Men usually do," Elisabeth said.

All the women made little *hmmmss* and *huhhhs* of agreement.

"And poor Onyx hasn't been right since her sister died." Elisabeth dropped her voice to a breathy whisper, lest the sticky breeze pick up her words and carry them to Onyx's ears.

"That's right," the strawberry blonde hissed. "And she got caught in all that hoopla with SorcerSoft."

"*SorcerSoft?*" I gaped. "My company used to work with them. Before they…you know…" I dragged my finger across my throat.

"Yeah, what a *mess* that was." The woman shook her head. "Onyx is lucky she didn't go down with them."

"Rune helped her," Elisabeth added. "And she helped him. And now they're glued at the hip, whether she likes it or not."

My eyes found Onyx as she jiggled her knee and flipped to a

new page, her eyes never leaving the book. "Poor thing. Was she close with her sister?"

"They were twins," Elisabeth said.

And my heart bled a little for Onyx. "That's *awful.*"

"Yeah." Elisabeth pinned a section of my hair to the back of my head. "I guess if anyone's entitled to a bit of fussiness, it's her."

My gaze swung from Onyx to where the men were strewn around the VIP section, some perched on benches, some leaning over the railing, watching the sea. Like Jackson, who leaned against the planked wood with a drink in one hand and a smoking cigar in the other. He was red-faced and a little loose in the way he moved, a sign he'd probably had a few drinks too many. And although he was talking up a storm to the men around him, his gaze never left Rune Bloodworth.

Rune, for his part, was out in the middle of the ship, entertaining the other tourists with his magic. Big, blobby bubbles floated in the air around him, bouncing and jiggling in time to the sea shanty he chanted. The kids were mesmerized, clapping along to the music, and squealing whenever one of the bubbles burst, dousing Rune in glimmering water. Occasionally, a bubble broke away from the formation to super soak someone from the audience.

"That one's got a big personality, huh?" I said to Elisabeth.

"Who?" She followed my gaze. "Rune?"

"Yeah."

"Oh, for sure." She shifted my hair into one hand so she could use her other to lift her drink. "Always. Big and boisterous. And he uses that charm too, make no mistake. He was born with a damn good weapon, and he knows how to wield it."

A gale of laughter swelled around the boat as a bootylicious bubble did the mambo around Rune's body. And then a voice twined over the hubbub, shooting into the air at an almost unnatural volume.

"Alright, may I have your attention. Eyes to me, please, ears as well…both, if you can spare them." A tall, beanstalk of a boy stood on a platform on the other side of the ship, waving his arms. "Eyes and ears please—oh, and bubbles too." He laughed, along with everyone else, when Rune's bubbles formed an arc around the bottom of the platform.

"Very good. Very good." The boy patted one of the bubbles, grinning when it jiggled. "We're going to be putting the anchor down here. And we've got a mighty fine meal cooking for y'all, so I sure hope you brought your appetite, but there's still time yet to work it up if you haven't. Now, I'll be asking each of you to pick a side of the boat. Try to split yourselves evenly, please. And leave room, eh? There's no need to crowd, certainly no need for pushing and shoving and the like. The Loch Ness Monster swims around the whole ship, so it doesn't matter where you stand, you'll be able to see him."

Excitement plumed into the air as people began to move, sorting themselves in groups and making a beeline for the railings.

"Ahhhh, don't you go rushing off," Elisabeth muttered to me, even though I hadn't moved. "Let me get this last weave in your hair."

"We ask that you wait until you are settled at the railing," the attendant continued, "*before* you put your goggles on. You may notice some distortions in your vision while wearing them, so please be mindful of that. If you feel unsteady, please step back and lower onto one of the benches."

I glanced down at the splash goggles, dangling from where I'd hooked them over my elbow.

"Parents, mind your little ones." The attendant raised his voice, so it didn't get lost in the mounting fervor. "If you have food with you, we ask that you please keep it secure. Do *not* feed the Loch Ness Monster. Do not lean over the railing either. Our Loch Ness Monster has a strict diet, and we do not want him to rot his stomach because a delectable little human fell into his jaws." He made an overly exaggerated "oooohhh" motion with his hands, like an actor at a cheesy haunted house.

My stomach clenched.

"*Strict diet,*" the boy called it.

I called it cruelty.

Even if Alistair had *wanted* to snack on some of the humans, he *couldn't.* He'd puke them back up.

"And, done," Elisabeth chirped. "*Gorgeous.* You've the perfect hair for this kind of weave bun, wouldn't you say?"

I thought she was talking to me, which seemed a silly question, when I couldn't really see the updo. But as a "yes" was rolling off my tongue anyway, Jackson's curt "sure" dragged my response to a halt.

"You should wear your hair like that more, babe," he continued. "Instead of always leaving it down."

"Oh, I'd wear my hair down all the time too, if I had curls like hers," Elisabeth said. "I'd want to flaunt them. But this'll keep the salty humidity from frizzing it."

Jackson gave a good-natured huff. "I gotta say, I never thought much about how weather and humidity can affect hair. Not until I started dating Pippi. My hair's always the same."

"Such is the way with men." Elisabeth sighed, and then gave me a light tap on the shoulder, whispering, "I think your man wants to take you to see the show."

"I think he wants to protect me from the monster," I whispered back.

Elisabeth laughed.

Jackson managed a thin, but charming, smile.

We took our spots along the railing near the front of the ship, on the opposite side of Rune, which made Jackson grumble. And he would've tried to zoom me to the other side, if one of the attendants hadn't swooped over and forced him to stay put.

The air thickened as the ship slowed, the geriatric wood grinding when the weight of the anchor pulled on it. Some people were discharging globs of anticipation, others were throwing fear into the pot; Jackson had added a big handful of disgust, and all of it simmered together to create a chunky soup.

A *sour*, cream-based broth that'd curdled before it was lugged into the pot.

I choked on it, as I slipped the splash goggles over my face.

But that cough turned to a surprised *"oh"* when I peered through the enchanted plastic. The world curved, as though it was looping itself around a big fishbowl, but the churlish grey waters were as transparent as glass. Hundreds of green, blue, and yellow fish scuttled beneath those crystalline waves, flashing googly-eyed expressions at the groaning ship. Jouncing tendrils of sea grass, coral, and other vegetation danced atop of the seabed.

I could see everything. Straight down to the ocean floor.

It was *freaky*.

Shrieking laughter billowed into the misty sky as people gawked over the edge of the boat, peering down at the seabed.

Thankfully, the magic *only* worked for the ocean. The wood of the ship, bowed slightly because of the shape of the goggles, remained solid. People did too, although several of our more *mature* individuals wondered out loud if they'd have X-ray vision through clothing.

Spoiler alert: they didn't.

I couldn't imagine what a lawsuit that would've been if the goggles gave people the power to view their neighbors' genitals.

Voices boinged between my ears as I leaned against the railing.

"That is *gorgeous*."

"Look at the fish!"

"Fishies!"

"That is one ugly effer!" This said as a long-bodied creature sleazed its way near the surface, flashing its wide-set eyes and pronounced underbite at us.

"Is that an eel?"

"Who ran him over with a truck?"

I *wanted* to be on the same level of awe and joy as everyone else. I really did. And I had been, for a hot second, after I'd first seen the sea bottom. But the more I looked down, watching the ocean life rippling beneath the waves, seeing how *very big* it all was…

A bulbous shark swaggered on to the set, chasing half the fish away and making the tourists shriek with delight.

A cold sweat prickled at my forehead.

That shark was decent-sized—fifteen or twenty feet, or more—but it looked *tiny* in the vast waters.

I'd been in this ocean. Had swam in it, played in it, nearly drowned in it, and had always, always, *always* been aware of its scope. But knowing it and *seeing* it were two completely different things.

"There he is!" a girl on the other side of the ship screamed.

"Ho-lee shit. He's *huge!*"

"He looks hungry, huh? Should I throw him a snack?" This joke warmly uttered by a man who laughed when a small child bleated, "*Noooo*, Dad!"

"Oooooh buddy, the pictures shortchange the shit out of this bastard," Rune boomed.

Alistair quietly meandered beneath the ship and emerged on our side.

The fish scattered when they saw him. Even the doofus eel, with its big underbite, got all bug-eyed and started scrambling.

People cheered, drumming their hands against the rail.

Alistair flipped himself sideways, scrunching his neck into a U-shape so he could scan his orange eye over the crowd.

He blinked when he saw me.

"Is that f-f-fear, Pippi?" His playful voice soothed my very soul.

I exhaled and almost responded out loud, which would've made me look like a mad little hatter, if no one else could hear him talk. So I gobbled the words back down, making a garbled noise that had Jackson snapping his eyes to me.

"Oh dear, that is fear," Alistair teased gently. "Of little old me?" He did a graceful arch into a backflip, flicking his tail above the surface, and splashing everyone along the railing.

I laughed along with them—how could I not, when I had Alistair's joy nourishing my heart.

He twisted back around, his eyes scanning the group, but always, *always* coming back to me.

My heart gave a hard, happy thump.

I smiled.

Alistair tucked his serpentine body into a ball, spinning in a series of underwater somersaults that had everyone cheering.

"Those guh-glll-glasses are *lovely*, Pippi," he said once he'd arched gracefully out of the spin cycle. "They make your eyes as big as mine."

I clapped a hand to my mouth to shove the giggle back.

"I've always wondered, so be h-honest, please, Pippi—do those glasses make my b-b-b-butt look big?" He wiggled his body as he lazily glided beneath the ship

I tried to swallow my mirth, but ended up gagging on it.

"Unbelievable." Jackson clapped his hand over my elbow. "The ship's *barely* moving, Pippi..."

I blinked at him, the giddy haze twining around my brain making me a little loopy. It took a full thirty seconds to understand why Jackson was looking at me with such *annoyance*.

He thought I was going to be sick.

Which, I probably had looked a little sick, with the way I'd been cackle-choking.

But he wasn't concerned, wasn't holding on to my elbow to keep me steady, or staring at me to make sure I was okay. He was *livid*.

A toxic mix of disappointment, disgust, and anger sizzled in my stomach.

I jerked my elbow out of his hand. "I'm fine, Jackson."

He scowled.

I leaned back against the railing. "I'm okay," I said this last bit to Elisabeth, who'd peered over a group of people to look at me with *actual* concern. "The alcoholic seltzer...you know." I made a vague circle-y motion with my hand that could've been a symbol for being bloated or tipsy, and both would've worked.

She laughed, and then tapped her head, indicating that she felt the same.

In truth, I hadn't even finished the first drink I'd been given. The half-empty glass still sat on the stool where I'd left it.

"You were drinking?" Jackson asked. "When you already get seasick. Real smart, Pippi. Absolutely genius…"

"I had *a* drink," I said. "And I'm not going to get sick. Jackson! Hey!"

He grasped my elbow again, this time forcibly hefting me away from the railing, just as Alistair made a trip back to our side of the ship.

"Pippi?" Alistair called.

A few people turned away from the ocean, fixing their goggle-covered eyes on me and Jackson.

"My girlfriend doesn't have great sea legs." Jackson laughed and tucked me against his side—a motion that *looked* like a comforting hug but *felt* like he'd zipped me into a straight jacket. "Real landlubber. I'm gonna get her to the bathroom."

"It's right this way, sir." One of the attendants, a round-faced woman in her early twenties, rushed forward.

"Everything okay?" Kian pushed away from where he'd been pressed to the rail next to Elisabeth.

No. I wanted to scream.

"Fine, fine." Jackson smooched the top of my head.

"Pippi?" Alistair's voice grew thin. Worried. "Who was that? The man who d-d-dragged you away?"

"Does she need to lie down?" Elisabeth walked toward us, her worry fermenting in the sour emotion soup.

"We do have some seasick patches onboard if she needs them," the attendant added.

"Pippi, I can't see you," Alistair called. "Are you alright? Please…if you can give me a sign…something."

There was just *too much*.

Too many voices.

Too much movement, with some people rushing toward me, legitimately worried I was about to have a medical emergency, and some people rushing *away*, afraid I'd get puke on their shoes.

And I did feel a little (lot) sick now.

I was either going to vomit or explode.

My free hand joggled, a futile attempt to soothe myself.

Jackson seethed and tucked that hand against his side, stilling it.

Alistair's concerned voice kept pinging off my brain.

And Onyx...

At some point she joined the flurry of movement as she stood on top of her bench and stared at me, her head cocked to the side. A strange, knitted emotion gripped her face.

And I...

I couldn't *breathe*.

Couldn't *think*.

"Pippi?" Alistair called again.

Jackson hustled me across the boat and down the rickety little steps that led to the bathrooms below deck. All while flatly muttering, "It's okay" and "I gotcha."

But once we were below deck—in a dark, musty area that smelled like brine, and piss, and damp—I snapped. And shoved at Jackson. *Hard.* "What is *wrong* with you?"

"*ME?*" he spat. "Fuck, Pippi, you were about to fall over the railing."

"I was *not*."

"And, c'mon, babe." "*Babe,*" in this case, being a word he lashed at me. "Have some fucking decency. People don't want some random chick hurling her guts all over their tour."

"I wasn't going to be sick. I—" Well, this was a pickle, eh? Couldn't well say that I was fighting a laugh because my sea monster friend had shaken his tail feathers at me. "I had to burp."

"Burp?"

"Yeah. I mean...I only had one seltzer, but they're fizzy and it was...you know...fizzing back up."

"Pippi? Please, *please* let me know if you're alright." The distress in Alistair's voice hurt me.

I ripped my goggles off, moving to hide how hard my hands were shaking.

Jackson slipped one of his hands over his head and then crossed his arms over his chest. "A burp. Really?"

"Yes."

"The fuck didn't you just say so?"

"Because you didn't let me." I pinched the bridge of my nose. "You just hauled me off. That wasn't okay, Jackson. That…You shouldn't treat me like that. And I-I don't want to be down here. It *stinks*."

I started toward the steps.

He snatched my elbow.

"Don't!" I arched back, preparing to rip away.

He sighed gustily and shoved my arm back at me.

Between his push and my overexaggerated pull, I stumbled, crisscrossing my feet. My arms pinwheeled, and I tried to right myself, but then the ship lurched, and down I went.

DING!

My chin drilled into the edge of the step.

Ouch.

Stars, that was a *bad* spot to hit.

My neck gave a sickly crunch as my head snapped back, and big, neon checkerspots dropped in front of my eyes.

"Shit, babe!" Jackson rushed to me. *"Fuck."*

He grasped my shoulders.

I batted him away.

"Babe, I'm sorry." He tried to heft me onto my feet.

I shrugged him off and stood on my own. My legs shook though, and I had to grasp on to the stair railing when my knees threatened to nope out.

Pain mushroomed along my jaw and fanned across my skull.

And this was all my stupid fault for overreacting the way I had.

So why, *why*, did I feel a gnawing fear in the pit of my gut?

Was it Jackson's fear?

Mine?

Alistair's?

Someone else's?

I couldn't tell.

But with my face throbbing and terror stabbing at my insides, all I wanted to do was curl up somewhere quiet and safe. Like the top of Alistair's head.

Instead, I rubbed at my jaw and mumbled, "I'm going back up, Jackson. I promise I won't blacken your reputation by puking in front of the people you're trying so hard to impress."

"Pippi?" Alistair continued to call for me.

The sea salt air caressed my face as I clambered back up the steps, soothing the raw, throbbing ache in my jaw.

Jackson followed me up but said nothing.

"Feeling a bit better?" the attendant asked.

I nodded again. A lie. But I didn't care.

A few people looked at me as I shuffled back over to the railing.

I snapped the goggles back onto my face—a process that *hurt* this time—and smiled at them.

Or, well, *tried* to smile.

The slight muscle contraction around my jaw drilled a deep, molten pain into my bone. My eyes watered. When I gingerly pressed my fingers to the area, the skin there felt red hot. It would bruise. Badly. But it likely wasn't discolored yet.

I leaned back on the railing.

"Pippi." Alistair blew out in relief as he shimmied back to our side of the ship. "I was scared. I…Who is that? The man? Your b-b-boyfriend? Why did he drag you like that?"

Alistair turned in an elegant, looping dance beneath the water. But he never took his eye off me.

"You're not alright. Are you?" he asked.

All I could do was shake my head.

"What's wrong?"

I closed my eyes.

Jackson shimmied up to my left side and draped an arm over my back. "I am sorry, Pippi," he grumbled.

"Would you tell me?" Alistair pressed. "Later?"

I tucked my chin down.

Jackson tugged me against his side.

I opened my eyes to find Alistair frozen in the waters, staring at me and Jackson.

"He was rough with you," Alistair said. "It s-scared me. Seeing that. Not being able to…Did he *hurt* you?"

I should've shaken my head.

But I couldn't.

A low growl went through Alistair, one that had people cackling in mock horror.

And two things happened simultaneously.

Onyx stood on her bench again and fixed me with a stare intense enough to sear my skin. I looked at her—I had to, with that intense gaze scalding me—and I *swore* she knew. Swore she'd heard Alistair's one-sided conversation with me. Her beautiful face contorted into a smug sneer.

But then Alistair exploded from the surface, twining his neck up, up, and up, along the side of the ship, looking for all the world like the insidious sea beast painted on the side of the building.

People shrieked.

Alistair shot a stream of water out through his mouth, blasting everyone standing to my left side, making sure to get the bulk of it on Jackson.

As Jackson yelped and leapt back, swiping the water from his face, Alistair bellowed in pain.

I turned to him, just as his head disappeared beneath the surface, and saw the hooked rune above his left eye light up an angry red.

36

Alistair stayed near the ship, even after his entertaining duties had ended, and everyone on board turned to the lunch spread that was set out for us. I couldn't see him—the goggles were collected at the end of his show—but I heard him.

"I wish I could do something."

"Is there good food?"

"Have some chips. For me."

"You are alright. Right?"

"I hope you can hear me."

His voice comforted me. Gave me something good to cling to.

Jackson kept me by his side and spent the duration of the trip chatting with Kian and some of the others. Never with Rune, though, much to his chagrin.

I, however, had watched Rune most of the ride back. He was suave with the way he avoided conversation with anyone who wasn't in his "inner circle." He talked *to* people, sure. Had spent 75 percent of the tour providing entertainment, making toasts, and telling stories. His enigmatic personality was a beacon of energy and light. Everyone gravitated toward him and listened. But he never talked *with* people. If someone tried to rope him into actual conversation, he'd smile and laugh and smoothly, oh-so-smoothly, navigate himself away.

A five-minute conversation with Rune might've been the key to changing your life, according to Jackson. But getting that five-minute conversation was as tricky and impossible as finding Willy Wonka's golden ticket inside a random chocolate bar.

We arrived back at our cottage late afternoon—although all hours of the day looked the same behind the dense wall of fog—and Jackson's mood had turned vinegary.

Unfortunately for him, my mood had gone *more* acidic. Because my jaw ached something fierce—it'd hurt to eat earlier, when every bite drove white-hot needles into the side of my face—and my heart, which had taken so many batterings since arriving on this isle, wouldn't stop bleeding. It was drowning me. This sorrow. Guilt. *Dread.* My head was barely above it all, and I didn't have the strength to keep swimming.

If this went on until tomorrow, it would destroy me.

I had to plug the flood of emotions.

And the biggest source of hemorrhaging was the gorgeous, god-like man before me, who was currently kicking off his shoes and stomping into our bedroom.

I rolled my tongue around, trying to wrangle the words, before saying, "Can we talk now, Jackson? Please?"

"About?"

"Us."

He paused, midway through rooting through our little closet, where he'd hung most of his clothes.

"I don't want to argue anymore, Jackson," I said.

"Good." He pulled a pair of jeans off a hanger. "Neither do I. You should get some more ice for your jaw, babe. It's all red." He slapped his jeans against his thigh. "I *am* sorry."

"I know. And I'm not mad, Jackson. Honest."

I'm tired.

And sad.

And scared.

"But we do still need to talk," I finished.

His irritation clawed at me, but he was outwardly the picture of calm as he closed the closet and draped his clothes over his arm.

"I—we—" The words stuck their thorny edges into my

throat. The more I tried to clear them, the more they stabbed their spikes into me.

Jackson raised his brow and wiggled his clothes in a "go on" motion.

"I…Haven't you been feeling that something's *off?*"

His brow arched higher, almost disappearing into the wind-blown locks of his hair. "That something's off with *you?*"

"No. With us."

He scoffed.

"Jackson, please…" I stepped toward him, reaching for his hand.

He grunted and swatted me away.

I shoved the hurt down as I tucked my hands against my sides. "I love you, Jackson, and I always will. But I don't think we work anymore. Maybe we never did, but we cared too much to see it. I just have this *feeling*…that we're too different. And we want different things out of life. And the common ground we used to meet on is getting narrower." A hot tear scorched my cheek. I swiped it away. "Maybe we needed this trip. To shake things up and make us realize our common ground has shrunk so much. I don't know. But…I think…I think what we have just isn't working. For either of us."

Jackson opened his mouth. Closed it again. Opened it. "You're…Lemme get this straight, *babe,*" he hurtled the word at me. "You're breaking up with me?"

I hated the way that sounded.

Breaking up with me.

Breaking my heart.

Breaking my life.

"Yes." The word tasted metallic. Like blood.

Jackson's face reddened. A vein pulsed on his temple. Disgust cascaded off him.

He pinched the bridge of his nose. Scowled. Ran a hand through his hair. Scowled some more. Twisted his jeans in his fist. Continued scowling.

"I'm so sorry."

"You better be fucking sorry! This is unbelievable. It's—" He turned and rammed the heel of his palm into the doorframe. It connected with a painful *SMACK*, a sound like a pellet ricocheting off a solid rock.

I flinched.

Jackson *fumed*.

"*Fuck*, Pippi!" He winced and shook his hand, growling at me when I tentatively reached for him, to see if he'd hurt himself. "You've got some fucking gall to stand here, in the cottage *I paid for*, on the island I footed the money for you to be at and say you're breaking up with me."

"I—"

He moved away, chucking his clothes onto the bed, and fisting both hands in his hair. "This is…For fuck's sake, Pippi."

"Jackson—"

"I mean, how *ungrateful* can you fucking be? I buy you the trip of a lifetime. And this is the shit you pull?"

I buy you.

The island I footed the money for you to be at.

The cottage I paid for.

His words clicked together in my head. And my blood froze. "I thought you said this'd all been paid for? That you just took Zohar's spot?"

Jackson flashed me an incredulous "are you for real right now?" look. "Pippi, honestly, sometimes I wonder if you have a brain in that pretty head of yours. People don't just *give* shit like this away. Zohar *sold* me this trip."

My stomach swilled. With rage. And hurt. "That is *not* what you told me a few weeks ago."

"Because I didn't want you to get uppity about the money."

"We don't *have* this kind of money, Jackson!" I breathed.

"I made it work! *Barely*, thanks to your visit to the health clinic. But with Magix here, I figured…well, I've been working non-stop to recoup some of the financial loss and open some fucking doors for us." He sighed and leaned heavily against the bed. "You see why I'm upset? After all I've done." He shook his head.

After all I've done.

Like lying to me.

I'd severely, *woefully*, underestimated how much we'd been spending on this trip. He'd taken out a loan. Must have. Because I knew what we had in our bank accounts, and even if we'd pooled every cent together, it wouldn't have covered the cost of this trip.

I felt sick.

And why? *Why?* Why go into debt over this stupid island?

For prestige?

To show off? Flaunt that he'd been to an elite vacation spot?

For opportunity?

Had he *known* Rune was going to be here?

Had he dumped all our money into the one-in-a-million shot that he'd find the golden ticket?

I didn't know.

And I didn't ask. Because I'd lied to him too—he *still* didn't know about my friendship with Alistair—so I had no moral high ground to stand on.

But it *hurt*.

"I'm sorry," I muttered. "I...I *do* appreciate you, Jackson. *Everything* you do, everything you've done. And this timing is awful. And I'm *sorry*, but"—I fought to dredge the words from the pit of my stomach—"this has been coming for a while."

"The fuck it has."

"And this trip...we've not been happy. It's frankly been a *nightmare*. So I figured rather than stewing in this tension, it's better to pull it off the burner. Let it air out."

My hand started to jiggle. So I clasped my fingers together, twisting my knuckles until they crunched and popped.

"Oh, sure. Because you haven't done enough to fuck up this trip, why not add a breakup into the mix?" Jackson made a *huck* of disgust, picked up his clothes, and went to the bathroom, where he set about freshening himself up: pulling his deodorant and cologne out of his travel bag, washing the sea salt grit off his face, and tidying his hair.

His blurred figure moved and bounced through my teary eyes.

I'd seen Jackson freshen up dozens of times over the years. *Hundreds.* I knew his routine by heart. Had memorized the crisp scent of his deodorant and the clean fragrance of his cologne. And there was something devastating about watching him now, knowing it might be one of the last times I'd ever see his routine.

My heart rubbed its bloody hide against my insides, begging me to do something to take away the hurt.

But I just watched.

And cried.

I figured I'd spend my life with this man.

I loved him.

And I'd made the decision to leave him.

"Oh good, turn on the fucking waterworks. It's not gonna work, Pippi." Jackson's eyes met mine through the mirror. "*You're* the one who broke up with *me*. You don't get to be upset." He plucked his toothbrush out of his bag and set about cleaning his teeth in short, jerky motions.

His emotions crowded me, bludgeoning my wounded heart. But none of them were sorrow or heartache.

Disbelief.

Denial.

Disgust.

Rage most of all.

People often hid their hurt behind walls of anger—sometimes that was the last shield folks could erect to protect their heart. But there was a difference between a malleable buffer, weakly hoisted by a bruised soul, and the steel-solid door of Jackson's fury.

Jackson, can't you see *that the affection and adoration most couples have doesn't exist between us?*

Can't you feel *how empty our relationship is?*

You probably can't.

And I get it. Because I didn't feel it either.

Until I found that connection I'd been missing in someone else.

"I'm going to go to dinner. *Alone.*" Jackson spat toothpaste into the sink and rinsed his mouth. "And I'm going to enjoy whatever part of this vacation I can."

A tear tickled my cheek. I swiped it away. But more followed.

"You can head to your goofy friends next door. Or stay here. I don't care. I'm not giving up the bed, though." He turned, leaving his bathroom stuff scattered haphazardly along the counter, and bulldozed past me. "Don't wait up, *babe.*"

And then he was gone, slamming the door shut behind him.

Two of the watercolor paintings on the wall bounced right off their hangings and crashed to the floor.

RIPPING off a Band-Aid lashed some intense pain into your skin.

But after? Once the adhesive was gone and the sting had receded...

Relief.

Your flesh was clean and *new.*

The absence of pain left you wide eyed. *Alive.*

It was that rejuvenation that set me bolting out of my cottage at midnight, running down the cliff path—at a pace far too quick to be safe—and blurting to Alistair, "Let's go. Please. Somewhere. Anywhere. Where it's just the two of us."

He hadn't even said anything. I hadn't given him the chance to.

But I'd felt him there—his happiness, and sorrow, and relief, and hope, and all the wonderful, tentative emotions he had. They'd cradled my heart as soon as I'd slid to a precarious halt in my usual spot.

His answer massaged my brain, healing the pain that'd been mounting all day. "As you wish, Pippi."

I slipped out of my shoes and climbed the rest of the way down to him.

"Your clothing is lovely today," he added. "It always is. But those colors. All of them. They're..." he paused. Considering. "*Beautiful*. But that's not a strong enough word. And...and... your hair is different."

I still wore the rainbow blouse and pink skirt from the boat tour—I figured there'd been no point in getting changed just to get fresh clothes soaked in the sea—and my hair was still twisted into the woven bun Elisabeth had done for me.

"Thank you." I beamed as I clambered to my usual spot atop Alistair's head.

"I should have told you earlier. About the clothes. But I... When you d-d-disappeared...When he *pulled* you. You were gone. And people were speaking...*saying*...someone was s-s-s-sick. And...I worried." This was all said in a stuttering rush and accompanied by a residual sprinkle of fear.

Stars, he was *so* sweet.

I really, really, *really* liked him.

Too much.

"You're sure he didn't...hurt? He looked...ru-ro-rough," Alistair continued.

"I'm okay. Really." And, thankfully, my pulsating jaw was only a little red. The bone was definitely bruised, but the purple blotching hadn't spread to my skin. With the way Alistair grumbled disbelievingly, he never would've bought my *"no"* if I'd said it while sporting a shiner.

"Honestly," I insisted. "I'm fine."

"He seemed a-angry."

"He was. A little."

"That was your boyfriend?"

"*Was*. Yeah. Good choice of word, Alistair. *Was*. Although technically he might still be? It's a long story."

"Would you like to tell me?"

And I did.

Alistair took me to the other side of the inlet, where I sat on the cliffs, safely away from the sea, and he kept his head out of the water, resting it near me.

And I told him everything.

The fights. Plural. *Fights.*

The breakup.

The aggravation. The frustration. The sorrow. The heartbreak. All of it.

I didn't cry—pretty sure that well was bone dry—and the sound of my own voice as I spoke was eerie. I was too calm. Too detached.

But the anguish was there, circling my heart like a shark, waiting until I let my guard down before it swept in and consumed me.

"I'm so very sorry, Pippi." Alistair blew out, letting his warm, fish-scented breath stroke my body.

I was shaking.

And I hadn't even realized it.

I scooted over, pressing my hip into the side of his nose, wanting, *needing*, the contact.

He whiffled and nuzzled against me, giving what he could. "Is there anything I can do?"

I ran my hand over the coarse scales above his nostrils. "You could tell me that I made the right call, and I didn't just demolish my life on a whim. Even if it's a lie and you're really sitting there thinking I messed everything up. Tell me..." My fingers trembled. "Tell me I did the right thing."

"I think you did. And that's not a l-lie, Pippi."

"It just...we weren't *working*. Together."

"It doesn't sound like it."

"And I gave up so much of myself for Jackson. But it never felt like he was giving for me. And I was tired of our relationship being like that, all hollow and one-sided. Stars, what a selfish thing to say."

"You are *not*. S-selfish," Alistair huffed.

"I keep thinking it was kinder to let him go. But maybe it's cruel? Oh, goodness, I don't know." My hand curled into a fist. "It just wasn't working. And actually…the sex wasn't even that good."

A shocked laugh boomed out of Alistair.

"I'm being serious." A grin tugged at my lips.

"I didn't say you weren't." He wrestled to quiet his laughter. "I wasn't e-e-expecting that."

"I wasn't expecting to say it. It just sorta"—I touched my hands to my chest and then threw them outward with a low *blll-lluuuggggh* sound—"burst outta me. But yeah, it was pretty average. I mean, Jackson is *hot*—"

"Is he?" Alistair whiffed, as though I'd just rooted through the trash, pulled out some moldy five-day-old leftovers and called them art.

"*Yes*. Very. Unfairly. And I liked looking at him, y'know? Liked *feeling* him. So I'd drink all that in. The sights, the feelings, the noises he'd make, *everything*. And I'd tell myself the sex was good. Great, even. When it was…"

One-sided.

Underwhelming.

"…bland."

Bland.

Stars.

Could I have picked a *blander* word to describe the experience?

"Jackson never really cared about what I wanted," I prattled on before Alistair could say anything. "I gave him more flipping blowjobs than…" I shook my head, grunting in annoyance. "But heaven forbid I asked him to go down on me. Or for any foreplay. Or even cuddling…he *never* cuddled. Ever. I cuddled him. But he never cuddled me back. And I *love* cuddling."

This said as I moved even closer to Alistair, gluing every inch of my body to his head.

And he'd shifted closer to me, as though trying to do the same.

"I love c-cuddling too," he said.

"It's awesome, right? Jackson barely tolerated it. And..." I scoffed. "Talking about all this now, it's no wonder I had that dream about you. My brain was trying to tell me something. And you...I get that I don't know you all that well, and I'm really, *really* sorry if this is crossing any lines. You can tell me to shut up if it is. But I can't see you leaving a woman hanging. If you know what I mean."

"Ah," Alistair cooed. "No. I would not, never, leave a woman h-h-hanging."

"Didn't think so." I stroked his jaw, smiling when he purred. "This is getting weird, though. Isn't it? I'm sure you don't want to hear about my sexual blues. I'm sorry, Alistair."

"It's not," he said. "Weird."

"Only sad and pathetic, right?"

"No." He nestled his nose more firmly against me. "I un-under...stand...understand. Pippi, you forget...I had a dream too."

"Ah, that's right. The one you said I was naughty in."

"Hmmm. But you never c-c-confirmed if I was naughty in *yours*." His eye shifted, fixating on my face. "Was I?"

That *voice*...

Combined with that intense stare that stripped right through my flesh and peeped into my soul...*Goodness.*

My belly quivered as heat flooded it, making me ache.

I laughed. Tightly. And it was a delicious torture as it vibrated through my body.

"You were," I rasped. "Plenty naughty."

"Oh, yes?"

"If you want more details"—I booped the tip of his nose—"I think we'll have to agree on a fair exchange. You tell me the naughty things I did in your dream, and I'll tell you what you did in mine."

His nostrils billowed. "You r-r-rode me."

Which...

I didn't know what I'd expected him to say. But it hadn't been that.

"*I rode you?*"

"Yes." A shudder quaked his body.

"I...*Interesting.*" Hot. Okay. That was *hot.* Although... "I don't quite think the mechanics of that would work."

An image flipped into my head.

There and gone, in less than an instant. So fast, I couldn't absorb it. But fragments of the flash lingered.

Me straddling the tall man from my dream. *Riding* him. Watching his sweat-slick body strain beneath me and savoring his anguished mewls and grunts.

Well...

I was officially, thoroughly, and *uncomfortably*, turned on.

"Anything can work. In a dream," Alistair said.

"Yeah." I gulped. "Guess so."

"And you?" Alistair asked.

"Me?" I parroted dumbly.

"What naughtiness did I do? In your dream?"

"Oh. *OH.* I...We...we...There was...kind of a lot. But the bulk of it...you were...pleasuring me. Under the stars."

"I was?" Alistair's voice deepened. Roughened. "How?"

Stars. Help me.

"With your mouth."

He rumbled, and his arousal plowed into my side like a javelin thrown by an Olympic athlete. It stole my breath, leeched every ounce of blood out of my head. All of it. Every single drop. It all rushed down, pooling between my legs.

Brains *needed* blood to operate.

Because otherwise, they blurted stuff like this: "Would you... since we both...you know...had wet dreams...would you wanna...*not* have them be dreams? Make them real?"

Alistair sucked in a big breath, one that fanned out the gills along the side of his neck.

"Obviously some things we can't...but other things we can. Right? If we get imaginative. Would you want to?"

Blackness pooled across his eyes as his pupils dilated, almost choking out the orange. "I would love to."

Thank the stars.

Because in the half a second between me finishing the question and him answering it, I'd started to feel mighty stupid. And almost predatory, propositioning him.

What was I thinking?

"But I want you in the water," Alistair continued.

"Oh."

"These rocks are n-n-narrow. I don't want you to fall."

"I mean." I gulped. "We don't actually *have* to do anything. I was..."

Wishing out loud.

Letting my ravaged emotions turn me into a horndog.

Alistair barked a pained-sounding laugh. "I *want* to. More than anything. I want to *t-t-taste* you."

A tinny *eeeeep* squeaked out of me.

He chuckled.

"You can't *say* stuff like that," I muttered.

"Why?"

And I had no answer for him. Because if I told him I liked it —too much—he'd milk it for all it was worth.

But I think he knew anyway, with the way his delight coursed through me.

"The waters are calm." Alistair rubbed his nose soothingly against me. "There are rocks you can hold on to. I can p-p-p-pleasure you. Like in your dream. In the water—you'll be safe, Pippi. I promise."

Safe.

He never needed to remind me of that. The security was there with him, always, wrapped around me like a cushy blanket. It was the only reason I clambered down the side of the cliffs, holding on to his nose for balance.

But some uncertainty snuck into that security blanket as I neared the bottom, where the water sploshed against the rocks.

I shook. My legs trembling, fingers numb, as I slid my

panties down my leg. Not teasing or putting on a strip show, just fighting for composure and balance.

Alistair groaned softly.

I felt like the sexist stripper in the world, with the way Alistair watched me. With the soft noises he made. With the way his breathing deepened.

He rubbed his nose against me once the panties were gone, in a sweet, affectionate pet.

I folded my panties—actually took the time to tuck them into a neat little square—before I placed them on a rock. It was the few seconds I needed to convince myself that I really *did* want this. That Alistair really wanted it too.

And when guilt started circling my heart, reminding me that I'd only just broken things off with Jackson, I told it to stuff itself.

37

I decide I *do* hate Onyx.

For filling my head with words and taking them back.

For leaving me in this moment without a way to…*express* myself.

"Would you want to not have them be dreams?"

"Make them real?"

There is so much…

So much *feeling*.

I am *alive*.

Pippi removes her…

I know this word.

Know it.

The cloth that sits under her clothes. Protecting that soft, forbidden area.

I *know* the word.

But it's slipped.

She shakes. As she unclothes. There's fear in her eyes again.

I don't want her afear…afraid.

I breathe. Heavily. Warming her. Letting her feel the things I don't have words for.

She smiles.

And it *hurts* to see her this way. A good hurt. A hurt that is sharp. Consuming. But also…*pleasurable*.

It's been so long.

So long since I've felt touches from another human.

So long since I've laughed.

Talked.

Cuddled.

Desired.

So long since I've felt like a living *man.* Rather than an empty beast.

Pippi has given me all this. Given me life. Wants. *Dreams.*

I touch her. My nose against her arm. Her *skin.*

The contact *hurts.*

I want more. To touch everywhere. With my human hands. And human body. I want to *feel* her.

But what I have now is…

It's…

Precious.

Her looks. Her touches. The scent of her…she's…around… *aroused.* As am I.

She can feel mine. I can smell hers. And it's enthralling.

That she trusts me.

That she *wants* me.

I can't…I don't have the words.

And when she slides into the water, I stop looking for those words.

I just…*feel.*

listair disappeared.

He'd carried me into the sea and waited until I had a secure handhold on a stooped rock. And then he'd gone under, leaving me bobbing up and down with the lazy waves, my skirt pooching in the water around me, my underside floating bare underneath.

Fear might've crept in then. Even though I was securely holding a rock, the ocean and I would never be on friendly terms. But I *trusted* Alistair. And—

Something slithered up my leg.

"Oooh!" I squealed, jumped, and whacked my shoulder against the rock.

"It's me, Pippi," Alistair laughed.

"Don't *do* that. I thought it was a *snake*!"

"A snake?"

"Some of them swim, don't they?"

"Yessssssssss." He sucked the S between his teeth.

"You're too much sometimes." I dug my nails into the porous rock. "Has anyone ever told you—" I jolted and kicked out when that slithery thing danced along my inner thigh.

"Oh dear," Alistair said. "You're very…s…s…j-j-jumpy."

"What—is—is that your *tongue*?" I squawked.

"Yes."

Stars help me.

He had to hold the Guinness World Record for the longest tongue known to man or beast. Because the organ was wrapped around my thigh, and still had enough excess to dribble down to my calf.

I gulped.

Alistair chuffed and massaged the tip of his tongue against my shin, calming me.

"In my defense," I said, "this feels...*strange*."

"Strange how?"

The sheer length of it was odd, for one.

The textures, for another. Its topside was as abrasive as a cat's tongue. But Alistair wielded it gingerly, letting me feel the scrape of the organ against my skin, but not allowing the bristles to dig or gouge.

"Pippi?" Alistair pressed when I didn't answer. "Strange how?"

His concern fluttered in my belly.

"It's different," I managed. "I guess. And *weird* that you can talk while doing that."

"Ah...Well..." His tongue arched up, brushing my upper thigh before receding. "I'm not talking."

"That's right. You're—"

I froze.

Because his snake-like tongue vanished.

And I *did not* like the sudden burbling of mischief in my chest.

Okay, no, I liked it. A lot. Too much.

"Alistair?"

He hummed.

"What are you—" A groan burst out of me when he dragged his tongue between my legs in light, quick strokes.

It was shocking, having a rough appendage caressing that delicate area.

Shocking how *good* it felt.

How quickly it left me aching. Wanting.

Alistair disappeared again.

My nails clawed into the rock as I instinctively bucked my hips, searching for him.

"That sound"—he dropped his voice to a gravelly octave that had me shivering—"was *lovely*. What others do you make?"

"I—*ummmpfffff!*" I gasped when his tongue returned, tickling and teasing until I writhed.

And then he was gone. *Again.*

I whimpered.

He returned, slithering that tongue around my bum, tickling the lower part of my back, but leaving without touching that throbbing area between my legs.

I hefted myself more firmly against the rock.

Alistair twined that devilish organ around my midsection, beneath my blouse, and lavished at my belly button until I squiggled, laughing, and *aching*.

He left again.

I hissed.

He chuckled.

And, this time, it was the hard, craggy shape of his nose that touched me. It rubbed against my legs. My belly. My butt. Not in a way to amp me up, this was a reassuring touch.

I leaned into it.

He purred.

"Could you turn, Pippi?" His tongue touched my back in a soothing swipe. "Face away from the cliffs."

I did. Because how could I not, when he asked in such a seductive drawl?

"Yes," Alistair croaked. "Like that. Open your body more."

I shivered, but some of the delight withered when the angle dipped me a little farther into the water.

My paddling feet connected with something solid and squishy.

Alistair.

"You're still safe, Pippi," Alistair said as I dragged my other foot onto...whatever body part I was standing on. "But if you ever feel not...safe...tell me to stop. Okay?"

"Okay." My overfull heart struggled to stay afloat over the

flood of affection, and excitement, and nerves, and...*everything*. All the vibrant emotions pulsating through both of us.

"Good," Alistair rasped.

His tongue wormed up my legs, the tip gyrating over my clit. Stroking gingerly—so, so gingerly.

Stars...

I arched back, one hand clenching the rock, the other paddling frantically through the water.

Alistair explored. Slowly. Lazily. Fondling every inch of my body he could get his tongue on and lavishing that sensitive bundle of nerves until I strained and panted.

My pleasure rose to a frighteningly fast boil. It stole my breath. Made my vision go all bright and fuzzy.

"Oh, Alistair." I arched my back, heaving, when he applied enough pressure to have me seeing stars. Zaps of ecstasy electrified my blood, bringing me so, so, so very close to boiling over.

His arousal answered, spiking into me with enough force to steal my breath.

We were feeding each other. Alistair and I.

The more pleasure he gave me, the more aroused he got.

The more aroused he got, the more pleasure I felt.

It was intoxicating.

Had it *ever* been like this before?

He dragged the bristles of his tongue over my legs, my butt, my clit. Letting me feel the prickling sting. Then he quieted the movements, soothing the light scrapes he'd left.

My head swam. And the heat inside my belly wrapped into a painfully tight coil. I *keened*.

"Lovely," he murmured.

He turned his tongue in long, lazy strokes, alternating between light and hard pressure. Soft and scraping.

My poor body was so confused.

The pleasure was unlike *anything*. It blacked out my mind. Made me see stars. Everything fell away—the waves, the rumble of the ocean, the harsh bite of the stone under my hand, the cold claws of the water. The world shrank to that sensitive bundle between my thighs, and the way it *throbbed* beneath Alistair's tongue.

The coiling pressure in my belly mounted to an uncomfortable burn.

I strained for release. Reaching for it. Moaning as Alistair dipped his tongue between my legs, fanning the heat, the ache, until I was ready to explode.

But the release wouldn't come.

I grunted. And bucked. And cried. Frustrated now. *Worried.*

I was dangling over the edge. But I didn't know how to fall.

"Relax, Pippi," Alistair murmured as I flailed, chasing the release, and crying as it escaped before I could reach it.

Relax?

Stars, how could I, when—

"Let me bring it to you," he whispered. "Trust me."

Water splashed over my face as I struggled.

His nose rubbed against my thighs. "Relax. You're safe, Pippi."

He pressed his tongue, hard, between my legs.

I wailed.

A deep purr ripped through him, rattling my entire body. "You are so lovely. I wish…"

Again, an image flashed in my head, like a splash of water, there and gone. Even trying to grab it this time didn't work—it trickled through my fingers—but some fragments lingered.

That lean, long-limbed man crouched between my legs, his silken mop of curly hair tickling my thighs as his mouth latched to my clit, suckling. His hands pressed into my lower belly, massaging, holding me still. Forcing me to feel every ounce of sensation.

I reached for that man. Wanting to look into his eyes as I came untangled beneath his ministrations.

But my hand only swatted at water.

"I wish I could. Hold you." Alistair's nose rubbed against my front, stroking my breasts, while his tongue continued to work between my legs.

A new emotion assaulted me.

Love.

I sobbed. And my overwrought body finally came undone.

I squeezed my eyes shut as the orgasm ploughed through me, hard enough to send my body twisting into bone-rattling shudders. To have me seeing stars.

It ebbed slowly, leaving me panting. Weak. Shivering.

My arm slid bonelessly over the rock. And panic spiked my gut when my sluggish limbs sank into the water.

But then Alistair was under me, placing me securely onto his head and lifting me out of the sea.

I flopped onto my back between his horns and panted. *Laughed.*

I'd never had an orgasm rip through me like that. *Never.* Even when I had found release before, it'd never left me…

Giddy.

Drunk.

Content.

"Goodness, don't let *anyone* else on the isle know you have a tongue like that." I idly smoothed my wet skirt over my legs. "You'll have all the women lining up. Married. Unmarried. Lesbian. Doesn't matter. You'll be licking until your tongue falls off."

"My tongue"—Alistair fluffed with pride—"is only for you, Pippi."

A tingle of pleasure snaked up my spine. I shivered.

"Are you cold?" he asked.

"*No.*" I was the opposite—feverish, almost. "That was…I mean…it…" I laughed. Again. "I think you broke me,Alistair."

"Good." He chuckled.

"Now"— I flipped over, pulling myself shakily to my feet— "it's time to brainstorm."

"I'm sorry?"

I breathed in, absorbing the arousal still simmering in him. "On how I can break *you.* Unfortunately, we can't reenact your dream. I don't think all the lube in the world, magic or not, would make that anything less than excruciating. Y'know? Assuming…I mean…No, I'm just gonna leave that there. But I can do other things."

Alistair trembled.

I grinned, even as his shudders nearly upset my footing.

"You do *not* have to," he said. Firmly. "What you gave me is enough."

"I *want* to, though." I bent and stroked his head. "At least as much as I can. I enjoy giving pleasure. Most of the time. When it's not one-sided…which it's not, with you. And I don't know realistically how much I can do for you, but would you let me try? Please?"

"Well"—his voice broke around a bubble of desire—"if you i-i-i-in..sist. *Insist*."

That voice was going to be the death of me. Especially with it all hoarse and needy.

"I do. Insist," I said.

"Then—" He broke off. Fear and excitement warred through him, murdering some of his impishness.

He was *shy*.

Worried.

And I'd never known that could be a turn-on—to have a strong, self-assured male *hesitate*. But lust *pounded* through me, responding to the bashfulness in his voice.

"I'll need you to come back in the water." Alistair lowered his head slowly. Almost dazedly.

"Okay." I slid off the side of his nose once the surf rose to my knees and scrabbled for the rock again.

"You're sure?" Alistair asked.

"Positive."

With a *schlooooopp*, he disappeared beneath the surface.

"I'll roll over," he said, "you can stand on my belly. It will be s-s-s-s-s…slippery. Be c-c-careful."

His stammering worsened when he was flustered.

And I was finding I *really* liked a flustered Alistair. It was adorable. Wholesome. And it made me feel *protective*. Over the forty-foot sea beast. What a hoot.

Under the water, something solid bumped against the bottoms of my feet. I shifted, spread my legs more evenly, and bent my knees. Alistair rose, allowing his behemoth body to float to the surface, leaving me standing on the gentle curve of his belly.

His heaving, quivering belly.

The soaked scales were a bit like wet tile—*treacherously* slick. And with his stomach rising and falling in such heavy beats, standing was almost impossible. My feet immediately skated sideways, grappling for purchase.

Concern flooded him when he felt me flailing.

So I parked my butt down. Once I was seated and secure, I got a proper look at the green scales blanketing his stomach. "They're *glittery!*" I rubbed my fingers over the shimmering flesh. "Oh, Alistair, this is gorgeous." It was the way I'd always imagined a mermaid's tail would look: iridescent and radiant, twinkling beneath even the fog-smothered light.

"It's a d-d-d-d-defense mek-mekh-a...mechanism. The color," Alistair stammered breathlessly.

"It is?"

"It s-s-shines above the surface. Below, it b-b-b-blends in."

"Ah, so you've got a camouflage belly." I kneaded my hands into him. Soothing him, the way he'd soothed me. Fanning my fingers along the swell of his stomach. Digging my knuckles in.

"Can you feel it? When I do this? Am I using enough pressure?" I pressed my palms into him.

"*Yes*. I can feel it." He shuddered and his flappers sloshed through the water, pushing him a little farther above the surface, exposing more of his underside to me.

But you know what I *didn't* see?

I peered around the mound of flesh.

Part of his tail was visible above the water. So was the base of his neck. The tips of his flappers bobbed above the surface.

But there was no penis in sight.

"Ermmm…" Doubt clawed into me. Had I just done something cruel? Offered to get him off when he had no *equipment* to get off with?

"Alistair, do you…I mean…You have one, right?"

A nervous laugh pulsated through him. "Yes. It's behind you."

I scooched my butt back to the dip where his torso melted into his tail.

There was nothing there.

"Below your hand," Alistair said. "It's a…sl-sl…slit."

"Oh. Ummm…" There was, indeed, a thin cleft splitting his glimmering scales.

"You can s-stroke that," he told me.

Interesting.

I rose to my knees and touched my hands to the slit. Slick heat spewed off it, and it spasmed when I pressed down, rubbing lightly.

A groan shook Alistair's entire body.

"Does this…oh…*Oh!*" A gasp shook me when the cleft gave a hearty, undulating pulse and peeled itself apart, opening into a yawning gap for a pale pink cock to wriggle out of.

Very, very interesting.

And *terrifying*.

Because the organ immediately engorged itself to impossible heights, stretching four…five…*six feet* into the air. At least.

His cock was longer than my *entire body*.

I gaped.

His penis throbbed as it flopped over his belly.

How on earth was this going to work?

There was no way.

None.

Nada.

My insides wept with pain at the sight of that monster dick, at the thought of putting it anywhere near my sensitive areas.

Genius idea, Pippi. Real Einstein move. He's forty feet long. What did you expect would happen?

I hadn't thought this far ahead.

I'd just wanted to make him happy.

And when his uncertainty pumped into my stomach—because he'd sensed me hesitate and likely knew where my thoughts had gone—I blew out a breath and steeled myself.

"It's alright," I murmured, stroking the side of his stomach—not yet brave enough to put my hands near that behemoth organ.

He sighed. Tightly. But his worry was still jumbling around in a big tumbleweed.

I hated feeling that.

Hated that I was wavering instead of reassuring him.

Hated that he'd put himself in such a vulnerable position, giving me his trust, and I was destroying it.

So I went all in, smoothing my hand along that throbbing pink root.

But another issue presented itself.

Alistair's cock took *rock hard* to a whole other level. The organ had no give in it. None. Not at the root, at least. It was as solid as a rod of steel. I'd break my fingers trying to knead it.

But when I shimmied myself up further, where the tip thinned into a loose curl, the velvety flesh became malleable.

So I focused there, massaging my fingers into the hot, quavering flesh, drinking in the throaty sigh that escaped him.

He twitched. Stiffened. And the tip of his cock moved, bending itself backward, and coiling loosely around my arm.

Oh gosh…

It was *flexible?*

Alistair groaned.

White-hot arousal punched itself through me. My vision hazed as my body locked in a tight convulsion, so very similar to the one that'd gripped me when I orgasmed. And I almost came again—from *Alistair.* From the delight and desire and *want* that burned through him.

The tip of his cock tightened its hold on my arm. A grip that should've been painful. But it was *exhilarating.*

And, suddenly, my body was moving. Drunkenly. Knowing

what it wanted, even if my pleasure-soaked brain was a little behind the eight ball.

I lifted my leg over the center of the undulating organ and straddled it, savoring the way its girth stretched and spread my thighs, even as my hips gave a feeble creak of protest.

He said he dreamed of being ridden, right?

Alistair's breathing froze. "Pippi?"

"This is as close as I can get to your dream," I said as I dragged myself up and down along the length of his cock—or, well, the length I could *reach*.

And Alistair's whimpered breaths said my instincts were spot on.

"Please don't stop." He groaned as the tip unfurled from my arm, clutched in a hard spasm.

"I won't."

Up and down, I went, squeezing my arms and legs around him. Rubbing my hands into that silky, silky flesh. Drinking in the sounds he made—all the moans, and growls, and mewls.

And when he arched the tip of his cock back again, clumsily sliding it between my stretched thighs...

"*Oohhh.*" I bucked.

I take back every bad thing I'd ever thought about his cock.

My eyes clenched shut as we pleasured each other.

This is perfect.

Better than perfect.

It's...

Alistair roared and gyrated—not hard enough to unseat me, but enough to send my hands grappling. His flappers beat at the water, splattering me with cold, fizzing surf.

"I'm close, Pippi," he grunted. "*Please* don't stop."

How could I? When his reactions, his pleasured whimpers, his squirming...It all had me *thrumming* with want again.

And with that thin tip wriggling between my legs...

I hissed and ground down on him until we both keened.

"Pippi!" Panic lanced Alistair's voice. "Pippi, I—"

Whoosh.

Another of those snapshot images slammed into my closed eyes. This one lingered for only an aggravatingly brief heartbeat.

I straddled that tall, long-limbed man. And his hot cock pulsed *inside* of me. He reached up as I rode him, pulling me down, capturing my mouth in a rough, desperate kiss. I touched his face, letting my hands feel what my eyes never seemed to be able to make out: the high, sharp cut of his cheekbones; the prominent brow; the damp ringlets of curly hair; and the lush curve of his lips.

He growled and pulled me closer, squeezing his arms around my torso, and pressing his face into my neck as he yelled through his release.

And my second orgasm *exploded* inside of me.

I gasped. Cried. My toes curled. My back bowed.

It almost hurt to come like this. This *fully*.

Alistair bellowed and his cock gave an almighty surge before it burst, *literally*, shooting buckets, *gallons*, of cum over his belly and into the sea. In a way that was dirty and unnatural and delicious and...

Everything.

This was everything.

I pressed my lips against his emptying organ.

Alistair gasped. "Oh, Pippi."

I stroked him—gently—with shaking hands.

He hissed. Twitched. And, with a heavy "Grugh," he sank back into the sea, leaving me alone in the water, sputtering and fighting to get my rubbery limbs working.

"I'm sorry!" He rose beneath me again—his head, this time, my feet recognized the curve of his brow—and then I was safely away from the sea's clutches.

"Ooomf!" My bottom smacked against the stone as he deposited me, as gently as he was able to, in his shaken state, back on to the cliffs. And then his snout was all over me. Nuzzling. Blowing warm air to dry me. Nuzzling me again. Whuffling through my hair. Nuzzling some more.

He was…

Alistair dragged the side of his nostril across my cheek.

Cuddling.

He couldn't wrap me in his arms and hold me against him. So he rubbed, warming me. Caressing and comforting my body as it crashed from its high.

I reached for him, twining my arm under his chin and pressing my forehead to his nose.

And then we held on to each other.

39

Alistair might have truly broken my brain. Because time mashed itself into a big, steamy vat of potatoes during the second half of my stay at Niverwick.

Jackson refused to talk to me.

We shared a cottage because we had to. But we'd become two strangers who occupied the same living space.

And I hated that.

Hated that this man I'd loved, and lived with for three years, suddenly seemed so estranged. As though the life we'd built together hadn't happened.

I tried to talk to him. He ignored me. So I wrote him letters and tucked them in the drawer with his boxers. And I poured *everything* into my writing, articulating my feelings.

I think when we met, I hadn't fully grasped who Pippi Long was. I didn't know what I wanted out of life. But I do now. And I'm sorry I had to string you along on the quest to figure myself out. Penning a hope for his future, and for mine: *Jackson, you'll be okay. You're smart and enigmatic and driven. This life is going to bow to you one day and give you everything you've ever wanted. You'll be happy, I promise, as will I, when we've been able to put this hurt behind us. Time will give us clarity. One day we'll look back on this and realize this decision was the best thing for us.*

So much love and care went into those words.

He crumbled them up and threw them away.

IN AN EFFORT not to dwell on Jackson, and the utter mess I'd made of our lives, I spent the last couple of days of my vacation...*vacationing.*

Chunks of time meandered by as I wandered the isle. Usually alone. And sometimes with Melany and Sarah, who knew what'd happened between me and Jackson, but were very careful to avoid talking about it.

On a soggy evening, when rain lolled in the air above our heads, threatening to fall, but never following through, they took me to a field on the northern part of the isle where they'd found the will-o'-the-wisps. And I'd awed at those beautiful, fluttering spirals of light. They were like jellyfish. The sort you'd see on an undersea screensaver, all glowy and ethereal, floating effortlessly through the air. Cajoling us into following their dance with an unspoken promise (a lie) that we'd float above our problems too, if only we'd join them.

"I can see why people get wrecked, following these things to their doom," I'd said.

"I've already tried to follow them." Melany turned her guilty grin toward me. "They're so pretty and squishy. I wanted to see what they felt like."

"Did you touch one?"

"I did." Another shamefaced smile. "And got the shock of a lifetime."

"Her hair was standing on end." Sarah laughed.

"Yeah, don't touch them, Pippi." Melany snatched my arm and tucked my hand against her side, as though shielding me from the mistake she'd made.

The next afternoon I went for a hike. Alone this time, although I met enough people along the path to whet my appetite for conversation. It was invigorating, winding along rocky trails through the mountains, weaving around the curtains of fog and mist, and finding fields and valleys blanketed with the greenest grass I'd ever seen. A spattering of flowers had begun to bloom, and the trees—all slanted and curved to accommodate the hilly and rocky terrain—were proudly showing off the first buds of their summer leaves.

It was a different world up there, on the northernmost point of the isle. And it was the first time things looked, and felt, *magical.*

Or maybe that was the spark of new love slipping rose-colored glasses over my eyes, making everything seem more vibrant and majestic.

Because my nights were spent with Alistair. And my heart was so far gone, lost to this creature from the sea, that I didn't think I'd ever get it back.

Sometimes we cuddled, with his nose nuzzling me as we sat in silence. Other times we talked about the things that made us sad, as well as the things that uplifted us. About the unfairness of life and the cruel irony fate often teased us with.

Sometimes we played and laughed and teased. Sometimes we seduced.

And the *sex*.

Oh my goodness.

The *s-e-x*.

One night, I lay up on the cliffs and masturbated while he brushed his nose against my arm, talking to me. Coaxing me. And I hadn't been entirely into it at first. But his *voice*—when he dragged that husky timbre over my brain, murmuring nonsense words and terms of endearment—it was enough to have me shoving my hand between my legs and working myself until I reached that spine-tingling orgasm.

And, somehow, my voice did the same for him, even if I was absolutely *horrid* at dirty pillow talk.

"Er...I'm going to suck you dry, and...Oh stars, I sound like a *vampire!*" I grinned and thumped his nose when he choked on a richly amused laugh. "'*I vant to suck vur blood.*' Goodness. I told you I'm awful at this."

"You're lovely, Pippi. Always." Alistair whuffled. And then groaned, when I rubbed my hands along his nose and muttered, "I wish I could actually get you in my mouth, though."

I couldn't see how he pleasured himself, and me asking, or trying to envision it out loud, usually made him writhe, so I asked a lot.

He told me I was lovely. Again, and again, and again, as he worked himself into a release. I'd never be able to hear that word again without either bawling my eyes out or flushing in embarrassment.

We pleasured each other as well, the way we had that first night. And every time I orgasmed, I saw visions of that long-limbed man. The one I dreamed about. The one who held me so tenderly and lovingly, while he kissed and suckled and yelled my name as he came undone.

And I knew this was the man Alistair had once been. Before the curse had gripped the island and twisted its inhabitants into new forms.

This was where the cruelty of fate came in.

Because I wanted that man. Wanted Alistair.

I laughed more with him than I ever had with Jackson. I felt sexy and free and content, as I dreamed and played and experienced.

For the first time in thirty-five years, I *lived*.

I'd had to nearly die in the jaws of the sea to find myself. To figure out what my heart and soul wanted.

But the rapidly closing week was going to snatch all those discoveries away.

"I DON'T WANT TO GO," I whispered on my very last night on the island. The final time Alistair, as he'd lamented, would get to wear his "favorite hat."

I hadn't stayed on his head though, because I'd been too antsy to see him. So I treaded water beside him, suffering the cold, for a chance to explore his body.

Alistair twisted his neck, watching me.

"I could stay. You know…" I palmed his side.

"You can't," he said.

"Who says?" I traced my hand along the swell of his back. "I'm sure the isle is hiring. And I'd probably like working in tourism. Getting to meet new people every week. Listening to their stories and sharing their experiences."

"Without ever living those stories and e-e-experiences yourself," Alistair said.

I paused. "This week has been *more* experience than most people get in an entire lifetime."

"But you shouldn't settle for one week. You should *want* more. If you stay here…the…they…the isle…" He shook his head, working at the words. "The isle s-s-staff…they came here because they had nowhere else. They stay, because they can't a-a-a-afford to go anywhere else. They talk," he added when I started to ask how he could possibly know that. "If you stay, you'd be trapped."

"There are worse places to be trapped. I'd at least have you." I peered up at him.

His nostrils billowed as anguish and longing curdled my insides. "No, Pippi. You freed yourself. Of that quagmire you spoke of. I won't be the reason you become trapped in another."

My nose twitched as tears tickled it.

He was right. Of course. A week on this isle, surrounded by the fog, had worn on me. A lifetime of staying on this little slab of rock, surrounded by the sea, suffocated by magic, never seeing the sun or the stars or the moon—it would destroy me. Eventually.

But leaving Alistair behind would destroy me as well.

"What will happen to you?" I whispered. "When I leave?"

"I'll stay here." He touched the tip of his nose to the top of my head in a soft, lingering kiss.

"Alone?"

A consoling purr tumbled out of him.

"Do you have other people you can talk to? People who can keep you company?"

"None who can hear me," he said. "I'll be okay. Pippi. I p-p-promise."

But a deep sorrow hammered into my bones, nearly sending me sinking into the water.

Alistair hastily recalled his errant emotion, murmuring apologies as he nuzzled the top of my head.

"I'm so sorry, Alistair, I—" I yelped when something slithery and solid swatted my butt beneath the water.

Alistair's laugh warmed my insides.

"What"—I puckered my lips at him—"body part was that?"

With a *whoosh,* the whip-like tip of his tail popped out of the water and waved at me.

"We haven't ex...ex...experimented with this. Yet," Alistair said.

"I'm not sure if we should. I'm pretty open-minded—" I squealed when Alistair snaked the tail along the water and gently flicked water in my face. "But I might have to draw the line at getting banged by a butt extender. Who knows where that thing has been—"

"A *butt extender?*" Alistair sonic boomed that laugh.

I hefted myself against him to avoid the angry onslaught of waves.

"You're safe, Pippi." He wrapped his tail around me to keep me steady. "Always. Even from my d-dirty butt extender." The tip of his tail caressed my cheek as his mouth brushed the top of my head.

"Pippi..." He chawed on my name, savoring it until it gummed up his tongue, making it hard for him to get the rest of the words out.

"Pippi...Pippi, you...I..."

I craned my head, kissing his nose when I felt his aggravation burbling.

"I'll miss you," he finally said.

"Oh, Alistair." I leaned into him, sighing when his tail gave my midsection a comforting smoosh. "I'll miss you too."

40

Dawn came too quickly.

I hated when time did that.

I'd stared at my phone calendar before we'd left home and had wanted to weep at how far away the end of this trip had seemed. But now it was here, and I wept at how frustratingly short that final night had been.

I'd started crying when Alistair mumbled, reluctantly, that he'd have to take me back through the inlet.

"The waters…the *tide* will lower. Soon. It's time, Pippi."

The tears only worsened as he swam slowly through the rocks. And by the time he dropped me off at our usual spot, I was fully in the throes of big, snot-faucet central sobs.

"Oh, dear," Alistair said as I stepped off his head and clambered up the rocks. I slipped once. Twice. Both times he made sounds of distress. So I gulped a breath down, squeegeed the tears away, and got my feet back under me.

"You'll be alright, Pippi," he murmured as I popped my feet back in my shoes. "C-c-c-chin up…that's the saying. Yes?"

"Yes." I sighed and stared at the sloshing water beneath the rocks. "It feels wrong to say goodbye when I can't *see* you."

"Hmmm, it's for the best. I turn into a beast. With the sun. Didn't you know?"

I huffed.

"A huh-horrible, ugly beast. With big, ugly feet."

"I hate to break it to ya, but your feet were ugly under moonlight too."

He extruded a mock gasp. "*Oh no.* And I thought I'd…c-cast a spell. To make me seem dash-dashing to your eyes. Didn't it work?"

Gosh, what a goofball.

"It worked," I said, "a little *too* well." I paused, chewing on my next words, hoping they wouldn't hurt him too badly. "I think I love you, Alistair."

Euphoria seeped into every core of my body, making my limbs feel light and springy, as though I could leap off the cliffs and soar to the sky. But sorrow followed, grinding into my bones, reminding them they belonged planted on the earth.

"I think I love you as well," Alistair whispered.

"Then why...? I should *stay*."

"No."

"I can head to the lobby and ask for a job application. I—"

"Go home, Pippi. Please. This...here...*staying* here...it's not a life for you. I want you to *live*. Please."

"I don't want to leave you here alone."

"I'll be okay. I promise."

But he felt so sad.

All I wanted to do was hug him. Hold him. Protect him. Burrow myself into him and never come back out.

"They torture you here, Alistair," I croaked.

"I'll be okay, Pippi," he repeated adamantly. "Please. Go. Live. For me."

And there were so many other things I wanted to say.

I wanted to promise I'd see him again, even though I knew I'd never have the money to venture back out to the isle. I wanted to say I'd find a way to free him from the magic binding him here, even though that was a complete and utter pipe dream. Even if I understood how the magic worked, it wouldn't do me a lick of good since I was a plain ole Standie.

I should have done *more*. Dug into the mechanics of the isle. Verified if the other creatures suffered the same as him. Drilled the tourists to see if they knew how the main attractions were treated and raised the flag of awareness if they didn't.

I should've helped him.

And I wanted to tell him all of that—to apologize for all the things I hadn't done.

But he uttered a mournful, "Goodbye, Pippi." And then his emotions left me.

He was gone, returned to the sea.

And I had no choice but to return to the land.

THE COTTAGE DOOR shouted an overdramatic *eeeeeeep* into the quiet foyer when I pushed it open.

I froze.

But no movement came from the bedroom, where Jackson still slept. So I tiptoed the rest of the way in, trying to ignore the zesty-flavored guilt fish wriggling around the base of my throat, and squinted around the dark cottage.

Jackson's packed bags were still stacked where he'd left them in the living room yesterday. My stuff was strewn everywhere. Because I'd started to pack but had been distracted by Jackson's unusual silence as he'd gathered his own stuff, and the bitterness that'd filled our cottage like a noxious chemical cloud. And I'd been focused on Alistair, counting down the hours until I could see him, feeling wretched for thinking that way in Jackson's presence.

So my packing was not finished. I'd have to do a full speedrun once Jackson woke up.

But for now, I needed a shower. Desperately. The brine rising off my skin made my nose itch.

I crossed the room, untying the band I'd looped around my hair.

Something glittered on my right side. I turned. And jumped about a foot into the air when a luminous pair of jade green eyes blinked at me from atop Jackson's suitcase.

In the bedroom, Jackson grunted. Snorted. And carried on snoring.

Thank the stars he slept like the dead.

Because when Marvin the cat said, "Hello, Pippi."

I screamed.

Marvin flattened his ears. "You may not be aware of this, but cats have substantially better hearing than humans. Screaming hurts."

"I'm sorry. I—"

Jackson still snored away, but I clapped my hands over my mouth anyway.

Marvin sat up, yawned, and stretched, dragging his nails into the top of the suitcase.

"H-how..." I stared around the cottage—at the closed windows and the door I'd shut behind me. "How did you get in here?"

Marvin popped his bum down, waving his long tail idly behind him. His bottle-green eyes narrowed, as though he found me to be the dumbest creature who'd ever walked the earth. "I can get into *any* building on this isle."

"That's...I can't imagine that's okay. For you to squat in people's homes." I peeped through the half-open door to the bedroom, watching Jackson's sleeping form. "And my boyfriend's allergic to cats—"

"He's not."

"Pardon?

"He's not allergic to cats." Marvin apathetically licked his left paw and swiped it over his face.

"He is—"

"No. He's not. I've spent most nights in this cottage over the past week, and he never so much as sneezed."

"You...*what*? You could've made him sick! Because he *is* allergic. To all animals."

"He lies." Marvin rubbed at his cheeks. "If he had truly been allergic, I would've waited outside. But I saw little point in making myself uncomfortable for no reason."

"You…Wait…Hold on. You've been in our cottage *every night*?" That last part had taken a bit to register.

"Most of them." Marvin smeared his spit-coated paw between his ears.

"That's…You…There has to be *rules* against that."

"Sure, but there are no *runes* against it. So here I've been. Listening to the liar snore and waiting to see if Alistair would tell you anything. As much as he could, anyway, which I was sure wouldn't be much. He's not quite as restricted as we are, since he can't talk, but he's been stuck in the sea for so long, his memory's…And…well, he's not *heard* the things we have."

I blinked.

Marvin did a snobbish, slow blink back.

"You know Alistair?" I asked.

"The big, green Loch Ness Monster, who's the star attraction of the isle I *live on*?" Marvin slow-blinked again. "Never heard of him." He drooled sarcasm as he slathered up his foot and went back in for another round of face cleaning.

"There's no need to be rude," I chided. "You knew what I meant. Can you…can you *hear* him?"

"No. None of us can. That's by design, of course."

"What?"

"But *you* can." He dropped his paws and tucked his tail around them, as though trying to keep them warm. "Are you aware you're a Sensitive?"

"A what?"

"A Sensitive," he repeated slowly. "You can hear Alistair, and I'd wager you can also feel the energies of others, yes? Their emotions and such."

My heart stuttered. Almost stopped.

"I'll take that as a yes." Marvin's ear twitched.

"I-I mean…I'm sensitive, sure. But I'm not—"

"It's rare, what you are," he continued. "A Sorcerer without the ability to wield magic—"

"I am *not* a Sorcerer."

"Not fully. No. But someone in your family was. A grandparent, perhaps great grandparent. Gave you enough good blood to sense magic, but not enough to wield it. Alistair would've known this too...*should* have known it, if he remembered. I'm not sure how many patches he has in his memory now, since I haven't been able to talk to him."

I stared, thoroughly bamboozled.

"So he *doesn't* remember," Marvin sighed. "Or he didn't want to burden you with it. But I'm surprised he didn't...because I *know* he hasn't forgotten—"

Marvin's ear flicked and he bit himself off with a hiss. Frustration poured off him.

"I'm limited as to what I can say," he spat.

"I...You...Ugh!" I angled my head to the bedroom.

"He's still sleeping," Marvin told me.

"Maybe we should take this outside?"

"It's damp." He kneaded his claws into the suitcase.

"Isn't it *always* damp here?"

"Yesssss," he hissed. "It's a—being *stuck* here...I can't explain much. That's the rub. But you've heard the history we tell? About the Scottish island and the curse?"

"I...Yeah."

"It's hogwash. A story we spin for tourists."

Ice tumbled into my belly. "You're not reincarnations of people from 500 years ago?"

"Nope."

"Then—"

"If I say anymore, I'll activate the rune that compels me *not* to say more. And that is a pain to rival the worst migraine a human has ever gotten. So I would rather not say more. You'll need to fill in the gaps."

"These aren't gaps, they're craters. If you're not...If that story's not true—"

"Parts of it are true."

"Which ones?"

"What happened to the people?"

I exhaled. "But you *just* said—"

"What. Happened. To. The. People?" His whiskers fluttered.

"I…They were cursed. They died—"

"Scratch that second part—"

"—and became beasts."

"Take out the past tense."

"They *become* beasts? I…That…" But then it clicked.

The long-limbed man I kept seeing—the one I *knew* was Alistair.

The way the creatures here were so tightly controlled. Branded with runes that dictated what they could and couldn't do. What they could and couldn't say.

The way this isle scrambled my emotions. Because the creatures living here were in turmoil.

Alistair. Always fighting so hard for his words.

And the phrase that had tickled my brain on the night I first slept atop his head.

"I am human."

"You're cursed." Shock hit my belly the way a slushy did, when I sucked it down too quickly on a sweltering day. "You're people. From now? This time period? *Living people*, who are cursed."

"I knew you'd get there." Marvin's tail twitched. "Took you long enough, though."

I wrapped my arms around myself, suddenly wondering if I was going to upend my stomach over my feet. "But curses like that are illegal. They've been outlawed for centuries."

"People can break laws and get away with it, if they're crafty enough."

A foul, lemony taste flooded my tongue.

Alistair was *human*.

He hadn't just *been* the man I kept seeing in some once upon a distant time. He *was* that man. Now. In the present. A man stuck in another body—imprisoned there by a curse.

All of them were.

Marvin.

The alicorns.

The kelpies.

All of them.

They were *people*.

This was…

It was *sick*.

It was *torture*, what was done to them. I'd thought so before, when I'd believed them to be centuries dead. But now…

It was *malicious*, to round up a band of living, breathing humans. People with lives, families, and friends. And curse them—force them into different bodies. Strap them to this shitty island to entertain a bunch of tourists.

I staggered back. Hit the wall. Sank down it until my butt plopped onto the ground and buried my head in my hands.

Marvin watched me.

"I have to do something," I sputtered. "I can't…I can't leave him…or any of you. I'm…Oh *stars*. There's…Is there a way to reverse this? Is there *anything* I can do?"

"Yes," Marvin breathed. "Yes, I think you can—" But he cut off with a yowl, rubbing frantically at his head.

Beneath his fur, a squiggly rune lit up in neon orange, burning him.

Marvin *howled*—the sort of wailing screech cats made when they fought.

I rushed toward him when he tilted sideways and plopped off the suitcase.

And Jackson finally woke up.

41

Alistair

"*I* could stay."

"*There are worse places to be trapped. At least I'd have you.*"

"*I think I love you, Alistair.*"

I want to keep her.

It *hurts*. This wanting.

Hurts more when I watch her leave. Crying, as she does so, because she hurts too. Letting her stay would take away the hurt for both of us.

And I want to call to her.

Stay. Pippi. Please. I don't want to be alone again.

I love you. *All* of you. Your laugh and…hu-*humor*. Your kind-ness. And your dreams. *Everything*. I love how spending time with you feels…easy.

Stay. Please.

But I don't say any of that.

I want to tell her other things too.

What she is.

What I am.

What the island is.

Why we're here.

Why we can never leave.

But I can't. The words slip when I reach for them.

I remember *Sensitive* now. I know what I need to say to explain it to her. But when I hold her against me and try, the words aren't there anymore. They return when she is gone. Slip when she is near.

It's *maddening*.

The curse is the reason I forget.

It's why I *know* there are people I hurt—sorrow—*grieve* for. But they've slipped. Mostly. Some faces return, but no words... no names.

I try to hold the words I need for Pippi. But they slip. And holding *hurts*.

Not saying them hurts more.

But she leaves. And I tell her nothing.

After, I am called to feed, although I can't eat. I move. Restlessly—un-purposefully—through the waters. Never going anywhere. Because I can't.

But Pippi can.

I am trapped.

She is *free*.

So I wait for the shadow that will take her away.

I wait to see her again. For the last time.

I wait to be alone in the waters again.

I wait to hurt.

I wait to heal.

I wait to forget.

I wait.

And wait.

That is all I can do. All I will *ever* be able to do.

When the shadow arrives, the rune above my right eye burns, calling me to go to the surface.

Something isn't right.

A second shadow passes over.

I lower in the waters, worried.

The burn deepens, making me hiss, and my body moves on its own, wanting to get rid of the hurt.

Something isn't right.

I swim and the rune above my left eye burns, telling me I am too close to the shadow. But I am being called to be close to it.

I shake my head as I come above the surface. The hurt is... it's...

Awful.

The only word I have for it.

Awful.

"Well, Alistair!" someone calls to me as I am maddened with hurt.

I hiss again.

"You've gotten yourself in quite the pickle, huh?"

I know the voice, the man who speaks it.

Know him.

But his word…*name*…has slipped.

"You don't remember me, huh?" the man asks. "That's…well, it's kind of sad, but oh-so-satisfying. I'm Rune Bloodworth."

Jackson sprang out of bed and bolted into the living room, moving with a nimble-footed gait, sweeping his enrapt eyes over the room. His hands found a weapon almost immediately, fisting around a poker from the fireplace.

"Jackson!" I called.

He whirled, swiveling those calculating eyes to me, and growled, "Pippi, what in actual—"

Marvin scuttered as he picked himself off the floor.

Jackson caught the movement and spun around, his weapon whipping back to strike.

"Don't!" I yelled.

Jackson froze with the poker suspended halfway over Marvin's head. "It's the cat," he muttered dumbly. "The *cat*? The *fuck*, Pippi? You brought the *cat* in here?"

"I—"

"You're un-fucking-believable."

"We were"—Marvin turned his eyes to me—"having quite a nice cha—*ooooffff*!"

Jackson chucked the poker aside and hauled Marvin up by the scruff of his neck.

"Jackson!" I scrabbled to my feet. My knees knocked together, nearly sending me crashing back down. I gritted my teeth and forced them to hold.

Marvin yowled and hissed, his claws swiping at the air. "Unhand me, you buffoon!"

"Stop!" I swaggered over to him, touching his shoulder. "Please—"

Jackson snarled and snapped his arm back, whacking me across the chest and harpooning me into the wall.

My back cracked on impact.

I grunted as pain shot along my shoulders.

Jackson paused. Slid his eyes to me. Scoffed. And opened the door, chucking the screeching Marvin out.

"I can't believe you, Pippi." He slammed the door, drowning out Marvin's heated calls. "Do you really hate me that much? That you'd force an allergy attack? I'll be sneezing my head off all day." He sniffed. And swiped at his nose. And rubbed at his eyes.

His *clear* eyes. They weren't red or teary, his nose didn't sound stuffy or look runny, and he certainly wasn't launching into a sneezing fit.

He lies.

He was performing all the acts he thought an allergy sufferer would. But he wasn't actually suffering.

Anger frothed inside me. I gulped it down. Because this hashing argument had to wait. Something far more important needed to be aired out first.

"Jackson." I reached for him as he stomped past.

"What?" he snarled.

"Jackson…I-I need you to listen to me."

He gave a big, exaggerated sniff. "Unless it's an apology, I'm not interested."

"Jackson, *please.*"

And he must've seen the turmoil in my face when he deigned to bring his eyes back to me. I was crying—had been all morning—so my eyes were puffy, and I was jittering. And I was sure I'd gone whiter than a sheet.

He paused and crossed his arms over his chest, waiting.

"Jackson…there's something…This island is *wrong.*"

He rolled his eyes.

"They're *people!*"

"Who?"

"The creatures! Marvin and Alistair, and the alicorns, the kelpies, the banshees...they're all *people.*"

"Well...yeah. But they've been dead for 500 years—"

"No, they haven't! That's a story the isle tells, to hide the fact that they cursed *living people.*"

Jackson sighed and pinched the bridge of his nose. "I don't... Pippi, I don't have the patience for this bullshit. We're leaving in a few hours. Did you pack your things yet? Or did you waste time kissing the cat's ass in hopes he'd turn into a prince?"

"It's not—"

He walked away. Ignoring me.

And my anger, my hurt...*everything* boiled over. "DON'T YOU DARE WALK AWAY FROM ME, JACKSON!" I bellowed.

He pivoted, his eyes burning with rage. "What the—"

"Listen to me. Please. Just for a few minutes. This is...it's important. It's bigger than our fight. People, real people, are getting hurt by this."

Patches of red blossomed over Jackson's cheeks and a vein pulsed in his temple. But he stayed quiet as he jerked his arm through the air, motioning for me to go on.

"The creatures on this island are *humans.* They've been cursed—recently, I think. When the isle opened, or a little before."

He rubbed a hand over his face. "Do you hear yourself right now, Pippi? Do you actually comprehend what you're saying?"

I scowled. "Don't talk to me like I'm stupid, Jackson."

"Then don't say stupid shit."

"How dare—"

"Curses are *illegal*, Pippi."

"I know..."

"They taught us about curse laws in fucking grade school."

"*I know.* I thought that too. But laws can be broken—"

"That's a big law to break."

"Right. Yeah. But someone with a lot of money and power would stand a chance at breaking it."

"Of course." Jackson rubbed at his cheek. "Let me guess… Rune Bloodworth is the villain?"

"I—"

"And *how* would the logistics of this work? *How*, Pippi? No one noticed a big swathe of humans went missing?"

"They—"

"The talking creatures never shouted *'Hey! I'm Bob Nobody from Texas. I've been kidnapped'* to any tourist? Not a single one, in five years?"

"They *can't*. They have runes branded into them that dictate what they can do and say."

"Well, that's convenient."

"It's the truth. I've seen it. It burned Marvin before you woke up because he tried to tell me more about the curse. And Alistair—"

"Who"—Jackson's eyes glittered—"is *Alistair*?"

Ooof, well, I'd stepped in it now, hadn't I?

Jackson's expression turned cold—a human face etched into emotionless marble. "That's the second time you mentioned that name. *Alistair.* Who is he?"

My tongue thickened into a gelatinous blob. "Alistair," I finally managed, "is the Loch Ness Monster."

A knitted V formed in Jackson's brow. "It has a name?"

"*He*. And yes."

"How do you know that? Nowhere lists that name. How did you figure that out?"

My stomach corkscrewed into my throat. I clenched my teeth around my next words, in case something *more* than words came out. "He told me."

"He…*who*?"

"Alistair. The Loch Ness Monster. He told me his name."

"The Loch Ness Monster? The one creature on this island that doesn't talk?"

"He *can* talk. But nobody can hear him. But…"

Jackson's face reddened, making him look a bit like a pulsating tomato.

"I can," I continued. "I've been able to all week. Since that night we went skinny dipping. He's…I mean…he's the reason I'm alive. He saved me."

"What?"

"I-I'm sorry Jackson. I should've…I don't know why I didn't. I…I was confused at first. And then I didn't know *how*. I should have told you. But, yes, he saved me. When that tide ripped me out to sea. I was lost. And scared. He plucked me out of the water and protected me. And I found out he could talk. But I'm the only one who can hear him. And I don't fully understand why. It's awful, though, that his voice is silent to everyone else. Because he's sweet, and—"

Oh. Stars.

I'd said too much.

Far too much.

Jackson's emotions *slammed* into me, nearly bowling me off my feet.

These were dark feelings—frighteningly so. Pounding sensations that left my blood boiling and had me itching to hurt something. Some*one*. More than hurt them. *Murder* them.

"Sweet, and goofy, and charismatic?" Jackson drawled.

He sounded so very calm. A placid sheen of ice, concealing riotous waters.

"How much time did you spend with the sea beast, Pippi?" he asked.

I forced myself to meet his gaze. Forced myself to remain calm, even as terror flayed my insides. "I'm sorry, Jackson. Not sorry I did spend time with him—I wish I could say I was. But I can't regret getting to know Alistair. But it was *awful* that I went behind your back. And hurt you—"

Jackson turned away with a snarl. Paced into the living room. Stopped. *Seethed* when he noticed cat hair on his suitcase. Belched up a violent string of curses that had me instinctively flattening my back against the wall. And fisted his hand on the suitcase handle.

For a brief, heart-sickening second, I pictured him hefting that suitcase up and throwing it at my head.

And I figured if he did, I'd deserve it.

But then his savage emotions quieted. He knocked his empty fist against his thigh and *laughed*. "This explains it, doesn't it?"

"What explains what?"

"*You!*" he exclaimed. "All week I've been raking my brain trying to figure out what the fuck was going on with you. And now it makes *perfect* sense. That sea monster's bewitched you or something. Hasn't it?"

"What? *No.*"

"Precisely what someone who's been bewitched would say."

"I've not been bewitched, Jackson! That's not even a *thing—*" I bit off when he circled the living room furniture and stormed toward me.

I tried to move back, but I was pressed against the wall. Trapped.

Jackson slammed a fist into that wall above my head and snatched my chin in his other hand.

"Let me go." Panicked words burbled out of me. "Jackson. Please. Let—"

He squeezed my jaw until the pressure creaked my bone and left me yelping in pain.

"Luckily for you, *babe*, I'm not one of those assholes who chucks girls out to the curb over indiscretions like this. You're forgiven, Pippi." He touched his lips to my head in a kiss that felt more possessive than romantic.

"Jackson." My jaw crackled and ground as I fought to get the words out. "I *swear*, I'm not—"

"You're not thinking clearly. Of course. How could you, with that thing so close to the island?"

"He's not a thing!"

"And I wish I could say that getting you home would make

everything better. But bewitching is like a curse, right? Permanent?"

"I haven't been bewitched! Or cursed."

"I'm sorry, babe, you were trying to tell me, too, without being able to tell me. *'The beasts have runes that dictate what they can do and say.'* That's what happened to you, huh? I should've listened!"

"Jackson!"

"As far as I know, a surefire way to get rid of a spell is to get rid of the source. At least that's the rumor. Might be true. Might not be. Only one way to find out."

My blood morphed into freezing sludge, too thick to course properly through my veins.

"I'm going to take care of it. I promise." A smile quirked at the corner of his mouth.

"NO! Jackson, *no!*"

"But you'll have to stay here."

"No!" I screamed when he dropped his other hand and wrapped it in my hair.

"You were with him last night, weren't you?" He pulled on my hair until I squeaked. "Your hair's still wet, babe."

"I—"

But then he was dragging me, literally, by my hair. Ripping at the strands until my scalp burned, and I was sure he'd uproot whole chunks. Forcing me through the bedroom and into the bathroom.

"JACKSON STOP!" I screamed. Kicked. Bit at his hand—and got rewarded with a hair twist that had me seeing stars.

"I need you to stay here for a few hours, babe. That's it."

"NO!"

"You'll probably do or say anything to protect him, and I can't have that. It'll be okay, Pippi."

This said as he threw me, bodily, into the bathroom.

I staggered, crashed into the sink counter, cried when the edge of it drilled a bruise into my hip, and howled when Jackson slammed the door shut.

"Jackson! You selfish, stupid—" I wrenched the handle. It didn't move. There was scuffling from the other side as Jackson braced something against it.

"LET ME OUT!" I slammed my shoulder against the door, cursing when pain shot down my arm.

The door didn't budge.

I whirled, scanning the bathroom. There were no windows. *Nothing.* Only one way in or out.

And that way had been barricaded.

43

Pippi

Panic fizzed inside my gut, shooting a trickle of citrusy bile into my mouth.

I pounded at the door until my knuckles bled and left red smudges over the embossed wood and screamed until my voice mangled my throat, until all the sound I could manage was a wet rasp.

"A surefire way to get rid of a spell like this is to get rid of the source." Jackson had said.

I walked, pacing the area between the sink and the shower, my breath coming out in strained wheezes.

Jackson wouldn't—he *couldn't* hurt Alistair.

He *couldn't.*

Not by himself. Not without a boat, or a harpoon, or some big piece of weaponry.

Right?

Right?

So why did I have this awful, sinking, nauseating feeling that he was going to do something? And that poor Alistair was going to get hurt?ken

"Ouch!" I cried when I drilled my knee into the porcelain rim of the toilet.

Stupid.

Pain savaged my kneecap and rocketed up my thigh to brutalize my hip.

Stupid!

I yelled and smacked my hands against the top of the closed toilet seat. It discharged an awful, tinny twang that made my ears ring, and fanned the broiling agitation. So I kicked the toilet too, for good measure, and hit it again when a throbbing agony bit my toes.

I was a mess.

A shrieking, wild, messy-*mess*.

Calm down, Pippi.

I joggled my hands, sprinkling blood droplets all over the bathroom.

CALM DOWN!

I turned and plopped onto the toilet, pressing my forehead to my jittering knees. Breathing in the musky brine clinging to my clothes and skin—an odor that would've sent me scrambling for a place to upchuck a week ago, but was now so twined around memories of Alistair, it was a comfort.

Breathe, Pippi.

My lungs stuttered around each thin inhale.

Breathe. In. And out.

But with Alistair's scent tickling my nose, I kept seeing a horrific image of him being impaled by a harpoon, ala Moby Dick style.

My gut lurched.

Breathe, Pippi.

Jackson can't do anything.

Alistair is safe.

Tears splashed onto the tops of my knees.

He can't do anything.

But if he does *do something, I can't stop him...*

Because the selfish prick locked. Me. In. The. Bathroom!

And that...*that...*

The fact that Jackson had been so quick to jump on the idea that Alistair had bewitched me. So quick to believe the only reason I'd *"changed"* was because a sea beast had me in a thrall.

He'd refused to hear my side of it. Refused to listen to *anything* I'd said all week.

Because he didn't care.

How had I not seen this before?

The only person Jackson truly cared about was himself.

Relationship. Bah. That wasn't the word for what we had been.

A relationship was a thing two people built *together.*

Jackson had never built anything. He'd dictated. Taken for himself. Left me to do the heavy lifting until I decided I was done breaking my back. Then he got mad. Because he'd boasted about our relationship—this thing I'd built alone—and had taken great pride in it. And I'd had the gall to take it away from him.

I'd empathized with him when I pulled that plug. My heart had bled for him. I *hated* hurting him.

But now I saw the ugly truth.

I hadn't hurt *him.* Not his heart or his soul.

Just his pride.

A broken heart he might've endured. But he wielded his fractured ego as a weapon. He was lashing out, blaming an innocent creature for taking me away, rather than accepting the fact that I didn't want to be with him anymore.

What a *monster.*

I cursed at the Pippi I'd been—the Pippi who'd tolerated his bullshit for years and called it *"love."* But I also mourned for that Pippi who'd wasted her heart and a precious chunk of her life on a terrible man.

He won't do anything to Alistair.

He can't. I wished I believed it.

Time trickled by. An hour. Maybe more—impossible to say, while swaddled in the dark of the bathroom, watching the candlelight gyrate on the walls.

Magical candles. They lit as soon as someone entered the room and burned until they left.

For a while, I distracted myself by trying to snuff the flames out. Blowing on them. Squirting water over them. Even squishing some of my makeup tins over them.

The magical flames continued their merry dance, never missing a beat.

After that, I sat and cried for a while, until a manic fervor sent me pacing and punching at the door again.

Nothing helped. I wasn't strong enough to bust down the door. Whatever Jackson had barricaded against it refused to budge.

I tried, though. Until my body ached and my head spun. Then I leaned over the sink, watching as my shadowed reflection bounced and swayed unsteadily before my eyes, wondering if the tingling feeling in my face and stomach was a precursor to fainting or puking.

"He has her…bathroom…"

My head whipped to the door when a voice I recognized snaked underneath. *"Marvin?"*

"You'll have to move the table," Marvin the cat drolled. "It's heavy."

"It should slide. We'll scuff the floors, though."

"Fuck the floors. They can take it out of lover boy's deposit."

I recognized those voices too.

Melany and Sarah.

Relief flooded me as I staggered forward, knocking my bloody knuckles against the door. "Help!"

"Hold on, girl," Sarah called.

"We're coming!" Melany added.

Heavy thunks and knocks rattled the door. I took a step back. Waiting. Jittering. Twisting my knuckles until they ached.

"That should do it!"

With a soft *click*, the door swung open.

I bolted. Zooming past Melany and Sarah. Past Marvin. Stopping only once I reached the cottage's front door. It took me several *painful* seconds, whacking my bleeding, shaking hands on the handle, before I was able to open it. Then I was outside, in the dull pallor of a foggy morning. Breathing the salty air. Feeling the tickle of the tepid breeze against my cheeks.

I braced my hands on my knees and focused on breathing— on keeping myself conscious.

"Oh, honey, you've got a lot of blood on you." Melany reached my side first and rubbed at my back.

"I know." I sniffed. "I banged my hands up."

"Well, you certainly did. But most of the blood is from here." She gingerly touched the side of my head.

I yelped when pain zapped my skull and pulsated down the side of my neck. And then I reached up to check my hair.

Tacky streaks of blood painted the strands.

I prodded the seeping gash arching along the crown of my head.

He'd torn some of my hair out.

That *jerk*.

Something soft brushed against my bare calves, making me flinch.

Marvin twined himself between my legs and sat in front of my feet, fixing me with that judgmental stare.

"Darling Marvin," Melany said, "told us you were in a spot of trouble. And…Pippi, your boyfriend was in Brew & Bites raving about—"

"Jackson?" I straightened sharply. Too sharply. My head fizzed. I staggered.

"There, there, honey. Take it easy." Melany touched my arm. "Sarah was getting you a—"

"Already have it." Sarah strolled up to my side and shoved a glass in my hands. "Drink this."

I took it from her, surprised at the fierce thirst scraping the inside of my throat, and downed the glass in a few big sips.

"What was Jackson doing?" I swung my gaze between the three of them.

"Telling lies," Marvin said. "As he does."

"He was raving about the Loch Ness Monster," Melany clarified. "Said…Oh, it was *awful*." She tutted as she touched a blood-streaked strand of my hair.

"He was saying the monster took you," Sarah finished.

"*What?*"

"The way he told it, you wanted to explore the cliff

trail. He asked you not to, but you went anyway. You slipped and fell, and the Loch Ness Monster took you away."

"He seemed very upset," Melany added. "Thinking you were dead. I believed him, Pippi. I was bawling my eyes out."

"He said I was dead?"

"No. He worried you were dead," Sarah said. "But claimed he didn't know for sure. He's a rotting bastard for saying something like that."

"But it was very convincing." Melany chaffed my arm.

"It was," Sarah agreed. "That's why he got so many volunteers."

"Volunteers?"

"To hunt the Loch Ness Monster"—Sarah's lips pursed—"and find you. More than half the isle went with him."

My knees buckled.

Marvin hissed, reminding me he was beneath my feet. Melany and Sarah grabbed for me, keeping me upright.

"You should sit down," Melany cooed.

"No."

"Before you fall down," Sarah added.

"No! I—" The glass slid from my numb fingers and shattered all over the ground in several big, bloodstained pieces.

Marvin flattened his ears as he shimmied away from the shards.

"I-I have to stop them." I ran a hand through my hair, biting my lip at the pain. "They can't hunt Alistair. He hasn't *done* anything!"

"Alistair?" Melany and Sarah echoed.

"That's his name," Marvin told them.

"He's my *friend*!" I exclaimed. "I…They can't hunt him. He didn't take me, I—"

"They already are hunting him," Sarah said.

I blanched.

"They suspended the ferry off the isle. As soon as it arrived to pick us up, they took it. Because the tour ship wasn't big enough to hold everyone, and people wanted to see..." She stopped and sucked her lips between her teeth.

"What?" I asked. "Wanted to see *what?*"

"Well, Jackson's lie was convincing. Very. And Rune Bloodworth got concerned the magic containing the beast might have failed."

"They wanted to re-brand him," Melany said tentatively.

"No. *No. No. No. No.*" I shrugged away from them, shaking so hard my teeth clanked.

And at that moment I didn't see Melany and Sarah. All I saw was an image—an awful, heartbreaking image of poor, gentle, goofy Alistair bellowing in pain as more of those malicious runes were seared into his skin.

"They can't do this!" I yelled.

"They *are* doing it," Melany said. "I'm sorry, Pippi, I—" She glanced down at Marvin as he skulked around, his eyes fixed on me. "Marvin told us you had a relationship with the Loch Ness Monster...you really do, don't you? You care about him?"

I love him.

"Yes," I said. "I need to stop them. Alistair is...he's *innocent.*"

"Well now I'm wondering"—Sarah crossed her arms over her stomach—"is he being attacked because lover boy found out about your relationship with him?"

Guilt tasted like rotted eggs. "Yes."

Sarah harrumphed. "So he's one of *those* bastards, huh? Gets all prideful and spitting spite if his girl dares to look elsewhere."

"I could've handled it better."

"He still would've gone to an extreme," Sarah said. "If he's that type. Well now, you're in a real spot of trouble, hun. No way to sugar coat that. Luckily for you, the captain of *Valiant* abandoned his ship."

"Caleb?" I asked, remembering the kindly man who'd given me the peppermint balm on the ride over.

"That his name? He didn't seem like he cared for Rune too much and wanted no part of this hunt. When Rune insisted on taking the ship, the captain stepped off. I don't know how much *help* he's going to be, but he might be all we have. You feel steady enough to walk?"

No.

But I gritted my teeth around a "yes."

"Oh, hun, that's a lie if I ever heard one," Melany said.

"Alrighty. Well"—Sarah scooted to my left side, Melany to my right—"let's see what we can do to save your friend." They linked their arms through mine.

Gratitude ballooned in my chest, nearly choking me. "Thank you."

Melany patted my arm.

But the little comfort I'd suckled from them perished as we started walking. Because radioactive panic spilled into my chest.

Alistair's.

It was thin, with him so far away, but he'd been scared enough to shoot his emotions clean across the sea and land.

My stomach twisted itself into a pretzel.

Hold on, Alistair!

44

Caleb sat alone in Brew & Bites, nursing a beer that'd already gone flat, looking a little glum and a lot irritated.

But he exuded calm. Even when I rushed up to him and started babbling my story, Caleb's emotions stayed steady. When he took my cold, shaking hand between his warm, calloused ones, some of my panic ebbed.

He didn't prod or question anything. Just listened, and jumped into action as soon as I'd finished.

"The ruddin' sods took *Legacy* as well," he said as he led me through Brew & Bites, barreling into the RESTRICTED: ISLE STAFF ONLY doors.

"*Legacy?*" I asked.

"The ship they use for the tours," he amended.

"Oh."

Some of the isle attendants, noticing we'd burst into their corner of the building, sputtered and tried to wave us out of the area.

Caleb ignored them.

"There's a boat somewhere, though? Right?" I had to jog to keep up as Caleb cut through a rather dingy-looking cafeteria and lounge. The floors here were a slate grey streaked with black scuffmarks from the employees' shoes. Ratty furniture dotted the area—couches, recliners, tables and chairs that looked like they'd spent a chunk of time festering on a curbside.

"There's not," Caleb had gruffed.

My heart sank. "But...how..."

He shoved against a door on the far side of the lounge and pulled me into a massive storage room.

As the flame sconces flicked to life, illuminating the rows of supplies, Caleb took me to a rack in the center of the room, where life vests and floatation devices hung.

Oh no.

My stomach plopped stickily.

"This'll keep ye floatin'." Caleb popped a life vest off its hanger. "And this'll take us out to sea." He handed me one of the round floatation devices. "They're enchanted, mind. Dunna rightly know how it works, but they're made to go to the isle or the ship. Takin' ye somewhere safe and the like. We may have to force them away from the isle since they'll be thinkin' we're already safe." He slung one of the life vests over his shoulder. "But we'll get to yer beast. One way or another."

Stars, this man was a blessing, wasn't he? A true gentleman. A shining example of the male species. We needed a hundred more like him.

Which was why I wasn't willing to risk the one our society *did* have.

"Thank you," I whispered. "But I...I think I should go alone. I —" Thin tendrils of Alistair's fear still gyrated in my belly. "I'd hate to put you in the middle of this. When I don't know what they're doing, or what it'll do to him. I should go alone."

Caleb paused. "No. I dunna like that, lassie. What if yer hurt, eh?"

"Alistair would never hurt me."

"Aye, I wasna talkin' 'bout him. But, as ye said, ye dunna what they're doin'. Might be drivin' him mad, whatever it is."

"He still wouldn't hurt me. He *knows* me. And he won't hurt me."

The same probably couldn't be said for the people on those ships, unfortunately.

But I didn't say that.

Caleb was already looking none too pleased at this arrangement.

But he let me go. Alone.

He helped me into the water, making sure the life vest was fitted properly, and then he stayed on the isle, watching from the dock with Melany, Sarah, and Marvin as I waged war with the sea.

"Ye'll have to fight it, lassie," he called.

The surf bit at my ankles, trying its darndest to rip me off the floater I clung to. And the rubber floaty hummed and burned red hot beneath my arms and chest as it shimmied, trying to take me back to the isle.

"Push, girl. Show that fucker who's boss." Sarah whooped.

Water slapped my face, making me cough.

The boiling floater smacked my stomach as it tried to spin around. Like, "Hey, you coo-coo crazy chick, land is this way."

I kicked. Hard. Pummeling my legs through the water. But it was like trying to move a brick wall.

The floater dipped sideways with a wave and did a quick turn and burn, whipping me around to face the isle again.

My little cheering squad waggled their arms, motioning for me to keep going. But it seemed impossible.

Everything did.

Swimming out to sea. Winning against this stupid floater. Getting to Alistair in time. Hauling Jackson and the others off him.

It all seemed too big. Too much.

But then Alistair's fear clawed at my belly again. Viciously, this time. And I could *hear* him. Whispered words of confusion. Of hurt.

I ground my teeth and shoved my full weight into the floater, forcing it away from the isle.

"Attagirl!" Melany whooped.

Hold on, Alistair.

I'm coming.

My legs propelled me through the water.

When the floater scorched my skin and started to rattle,

angry at my disobedience, I smacked one hand over its rubbery surface and cursed at it to stay straight.

Onward we went, slowly, the floaty whining in protest the whole way.

The fog swallowed the end of the dock, taking my cheering squad with it. I could still hear them for a while. And I grasped on to their voices, their encouragement, suckling them up. Fuel to keep me moving.

Until the fog stole that too.

I was alone. Out in the middle of the ocean, where the curdling fog drooped low over the undulating hills of pewter green, making it seem as though the sky and sea were converging.

I swam, fighting the tears, the exhaustion, the *fear*. My heart still stuttered if I let my eyes wander too far around the ocean's scope.

So I didn't let my eyes wander.

The waves rolled me up and down. The undercurrent dragged at my feet, making it feel like I was trying to carry a boulder through a swamp with every paddle. Fatigue dragged its nails over me, making my muscles quiver, and my joints scream with pain. White curled around the edges of my vision, and little color bursts speckled the front.

I ground my teeth against my tongue and lips, using the sting of pain and the washes of blood, to keep myself focused.

The floater gave a sudden, violent shake, nearly bucking me off.

I grappled to keep a hold of it.

It bounced. Hummed. And abruptly shot forward, zipping across the ocean.

Oh, stars.

This was *fast*.

Why was it so fast?

My lungs heaved as the floater rode up the crest of a wave and caught some air, popping me out of the water for a terrifying heartbeat, before slamming my bottom straight into the next wave. The impact stung.

But the throbbing welt on my rump vanished when I glanced forward.

Burly shadows smudged the murky horizon.

Alistair was close, his emotions so thick, they were almost tangible.

Confusion.

Worry.

Anger.

Sorrow.

They all wrapped their thorny vines around my heart and pulled.

Yells punched through the fog's muffling veil.

"What did you do with the girl, Alistair?"

Rune Bloodworth.

But this was not the same boisterous, happy-go-lucky Rune who'd declared a gazillion toasts and regaled stories to a captivated crowd. This version of him was cutting. Cruel. A silken slip covering a bushel of thorns.

The curtains of fog parted as my floater scuttled through. And my heart turned ice, ice cold.

The two ships were parallel to each other: the smaller *Legacy* closest to me, *Valiant* on the other side. And my floater picked up speed as it headed for the center of *Legacy*.

"Oh—*shit*." I squeaked and whisked my hands off the floater and bailed. The sea snapped at my feet, keen on ripping me under, but the life jacket snagged around my armpits, keeping me afloat.

The floater skipped merrily forward and *THWACKED* into the broadside of *Legacy*.

That was the *worst* safety device ever. My goodness.

I'd almost been pancaked.

"Alistair," Rune called again, "what did you do with the girl?"

Alistair said nothing.

"Onyx," Rune boomed, "is he answering?"

So Onyx *could* hear him?

I'd have to mull that tidbit over later, when I wasn't being slogged by the sea.

If Onyx responded, her voice didn't reach my ears. But Rune snarled, "This isn't good, Alistair. I'm trying to help you out here. But if you've taken this fine fellow's woman—"

Fine fellow.

Jackson?

Blegh.

"—that's unacceptable. Tell us where she is. What happened? And maybe I won't add this new rune."

Oh, no.

I pawed at the water frantically, trying to swing around *Legacy.* Alistair was on the other side. I felt him. But couldn't see him.

And the people on the ship couldn't see me.

I flailed in the bobbing sea, choking on it, and waving my arms, occasionally coercing my waterlogged lungs into jetting out a squawk. But no one noticed me.

They *needed* to notice me.

They needed to stop this.

But no matter how furiously I doggy paddled, the front of the ship never seemed to get any closer.

"Alistair!" Rune shouted.

And this time, Alistair's response smoothed across my brain. "I haven't taken her. I would *never.*"

"Onyx?" Rune snapped. "Anything?"

Ssssuuuuccckk.

I cried when the ocean slurped me into the side of the ship. My head cracked against the wood, and my knees popped as my feet got dragged halfway under. The lifejacket cut into my armpits, chaffing me raw.

"I'm really surprised at you, Alistair." Rune's words barely rose above the rushing of water and the creaking of the ship as I flattened my hands against the hull.

"I can't say I'm surprised at you, Rune," Alistair bit back, his voice more bitter than I'd ever heard it.

Push, Pippi! I screamed at myself. *Push!*

It took everything.

Every ounce of strength, shoving against the ship, scraping my palms on the surface. Straining my shoulders until they popped. But I freed myself from the suction.

Go, go, go, go!

I clawed through the water, forcing it to yield to me. To let me pass. And finally, *finally*, I pushed myself around the front of *Legacy*.

And there he was, floating between the two ships. His serpentine body was painfully contorted, with his neck all bunched in a vertical U-shape, pinning his nose to his chest, while his right shoulder lilted into the water, leaving him cock-eyed. As he teetered, he squiggled his left flapper in the water, using it as a counterbalance.

Three jagged runes glowed neon red on his head: two curved above his eyes, the other on the tip of his nose. And bright rouge popping against his green scales gave the impression that he was bleeding.

Pain cascaded off him—I'd felt it all the way here. Internally, he was withering and wailing, in incomprehensible agony. But externally, fluttering his flapper seemed all the movement he was capable of.

I wondered if one of those runes was immobilizing him.

"I think we can arrange a quick check." On *Valiant*, standing with his feet laced through the railing, raising him above Alistair and all the other people, was Rune. Blue magic glowed over the tips of his fingers, casting crevicing shadows over his face, leeching out all the features that had made him handsome and boyish.

He slashed one of his blue sparkled hands through the air.

Alistair stiffened. Cried.

The rune on his throat sizzled, ringing his neck like a macabre glow necklace.

He retched, upending bile and fish all over himself.

"Alistair!" His name came out in a breathless whisper.

No one heard me.

They hadn't seen me either, as obscured as I was in *Legacy's* shadow.

"Nope," Rune chirped and turned to someone on his left side. "That rune is working—he wouldn't have eaten the girl."

Jackson's golden head appeared at the railing, sneering down at Alistair.

I hate you. I wanted to scream at him.

"We'll find your girl, Jackson," Rune boomed. "In the meantime…" He raised his glowing hands.

Alistair flinched.

"I'll make sure he doesn't do this again. She was pretty, huh, Alistair? The redhead? That's why you wanted her? I get it, man. But it's not cool. So, to be kind, I think we'll remove all future temptation."

No, no, no.

I didn't know what that meant.

But the *look* on Rune's face…

The *fear* in Alistair's heart…

STOP!

My mouth gaped, trying to push the word out.

The sea rushed in, gagging me.

STOP!

I raised an arm. But it threw me off kilter and I went spiraling sideways when the ship tried to glug me back under.

Alistair saw me.

His wild, panic-stricken eye rotated toward me.

"Pippi!" he gasped. "Leave. Pl—"

Rune drew a pattern in the air with his glowing hands.

And that pattern burned into Alistair's left eye.

He *screamed*. Blood belched from the rune and trickled down his cheek, painting swirling crimson patterns into the sea.

"STOP!!!"

I didn't recognize my voice when it finally burst out of me.

Wasn't even sure if that animalistic wail was mine, until people on board the ships scurried, leaning over the railings, watching me as I wrenched free of the ship's suction and made a panicked dash to Alistair's side.

Several screamed.

"Shit! Rune!" Kian's voice boomed. "Back off. She's in the water!"

"Pippi?" Jackson's anger exploded over me, making my gut twist.

I ignored them both.

All I could see at that moment was Alistair. The sad, heartbreaking state of him, floating lopsided and mewling as blood bubbled from his ruined eye.

His head was pinned low enough, with his chin just above the water, that I could reach up and touch him.

He hissed.

"It's me, Alistair," I soothed. "It's me."

"Pippi." A broken sigh escaped him.

Voices twined over my head as people from both ships shouted speculation at each other.

"Where the fuck did she come from?"

"Did he have her with him the whole time?"

"Did she jump off the ship? She's got a life jacket."

"I swear I didn't see her."

Alistair leaned into me, shivering. Blood still bubbled from the gummy hunk of flesh where his beautiful orange eye had been only seconds before.

"Pippi, get away from it!"

Jackson.

I bristled at the sound of his voice.

"I haven't finished the rune," called the man who was as awful as the malicious magic he was named after. *Rune.* "I have to do the other eye. But she needs to get out of there. The spell can only do so much to hold him."

I plastered my body to Alistair's head.

"Pippi?" Alistair murmured.

I stroked his scales.

"I...I have a question."

"Okay..."

"It may mean the d-d-difference between life and death," he continued.

My stomach dropped.

"Does this rune..." He flinched as his mangled socket convulsed. "...make me more or less a-a-attractive?"

A surprised, sobbing laugh burst out of me. "Oh, you goof." I rubbed his face, gingerly swiping some of the blood away. "But you're *more* attractive. It makes you look like a ferocious warrior."

A life preserver pinwheeled off *Valiant*, bonking me in the head before plopping into the water beside Alistair's chin.

He hissed again.

"It's a floaty," I said. And then I picked the donut ring up and chucked it back.

It didn't land anywhere near the ship—stars knew my throw and aim weren't that good— but the message was received. Loud and clear.

"Pippi!" Jackson cried. "Grab the life preserver!"

And, oh, he was playing a part. Wringing his hands. Mussing his hair. Jiggling his knee. Acting very much like a concerned boyfriend trying to get the love of his life out of a dangerous situation.

It was bullshit.

And he and I...we were long past the point of niceties.

"Fuck you," I bellowed.

A cloud of murmurs and incredulous laughter spritzed from the ships.

Jackson's face reddened. "See what I mean? It's *done* something to her—"

"The only thing Alistair did was care about me." Yelling scourged my throat and took more oxygen than my overworked lungs had. My vision got checkerspotty. But I cranked the volume up a little more, because I wanted to make sure he heard me. "Which is more than I can say for you!"

Jackson gripped the railing in both hands and leaned halfway over, almost as though he'd considered jumping into the water to wring my neck. Then he thought better of it, straightened up, and called down, "Grab the life preserver, Pippi."

"So you can *get me out of the way* before the asshole you idolize mauls an innocent person? I think not."

"Pippi."

"I won't do it, Jackson." I jutted my chin up. "If you want to keep gouging his eyes out, you'll have to gouge mine out too. Because I *won't* leave him."

Dozens of faces dotted the ship's railing now as people swung their gazes between me and Jackson, murmuring things like *"Did I hear her right?"* and *"Oof, this might get good."*

Rune placed a placating hand on Jackson's shoulder as he wiggled his fingers, calling the life preserver to him. "Pippa, we can't risk Alistair hurting people."

"Do I look hurt to you?" My throat burned.

"No. And I'm very glad you're not. But you've clearly interacted with him before, and he should not be able to interact with tourists. Ever."

"Why?"

"These runes keep him safe too," Rune spoke over me. "They keep him from doing something that would bring a hunt like this down on his head."

"And what about the curse?" I spat. "Was that done to keep him safe?"

"I'm sorry?" Rune tapped at his ear. "It's hard to hear you, darling."

I was certain he'd heard me just fine. But I threw my head back and upped the volume a few more degrees. *"What about the curse?!* The one that turned him into this. And is keeping him trapped here?"

"Oh, Pippa, I think you may be confused—"

"Pippi!" I screamed. "It's Pippi. Not Pippa. At least get my name right if you're gonna act like a condescending sack of shit."

Alistair's shocked laugh was music to my ears.

Other people chuckled too. Nervously, the sort of way folks did in those awkward situations that made them feel so uncomfortable, they had to giggle to release some of the tension.

"Pippi, then," Rune said. "I think you're confused—"

"I'm not. And don't spin this like I'm some traumatized little woman who's too scrambled in the head to know what she's saying. My head has never been clearer. Alistair is *human*." My voice crackled around that word. I paused. Swallowed, to soothe the lacerations in my throat, and bellowed, "And you cursed him."

Jackson's voice trickled down. "See, this is the nonsense she was blabbering about."

"My ears work, Jackson." I whipped my eyes to him. "And if anyone is blabbering nonsense, it's *you*. Why don't you tell them the truth behind today—or this whole week?"

His face turned stony.

"That's fine. You don't have to. I will." I pivoted my gaze between the two ships, meeting each set of curious, worried, and shocked eyes that peered down at me. "Jackson's mad because I broke up with him. Because I finally realized he's a selfish leech who's been draining me for *years*. And he threw a tantrum and fabricated this bullshit story where he's the hero, and I'm the simpering damsel who's been bewitched by a horrific beast. Because that's easier for him to accept than me not wanting him." I turned back to Jackson.

He exuded so much fury, it lit a full-fledged fire in my belly.

"Did that cover everything, *babe*?" I tried to bring my speech to an epic mic drop conclusion. But my blistered throat crapped out on me, and those last words were barely a hiss.

"Pippi." Alistair nuzzled his head into me. "You're so lovely when you're m-m-mad. Has anyone told you that? It's s-s-s-*sexy*."

I sputtered.

He chuckled.

"You should be mad more," he whispered. "Especially toward people who use you. Save your k-kindness for people who earn it."

I turned and pressed my lips to his face.

Chaos erupted over us.

Kian screamed at Jackson, demanding if I was telling the truth.

Rune shouted that he couldn't leave his magic unfinished, and that, "Alistair had still been allowed to get too close to a human."

People speculated.

I heard it all. But didn't care.

At that moment, my world shrunk.

It was just me and Alistair, floating in the water, as we'd done so many nights before. Soaking in each other's company. Feeding each other comfort.

After a long stretch of silence, Alistair groaned. "Pippi, I do love you. And I'm...I'm sorry."

"Sorry for—Whaaaaa...Alistair!" I scrabbled for balance when he abruptly ducked his head underwater and shoved it beneath my feet.

"Alistair, what are you—" I blanched when he lifted me up and swung his head toward *Valiant*. *"No."*

The runes on his head bubbled and popped, boiling into his flesh until he bled. Heavily. Thick ribbons of crimson meandered down his face.

He bellowed and kept going.

"Alistair!"

With a thrust that was a little too shaky to be gentle, Alistair bonked his nose up. And sent me spiraling against the side of the ship.

Hands immediately snaked down and encased my arms, my shoulders. Fingers grasped on to the back of my vest.

"Stop!" I croaked. "Alistair!"

He sank back to the sea while I was hauled up and over the ship railing.

"I'm sorry, Pippi," he whispered.

My butt kerthunked against the deck. And an ocean of worried faces swarmed me, people asking, with full sincerity, if I was alright. If I'd been hurt. Most were strangers, but I recognized some of them.

"She's covered in blood." Elisabeth knelt and fussed over the state of me.

Dazedly, I stared at the crimson splotches decorating my clothes. *Not my blood.*

Not all of it, anyway.

"Get her some water."

"Grab a blanket too."

I panted. Panicked. As I shifted my eyes between all the unfamiliar gazes, trying to work up the strength to force the words past the ball of dread that'd lodged in my throat.

"I need to get his head secure again to finish the rune!" Rune shouted.

"Move! For feck's—I said MOVE!"

I blinked sluggishly, as Onyx barreled her way through the throng of concerned people and zipped to my side.

"Back up," she snarled at them when they pressed in, trying to fiddle with me. *"Back up!* How many feckin' times must I repeat myself?"

And they did, because the cutting command in Onyx's voice was the sort you obeyed without question.

"Pippi, is it?" Onyx crouched by my side.

I didn't answer.

I couldn't.

At that moment, with so many emotions and voices gunking up my head and heart, I barely remembered my name.

"Pippi? Yes?" Onyx shook me roughly.

"I…Yes."

Alistair's desolate keens filled my head. The bleats of a suffering person begging for the end.

"I need ye to look at me, Pippi." Onyx slapped my cheek. "Look at me!"

I did, but her face swam meaninglessly before my eyes.

"Do ye love him?"

"I..."

"It's a yes or no question," she said. "But yer heart hasta answer it. Not yer head. Do ye love him?"

"Yes," I said. With no hesitation.

She smiled, bitterly. "Then they can't hurt him. Not anymore."

"They *are* hurting him!"

ZZZAAAAPPPP!

White light exploded over the ship. A blinding, all-consuming flash that wrenched the sight from my eyes—there was *nothing* anymore, beyond the bleached haze. No shadows. Or colors. Or shapes. Only an endless sea of white.

For a terrifying heartbeat, I wondered if I was still alive.

If the wails around me were from the people aboard the ship, or the souls trapped in this glaring afterlife.

But color returned. Slowly. Spilling back into the world one tendril at a time.

I saw the black of Onyx's hair as it billowed in the wind. And then the soft, ivory curve of her cheek, and the deep jade green of the dress she wore.

Around us, other people began to take shape and color as they sorted themselves out. Several of them had fallen—as I would've, if I hadn't already been sitting.

"What—"

SLOOSHHH!

A wall of water plumed into the air, rocketing well above the tallest sail on *Valiant*.

The frightened screams swelled.

I gaped, silently.

The water was...No.

Surely not.

This was terror making my vision funny, right?

That funnel of water was *not* really a shimmery periwinkle. *Right?*

I blinked.

The colorful cyclone remained glistening periwinkle as it bashed against the sides of the ship, flecking off several layers of old, splintered wood.

My heart hammered against my ribs. "What's happening?" I yelled.

"The curse is breakin'," Onyx said.

I whipped my head to her. "There *was* a way to break it?"

"Aye. Ye canna lock a door without a key," she said. "Curses need to have a way to be broken. It's the nature of magic. And I made this key meself."

The water twister roared and whipped the fog into a frenzy.

Movement fluttered across the ship deck as people ran and then panicked when they realized there was nowhere to run *to*.

Their fear mingled with my own terror frothed into a noxious vat of hot, sour milk.

We're going to die!

The undulating periwinkle tornado swarmed the ship.

Wood shuddered beneath our feet. Boards came loose. Anything that wasn't bolted down went flying—and some of the bolted stuff did too, when the watery typhoon ripped the nails up.

Onyx and I ducked when half a bench careened past us.

The water funnel slurped it up.

The wet, viscid air grappled for body parts next, clamping on to legs and arms, and hauling people bodily across the deck.

It hooked around both Onyx and me and shoved us into the railing.

"Curses don't *like* to be broken, ye ken." Onyx seethed.

BOOM! BANG!

A shard of wood clipped the side of my head on its trip to the typhoon.

Terror left a foul taste on my tongue. I gagged.

ZAP!

The water twister vanished.

It didn't shrink back to the sea.

It just...poofed out of existence. Leaving the air still and eerily silent.

People didn't dare speak as they peered wild-eyed at each other. Even the sea seemed afraid to make a noise. So it was easy to hear that feeble, plaintive voice as it snaked over the ship.

"Pippi?"

My heart leapt.

"Alistair?" I scrabbled, my feet moving too quickly for the rest of my body to keep up, and half stood, half fell onto the railing, peering down.

But Alistair's mountainous body was gone.

Instead, a man treaded water, his mop of black hair sopping into his pale blue eyes as he stared up at me.

45

Alistair

I see my life. All the moments I've lost. And the ones I fight to cling to. It's all there.

This happens at the end, I think.

Is it the end?

It feels like it.

My body *hurts*. Everywhere. A hurt worse than the one I felt when I became what I am. When I changed from man to beast.

Pippi touches my face. On the side where I see nothing but dark and feel nothing but hurt. She speaks. Not to me—to the others. Speaks with *rage*. With…

Passion.

Defending me. While also defending herself.

And I think she has never been more lovely.

I feel joy for her, even as it becomes hard to hold on to the words she says. Most slip, meaninglessly, as my life returns to me.

I am a child again, and the adults in my life are scolding me. For my energy. For how lost I become in one thing, while being oblivious to others. For my outspokenness—it makes me happy when others laugh. It always has. So I *try* to make them laugh, to the…

Madden…nation?

No.

Frustration.

To the *frustration* of the adults.

"He's a brilliant young man. But he takes nothing seriously, and we can't get him to stay in the classroom."

A woman's face fills the darkness of my ruined eye. A…

There's a word.

Teacher.

A teacher.

My teacher.

"It's Pippi. Not Pippa. At least get my name right if you're gonna act like a condescending sack of shit." I try to hold on to Pippi's voice.

But she keeps slipping.

And my life returning.

I am older, trapped between being a boy and man, and I am lost. Not knowing where I belong. Being told my dreams are too big, and my heart too soft.

"You're too emotional, Alistair. And too…all over the place. It's admirable, what you want to do, but something like that takes resolve. Grit. You don't have either. You're aiming too high, son."

That face…That *voice.*

My father.

A man as cold and strict as I am emotional and energetic.

I don't listen to him.

Actually, I decide he's an old stiff who needs to get his nose out of my life.

And I keep my dream.

It grows, as I grow. And, at times, it seems too big for me. But I continue to chase it.

"My ears work, Jackson," Pippi says. *"And if anyone is blabbering nonsense, it's you."*

I am an adult.

I am in love. With Indigo.

And the dream has a name.

SorcerSoft. Putting magic at everyone's *fingertips.*

It is real now. A dream no longer, but a company I own. A company that is changing lives, as I hoped it would.

But it is destroying me.

I am lost in it. In the work. The projects. The passion of my team. In my customers. I am lost. My heart is slipping.

Pippi pauses. And I miss her words. Her voice.

I lean into her touch and say, *"You're so lovely when you're m-m-mad. Has anyone told you that? It's s-s-s-sexy."*

Her laugh chases some of the hurt away.

I am a beast—broken and empty.

I don't dream anymore. Only nightmares come to me.

Until Pippi finds me. Until I dream, again. And love. And live.

She *gives*. Pippi gives. Too much.

And people take from her. Too much.

I've taken too. Her kindness. Her laughter. Her smiles. Her dreams. I've taken them and used them to make myself feel alive.

I don't want to take anymore.

I don't want to be so lost, so *distracted*, that I hurt the ones I love.

Never again.

"Pippi, I do love you. And I'm...I'm sorry."

I am a beast.

And I've sent my heart away, where it will be safe.

And then I am in pain—unlike any I've been in. Pain that consumes. And...*ravages*.

I am screaming.

Crying.

The pain burns throughout my entire body.

I am begging for an end.

Begging for death.

But it does not come for me.

Instead, life does. It wraps me in a soft embrace—a hold that feels so very much like Pippi's—and tells me I am not done.

And then the pain is gone.

I am surrounded by the sea. Struggling to swim with limbs that feel small and insignificant against the watery titan.

I am confused. Disoriented. I don't understand why I am in the sea, in my skivvies, as it were, or why ships surround me. I don't understand why my arms and legs feel strange, or why my neck seems frustratingly short—how am I to see my surroundings when I can only twist or tilt my head a few measly inches?

I don't understand *who* I am.

Her name is the first word that returns to me.

I call it.

And there she is.

The sea has stained her hair a darker crimson, and blood decorates her face and neck—*my* blood, I think, although I'm not certain.

She is so lovely. A goddess—one who radiates so much beauty and light, it hurts to cast your eyes upon her.

I want to hold her, and I weep as I realize I have arms that *can* hold her, but I'm too far away.

"Alistair?"

My name tumbles out of her mouth.

Alistair.

Me!

I am a man again.

Somehow my life has returned to me.

46

Pippi

Those first moments after Alistair turned human were a whirlwind of activity.

Alistair pleaded for help as his long-limbed body struggled against the sea. Confusion rippled around the ship, and there was a flurry of movement as people scrambled to throw him the life preserver and hauled him aboard.

He collapsed onto the deck, naked and shuddering, and his eyes found mine again.

And I didn't even *think*. Didn't care that Jackson was on board, or that the people around me were belching up bubbles of horror and shock. I let it all slide off me as I ran, plopping into a sitting position and smashing into Alistair's side.

He gave a hollow "*Oomph*." But then his jittering arms closed around me, smooshing me against the solid wall of his chest in the biggest bear hug—the sort that was pure comfort. Like being wrapped in a fuzzy blanket after a long day out in the snow.

And we did, actually, get bundled into blankets. From Elisabeth, who stammered apologies in my ear. And Kian, who was too shocked to say anything. And others—a nameless carousel of faces.

Alistair pressed his face into my hair.

I flinched when his cheek brushed against the section of scalp Jackson had mangled.

Alistair stiffened and made a sound of distress when he carefully parted my hair and found the wound. "I'm sorry." He touched his lips to the gash. "I'm sorry." The words quavered off his lips as he gathered me more firmly against him. "I'm sorry." He cried. Tears of joy and relief and heartache.

And I cried too. Because this was a dream, being held by him, but better. Because it was *real*.

I could have stayed there for the rest of my life. Wrapped in his warmth, with the secure weight of his arms around me. Smelling his scent—the briny tang I was so accustomed to—combined with a crisp musk of his human skin.

But the mottles of terror dragged my head away. Had me turning.

People ran from the other side of the ship, trying to avoid the massive eel wriggling around the deck.

Massive, as in that grey-skinned creature had to be *at least* eight feet long.

It flopped, smashing its body against the wood, and writhed, swinging its beady eyes around the deck.

"Help! I...Don't *run*. For fuck! *Help me*."

Rune.

That was Rune's voice.

Coming from the *eel*?

Alistair caressed my back. "He d-d-didn't read the fine print."

Stars, it was an incredible feeling to have his words ghosting over my skin with his breaths.

"What?" I asked.

"Rune." Alistair nuzzled me. "It's a figure of speech. Although there are warnings in old textbooks—which I assumed he read, since he likes dabbling in old magic, but he probably skipped over the warning sections. Curses are...well, there's a reason they're outlawed. One being that they're h-h-horrific. The other being that if they're broken, the magic rebounds onto the caster. Rune made me and my employees beasts. The curse is broken. So now *he* gets to live as a beast."

Alistair had not been lying about being a fast talker. Words zipped out of him—almost too quickly for me to grasp. Which made me laugh. Because I realized this was how he'd felt when

I'd talked before: like his mind was in rear-wheel drive, spinning itself stuck in muck.

And my mind *really* churned fruitlessly through that mud. Because it took me several seconds to register what he'd said.

"Rune Bloodworth is an *eel*?" I gasped.

"Aye, likely forever. In all the texts I'd read, none say a rebounded curse can be reversed."

That drawling response came from Onyx.

I whipped around. Too fast. Not only did I crack my shoulder against Alistair's cheek—he laughed as I blabbered an apology—but I put a wicked crick in my neck.

Onyx stood back, watching the melee with her hand propped on her hip and her lips pursed.

"I'm glad you couldn't wield that curse, Onyx," Alistair said. "It would've been *terrible* to see it rebound on you."

Onyx flashed him a look that could have melted the skin right off his face, and then barked at the crowd, "Oi! Ye lot wanna keep standin' and wringin' yer hands while the eel suffocates? How about ye make yerself useful and throw him overboard?"

And when Onyx commanded, people obeyed. *I* was half tempted to spring to my feet and go help them heft the massive, wriggling eel over the railing—I might've, if Alistair hadn't been holding me with an iron grip.

"Rune Bloodworth, though, Onyx. Why?" Alistair prodded gently.

"He was willin' to do it."

"Of course he was. Rune would do *anything* to put money in his pocket. He doesn't care who he hurts along the way."

"You know him?" I asked.

Alistair squeezed my hip. "I knew Magix. They gave me some wicked headaches...I...hmmmm...I don't know how many years ago. Onyx! How long have I been a sea monster? I swear I knew this before, but I'm blanking now."

She scowled. "Six years."

"Oh, damn. I'm almost *forty* now. Right?" He muttered

numbers under his breath. "Uggh, it's May? I'll be forty in August. Pippi, be honest, do I look like an old man?"

He tucked one of the blankets around his naughty bits before he leaned back and spread his arms, giving me an open view of his leanly muscled and long-limbed torso, which was exactly as I'd remembered from the dreams. But his face—the one thing that had always eluded me before—was *ethereal*. The more I stared at it, the more the shapes fascinated me. High and wickedly sharp cheekbones curved toward his pale eyes, giving him a rather severe expression. The wet-and-grey speckled hair plastered to his head didn't help to soften that impression, although he'd have a proper mop of curls when the strands dried.

His mouth was his defining feature, though. Those plump, luscious lips formed a sexy smolder when at rest, but they also shaped themselves into the derpiest smile I'd ever seen.

And he smiled at me now, watching me inspect his face.

"I think you're handsome," I said.

He beamed.

"A perfect silver fox."

His lips flattened into that smoldering line. "I've grey hair now?"

And he looked so adorably flustered, as though someone had snagged a cookie right out of his hand.

I kissed him.

My lips caressed that fascinating mouth of his, drinking in the soft groan as it lumbered out of him. Lavishing over the shape of him, all the hard angles and soft flesh.

His hand went to my cheek, stroking feather-light patterns.

Mine smoothed over his pecs, and a tingle of delight shocked me when the long lines of delectable muscle bunched and rolled under my palm.

He murmured, breathing nonsense words against my mouth, as he suckled and nibbled on my lips. Words meant to be felt more than heard. Expressions of love, of adoration, of relief, and of sorrow, all branded into my very soul.

And it was too much.

His vibrant emotions overwhelmed me.

Which, if I was being honest, I was already overwhelmed, with the frenzy still happening around us. Alistair made me over-overwhelmed.

Tears burned my eyes. Clogged my throat. Made it too hard to breathe.

I ripped myself away from the kiss and buried my face in the crook of his neck as the tears took me.

"Oh dear." Alistair stroked my back and wrapped a blanket around me.

And I loved the way he said that, "*Oh dear*," in his hemming and hawing way.

I loved the way he felt. Physically, of course, but emotionally most of all—so squishy and happy. A big teddy bear.

I loved how easily he gave affection. Kissing my brow. Nuzzling me. Soothing me.

And when he sniffled, shedding tears alongside me, I loved that too.

Alistair was warm and open and soft and kind. All the things Jackson hadn't been. All the things I'd been missing but hadn't realized I was missing. Hadn't realized I'd *needed*, until now.

We soothed each other's tears. And calmed each other, resting brow to brow, breathing each other in.

"Ye two make me sick," Onyx grumbled.

Alistair sighed and kissed my forehead. "Why did you use love as the key then, Onyx? That *is* what broke it, yes? Or am I barking up the wrong tree?"

Irritation boiled off her. "Because I figured no human'd be mad enough to fall for a feckin' sea monster. And I figured even if ye did love, and were loved, ye'd never be *selfless*."

"Ah. So it wasn't that Pippi needed to fall in love with me. I had to...?"

"Put her ahead of yerself. Like ye *didn't* do for Indigo."

Alistair hummed thoughtfully. "That was a good key, Onyx.

Complex, but not impossible. I'm surprised Rune let you build it in."

"He didna have a choice. There needed to be one. And he figured the same as I. For what it's worth, Alistair...I'm not entirely mad I was wrong. I dunna know that ye deserve to be absolved. I guess time will tell. But I didna like ye bein' used the way yer were—a clown for tourists. *Blegh.*" Her heels clinked as she stomped along the deck away from us.

"For what it's worth, Onyx, I'm still your friend," Alistair called. "And always will be."

She muttered a thick, "Feck off," and kept walking away.

"Was I supposed to follow any of what just happened?" I murmured.

Alistair cupped my face between his hands and kissed me. *Hard.* "I'm afraid I got distracted telling you the first half—I do that, sometimes. Actually, I do it *a lot*. But—Pippi, your hands!"

I'd reached up, swiping my floofy hair out of my eyes, which gave Alistair a gander of my mangled knuckles. He hissed lightly and drew my hands to his mouth, peppering feather-light kisses over the cuts. "I'm so sorry," he murmured.

I freed one hand and touched his cheek. "They're okay, Alistair."

"They're swelling," he murmured. "I'll get you a tonic. As soon as we're...not on this ship." He peered around us blearily. "Hopefully they'll not have issues sailing it. Anyway, what was I saying before? Oh! I wanted to fill you in on the basics."

And he did.

People scuttled around us, wild-eyed and pale-faced as they looked at Alistair—the man who had been a beast—and then leaned over the railing, ogling at Rune—the beast who'd been a man. There were spiels of confusion. Calls to sail the ship back to the isle. The crackling and popping as the anchor was raised and the geriatric vessel, damaged by the breaking of the curse, began to move. From the sea, Rune exploded with curses, demanding that someone help him, and whining plaintively when the ships sailed away.

Through it all, Alistair smoothed his hands over me, fretting and fussing over my bumps and bruises as he told me his story. Of Indigo, the woman he'd loved, who perished on a ship he'd championed—and the grief and guilt he'd felt after, unable to understand *why* the tragedy happened. Although, after seeing Rune's involvement in the curse, he now suspected foul play.

He told me of Onyx's rage, as she believed Alistair's negligence had stolen her twin. He told me of her powers, and of mine. *Sensitives.* I still couldn't wrap my head around that. And he held me, vowing to teach me to better guard my heart.

Rune's tale was a more complex one—an insidious yarn of a man who bent and broke rules on a whim and charmed his way out of the lawsuits.

"Rune's operation didn't take kindly to mine," Alistair said. "Which is why I'm wondering if he did something to *Saturn*. And maybe I should've wondered about it before because he lobbed *so many* empty claims against SorcerSoft over the years, and lost all of them."

"SorcerSoft?" I asked.

"Yup." Alistair popped the *p*. "My pride and joy. Or it *was*."

I gaped. And squealed. "Oh my goodness, I used to work with you! Well, not you…but your company. That's…You were my favorite supplier. You were so efficient and everyone on your staff was always so sweet. I *hated* seeing your company go belly up. But…Oh. Oooh. Oh no, I didn't connect that." I clapped a hand over my mouth. "The *curse* sent you belly up?"

Alistair's mouth thinned slightly. "We might've been heading there anyway, with what happened to *Saturn*, but the curse made sure the company rotted. Because it wasn't just me, some of my employees were cursed too. The ones who worked with me on the *Saturn* project." He quivered with nerves and excitement. "I owe them all an apology. More than an apology. I'll need to round them all up and take them to dinner. Multiple. Open bar, five-course meal, dinners. I'll probably need to grovel…*lots* of groveling. Do you think they'd forgive me if—no, that probably won't work. It'd be like trying to buy forgiveness."

He heaved a lumbering sigh. "I just want to see them. And hug them. And promise I'll never put them in the middle of my shit again. I'll never put *you* in the middle again." Alistair's knuckles grazed my cheeks. "*Ever*. Pippi, I...My life is going to be a mess. For a while. So I don't want to...When this kind of news gets out...the legal ramifications...I'd rather not start our relationship—if you still *want* a relationship—by dumping all this on your shoulders. I—"

I kissed him again. Briefly. *Sweetly.* Quieting his spiraling thoughts. "Of course I want to be with you, ya goof. You're my person. Y'know?"

"I do." He pressed his brow to mine, exhaling. "You're my person too. I love you, Pippi."

His adoration nuzzled against my heart, making me feel buoyant and euphoric and giddy. I pecked a kiss to the tip of his nose, grinning when he made a purry sound. "I love you too, Alistair. But my life is going to be a mess too. I nuked it, remember? So we'll take things one day at a time."

"That's a plan I can follow. One day at a time." He gave my brow a lingering smooch. And then asked, "Do they have chips on the isle? I really, really, *really* want chips. You don't understand, Pippi." He laughed when I burst into giggles. "I've been craving them for *six years*."

At some point—I couldn't quite remember when, with fatigue and shock making my brain woozy—Jackson wandered near us.

I called to him. Untangled myself from the blankets, and the warm security Alistair provided, to reach for him. I would've tried to set things better between us, so we didn't go our separate ways festering on hate and hurt and rage.

But he spat at me.

Which made me mad, so I spat right back at him.

As Alistair boomed with mirth, Jackson wrinkled his mouth into an unattractive pout and walked out of my life.

The rest of that day?

A blur.

We arrived back to the isle and found it in shambles. A water cyclone had struck here too when the curse broke and ripped a big chunk of the dock up. The tourists were in a frenzy, traumatized from the periwinkle twister, and scarred from seeing hordes of mythical creatures transforming into naked humans. Most of the guests loudly demanded refunds, claiming they and their children would *have nightmares forever*.

And the freshly turned humans were dazed, as they huddled inside Brew & Bites, wrapped in blankets, most dressed in a ghastly mix of lost-and-found clothes or garments some of the kinder visitors had donated.

Caleb had offered his captain's coat to a tall woman with dusty-grey hair. Melany and Sarah had given away most of their luggage—and they cheered when they saw me, bulldozing right past Alistair to fold me into congratulatory embraces.

Alistair, meanwhile, ran up to each of the transformed people and folded them into great, galumphing hugs—whether they wanted a hug or not.

Marvin, a tall, elegant man, recognizable only because of his auburn hair and bottle-green eyes, cringed when Alistair flopped his arms around him.

"Oh, good," Marvin drawled. "You're back to violating my personal space."

But I felt the joy coursing through him, and I saw the sly smile he threw at Alistair.

There were lawsuits.

Stacks of them.

The lawsuits had lawsuits.

There were court dates. And media attention.

There were questions.

Alistair had been *quite adamant* that I was to be left out of all inquiries, and everyone respected that...*after* he flashed a spell at the gaggle of reporters that'd tried to follow me home from the airport, making big warts bubble over their hands.

"That's horrible," I'd chastised him gently.

"Eh"—he rolled his shoulder—"it'll only last an hour and cause them no pain. But it'll get my point across well enough." He pulled me in for a one-armed hug. "I'm done letting innocents get caught in my cross fires."

But that didn't stop the people in my life from pelting me with all the questions the reporters would have asked.

The months following the vacation were a bigger blur. Of questions. Explanations. Of watching news alerts on the mountain of lawsuits.

Alistair traveled a lot in those early months, to speak on the lawsuits and dissolution of Magix, and to clean up the disarray of his own company—which also involved him helping the employees who'd been cursed and trapped on the isle get their lives back. A tremendous task that he tackled relentlessly, driving himself to the brink of exhaustion, stopping only when he was satisfied everyone was settled, compensated, and ready to move on.

And his employees loved him for it. When I met them—Alistair made a point to introduce me to all of them—their adoration and affection for him poured off them in droves.

Alistair initially wanted to leave SorcerSoft terminated, but they encouraged him to rebuild. And so did I.

"You believed so hard in it," I said. "Please don't give up your dream. You can pursue it without having it consume you."

So he set about reopening, promising me he'd limit his involvement.

And Marvin, who'd been Alistair's assistant before the curse, and jumped at the opportunity to be so again, promised me he'd cattle prod Alistair if that promise was ever broken.

But, for a time, we both agreed to continue living separately. To take our relationship slowly, one day at a time, while we sorted our lives out.

I started over, taking the (alarmingly meager) funds that I had left to my name and began my new life. Alone. First by spending a week in a motel—paid for by Alistair, although I hadn't realized that little tidbit until I noticed my card hadn't been charged—until I got up the nerve to go back to the house Jackson and I had rented. Then I finally made that trip, with Jessa, Kai, and Alistair at my side, to pack up everything I'd owned. Which wasn't a whole heck of a lot. Most of the knick-knacks and bobbles belonged to Jackson, who was pointedly absent on the day I packed.

Afterward the group of us celebrated the successful packing day with a four-course Italian dinner. And sitting in that restaurant, sandwiched between the man I loved and my two best friends, listening to them joke, laugh, and enjoy each other's company…

My heart had never been more content.

I drank extra wine, ate until my stomach felt ready to explode, and made a vow that I'd *fill* my next living space with random stuff. *My* random stuff.

Something Alistair *enthusiastically* encouraged.

I got slews of messages from him, coaxing me to indulge myself.

Alistair: This would look lovely on that little shelf you have above the sink.

Attached was a picture of an artfully sculpted wine decanter.

Alistair: Look how cute it is! You *need* to give him a home.

Attached was a picture of a little dragon toy, a replica of the one I'd *oohed* over at a farmer's market the weekend before.

Alistair: Yay or nay to the adorable keyboard?

Attached was a picture of a sparkly, multi-colored keyboard.

Earlier that week I'd mentioned I'd been so *inspired* to write —that I'd pounded my old keyboard (a drab, functional, black thing) into an early grave.

At one point I told him I missed having a pet, and I got *bombarded* with pictures of cats and bunnies and ferrets, and all sorts of fuzzy, adorable critters for adoption.

He went with me to the shelter, and I pulled the trigger and adopted a middle-aged calico with the sweetest eyes. I named her Cocoa. Alistair snuggled with her all the way home, cooing and kissing her head, and then kissing me once I got back to my apartment.

And when Melany and Sarah flew in for a visit, Alistair was there, easily adopting my friends as his own. And he stammered "thank you" at them every chance he got, since they'd helped me on that last day at Niverwick Isle.

"What an *incredible* love story you two have. I'm so glad you found each other." Melany gave me a big hug and whispered those words in my ear after I'd dropped them off at the airport.

"Me too." I hugged her right back and hadn't stopped smiling the rest of the day.

Alistair slipped into my life so easily.

He was exuberant.

Goofy.

Kind.

Friendly.

Easily distracted. Conversations with him could be exhausting, because he veered off into the weeds so often, sometimes he and I forgot where the road was. But those weeds...we had some *deep* talks in those weeds.

He laughed easily and loudly—still sonic booming, even as a human.

Tears came nearly as frequently to him as laughter. Even

watching a sappy movie could have him welling up and pulling me close.

He loved to snuggle and always needed to touch; he would brush my knuckles as we sat together at dinner, stroke my hair as we perused the shelves in a store, hug me every chance he got —and he gave the *best* hugs. They were big and boisterous and warm and secure. Just like the man himself.

He was high energy, though, likely because his diet consisted of sugar, more sugar, extra sugar, and French fries (or "*chips,*" as he called them). He was a junk food junkie, and he was always wired. Those long legs of his didn't have a walk mode. He ran everywhere, only slowing down when he found me struggling to keep up.

"My legs are littler than yours," I'd grouch at him.

"Ah, you may have little legs, but you've a big heart," he'd throw as a sappy response, knowing it would make me smile. "And I'd not have you any other way."

It was incredible.

Being with someone who suckled my affection, my love, and fed it right back to me. Someone who *gave*, instead of took.

And I'd never known, never realized, life could be this way. That it could be so full of joy.

I squinted at the screen, my eyes blurring, smooshing the words together in a big glob. I honestly couldn't tell if what I'd written was English or jabberwocky.

But jabberwocky or not, it was *done*.

I rolled my shoulders, wincing when they crackled (spending multiple hours crouched over a desk was a dangerous activity for those in our late thirties) and gently wiggled Cocoa out of my lap.

Cocoa mewed tiredly, yawned, and curled into a tighter ball.

"Uh-uh, ma'am," I murmured. "This is your official eviction notice."

Cocoa rolled herself into a bone-shuddering stretch, flashed me a look that said she was cursing me and all my unborn offspring for daring to inconvenience her, and slithered to the floor, dragging herself into the cat hut under my desk.

Such a tragedy, the things I put this cat through.

I stood, stretched, winced when that stretch made me sound like a bowl of Rice Krispies, and strolled from my little corner writing nook to my airy, open-concept kitchen.

Finishing a book—a full-length doorstopper of an epic romance—called for some wine.

And maybe some chocolate.

And—

With a soft *clink*, the door to my apartment opened, and that was all the warning I got before my two-legged golden retriever (a.k.a, Alistair) barreled into the room and swept me into a bone-crushing hug.

"The key worked okay, I take it?" I laughed.

"Like a dream." He beamed and cupped my face. "Hi there."

"Hello yourself." I frowned a little when a twinge of sadness rolled through him. "Are you alright?"

He stroked my cheek. "It was a hard day. I was in the bank earlier and they had a big vase of orchids. And...well...Some days are like that, you know?"

They were.

We'd talked about this before. Openly.

Some days he still mourned for Indigo...*wept* for her. And I wept with him, because I hated seeing him in pain. The ache of losing a loved one like that was an excruciating wound that would never fully heal.

Some days I still found myself searching for Jackson in a store and got a kick in the gut when I remembered that part of my life was over.

It was hard sometimes. Healing from past relationships. Past hurts.

I stood on my tiptoes and kissed him. "Do you want to talk?"

"Later." He petted my hair. "Later." His mouth quirked. "Your eyes are *sparkling* tonight, Pippi. Did you finish it?"

I squeezed his midsection. "Mission accomplished."

He whooped. "Congratulations! Can I read it?"

"No."

He pouted.

"It's probably awful."

"Oh psssst…" He swatted my bottom. "I'm sure it's not *awful*. Unless it ends with the girl dying." Alistair cupped my cheek and flashed me a serious look. "Is your book going to make me cry?"

"No. Happy endings all around in this one. For everyone. Even the villain…somewhat. Which is a sight better than the villain of *our* story."

Rune Bloodworth still lived in the sea near the defunct Niverwick Isle. As far as we knew, anyway. That was the last place he'd been spotted six months ago.

No one had heard from Onyx since she'd left the isle last year.

"Excellent. Well…" Alistair tugged me in for a kiss that had my toes curling, and then whirled away.

"Gosh…*slow*, Alistair. We've talked about this." I laughed as he sprinted back to the door. "Walk mode. I know you've got one."

"That's boring." He waved his arm dismissively and snatched a bag from the doorway. "I've got a gift for you."

"Oh yeah? What a coincidence. I've got one for you too."

Which, it wasn't a coincidence.

Today was May first, after all.

A full year since I'd dipped my bare-naked bottom into the water and somehow caught the love of my life.

Alistair leapt onto the countertop, parking his butt against the end and swinging his long legs along the side.

That poor countertop…

One day, when my landlord asked *"How did you dent a solid piece of marble?"* it would be *very* hard to explain that I lived with a six-and-a-half-foot golden retriever who bounced off *everything*.

"I actually have *two* gifts for you," Alistair said. "One serious and one, well…" He grinned coyly. "Which would you like first?"

"After that face you just pulled? Might as well lay the good one on me first."

He gave his butt an excited wriggle—almost exactly like a dog wagging its tail—and plucked a neatly wrapped clothing box from the bag.

"Now," he started, barely even giving me enough time to pull at the wrapping paper, "you don't have to wear it. Of course, if you *want* to, I won't complain. But it's completely optional."

"I have to open it first…I…Oh my freaking—" I gasped when I pried the lid off the clothing box and peeped the teeny bikini draped inside.

Not *just* a bikini, though.

"Is this seaweed?" I choked.

"Well, it's designed to *look* like seaweed." Alistair waggled his eyebrows. "But it'll stay on better than the real stuff."

And the giggles got me. I laughed until I doubled over and had to clutch at Alistair for support.

"Like I said, you don't need to wear it," Alistair chuckled.

"Oh, I'll *definitely* wear it. But it'll be for your eyes only."

Arousal squiggled through him.

I placed the box gingerly on the counter and hugged him. "But this is actually hilarious because, well, we must've been on the same thought train."

"Great minds usually are." He bit his lip in a hammy, yet seductive, sort of way. "Did you get me a bikini too, Pippi?"

"No. Better." I crossed into my living room and grabbed the wrapped shoe box from where I'd placed it on the sofa.

It took him a second, when he took the box from me, opened

it, and pulled out the red paddy hat. I started to get nervous that maybe he *wouldn't* get it.

But then I felt his glee, burbling off him a half a second before his sonic boom rattled the paintings in my apartment. "This is your *blouse*?"

"Sure is. I found someone who could custom-make the hat. I think she thought I was crazy, having her use the blouse. Especially since it was still in such nice condition."

Alistair shook the cap loose and popped it over his curls, tilting his head to the side to model it for me. "How stylish do I look?"

"Oh, very."

Stars, he was adorable, with the hat perched precariously on top of his wild mop of hair. It joggled, clinging on for dear life, when Alistair reached over and hauled me into his arms, settling me between his thighs, so I could rest my hip against him. "Thank you, Pippi," he murmured into my hair. "I love it. It'll be my favorite hat forever."

For a minute, two, three…we stood there. Cuddling. Kissing. Petting and arousing each other.

"Would you like your serious gift now?" Alistair mumbled against my lips.

"Does the serious gift involve you naked in bed?"

He clicked his tongue and nibbled on my jaw. "That's the *after*-gift, Pippi."

"Ah."

"The serious gift is actually serious. And not really a gift, more of a suggestion." He nudged me away slightly, so he could reach into his bag and pull out a wad of papers.

It took me a minute to leaf through those papers and register what they were.

"This is a house," I said dumbly.

"About forty-five minutes from here." Nerves rolled off Alistair—a rarity for him—as he drummed his heel against the bottom of the counter. "Might be too far for you to commute to work? But…well, I figured we could take a look at it tomorrow.

It backs right up to the state park, which is what appealed to me. I know you like hiking. You could literally walk out the back door and go. And Cocoa"—he bent his head, peeping at the snoozing cat under my desk—"would get lots of birdwatching in. But…" He exhaled. "Like I said, it's only a suggestion. I have a connection. I told them I was interested, but nothing's been done beyond that. If you hate the idea, or hate the house, I— *ummmpfffff!*" He bit off, moaning, when I wrapped my arms around his neck and latched my mouth to his.

I fondled him as we kissed, dragging my nails over his navy blue button-up and clawed them into the black jeans cradling his thighs. He squirmed and mumbled into my mouth.

It was so easy to make him writhe. So easy to coax delectable little grunts and mewls out of his chest. And I loved that about him too.

"I guess you're not opposed to the suggestion?" he panted when I drew away.

"You'd guess right." I shimmied my body between his legs, rubbing at his crotch, grinning when he gave a breathy sigh. "This is…Gosh. I'm…I might be a little overwhelmed. And a lot horny."

"You don't say?" He bent, nipping, not so gently, at my earlobe.

"Should I slip into that little bikini…?"

His eyes darkened. "Oh, I'd *love* it if you would."

"And let you take it off me?"

"I'd love that even more." He scooched me against him and tugged at the collar of my shirt, hauling it to the side so his mouth had full access to that ticklish area between my neck and shoulder. And it was my turn to groan and pant as he lavished the area, suckling until I strained, aching for more.

A shot of mischief punched through my chest a half a second before he puckered his lips against the side of my throat and blew an obscenely loud raspberry.

"Alistair!" I shrieked, turning to give him a playful swat.

He beamed and dodged my blow, which sent the dang hat weebling over his head, and spiraled me into another giggle fit.

"I think we need to lose the hat," I wheezed.

"Never." He clamped it more firmly on his head and then gave me a lopsided grin. "You're my favorite, Pippi. Always."

"And you're a sappy goof," I chucked his chin, "but you're *my* goof."

THE END

ACKNOWLEDGMENTS

Gosh, I don't even know where to begin with this.

This was a book I was *convinced* wouldn't happen. I'd signed up to be a part of the *Bewitching Hour* collection because the idea of writing a Loch Ness Monster romance sounded too fun to pass up. But a lot of life stuff happened while I was writing it, and I choked on the fact that this book had a deadline (me and deadlines *loathe* each other). So I struggled. A lot. I *hated* this book at first and almost chucked it in the garbage multiple times.

But then...I had my lightbulb moment. Everything clicked into place, and it was *magic*. And by the time I got to the end of my draft, I had a story I was utterly obsessed with, and characters I was head over heels in love with.

Funny how things work like that, huh?

But because this book was such a challenge for me to write, I called in a team for help. And boy did they come through.

So thank you.

To my alpha readers: Olga, Amber, Melissa, and Rose. Y'all don't even realize how vaulable your feedback was. Whether you were giving critiques, or just offering your commentary/reactions to a scene, it was all crucial in shaping this story.

To my editing help: Joyce and Betty. You two are incredible. I know this book was a rush and I kinda pulled you both in at the last minute, but you came through. And I will forever be grateful that I had you on my team.

To my friends and family, who offered comfort when I was frustrated, and offered an ear whenever I needed to bounce ideas off of someone. I never would've gotten unstuck without you.

And to you, my wonderful readers, who chose to give my books a chance when there are millions of other stories you could be reading.

Thank you all. From the bottom of my heart.

OTHER BOOKS BY STEPHANIE E. DONOHUE

Standalones

Windsong (2022)

Bewitched by the Sea Monster (2025)

The Across Time Series

Fires of the Forsaken (2023)

Ashes of the Earth (2024)

Embers of the Damned (2026)

The Across Time Companion Novellas

Hunted by Fire (2024)

Betrayed by Ash (2025)

Cursed by Ember (2027)

She just wanted a gosh-darn pizza. The apocalypse had other ideas.

Addie did not have "getting plucked from the 21st century and thrown into the apocalypse" on her "things to do after work" checklist. Yet here she is, trapped in the hellscape known as Sakar–a world torn apart by a Celestial war. Now she's dodging soulless Wraiths, getting chased by venomous horses, and trying her darndest to avoid a meltdown.

Thankfully, Cheriour, the gruff and grumpy commander of the human army takes her under his wing. He's blunt, brutal, and socially awkward. *Totally* not Addie's type.

So why does she find him so infuriatingly attractive?

As Addie's connection with Cheriour grows so does the danger. Wraiths threaten to eliminate the last dregs of humanity and secrets about Addie's past are about to surface that might just make her the key to saving everything... or destroying it.

Darkly thrilling and laced with biting humor, *Fires of the Forsaken* **is perfect for fans of** *Game of Thrones, Deadpool* **and** *Supernatural.*

446

Darkly thrilling and laced with biting humor, *Fires of the Forsaken* **is perfect for fans of** *Game of Thrones, Deadpool* **and** *Supernatural.*

Earth's last hope has anxiety, a lethal power, and absolutely no idea what she's doing.

Addie is having a colossally bad year. She's stuck in a bullshit biblical war, her friends keep dying, and her newfound power might be slowly eating her alive.

At least she has Cheriour, the gruff, battle-scarred commander of the human army, who is secretly a teddy bear hiding beneath a grumpy face. But even their budding relationship is threatened as the war rages.

With Wraiths scavenging the ailing country of Sakar, and the Celestials tightening their grip, Addie must lead a desperate mission to save what's left of this world. But the deeper she dives into the secrets of Sakar—and the reason she was brought here—the more she realizes some truths should stay buried.

Gritty, emotional, and packed with sharp humor, *Ashes of the Earth* is a thrilling grimdark romantasy perfect for fans of *Game of Thrones*, *Deadpool* and *Supernatural*.

448

Gritty, emotional, and packed with sharp humor, *Ashes of the Earth* is a thrilling grimdark romantasy perfect for fans of *Game of Thrones*, *Deadpool* and *Supernatural*.

ABOUT THE AUTHOR

As a child, Stephanie E. Donohue roamed Narnia with the Pevensie siblings and rode the Hogwarts Express with Harry and his friends. She never tired of discovering new and magical worlds through the pages of a book. And, when the yearning to explore still wasn't satiated, Stephanie turned to writing. With a pen and a few sheets of paper, she learned to craft new worlds, and vibrant characters to explore with.

That passion has never died. Stephanie still enjoys writing stories that take readers on exciting, and sometimes dangerous, adventures.

When she's not writing, Stephanie can usually be found cuddling with her two cats, obsessively re-watching The Office, or rocking out to a Pound Fitness class.